Tiger and Del

My home was built of walls I fashioned in the circle, because only here could I find my worth in the world. *Only* here had I become a man. Inside the circle I was whatever I wished to be, and no one at all could alter that.

"No—" Del said.

I grinned.

"Tiger—"

I laughed.

With an expression of determination, Del tried the maneuver I'd chastised her for.

Disgust. I couldn't help it. Because now I had no choice. I broke her guard, went in, tore the sword hilt from her hand. "What did I *tell* you?" I roared. "Did you think I was joking? That kind of move could get you killed!"

Furious, she bent and retrieved the sword. "Again."

"Del—"

"*Again,* curse you!"

I stepped back, renewed the assault. Saw Del begin the maneuver again. I moved to block it, destroy it—and this time something entirely different happened. This time it was *my* sword that went crashing to the tile. And I was left nursing a wrenched thumb.

"Shall I kiss it?" she asked, with heavy irony.

DAW Titles by Jennifer Roberson

THE SWORD-DANCER SAGA

SWORD-DANCER
SWORD-SINGER
SWORD-MAKER
SWORD-BREAKER
SWORD-BORN
SWORD-SWORN*

CHRONICLES OF THE CHEYSULI

SHAPECHANGERS
THE SONG OF HOMANA
LEGACY OF THE SWORD
TRACK OF THE WHITE WOLF
A PRIDE OF PRINCES
DAUGHTER OF THE LION
FLIGHT OF THE RAVEN
A TAPESTRY OF LIONS

THE GOLDEN KEY UNIVERSE

THE GOLDEN KEY
(with Melanie Rawn and Kate Elliott)
THE WARRIOR*
(solo novel)

ANTHOLOGIES

(as editor)

RETURN TO AVALON
HIGHWAYMEN: ROBBERS AND ROGUES

*forthcoming from DAW Books in hardcover

SWORD-BORN

A Novel of Tiger and Del

JENNIFER ROBERSON

DAW BOOKS, INC.

DONALD A. WOLLHEIM, FOUNDER

375 Hudson Street, New York, NY 10014

ELIZABETH R. WOLLHEIM
SHEILA E. GILBERT
PUBLISHERS
www.dawbooks.com

First Paperback Printing, March 1999

2   3   4   5   6   7   8   9

DAW TRADEMARK REGISTERED
U.S. PAT. OFF. AND FOREIGN COUNTRIES
—MARCA REGISTRADA
HECHO EN U.S.A.

PRINTED IN THE U.S.A.

For Debby,
in memory of Pib.

Acknowledgments

I would like to thank the excursion tour guides and ship's personnel affiliated with *Renaissance VIII* of Renaissance Cruise Lines, who helped make my visit to Greece and Turkey in the summer of 1996 not only immensely enjoyable, but also a true education for someone undertaking research for a new book. The back-burners of my brain are already sorting through ideas for novels yet to come.

Special thanks go to Pat Waldher, an old college buddy, who first proposed the trip, talked me into it when I waffled, taught me the first night on board how to play Blackjack, and who, like me, enjoys a good storm at sea; to Marta Grabien, Melanie Rawn, and Susan Shwartz, for suggestions regarding travel and historicity; and lastly to the cruise-tour participants who only occasionally—and very politely—murmured to one another as I clambered gracelessly over segments of Corinthian columns lying about like poker chips, ancient libraries, latrines, and bordellos, Crusader fortresses, akropoli, and Biblical amphitheaters: "Now why in the world is she taking a picture of *that?*"

Prior Knowledge, or:
"A Note From the Author"

One of the more formidable challenges facing an author returning to a universe featuring familiar characters—in this particular instance, eight years and six novels later—is the necessity of presenting previously established information to new readers. On one hand, the author doesn't want to bore by writing one of those potentially tedious prologue summaries . . . *When last we saw Our Heroes* . . . , etc., which may be repetitive and unnecessary for readers familiar with said universe and characters. On the other hand, some reintroduction is essential. Particularly for new readers who may begin with the equally new novel, or those who haven't reread the first volumes prior to starting the latest.

The method I consider most effective is a technique I call the "context method." Authors do the summing up of elements previously established by means of an explanation *within the context* of the story. The characters will themselves from time to time discuss things that happened in earlier volumes, or perhaps the author will drop in some explanation within the narrative exposition.

Therefore, in tackling this task, I have *not* done two things:

a) Assumed everyone on the planet has read the previous four volumes;
b) Presumed readers are too stupid to catch on, so that they must be spoon-fed infinite details regarding What Happened Before.

"Even today the rocks . . . are no less than spiritual training grounds and arenas where faith is fashioned, sin is driven out and the personality is forged."

—THEOCHARIS M. PROVATAKIS
Meteora: History of the Monasteries and Monasticism

PROLOGUE

*S*WORD PIERCED FLESH,
broke bone. I felt it go in, felt the give, the tension in my
wrists as steel cut into body. Heard my own hoarse shout
as I denied again that this was what I wanted, what I
meant—

—and awoke with an awkward upward lunge that
smashed the back of my skull into wood.

One way to stop a dream, I guess: knock it clean out
of your head.

Driven flat by the force of the collision, I lay belly-
down on the threadbare blanket and scrunched my face
against pain and shock, locking teeth together. I couldn't
manage a word, just swore a lot in silence inside my rat-
tled skull.

From above, warily, "Tiger?"

I didn't answer. I was too busy gripping the back of
my abused skull, trying to keep it whole.

"Are you all right?"

No, I wasn't all right, thank you very much; I'd just
come close to splattering my brains all over the tiny cabin
we shared aboard a ship I'd learned to hate the day we
sailed. But to *say* I wasn't all right?

I turned my head, carefully, into a slotted streak of
brassy sunlight skulking fitfully through creaking boards
bleeding dribbles of sticky pitch. "—fine." From between
gritted teeth.

Movement overhead. A moment later a wealth of fair
hair barely visible in fog-tendriled morning light spilled

1

over the side of the narrow bunk looming low above me, which was precisely what I'd cracked my head against. (The bunk, that is, not the hair.) Then the face appeared. Upside down.

Del is beautiful from any direction, in any position, wearing any expression. But just now I was in no shape to appreciate that beauty. "Was that your *head?*"

I unclamped my jaws a bit and removed my cheek from the lump of mildewed material that served inadequately as a pillow. It stank of salt and fish and, well, me. "I suppose I could point out that sleeping apart for months on end in bunks barely big enough for a dog makes it hard for a man to, um, *demonstrate his admiration and affection*—"

"Lust," she put in, stripping away euphemism neatly. "And it's only been two weeks. Besides, we had the floor." She paused, correcting her terminology. "The deck. Which we've used. Several times. Or have you forgotten already?"

Not to be thwarted by an annoying and convoluted interruption intended solely to sidetrack me into defensiveness, I continued with laborious dignity. "—and therefore I could claim it was something else entirely that smacked the underside of your bed with such force as to make the earth move—"

"Embroidering the legend of the jhihadi, are we?"

"—but considering that I'm always an honest messiah, er, man—"

"When it suits you."

"—I'll admit that, yes, that was my head." I moved my fingers gingerly through wiry hair. "I *think* it's still in one piece."

"Well, if it isn't, it matches the rest of you. Age does that to a man." And she withdrew her head—and the hair—so I had nothing to glare at.

"Your fault," I muttered.

She swung down from her bunk over mine. Short, narrow bunks, too small for either of us together or apart; Del is a tall woman. She landed lightly, bracing herself against the ship's uneasy wallowing with a hand on the salt-crusted, battered bunk frame. "*My* fault? That you're feeling your age? Really, Tiger—you'd think it was always my idea that we, as you put it, 'demonstrate admiration and affection.' "

"Hoolies," I muttered, "but I'll be glad when we're on land again. Room to *move* on land."

Del sat down on the edge of my bunk. It wasn't a comfortable position because she had to lean forward and hunch over so she wouldn't bash *her* head against the underside of her bunk. I rearranged bent legs, allowing her as much room as I could; I wasn't about to sit up and risk my skull again. "Any blood?" she asked matter-of-factly, sounding more like man than woman preparing to blithely dismiss an injury as utterly insignificant unless a limb was chopped off.

Someone once asked me what it meant if Del was ever kind. I answered—seriously—that likely she was sick. Or worried about me, but that wouldn't do to say. For one, I hated fuss; for another, well, Del's kind of worrying doesn't make for comfort. A smack on the butt is more her style of encouragement, much like you'd slap a horse as you sent it out to pasture.

I inspected my skull again with tentative fingers, digging through salt-crusted hair. No blood. Just a knot coming up. And itching. But too far from my heart to kill me.

Then I dismissed head and irony altogether. I reached out and clasped her arm, closing the wrist bones inside my hand. Not a small woman, Del, in substance or height (or in skill and spirit); but then, neither am I a small man. The wrist fit nicely. "I dreamed about you," I said. "And the dance. On Staal-Ysta."

Del went very still. Then, eloquently, she took my hand and carried it to her ribs, where she opened it and flattened the palm against the thin leather of her tunic. "I'm whole," she said. "Alive."

I shivered. Felt older still than thirty-eight years. Or possibly thirty-nine. "You don't know what it was like. You were *dead*, bascha—"

"No. Nearly so. But *not* dead, Tiger. You stopped the blow in time. Remember?"

I hadn't stopped the blow in time. I managed only to slow it, to keep myself—barely—from shearing her into two pieces.

"I remember being helpless. I remember not wanting to dance with you in the first place, and that cursed magicked sword making me fight you anyway. And I remember cutting you." Beneath my palm I felt the warmth of flesh, the steady beating of her heart. And the corroded crust of scar tissue mounded permanently in the skin beneath her left breast. "I remember leaving—no, *running*—because I thought you would die. I was sure of it . . . and I couldn't bear to see it, to watch it—" I levered myself up on one elbow, reached out, and slid my free hand to the back of her skull, urging her down with me. "Oh, bascha, you don't know what it felt like, that morning on the cliff as I rode away from the island. From you." But not from guilt and self-recrimination; I was sure she had only hours. While I'd have years to remember, to wish myself dead.

I shifted again as she settled; it was too small, too cramped, for anything more than the knotting of bodies one upon the other. "And then when you found me later, me with that thrice-cursed sword—"

"It's over," she said; and so it was, by nearly two years. "All of it is over. I'm alive and so are you. And neither of us has a sword that is anything *but* a sword." She paused. "Now."

Now. Boreal, Del's jivatma, she had broken to free me from ensorcellment. My own sword, the one I myself had forged, folded, blooded, and named on the icy island called Staal-Ysta, lay buried beneath tons of fallen rock. We were nothing but people again: the sword-singer from the North, and the sword-dancer from the South.

I flinched as she put her hand to the scar I bore in my own flesh, as gnarled and angry as hers over ribs now healed. She'd nearly killed me in that same circle. But it wasn't her touch that provoked the visceral response. The truth of it was, I wasn't even a sword-dancer any more, not a proper one. The Sandtiger was now *borjuni*, a "sword without a name." And no more proud—and proudly defended—title won in apprenticeship and mastery through the system that ruled the ritualized combat of the South, the oaths and honor codes of men who danced with swords within the circle and settled the wars of the tanzeers, princes of the Punja, the South's merciless desert.

Deserted at birth, then taken in as a slave; freed of that by oaths sworn to the man, the shodo, who taught me how to fight, to dance according to the codes; and now deserted by others who swore the same oaths and thus had to kill me, because I'd broken those codes.

Yet despite the price it had been easy to break them, because it was for Delilah. For *her* oaths and honor.

And so in the South, my homeland, I was prey to be hunted by any sword-dancer alive, to be killed without honor outside of the circle because I wasn't part of it any more. In the North, Del's homeland, I was a man who had turned his back on the glory of Staal-Ysta, the Place of Swords, and the sword-singers who danced in the circle with enchanted blades.

But here, now, with her, I was just me. Sometimes, that's enough.

ONE

WE LEFT the North because Del agreed to go, if only because I forced her hand by winning a dance in the circle according to Northern rites. But I'd forced their hands, too, those blond and bitter people who'd sooner see Delilah dead even by deception because of broken oaths; once healed, once reunited, once free of Staal-Ysta and Dragon Mountain with its demon-made hounds of hoolies, we had eventually headed South—where within a year I'd broken the oaths I'd sworn to *my* people.

Now both of us were nameless, homeless, lacking songs and honor, abandoning our pasts in the search for a new present, but one linked uncannily to a past older than either of us knew: a baby's begetting, a boy's birth. The woman who had whelped me there on the Punja's crystal sands, and the man who had sired me far away in foreign lands.

Skandi. Or so we thought. So *Del* thought, and declared; I was less certain. She said it was only because I was a self-made man and didn't want to know the truth of my presence in the world, for fear I was lesser or greater than what I'd become.

Me, I said little enough about it. Mild curiosity and the dictates of the moment—the need to retreat, rethink, escape—had been diluted beneath the uncertainties of sailing, of odd, misplaced regrets, and something akin to confusion. Even homesickness. Except it was all very complicated, that. Because the South maybe wasn't my home at all. My birthplace, yes. That much I knew. Sou-thron-born, Southron-reared. But not, we now believed, Southron-begotten. Which is one of the reasons we were *on* this thrice-cursed boat, sailing to a place where I could have been conceived.

Or not.

Someone might have told me, once. Sula. A woman of the tribes, of the Salset, who'd done more than any to make me a man in all the ways one can be. While the rest of the Salset ridiculed me as a chula, a slave, as an over-tall, long-limbed, big-boned boy awkward in body, in mind, wholly ignorant of grace, Sula had valued me. In her bed, to start with. Later, in her heart.

Mother. Sister. Lover. Wife. Yet neither bound by blood, rites, or ritual beyond the one we made at night, when I was allowed to sleep somewhere other than on a filthy, odorous goatskin flung down upon Punja sand. But Sula was dead of a demon in her breast, and there was no one to tell me now.

We left, too, because I was, well, a messiah. Or so some people believed. Others, of course, didn't buy any of it. People are funny that way. Some believe because of faith, needing no evidence; others have faith only *in* evidence—and I had not, apparently, offered any of worth.

At least, not the kind they believed in. After all, turn-ing the sand to grass—or so the legendary prophecy went—was not the kind of imagery that really grabs a man, especially Southroners. It was a little too, I don't know, *pastoral* for them, who suckled sand with their mother's milk.

Whether I was the messiah, called jhihadi, and whether I had turned the sand to grass (or at least begun the process), was open to debate. Both were possible, I'd decided in a fit of self-aggrandizement fostered by too much aqivi and too little of, well, Del's admiration and affection one night beneath the moon, if one took the magic out of it and depended on a literal faith.

That's always a problem, dealing with religion. People take imagery literally. Or when the truth is presented as something unutterably tedious—such as digging canals and ditches to channel water from places with it to places without it—no one wants to listen. It's not flowery enough. Not *magical* enough.

Hoolies, but I hate magic. Even when I work it myself.

Having established once again that my bunk was not a particularly promising location for assignations of admiration and affection—I nearly smacked my head again, while Del cracked an elbow hard enough to provoke a string of hissed and dramatic invective (in uplander, which saved my tender ears)—we eventually wandered up onto the deck to greet the morning with something less than enthusiasm, and to placate discontented bellies with the sailor's bounty the crew called hardtack. Hard it was; anyone lacking teeth would starve to death. Fortunately neither Del nor I did, so we managed to gag it down with a few swallows of tepid water (Del) or a belly-burning liquor called rhuum (me). Then we stood at the rail and stared in morosely thoughtful silence at the wind-rumpled water, wondering when (or if) we'd ever see land again. It had been two days since we'd left behind a string of small islands where we'd stopped long enough to take on fresh water and fruit.

"Maybe it's not a real place," I observed, only half-serious, which, as usual with Del, provoked a literal response.

"What—Skandi? Of course it's a real place. Or they wouldn't have taken us on as passengers."

I slanted her a glance. Del couldn't possibly be any part of serious. "Are you any part of serious?"

"I didn't ask about Skandi in particular." She dismissed without rancor my unspoken suggestion that someone, somewhere, had done the impossible and taken advantage of Delilah. "I asked where the ships were going. Nothing more. So no, I did not play us into someone's greedy hands by planting the idea we'd go anywhere so long as we *thought* it was Skandi. They told me this one was going there, without prompting."

I vividly recalled the day she'd have scoured and

scaled me with tongue and temper for even hinting some-one had gotten the best of her. But the bascha had settled somewhat in the past three years, thanks to my benign influence. Now she *explained*.

Grinning, I settled once again against the rail. It creaked and gave. I moved off it again, promptly, scowling at damp, stained, salt-crusted wood. The ocean troughs were deepening, smacking unruly waves against the prow. So much water out there . . . and so little of anything else. Like—land. "You know, I just can't see how a pregnant woman would sail all the way to the South from a place so far away just to have a baby."

"Maybe she didn't."

"Didn't?"

"Well, maybe she didn't leave Skandi to have her baby in the South. Maybe she got pregnant *on* the voyage. Or maybe she got pregnant after she reached the South." Del eyed me assessively. "After all, half of you could be Southron. You look like a Borderer."

I'd heard that before, from others. I wasn't right for pure Southron blood, because the desert men were small, neat, and trim, dark-eyed, and swarthier than I. By the same token, I was too dark for a Northerner, who were routinely much fairer of hair than my bronze-brown. I was somewhere in the middle: tall and big-boned as Del's people, but much darker in skin and hair; too big, but not dark enough for a Southroner, and green-eyed to boot. Borderers, however, were halfbreeds, born primarily to folk who lived either side of the border between the North and the South. It made perfect sense that I was a Borderer. Which meant I wasn't Skandic at all, and this entire voyage of discovery was sheer folly.

But a man in Julah, where Del and I had stopped before going over-mountain to Haziz-by-the-ocean-sea, had thought I was of his people. Had spoken to me in his tongue. And he *was* Skandic. Or so he seemed, and so Del believed; she'd sworn he looked enough like me to be my brother. Which was possible—if I was Skandic, and *he* was—if not probable when considering the odds. Still, it was better odds than I'd been offered before beyond a dance in the circle—which I couldn't do anymore, thanks to me breaking the oaths and codes of Alimat. And departing the South altogether. It was as good an excuse as any to leave a place where men who'd trained as I had, where men as good as I was, were hunting my head.

So. Here we were on a ship bound for Skandi. Where maybe I was from. Or not.

"Scared?" Del asked, following my thoughts.

Yes. "No."

She smiled slightly. Still following. "You are."

"Scared of what, bascha? I've fought I don't know how many men in the circle, killed a dozen or more fools outside of it; ridden to a standstill a stud-horse who kills *other* fools, fought off hounds of hoolies, an evil sorcerer who wanted to steal my body and my soul—or maybe just my body; we've argued enough about whether I *have* a soul—survived numerous deadly simooms bad enough to strip the flesh from my bones, withstood afreets and loki, sandtigers and cumfa, not to mention various tribes wanting to sacrifice me to some god or another; escaped murderous women and angry husbands . . . and I share your bed. Regularly." I paused. "What's to be scared *of,* after all that?"

"Knowing," she said. "Or—not."

Oh. That.

She waited, wind stripping unbound hair from her flawless face. Such blue eyes, had Delilah.

I spread legs, bent knees, set my balance to ride the lalloping sway of the boat and crossed arms against my chest. Tightly. Somehow, this mattered. "I suppose you *wouldn't* be. Scared. Of knowing. Or—not."

"I am scared of many things," she said simply, "and not the least of them is of losing you."

That shut me up in a hurry. After a moment I even managed to close my mouth.

Del, strangely satisfied, merely glanced sidelong at me, smiling, then looked across the bow again. "Ship," she said lightly.

So there was. With blue-painted sails. Behind us, above us, the crew of our own ship noticed the other also.

Well, it wasn't land, but it was better than empty ocean. At least, until the crew swarmed like sandstingers over all the sails and ropes and timber. Next I knew, we were turning. Hard.

"Hey—" I grabbed the rail and latched on, not happy to hear it creak again ominously, but even less happy to feel the accompanying protests of the boards beneath my feet. Sandals slid, scraping on dampness and salt. The shift in wind filled my mouth with hair; I spat and stripped it out, then tucked it behind my ear, which did no good at all. Swearing inwardly, I resolved to have Del cut it as soon as possible. Or to hack it off myself.

Del also grabbed at the rail as we swung heavily through the choppy waves, grasping wood firmly. Even as she opened her mouth to make a comment or ask a question, a babble of shouting behind us pretty much answered it. I knew fear when I heard it. The whole crew suddenly stank of it.

"Trouble," I observed, wiping the slick of foamy spray off my face. Salt stung in my eyes.

The crewman nearest us looked away from the blue sails long enough to gesture urgently. "Below," he said. "Below. *Below.*"

"Trouble," Del agreed.

Of course, the last place I wanted to be was immured in a tiny cabin near the waterline as the ship wallowed and bucked. I hung onto the creaking rail, maintaining a now-precarious balance against the violent undulance, and scowled at the sailor.

"I'll go," she said.

Startled, I stared at her. "Wouldn't you rather stay on deck and see what we're facing?"

"And I'd rather have swords to face it *with*," she declared. "That's where they are. Below."

Ah. So they were. "Bring mine, bascha."

"I had planned on it."

The sailor saw her go, looked relieved, then noticed I remained at the bow. His eyes bulged as the ship continued its wallowing, graceless turn. "Below!"

No, *not* below, thank you . . . but as we swung around,

the blue-sailed ship fell out of line of sight from my spot at the bow. I let the sailor believe I was following his suggestion; instead I made my way aft, moving so as to keep my eye on the other ship even as I clutched the rail, cursing in disgust as I caught a toe against a coil of prickly rope and nearly fell. This thrice-cursed boat, in rough seas, was harder to ride than the stud when he pitched a fit.

Still, I considered it curious that our captain would turn *around* rather than sailing on, especially as we were two days away from the last island, which meant there was no safe harbor within reach; but we'd been heading into the wind, which slowed us down. Now we moved *with* it. The sails bellied, cracking against the sky as the crew worked rapidly. Wind shoved us along the way we had come, but more swiftly than before. The question now was whether the blue-sailed ship truly wanted us enough to chase us—and, if it did, was it faster?

Well, yes. The latter was obvious by the time Del came up beside me at the stern. She'd braided her hair back into a pale rope hanging down her spine. Naked now of everything save intent, her face and expression were clean and lethal as a new-honed blade. I took the hilt she offered, felt better for having a sword in my hand. "Our captain seems to place no faith in the fighting abilities of his crew."

"You've sailed with them for two weeks," she said, squinting against spray-laden wind. "Would you?"

They spent more time drinking, dicing, and swapping lies than anything else. Point taken. "Well, he might have faith in *us*." I paused. "You did tell him we hire out for this sort of thing, didn't you?"

"He's seen you smack your head or trip over ropes and nets about nine times a day, Tiger. Why should he have any faith in you?"

This sounded suspiciously as if our captain viewed me pretty much the way I viewed his crew. I was stung into a retort—especially as I had acquired any number of scrapes and bruises since coming aboard. "I'm taller than he is!"

"And clumsier, he seems to think. Although *I* don't believe it." She patted my arm briefly, absently, as if comforting a child—which of course was exactly how she wanted me to feel. "It's catching up."

She meant the pursuing ship. "I wasn't made for water," I said aggrievedly, "or boats. *Ships,*" I amended, before she could correct me; the crew had been explicit. "I'm too big, or they're too small—"

"The world," she said gently, "is too small for you."

That stopped me cold. I eyed her, examined her expression closely, tried to figure out what in hoolies she was talking about.

Del burst out laughing. "Don't look so worried, Tiger! I only meant that you are large in all the ways so many men are small—"

"Thank you very much. *Many* men?"

"In all ways," she repeated, smiling peculiarly—and offering no answer. "Now, what were you saying?"

What *was* I saying—? "Well, look, bascha . . . I only mean I need land, something solid, something that stays put when I plant my feet—"

"Like the stud?"

Who was below, and not privy to this conversation. "Now that you mention it, I'd like to see what our esteemed captain, who thinks I'm so clumsy, would do on the stud . . ."

"Poor odds. *No* odds."

I scratched briefly at the salt-rimed scars in my face, four long clawmarks that scored me from cheekbone to jaw beneath a week's worth of stubble. "And anyway, the question now is not whether I'm clumsy on board a creaking hunk of flattened trees, but whether those fine folks would have come after us if we'd held our course—"

"The captain seems to think so."

"—or if we made ourselves look more attractive than we are *because* we turned tail and ran."

"The captain must have believed we had a chance at outrunning them."

"Or else he's just running scared."

"As well he might," Del observed as the blue sails swelled against the horizon. "We're losing the race."

I squinted across the narrowing gulf. "Maybe I should have a word with the captain about the benefits of standing your ground . . ."

"Unfortunately, as you've pointed out, there isn't any ground to stand *on*."

I spat hair out of my mouth again. "Well, *I'd* rather decide when there's to be a sword-dance than let the other man choose it," I reminded her. "There's merit to a good offense."

"Let me go," she suggested. "He's not much impressed by you. Me, he's impressed by; he comes up on deck to watch every morning when I loosen up."

"So do I, bascha—but watching you has nothing to do with fighting!" Well, I suppose it did; but so far no one had challenged me. Even if I did crack my head on timber and trip over nets and ropes. "And maybe it's time I loosened up, too, out on deck where everyone can see me."

"Why?" Her voice was deceptively guileless. "Do you want men to watch you?"

I slanted her a sour glance. "I just meant it might be best if they don't assume I'm a pushover."

"A *fall*-over, maybe." Del smiled sunnily. "Well?"

I flapped a hand. "Go. Maybe you can find out who our friends are, and what they want."

Del left, was gone briefly, returned. She wore an odd expression. "They aren't friends."

"Well, no."

"They are, he says, renegadas."

"What the hoolies is that?"

"I believe he means borjuni. Of the sea."

That I understood. "What have we got that they want?"

"The captain did not trouble himself to tell me."

"Did you smile at him?" That earned me a scorching glance. "Well, no, I suppose not, not you—why smile at a man when a knife in his gut will work?—but did he at least trouble himself to say what we can expect once they get here?"

Matter-of-factly she explained, "They catch the ship, board it, steal everything on board. Or steal the ship itself."

"*Her*self. They call the ship 'she.' And what about the crew and the passengers?" All two of the latter; this ship generally carried goods, not people. We'd been lucky to claim some room. Although just at this moment, luck did not appear to be an applicable word.

Del shrugged. "They'll do what borjuni usually do."

I grunted. "Figures." Although not all borjuni and Border raiders killed their victims. Some of them were just after whatever they perceived as wealth, be it coin, trade goods, or livestock. (Or, in the occasional circumstance, people, such as Del and her brother.) Still, it was enough to make you skittish about leaving such things to chance.

Del frowned thoughtfully, marking how swiftly the other ship sailed. It didn't wallow like ours but sleeked across the water like a cat through shadows. "He wasn't much impressed when I said we could help them fight them. In fact, he said they wouldn't fight them at all."

"Did you offer to fight *for* him?" I asked. "For a fee, of course. Passage, at the very least."

"He says if they catch us, we'll all die anyway, so why should they bother to fight?"

"Did you explain *we* hadn't died yet?"

"At that point he told me he had no use for a woman except in bed," Del explained. "I decided I'd better come back here with you before I invited him into a circle."

"Well, we know there's no point in trying to change any man's mind about that," I agreed. "We're contrary beasts."

"Among other things." Del, with a sword in her hand and action in the offing, was uncannily content. "But I did manage to change *your* mind. Eventually."

I begged to differ. "I beg to differ," I said. "I just learned to shut up about it. I *still* think the best place for a woman is in bed." I paused. "Especially after a good, nasty, nose-smashing, lip-splitting, teeth-cracking fight in which she shows all the foolish men she's every bit as good as they are with a sword. Or any other weapon, for that matter—including her knee."

"Kind of you," she observed. "Generous, even."

"Merely honest, bascha."

She smiled into the wind. "Among other things."

"And now that we've settled the way of the world again as we know it, what do you propose we do when those—those—"

"Renegadas."

"—reach us?" I finished.

Del hitched a shoulder. "Not enough room to carve a circle in the deck. A dance wouldn't be particularly effective."

"Nope," I agreed. "Let's just kill 'em."

TWO

UNFORTUNATELY, we never
got a chance to kill anyone. Because it became quite plain
very early on that the renegadas in their blue-sailed ship
weren't interested in engaging us. Working us, yes; they
drove us like a dog on sheep. But they didn't come close
enough to board, which certainly wasn't close enough for
us to stick a sword in anyone.

At least, not immediately.

First they drove us, then fell back as if to contemplate
further nefarious designs upon our ship. From a distance.
They lurked out there smugly, having shown us they
could easily catch us. And yet did nothing.

After all, why waste your efforts on forcibly stealing
booty when the booty rather foolishly destroys itself?

Not being much accustomed to ships or oceans, I
knew nothing about tides. Nothing about how a ship's
draft mattered. Nothing about how *things* could be lurking beneath the water that could do the renegadas' work
for them.

It didn't take long to figure it out. About the time the
captain and his crew grasped the plan, it was too late. And
I found out firsthand about tides and drafts and things
lurking beneath the water.

I have to give him credit: the captain tried to rectify
his error. Running for an island to escape the enemy is
not a bad idea. Except he either didn't know about the
reefs, which seems unlikely, or thought he knew the channels through the reefs well enough to use them. Because

I found out what happens when an ocean-going vessel with a deep draft sails into a series of reefs that, at high tide, wouldn't matter in the least.

At low tide, they did.

Maybe he thought the renegada ship was as deep-drafted and would run aground. It wasn't, and it didn't. They just chased us onto the reefs, where, even as our captain frantically ordered his crew to come about, our boat promptly began to break up into hunks and chunks.

Trees float, yes. But they also do a good job of splintering, cracking, bashing, smashing, crushing, and otherwise impaling human flesh.

I did everything I could not to be bashed, smashed, crushed or otherwise impaled. This involved using both hands, which meant the sword had to go—even with renegadas lurking outside of the reefs. Del and I both took to ducking, rolling, leaping, sliding, cursing, scrambling and grabbing as we snatched at ropes and timbers. About the time Del reminded me that I couldn't swim, which I knew already, and announced she *could*, which I also knew already, I realized there was someone else in our party who was unlikely to be particularly entertained by having a ship break up beneath his feet. Even if he did have four of them.

Del was in the middle of shouting something about tying myself to a big hunk of timber when I turned away and began to make my way toward one of the big hatches. This resulted in her asking me, loudly and in a significant degree of alarm, what in hoolies was I doing, to which I replied with silence; my mouth was full of blood from a newly pierced cheek. I plucked out and tossed aside the big splinter as best I could, and reached to grab the hatch next to my feet.

"Tiger!"

I spat blood and bits of wood, dragged open the hatch. If I could get down to that first deck, I could unlatch the big hatch in the *side* of the ship, the one above the water-line which, when opened, dropped down onto land to form a ramp. Which is how we'd gotten the stud on board in the first place. Cloth over his head had made him a bit

more amenable, and I'd managed to lead him up the ramp
and into the ship's upper cargo hold. Ropes had formed a
fragile "pen," layers of straw bedded him down. A cask
of water was tied to a timber, and I personally doled out
the stores of grass and grain. After two weeks he'd actually gotten pretty good about only kicking and biting occasionally.

"Don't go down!" Del shouted. "Tiger—you've got
to get off this ship now, tie yourself to something—"

We weren't all that far from the island. Del likely
could swim it, so long as she wasn't injured by the ship's
breaking up. So could the stud—but not if he was tied.
And I'd tied him well, too: a stiff new halter, a twist of
thin knotted rope around his muzzle for behavior insurance, and two sturdy lengths of thick rope cross-tying him
to two different timbers. He wasn't going anywhere . . .
which had been the whole idea at first, but now wasn't
quite the desired end. Or it *would* be his end.

I slipped and slithered my way down the ladder, un-
comfortably aware that water was pouring in from every
direction. I heard shouts, screams, and prayers as the sailors were trapped, crushed, impaled, or swept out through
gaping holes. It was pretty amazing how quickly a ship
can break itself to bits.

And a body, too, come to that.

"Tiger—"

I glanced back, shook wet hair out of my eyes; saw
Del coming down the ladder. "Get out of here!" I
shouted. "Go on—I'll bring the stud out . . ." I spat blood
again. "You can swim . . . get out into the water—"

"You'll drown!" she shouted back. "Or else he'll kill
you trying to break free!"

Water gushed against my knees. Over the screaming
of the crew, the roar of the water, the dangerous death-
song of a shattered ship, I heard the panicked beat of
hooves against wet wood and the squealing of a frightened stallion. I slipped, was swept aside, caught something and pulled myself back up.

"Go!" I shouted at Del.

But she has her share of stubbornness and nothing I

said could make her go where she didn't intend to go. For the moment it appeared she didn't intend to leave me. Fair enough. I wasn't about to leave the stud. He might yet die, but by any god you care to name he wasn't going to die tied up and helpless.

By now the ship was in pieces. There was no storm: blue sky and sunlight illuminated the remains uncompromisingly, so that I could see where our portion of the ship began and left off. Abruptly. A stiff wind shifted the wreckage against the reefs, pushing pieces of it toward the island, pieces of it out to sea. Larger portions remained hung up on the reefs. Ours was one. If it stayed steady long enough for me to reach the stud, to untie or cut the knots he'd undoubtedly jerked into iron—

I went down as the ship shifted, creaking and scraping against the reef. I heard Del's shout, the stud's scream. I clawed my way up again, spitting water, shaking soaked hair out of my eyes. Something bobbed against my knees, threatening balance again; I shoved the body away, cursing, and made my laborious way through rising water toward the thrashing stud.

He quivered as I got a hand on him, felt the heat of his flesh beneath the layer of lather. He was terrified. The knots, as expected, were impossible, and I had neither knife nor sword.

"Hold on," I muttered, "Give me a chance—"

The ship heeled over. What had been above the water-line now was not.

I came up coughing and hacking, one hand locked into the stud's floppy, upstanding mane; like me, he needed his hair cut. I hung on with that hand; with the other I reached over his muzzle and up between his ears, grabbing the headstall. "Don't fight me—"

But of course he did, which made it all the harder, and to this day I still don't know how I managed to jerk the halter over both ears. Once that was done, though, the rest came away easily. I peeled the knotted noseband off and tossed the halter, still cross-tied, aside. There was only one thing for it now.

Thigh-deep water makes it tough to swing up, so I

didn't even try. I just grabbed bristly hanks of mane and scrambled up as best I could, flinging a leg across his spine. He quivered and trembled beneath me, fighting the rising water, the enclosure, the stink of fear and death.

"—out—" I gasped, pulling myself upright. I slammed heels into his ribs, felt him leap and scrabble against the pull of the water. I bent low over his neck as he fought for balance and freedom, trying to save my head a battering. "—*out*"—

But out wasn't easy. And as he crashed his way through the shattered timbers and boards, I prayed with everything I had that nothing would spear him from beneath. He was loose, now; all we had to do was get clear of the wreckage, get off the reef, and head toward the island.

Even as I lay against him, I looked back toward the ladder. Back where Del had been.

Had been.

Oh, bascha . . .

"*Del*—"

The stud swam his way free of his prison as it scraped off the reef and sank. He scrabbled against the reef, grunting with effort. I had images of his forelegs stripped of flesh, tendons sliced—

"Del—?"

Where in hoolies *was* she—?

The reef was treacherous. I felt the stud falter beneath me, slipping and sliding. Felt him go down, felt the fire bloom in my own leg. I came off sideways, but did not let go of mane even as I fought for footing in the pockets and gullies of the reef. Sandals were stripped off entirely.

"—up—" I urged, trying to suit words to action myself. If we could get free of the reef, back into open water—"*Go*—" I gasped. "Go on, you flea-bitten, lopeared—" I spat out a mouthful of saltwater, sucked in air, "—jug-headed, thice-cursed son of a Salset goat—" I used the reef, tried to launch and jerk myself up onto his back again. Made it partway . . . and then he lurched sideways, hooves slipping, scrabbling; something banged me in the head, graying out my vision. More flesh came off against reef. And then he was free at last, lunging off treacherous footing into water again, swimming unencumbered, save for me. But if I let go—

Never mind.

I kicked as best I could, trying to hold up my own weight even as he dragged me. He swam strongly, nose thrust up into the air. A hoof bashed my knee, scraped off skin. I got my head above water long enough to gulp breath.

"If I live through this," I told him. "I'm either never going on board a ship again"—hoolies, there went the *other* knee—"or else I'm going to learn how to swim—"

But for the moment, luckily, he swam for both of us.

I twisted, peering in snatches over my shoulder, looking for Delilah. My immediate horizon was transient at best: I saw a lot of slapping waves, the looming hulks of unidentifiable pieces of ship, floating casks, chunks of wood bound with rope. And a blue-sailed ship beyond, swooping in now like a desert hawk.

It crossed my mind, even as I hung on with all my strength to a panicked stud-horse, that the renegadas could not have meant the ship to break up so definitively. I could see the intent: to run us hard aground, then come in for the kill. But surely it was next to impossible to find any of the supposed goods they were after, now that the ship was in pieces.

Then again, maybe they hadn't intended the ship to break up quite so—dramatically. Or at all. Could be they meant to trap her, and were as startled as any of us by her quick demise.

I heard shouting. Couldn't say if it came from members of our ship's crew, or the renegadas. All I knew was I'd swallowed a gut-load of saltwater and had left a strip or two of skin on the reef. But I was alive, and so long as I didn't lose the stud I'd stay that way. So long as he made it to land, that is.

The next moment I wasn't so sure he would, or I would. His hooves struck something substantial, and he floundered. One hand slipped out of his short mane as he jerked and flung his head, seeking balance; my feet banged on something hard and rough. My turn to fight for balance. There was land under us, or reef, or something. Enough for the stud to plant all four hooves, and for me to slip and slide and eventually lose footing *and* handholds.

Before I could blurt out a word, before I could get my feet under me, the stud lurched off whatever we stood on. He was in the water again, swimming as strongly as before. Beyond him I saw a rim of land, a line of skinny, tall, spike-headed trees. He'd make it, I realized. He was but ten horselengths away. I, on the other hand, well . . .

I managed to stand up. It was reef, not land. Water slapped at my knees. Most of me was out of it now. I was in absolutely no danger of drowning—so long as I stayed on the reef.

A body floated by. My heart seized up as I saw the blond hair, then realized it was one of the sailors. I turned, trying to look beyond, trying to see *anything* that might be Del. Then a floating piece of wood banged into me and knocked me right off the reef.

Ah, hoolies—

Timber.

Floating.

I snatched at it, caught it, hung on with everything I had. Kicked my way closer, tried to pull myself up on it enough to get part of me out of the water. It rolled, bobbed; I got a mouthful of seawater for my trouble. Finally I just locked my hands into a strand of rope and hung on, floating belly-down. So long as I kept a death-grip on the timber, I wouldn't sink, wouldn't drown. Of course I had no idea where it *or* I might wind up. For all I knew it would float back out to sea . . . so, I applied myself to working out the magic it took to aim and steer the timber, which I thought might be part of the mast. If I kicked just so; if I pointed the wood in a specific way, and *then* kicked . . . hey. Maybe this is how you learn to swim—?

Not likely.

However, it did result in the mast and me ending up closer to land than to open sea, and I let out a long string of breathless invective as at last I felt sand beneath me, not reef.

Water sucked it out from under me almost as quickly as I found it. I staggered, caught my balance, lurched forward. The wind had stirred up the water enough to make footing and balance treacherous. I dragged myself out of it, feeling sand sliding beneath bare feet. Eventually I got free of waves and managed to escape the ocean altogether, staggering up onto the packed, wet sand of the beach.

I turned back, looked for Del, for the remains of our ship: saw a ship, all right, but not ours. And people clambering over the sides, dropping down into a smaller boat. Several gestured toward the broken-up remains. Toward land. Toward me.

Throw the dice, Tiger. Let them pick you up, put you on board a fast, sleek ship, give you food, rhuum; or run like hoolies.

I ran.

At some point, after I had stopped running, I fell asleep. Or passed out. Or something. I only woke up when a hand closed on my shoulder.

I lurched upright from the ground, then finished the movement by springing—creakily—to my feet. I had no weapon, but I could *be* one.

Except I didn't need to. "It's me," Del said.

So it was. Alive and in one piece. Which gave me latitude to be outraged. "Where in hoolies have you been?"

"Looking for you." She paused. "Apparently harder than you were looking for me."

"Now, wait a minute," I protested. "I didn't exactly *plan* to fall asleep. It was after I escaped those renegadas"—and threw up half an ocean, but I didn't tell her that—"and I figured I'd better lay low for a while, *then* go looking for you." I sat down again, wincing; actually, I'd been so exhausted by the fight to reach land I hadn't the strength to do anything *but* collapse. "Are you all right?—no. You're not." I frowned. "What did you do to yourself, bascha?"

She shifted her left arm away from me as I reached out. "It's just a scrape."

The scrape ran the length of her arm from shoulder to wrist. The elbow was particularly nasty, like a piece of offal left for scavenger birds. "Reef?"

"Reef," she confirmed. "I think we both left skin back there."

Now that she mentioned it, I was aware of the sting of salt in various cuts, scrapes, and scratches. I was stiff and sore and disinclined to move, and yet move was exactly what we needed to do. "Water," I said succinctly. "*Fresh* water. We need to clean off the salt, get a drink." My feet were a mess. I suspected hers were as well. "Have you seen any of the renegadas?"

"Not since I got back here in the trees and brush." Del's hair hung in salt-stiffened, drying ribbons. There was a shallow cut over one eyebrow, and her lower lip was swollen. "I don't think they ever saw me. They saw the stud, saw you . . . I made like a floater in the water, hoping they'd miss me. Once they headed off after you and the captain, I got ashore."

"The captain's alive?"

"He was when I saw him." Del shaded her eyes and peered back the way I'd come. Seaward. "We could wait until after sundown."

I gritted my teeth. "We could. Of course, I might go crazy from the salt by then."

"Or get so stiff neither of us can move," she agreed, then eyed me sidelong. "There is one cure for that, though. And now that there's *room*—"

I grinned. "Hoolies, bascha, you do pick the worst times to get cuddly!"

Del sniffed. "I am not 'cuddly.' I am too tall for 'cuddly.' "

I reached out and very gently touched the scrape on her arm. Del hissed and withdrew the arm sharply. "And too raw," I suggested. "Sand on top of salt? No thanks."

I moved, wished I hadn't; got my legs under me. "Which way did the stud go?"

"That way." She jerked her head to my left. "He's not exactly a boat, Tiger. He can't very well swim us to Skandi."

"But he might take us *to* a boat." I stood up very slowly and couldn't bite back a blurt of pain. "Ouch."

"You're all sticky," she observed. "Is that blood? *Tiger*—"

"I got pretty intimate with the reef. With several of them." I worked my shoulders, waggled sore fingers. "Nothing but cuts and scrapes, bascha." I put out a hand. "Come on."

Del gripped it, used it. She set her jaw against any commentary on discomfort, but I saw it well enough in the extreme stillness of her face. Like me, she was sticky with oozing blood, fluids, salt, crusted with creamy sand.

I said it for her. "Ouch."

Del was looking at me. "Your poor face."

"My face? Why?" I put a hand to it. "What's wrong with my face?"

"First the sandtiger slices grooves in one cheek, and then you get a splinter through the other."

I'd forgotten that. No wonder my cheek and mouth were sore. I fingered the wound gingerly, tongued it from inside. "Well, it's just more for the legend," I said offhandedly. "The man who survives sandtiger attacks *and* shipwrecks."

Blandly, "But of course the jhihadi would."

I gifted her with a very black look.

Satisfied, Del smiled. "So, shall we hunt your misbegotten horse?"

"You mean the misbegotten horse who got me—nearly—to land, thereby saving my hide? That horse?"

"I'm only repeating what *you've* called him."

"I suspect he's called us much worse."

" 'Us'? I don't ride him."

"Me."

"Better." Del tucked a hank of sand-crusted hair behind an ear. "Water, or horse. Which one first?"

"Horse. He'll probably lead us *to* water."

Rhetorically she asked, "But will he drink?"

With much gritting of teeth but no verbal complaints, we moved slowly, quietly, carefully—and painfully— through the vegetation in the direction Del had seen the stud go.

THREE

‡

WE FOUND the stud. We found water. We found the wherewithal to clean off as best we could, stripping out of clothes to soak away salt from both fabric and skin, shivering and muttering and hissing and swearing vilely as we discovered various gooey scrapes, cuts, and gouges, and the promise of many bruises in places too numerous to mention. I put my leather dhoti back on, but nothing else was salvageable after introductions to the reef; I was barefoot and shirtless. Del's long ivory-colored leather tunic was scoured white in places, but remained serviceable. She wasn't as battered as I because she'd been able to swim *over* the reef—well, over most of it—but she had some nasty scrapes on her legs, and the one down her arm.

As expected, the soles of our feet were sliced up the worst because we'd both lost our sandals; Del scrunched her face in eloquent if mute commentary as she dangled sore feet in the water.

I was out of it now, checking the stud. His fetlocks were puffing, knees oozing, chunks were missing from shoeless hooves, and he stood with his weight on three legs, not four. "All right, old man—let me see . . ."

He didn't want me to. He told me so in horse language: pinned ears, swishing tail, bared teeth, an indifferent sideways snap in my general direction.

I popped him on the nose with the flat·of my palm, insulting the injury, and as he stared at me, wide-eyed and

29

aggrieved, I bent over the foreleg. "Give it here." I waited. "Give it *here*—"

He gave it to me eventually, if under protest.

"—hold still—" His head hung perilously near my own, but I ignored it and the quivering upper lip. "Let me just take a look . . . oh, hoolies, horse! Look what you've gone and done to yourself!" No wonder he was three-legged lame; he'd sliced open the tender, recessed interior vee of the hoof, called the frog.

"What is it?" Del was squeezing out hair darkened to wheat-gold by its weight of water.

"He's cut himself. Probably on the reef. It'll heal all right, but in the meantime he's no good for riding."

"We're on an island, Tiger. There's not much to ride *to*."

"Or from," I muttered, carefully looking for other signs of injury in the hoof. He was undoubtedly bruised as well. And every bit as sore and weary as we were. Plus there was a lot more of him to *be* sore. "It's going to take days for this to heal."

"I suspect we have days," Del observed gravely. "Probably even weeks, and possibly months—" She broke off. "What's the matter?"

I didn't say anything. Couldn't.

"Tiger?"

I was bent over the hoof. I don't know if that was it, or too much fresh water on top of seawater, or just reaction to nearly drowning. But my gut decided at that moment it was not happy with its contents. Very carefully I let the hoof back down, then slowly straightened up. Almost immediately I hunched over again, palms on knees.

"What's the matter?"

"Unnngffu," I managed. Unfortunately, my belly managed something else entirely.

Del had the good grace to wait until I was done retching and swearing. Then she said, politely, "Thank you for avoiding the water hole."

I scowled at her balefully, took the two paces to the water's edge. I huddled there miserably on aching, stinging, reef-scalped knees, rinsing my mouth out and my face off.

Hands were on my head, peeling hair aside so she might inspect the skull. "You smacked it on something," she said, fingering the swelling.

"I smacked it on several somethings." The ship, the stud, the reef. "I'm probably lumpy as a bad mattress—*ouch!*"

She patted wet hair back into place. "This reminds me of when the stud kicked you in the head in Iskandar. Before the sword-dance. That I ended up having to dance *for* you."

Well, yes. The stud had indeed kicked me. In the head. In Iskandar. I'd also ended up drinking too much aqivi on top of it, thanks to a well-meaning friend, and Del had indeed danced the dance for me against Abbu Bensir, before being interrupted. But there had been more to it than that. There'd been magic.

"You know—" But I stopped short. No one knew better than I what a bladetip set against the spine feels like. "Not worth it," I told her, feeling her tense beside me. And it wasn't. We were too stiff, too battered, too slow, in addition to being weaponless. They'd cut us down before we could even begin to turn.

Del muttered something succinct in uplander. The stud added a virulent, damply productive snort, then limped off a couple of paces.

Well, he was a horse, after all. Not a watchdog.

A big hand touched me, a rigid finger poked me—and with a garbled blurt of startlement I abruptly threw up again. Except there wasn't anything left *to* throw up, so all I did was heave.

Which served to amuse everyone but me. And maybe Del.

Someone cuffed me across the back of the skull, much as I cuffed the stud when he offended. "No sailor, this fool!" Amidst more laughter.

Well, no, so I wasn't. But then, I'd never claimed to be. I wobbled on my knees and one braced arm and thought very unkind and vulgar thoughts inside my abused head.

"Maybe you got stung by something," Del offered. "Something in the reef, maybe? Who knows what creatures could be lurking in those cracks and crannies. Or maybe something in the water itself."

I could think of many other things to talk about besides what was making me sick. I managed to cast her a pointed glance, then felt the meaty slap of a sword against my ribs. I winced as it connected with gnarled scar tissue. Lucky for me, it was the flat of the blade.

"Look." The same voice that had spoken earlier. "Look, fool!"

"I think you'd better," Del suggested after another blade-slap. "Look *at* them, I mean."

So I did, after a fashion. I sat back on my heels, let them see I was unarmed—which they probably knew already, but it never hurts to underscore such vital bits of information—then twisted my torso enough to look at them ranged behind us.

"Oh. Only six," I said, with carefully couched disdain.

"Four more than you," the closest man said, and thwapped me across the head with a broad-palmed hand as if I were an erring child.

"He's going to be sick again," Del warned as I clamped my jaws tightly. Which occasioned additional frivolity among the six renegadas.

"Maybe later," I said between gritted teeth, determined to impose self-control over an oddly recalcitrant stomach. "Hoolies, bascha—do you have to be so cursed helpful?"

"I just thought—" And then a sword lingered at her throat. Steel flashed, pale hair stirred—and a lock fell away. Nice warning, that. Sharp sword, that.

"No," someone said: a woman's voice, accented but comprehensible. "You will not distract us with foolish chatter." She paused. "Even if you are fools."

Oh, thanks.

"*We* are not fools," she went on. "You should sit very

still, very quietly, and pray to whatever gods and god-
desses you worship that we do not lose our patience. So
that you do not lose your lives."

I eyed them, marking swords, knives, stances, expres-
sions. Six. Five men, all fairly large, all quite fit, all
poised and prepared to move instantaneously. One
woman, not so big—in fact, she was rather small—but
every bit as armed, every bit as fit, every bit as poised,
every bit as prepared.

And there was absolutely no mistaking her for anything *but* a woman, either. Not in those clothes. Not with
that body. I blinked, impressed.

"No," the man said, and cuffed me yet again.

Three times was more than I let anyone whack me,
given a choice. So I ducked, rolled, came up with one of
his ankles in my hands. Twisted, yanked the leg up,
avoided the off-balanced sweep of his sword, cranked the
ankle back on itself and dumped him on his butt.

Of course, they stopped all that pretty quickly. Someone threw Del facedown onto the sand and sat on her, one
hand knotting up her hair in a powerful grip while the
other oh so casually set the knifeblade across the side of
her neck; three other men landed on top of me. By the
time we'd sorted all of that out, I was scummed with sand
once more, and grass, and my belly was turning backflips.
I discovered myself on my knees—*again*—while two of
the larger men gripped my wrists one-handed and yanked
my arms out from my sides, blade edges balanced lightly
but eagerly on sand-dusted ribs, muscle, and scar tissue
now standing up in rigid washboard relief, since the renegadas had me all stretched out in the air as if I were a
hide to be dried in the sun.

Del, sprawled face-down, managed to turn her head in
my direction. Slowly. Carefully, so as not to invite repercussions. She spat out sand, a piece of grass. "Nice
move," she commented briefly. "Forgive me if I don't
thank you."

"He deserved it." I smiled benignly at the big, tanned
man who sat on his rump in the sand, cursing, nursing a
twisted ankle. Like the woman, he had an accent; none of

the others had spoken. I noticed for the first time that he was bald, or shaved his head. Also that the head was tattooed. "And don't do it again."

He arched incredulous eyebrows. The woman burst out laughing. Like the others, she carried a sword. Like the others, she was tanned and tattered by wind, salt, and sun. Her hair, trailing down her back in a tangled half-braided tail, was a flamboyant red. The eyes beneath matching brows were hazel. And every bit of visible skin on face, arms, and legs was thickly layered in freckles.

"Better not," she said to the tattooed man. "He is a dangerous fool, this fool."

"With a weak belly," he growled.

Well . . . yes.

Del, cheek pressed hard against the ground, asked, "Do jhihadis *have* weak bellies?"

"I'm glad everyone here is having such a good time at my expense," I complained. "And what in hoolies do you people want, anyway? As you can see by the state of what remains of our clothing, we aren't exactly weighed down with coin. Or jewels. Or even weapons." I glared at the woman. "And just how did you find us, anyway? We didn't leave any tracks." In fact, we'd been extremely careful about that, and neither Del nor I were precisely bad at being careful. We'd traded sand for grass as soon as possible, and moved with deliberation rather than carelessness.

The red-haired woman grinned, crinkling sun-weathered skin by pale eyes. Her teeth were crooked. "There is only one place with good water," she said simply. "We knew any other survivors would come here. So we sailed around the island, hopped overboard, and waited." She flicked an amused glance at Del. "And so you came, and here we are. Dancing this dance."

She didn't mean that kind of dance, although I'd just as soon she did. Because then I'd have a sword. But for the moment I focused on something she'd said. "*Other* survivors?"

She jerked her chin up affirmatively. "The man cursing us—and crying—about his lost ship."

"Ah. The captain." I indicated Del with a tilt of the head. "You can let her up, you know, before the fat man suffocates her." Most of the meaty bulk sitting atop Del's spine appeared to be muscle, not fat, but an insult is worth employing any time, regardless of the truth. "I don't think either of us is going anywhere."

"But you are," the woman said lightly. "You are coming aboard our ship."

"Thanks anyway, but I'd just as soon not. The last one I was on had an accident."

The man I'd dumped got up. He tested his sore ankle, shot me a malevolent green-eyed glance from under bronze-brown brows—which were neither shaved nor tattooed, but were, I noted with repulsed fascination, pierced with several silver rings—then scowled at the woman. "Well?"

She considered him. Considered me. "Yes. He is nearly as big as you. It will be less trouble."

"Good." The man took three strides across the sand and smashed a doubled fist into the side of my jaw. "Oh, dear," he cried in mock dismay, "I *have* done it again!"

Fool, I said inside my head, not definitively certain if I meant him or me—and then the world winked out.

I came to, aware we were on a ship again, because after two weeks I was accustomed to the wallowing. I lay there with my eyes shut and my mouth clamped tightly closed, tentatively asking my body for some assurances it was going to survive.

It was. Even my stomach. For a change.

This ship smelled different. Handled differently. Moved with a grace and economy that reminded me of Abbu Bensir, a sword-dancer of some repute who was smaller than I, and swift, and very, very skilled. A man whom I'd last seen in the circle at Aladar's palace, which had become Aladar's *daughter's* palace, when I had shattered every oath I'd sworn, broken every code of an Alimat-trained, seventh-level sword-dancer, and become something other than I'd been for a very long time.

We'd settled nothing, Abbu and I, after all. He still

believed he was best. I believed I was. And now it would never be settled, that rivalry, because I could never dance against him *to* settle it. Not properly. Not where it counted. Because he would never profane his training, his sword, his honor, by accepting a challenge, nor would he extend one.

Of course, at this particular moment, none of that really mattered because my future might not last beyond the balance of the day.

"You there?" I croaked.

I heard movement, a breath caught sharply. Then, "Where else would I be?"

Ah. She was alive. I cracked an eyelid, opened the other. Rolled my skull against the decking so I could look at her. She sat across from where I was sprawled on my back on the deck of a tiny cabin, her spine set against the wall. There were no bunks, no hammocks. Not even a scrap of blanket. No wonder my bones ached.

"How long?"

"Not long. They lugged you on board, dumped you in here, pulled up the anchor, and off we sailed."

"The door bolted?"

"No."

"No?" I shot her a disbelieving scowl. "Then what in hoolies are you doing in here?"

Del smiled. "Waiting for you to wake up."

I put a hand to my jaw, worked it gingerly. I could still chew, if carefully—so long as they bothered to feed us. I undertook to sit up and managed it with muffled self-exhortations and comments to the effect that I was getting too old for any of this.

"Well, yes," Del agreed.

I jerked upright. "The stud!"

She poked a thumb in the air, hooking a gesture. "Back there."

I scratched at sand-caked stubble and scars. "How'd they get him on board? I figured he'd never go anywhere *near* a ship again—"

"They didn't. 'Back there' means—back there. The island."

"They *left* him there?!"

Del nodded solemnly.

"Oh, hoolies . . ." That image did not content me in the least. Poor old horse, poor old lame horse, poor old lame and battered horse left to fend for himself on an island—

"With fresh water," Del said, "and grass."

She never had liked him much. "Don't you dare tell me—"

"—he'll be fine," she finished. "All right. I won't. But he will be."

"We'll have to get back there and find him," I said gloomily. Then I frowned at her. "Are you all right? Did they hurt you?"

Del's expression was oddly amused, but she did not address the reasons. "I'm fine. No, they didn't."

"Did any of those men—"

"No, they didn't."

"Did any of the men waiting here on board ship—"

"No, they didn't." Del arched pale brows. "Basically they've pretty much just ignored us."

"Nobody ignores *you,* bascha." I tried to stretch some of the kinks out of my spine, winced as drying scrapes protested. And Del had her share, as well. "How's your arm?"

"Sore."

"How's the rest of you?"

"Sore."

"Too sore to use a sword?"

"Had I one, I could use it."

Had she one. Had *I* one. But we didn't. "Well, I guess now you can say that for the first time in your life a man took you seriously."

That set creases into her brow. "Why?"

"Because the minute I moved, that fat man sat on you. No one was about to let you try a move on anyone." I displayed teeth in a smug grin. "How's it feel to be treated like a man, instead of dismissed as no threat at all?"

"In this case," she began, "it feels annoying."

"Annoying?"

"Because if they'd ignored me, assuming I was incapable of defending you or myself because I am a woman, I might have been able to accomplish something." She rested her chin atop doubled knees. "I think it has to do with the fact their captain is a woman."

"She's their *captain?*"

"Southroner," she murmured disparagingly. "There you go again. And here I thought I'd trained you out of that."

Dangerous ground. I retreated at once. "Well, did they say anything about what they wanted us for?"

Del's eyes glinted. She knew how and why I'd come to change the topic so swiftly. "Not yet."

"Well, we're not tied up, and the door isn't bolted—what say we go find someone and ask?"

"Lead on, O messiah."

This messiah led on. Slowly.

The red-haired woman was indeed the captain of the ship. She explained that fact briefly; explained at greater length, if succinctly, that despite what we might otherwise assume, it was perfectly permissible for either Del or I or even both of us to try to kill her, or her first mate—she indicated the shaven-headed, ring-browed, tattooed man standing a few paces away, smiling at me—or any of the other members of her crew because, she enumerated crisply: *first,* if we were good enough to kill any of them, they deserved to die; *second,* if we tried and failed, they'd simply heave us over the side; and *third,* if we somehow managed, against all odds and likelihoods, to succeed in killing every single one of them, where would we go once we *had?*

The first point annoyed me because it presupposed we weren't good enough to kill any of them. The second part did not appeal to a man who could not swim, and now had no horse to do it for him. The third point depressed that same man because she made perfect sense: Del and I couldn't sail this ship. And unless we killed every man aboard once we killed their captain, we wouldn't even get a chance to *try* to sail this ship.

An idea bloomed. I very carefully did not look at Del.

The woman saw me not looking, saw Del not looking back, and laughed. "That is why he is chained up," she said, grinning broadly, "in a locked cabin."

Del and I now exchanged looks, since it didn't matter. So much for the captain of our former ship, who likely could tell us how to sail our present one. If we killed everyone else first, starting with this captain and her colorful first mate.

"You can try to get him out, I suppose," the woman said musingly, "but we would immediately kill him, which would undoubtedly upset him, and then where would you be?"

"Where *are* we?" I asked, irritated. She wasn't taking any of this seriously.

"Oh, about five days' sail from Skandi," she answered, "and a lot more than that from wherever you came from." True. "Now, to business: Who in this world would pay coin to keep your hides whole?"

Promptly, Del and I pointed at one another.

"No, no," the woman declared crossly, "that is unacceptable. You cannot pay *her* ransom"—this was to me—"because you have nothing at all to pay with; and she cannot pay *your* ransom"—a glance at Del—"because she does not either." She arched coppery brows and indicated the ocean beyond the rail. "So, shall I have you heaved over the side?"

"How about not?" I countered, comprehending a distinct preference for staying put on deck.

"Why not?" The woman affected melodramatic puzzlement. "You have no coin, you have no one but one another to buy your hides, and you are no use to anyone at all as sailors." She paused. "What would *you* do with you?"

The tattooed sailor grunted. "Shall I tell you, captain?"

"How's your ankle?" I asked pointedly.

"How is your jaw?" he asked back.

"Boys," Del muttered in deep disgust, which elicited a delighted grin from the—female—captain.

"No, I want *them* to tell me." She rode the deck easily as the boat skimmed wind-ruffled waves, thick tail of hair whipping down across one delicate shoulder. "If they can."

"I'm sure I can think of something," I offered. "Eventually."

"Well, when you do, come back and see me." The woman flapped an eloquent hand. "Now, run along and play."

FOUR

I SETTLED ON fat coilings of heavy rope and looked at Del, who stood at the stern of the ship with her back to the rail. Wind whipped her hair into a shrouding tangle until she caught and braided it, then stuffed the plait beneath the neckline of her tunic.

We consulted quietly, but with precision. "So, what do we know, bascha?"

"There are eight men, and one woman."

All eight men and the woman were busy sailing the boat through roughening waters and a potential storm, judging by the look of the sky; we'd made certain before taking up our present positions no one was close enough to hear. "And three prisoners."

"One of whom could sail this ship, but is chained and locked into a cabin." She paused. "While the other two are seemingly without recourse."

"Seemingly, yes. For the moment." I considered the odds. "Eight men, one woman. Nine swords we know about, probably more; double the number of knives and assorted stickers, I'd bet."

"And any number of things with which to bash us over the head," Del added.

"Yes, but those items are just as available to us." I patted the top coil of rope, thinking of chains and hooks and lengths of wood. "We can improvise almost anything."

She crossed her arms, swaying elegantly with the mo-

41

tion of the ship. "An option," she agreed, though she did not sound convinced. "And?"

"And . . ." I tongued the inside of my cheek where the splinter had pierced it. "Men are frequently taken by you, my Northern bascha. If the captain were male—"

"She isn't."

"No, but—"

"She also isn't so stupid as to be taken in by false advances."

"How do you know?"

"A woman who captains her own ship—*and* a crew of eight males!—is likely immune to such blandishments as a man might devise, who hopes to win her favor merely to serve himself." Del caught her balance against the rail. "She is a killer, Tiger. She would not have survived to captain a ship—and this crew of eight males—if she lacked wisdom or ability."

"But she might be taken unawares," I countered, "with just the *right* man. Command gets lonely after awhile."

"She might," Del conceded eventually, "and you do have a full complement of what some women call charm—"

"*You* certainly seem to."

"—so it's likely worth a try."

I contemplated her expression. Inscrutable. "Well?"

Del's mouth twisted briefly. "I saw you looking at her. I think you would not be opposed to undertaking this option."

I opened my mouth, shut it. Began again. "If she were ugly, she wouldn't believe it."

"An attractive woman is more accustomed to such things, and therefore is prepared for unwanted advances. And defeats them."

I knew a little about that myself. "But if the woman carries a sword, knife, and whatever else she might have hidden on that body, a lot of men wouldn't consider making any advances at all." Not if he wanted to keep his gehetties.

"Which means it is left to the woman," Del said. "As it was left to me."

I jerked upright. "What?"

"It was."

Bruises, stiff muscles, and various scrapes protested my too-hasty motion. "Gods of valhail, woman, you were cold as a Northern lake when we met!"

"*When* we met, I wanted only a guide."

"That's what I mean. Ice cold. That was you."

"Arrogant," she said. "A braggart. A man who believed women belonged only in his bed."

I relaxed again, leaned against elbows propped on rope and stretched out reef-scoured legs. "All I ever claimed was to be the best sword-dancer in the South. Being honest isn't arrogant, and mentioning it from time to time serves a purpose in the right company. As for believing women belong only in my bed, well . . ." I cleared my throat. "I think it's fair to say there are indeed times when a woman in my bed is a worthwhile, um, goal." I waggled eyebrows at her suggestively. "Wouldn't you agree?"

"Which is why it was I who had to convince you to get into mine."

"You did *not*—"

"Oh, you put on a good show, all that bragging you did about being the infamous Sandtiger, feared by men and beloved by women—"

"Hey!"

"—but when it came right down to it, when it came to the *doing,* you were reluctant."

"Was not."

"Were so."

I considered mentioning ten or twenty names I could rattle off without stopping to think about it, just from the year before Del showed up, but decided even as I opened my mouth that names of women were not truly the issue, and if I named them, I might get myself in trouble. "*If* I was reluctant—and that's not an admission I was, mind you—it was because you'd been very clear about wanting only a guide." I sniffed. "For a woman who rarely explains anything, you were definitely clear on that point."

"That *is* my point," she said. "When I let you know there could be more between us, you ran the other way."

"Did not."

"Did so."

Impasse. Finally I asked, "What does any of this have to do with getting off this boat? In one piece?"

"Your plan seems to entail seduction."

"I said it was an option, yes. And it is. One of the oldest in whatever book you care to read." Which meant it might not work; then again, it had been used with success enough times to end up *in* the book.

Del's turn to sniff. "You were quick enough to volunteer *me* for the option—except the captain isn't a man, so that won't work."

"It was *you* who said I was looking at her!"

"You were."

"So were you."

"Tiger, I do have some acquaintance with the look in a man's eyes when he notes an attractive woman."

She would. "It doesn't hurt anything to look."

"Of course not."

That sounded suspiciously like she was pulling my leg—or else saw my point. Which raised another issue. "Do you look?"

"Of course I look."

"At other men?"

"A woman looks at other men the way a man looks at other women."

"She does?"

"Of course she does."

I had never considered that. It was new territory. Negotiating carefully, I said, "You mean women who aren't married."

"I mean any woman, Tiger. If she sees a man she considers attractive—or thinks he *might* be attractive, but needs additional study—she looks."

"Even if she's married." I paused. "Or sharing another man's bed. For three years."

Del smiled. "Yes," she said gently, "I look."

"How often?"

She was laughing at me. "Ask yourself the same question."

"*That* often?"

She crossed to the coil of rope, sat down beside me. Leaned her shoulder into mine. "You look. I look. Looking is not leaping."

"And is there any man here you might *look* at? Without leaping?"

"Oh, I might look at the first mate."

"Him? He's bald!"

"He shaves his head; I've seen the shadow. And the shape of his skull is good."

"He's got those blue tattoos all over it!"

"They are beautiful designs, too, so intricate and fluid."

"He has rings in his eyebrows!" And, for all I knew, elsewhere.

"That, I admit, is not so attractive. But—different." She shrugged. "He's interesting looking."

"Anything else?"

Del nodded, then tipped her head into mine. Softly she said, "He has your eyes."

"My *eyes?*"

"Green," she said. "And while one can see the competence in them, the confidence and willingness to risk himself, one can also see the laughter."

I digested that. "I don't see that there's much to laugh about, in our present situation."

"He does."

"He should!"

"Then it's up to us to find a way to stop the laughter in his eyes, and put it back in yours."

I twisted my mouth. "Which brings us around to the captain again."

"So it does."

"And if she's as smart as you believe she is, it might take a while. This—seduction."

"It might."

I scowled into sea spray. "You don't sound all that upset about it, bascha."

"Because I will have my own task to do."

"What's that?" I asked suspiciously.

"Seducing the first mate."

"De-li-lah!"

"Think with your head," she admonished, "not with—something else. If you should succeed in winning the captain's favors enough that it gains you a knife or sword so you may take her hostage against our safety, her crew will come for me."

So they would. I'd never believed otherwise.

"And so," she continued, "I should arm myself as well so they can't take me to force the issue, and then they will have no choice but to let us assume command. And have our captain freed, so *he* can sail this boat."

"Ship," I corrected. "And this is about the silliest plan I ever heard."

"Men who want something have seduced women throughout the centuries, Tiger. You yourself admitted it."

"I hope you're going to point out that women have used seduction to gain things, too."

"Of course they have. Men are ridiculously easy to manipulate from between the blankets."

I glared at her.

She shrugged. "You only think it's silly because we'll both be doing the same thing at the same time for the same reason."

"This is your revenge," I accused.

"You have no problem with me going into the circle, Tiger. Or killing to save our lives."

"Of course not." Now. Once I had, on both counts.

"And you were suggesting that I might seduce the captain, were he a man."

"I said it was an *option*—"

"But now that I'm so willing to seduce this first mate even as you are seducing the captain, the plan makes you uncomfortable." She paused. "Why is that?"

My head hurt. "I don't know!"

Del sighed. "Small steps," she murmured. "But enough of them lead to the same destination."

She was being cryptic again. I hate that. "What in hoolies are you talking about now?"

"I can fight enemies with you, kill with you, sleep with you. But not seduce someone else even as you are engaged in the same activity." She arched pale brows. "You do not—yet—care to share this thunder."

I hunched over on the coil of rope, elbows on knees, chin in hands. Aware of aches and abiding frustration. "I have a better idea."

"Yes?"

"Teach me to swim," I growled, "and then neither one of us has to seduce anyone!"

"Ah. Well, that, too, is an option. And then there is yet another."

I turned my head to glower at her. "I'm biting, bascha. See me biting?" I displayed teeth.

The Northern bascha was innocence personified. "You're the jhihadi," she said. "Why don't you just magick us up whatever weapons we need?"

I put the plan into action on captain's watch, just before dawn. It wasn't particularly difficult: I wasn't sleeping well, was stiff and sore, and desperately needed the exercise. So, taking my lead from Del on the other ship, I went up on deck and began to loosen up.

I'll admit it: there are times when a man postures and poses merely for effect. I'd seen it in the stud around mares. I'd seen it in male dogs as they gathered around a bitch in season. I'd certainly seen it in cantinas when a pretty wine-girl was the desired object in a room full of men just in off the desert. Sometimes one can't help it. Other times one—can. But chooses not to.

This was one of those times.

However, I had reconnoitered before undertaking the plan. Even as I had counted the crew, I assessed them as well. Eight men. All tall, all strong, all in condition. A small woman, no matter her personal skill and abilities, had surrounded herself with large men capable of using brute strength individually or jointly to protect their captain. I didn't question their loyalty; if they were not loyal, she'd be dead already. And if not dead, she certainly wouldn't be in command of a ship, leading renegadas bent on stealing from other ships equally full of men.

In the South, I am taller, heavier, stronger, and faster than other men, not to mention very good with a sword. It afforded me tremendous advantage in the circle, as well as in most other circumstances. But here, in these circumstances, I was enough like her sailors in height, weight, and bulk, not to mention coloring, to *be* one of them. Therefore I had to offer her someone other than what she knew.

Though Del was frequently rough on me with regard to physical aches and pains—not to mention opinions— I'd seen her with enough babies, children, and animals to know what got to her. She was without a doubt the toughest woman I'd ever known in strength of will, mind, and sheer physical gifts, but she was, after all, a woman. She had her soft spots.

The captain was also a woman, and I was certain she had soft spots, too. I just had to find one.

I stood on the deck in the open and commenced loosening up. I did not bite my tongue against grunts of effort, of oaths sworn against stiff, slow muscles, of the favoring of particularly sore areas. I hurt all over. It affected the way I walked, the way I stretched, the way I twisted this way and that. Even the way I stood: within minutes my feet were bleeding. Any other time I'd have shrugged it off, told Del or anyone else I was fine, no problem, nothing I couldn't handle. It's easy to let pride replace truth. Sometimes it's necessary. This time, I thought, it was not.

Understanding Del was the key to this woman, this red-haired, freckled woman who had acquired a ship and eight men, not to mention various weapons and booty. Del had called her a killer: she likely was, although I had yet to see her personally kill anyone. That she'd ordered her crew to run us up on the reef, I knew. Whether she could stick a sword into a man and cut his heart out, I didn't know. Del could. Del had. Del, too, was a killer.

That stopped me for a moment. In mid-stretch I halted, summoned up that thought, that image again. Del in the circle, circumscribed by ritual, by song. Del out of the circle, circumscribed by nothing but her will, her skill, her determination to remain alive.

Hoolies, she'd nearly killed *me*.

And while I recalled that, put fingers to the misshapen sculpture of scars along my ribs where her sword had cut into me, felt again the pain, the shock, the chilling flame of Boreal eating into flesh and muscle and viscera, the captain came up from behind.

"The reef was cruel," she said.

I glanced sidelong at her, saw red hair knotted back into a haphazard braid, the shine of glass beads and gold at earlobes and throat, the snug fit of the wide belt buckled around a waist I could span with my hands, and the freckled upswell of generous breasts at the droop of her neckline. A thin tunic, rippling in the wind. Baggy leggings tucked into low, heel-less boots, but a curve of calf played hide-and-show in a rent. She *was* worth looking at. No question. And she was looking back.

So. The plan commenced.

"It wasn't the reef that drove us aground." I spread my feet again, bent to touch the deck with flattened palms. I let her see the effort not to show the effort, now that she looked. "Better to say you were cruel."

"So I am." She put a hand on my spine, into the small of my back above the dhoti, and pressed. "Does this hurt?"

I caught my breath, swearing inwardly. If she was *that* kind of woman . . . well, it made the plan problematical. To say the least. Maybe even impossible; I had not taken this quirk into consideration.

Queasy again, I straightened, felt the fingers walk up my spine. The hand, without warning, slipped around to the scar tissue, squeezed. "That hurt," she said. "Once."

Beneath that hand, beneath the dead tissue, the bones remembered. So did the softer insides. Indeed, it had hurt. Very much. And now I felt sicker than ever.

"Your feet are bleeding," she observed.

I swallowed tightly. "Forgive me for staining your deck." I waited for her to remove the hand. When she didn't, I removed it for her, lifting it off my ribs. She was close enough for me to consider making a grab for her sword or knife, but I was certain she wanted that. Therefore I decided not to do it. Not yet. Not yet.

"My deck will survive," she said. "Will you? Can you?"

"That depends on the alternative." I took a step away, then turned toward her. "A man will do many things to stay alive."

The skin by her eyes creased. "So will a woman."

"Does that include running other ships aground so they break apart?"

"You may blame your captain for that. His choice was to come about and allow us to take his ship, unharmed; instead, he misjudged and tried the reef."

"You knew he would."

"Other men have not made that mistake. I believed he would choose to let his ship and his crew live." She paused. "And his passengers."

"It makes no sense to lose the cargo, captain."

"No sense," she agreed, "but that is my risk. I throw the dice—" A quick reflexive movement of her right hand. "—and occasionally I lose."

"This time."

"Perhaps. Perhaps not. There is no coin of it, that is true. But there are two men and a woman."

"And you already know there is no one to ransom two of us."

A negligent shrug of her left shoulder. "Probably no one will ransom the captain, either. I doubt he is worth much even if he has a wife."

"So much for booty, captain."

"Booty is many things. It shines, it sparkles, it chimes, it spends." She smiled. "It breathes."

This time I hid my reaction. It took everything I had. "Slavers?"

Her eyes, intently clear under sandy lashes tipped in

sunbleached gold, were patently amused. "A woman will do many things to stay alive."

I drew in a careful breath. "So will a man."

"Then do it," she suggested. "Do what is necessary."

I turned sharply to walk away from her, thinking it necessary as well as advisable—and nearly walked right into the first mate, whom I had not known was anywhere nearby. Which didn't please me in the least.

Behind me, as I stopped short, I heard the woman laugh softly, saying something in a language I didn't understand. In morning light, the rings piercing the man's eyebrows glinted. He answered her in the same language, but did not take his eyes off my face even as she departed.

I didn't doubt for a moment that had I tried for the woman's weapons at any time, he'd have killed me instantly. That was the point of surrounding yourself with men such as this.

"What are you?" he asked.

Not who. What. Interesting—

And then my belly cramped. Hoolies, but I was getting tired of this. Maybe Del was right. Maybe I *had* been stung by something in the reef. "I'm a messiah," I answered curtly, in no mood for verbal or physical games.

Teeth gleamed as his lips drew back in a genuine smile. "I thought so."

Of course, at the moment I didn't feel particularly messiah-ish. After Del's comment about me magicking weapons out of thin air, which of course I couldn't do, I hadn't been precisely cheerful. And now this blue-headed man was playing the same sort of game. With much less right.

He said something then. I didn't understand it; it sounded like the same language he and the captain shared. He watched me closely as he spoke, searching my eyes and face. I couldn't very well prepare to show or not show any kind of response, as I had no idea what he was saying. I just looked back, waiting.

He switched again to accented Southron. "Where were you bound, when we took you?"

"Skandi." I saw no harm in honesty.

Something glinted in his eyes. "*Io*Skandi."

"Skandi." I shrugged. "That's all I know. Never been there before."

Ring-weighted brows rose consideringly. "Never?"

"Southroner," I answered. "Deep desert. Punja. Bred and born."

"No."

"Yes."

"Skandic." He sounded certain.

"Maybe," I said clearly, curious now as well as irritated. "Depending on what you intend to do with us, we may never find out—"

Without warning he clamped a hand over my right wrist. I felt the strong fingers close like wire, shutting off the blood.

I moved then, used strength and leverage, was free with one quick twist. He did not appear surprised; in fact, he smiled. And nodded. "*Io.*"

No help for it but to ask it straight out. "What is this about?"

He looked from me to the deck. He squatted then, put out a hand, fingered the blood left by my reef-cut feet. Rose again, rubbing his thumb against the fingers. Then he turned the hand toward me and displayed it palm-out, blood-smeared fingers spread. "*Io.*"

"You sick son of a—"

"*You* are sick," he interrupted. "Look at your arm."

Part of me wanted not to. But part of me decided to play the game his way until I understood it better, or at least knew if there were any rules. So I looked at my arm.

Around the wrist, where he'd shut his hand, the skin was blotched with a fast-rising, virulent rash. Even as I watched, astonished, clusters of small pustules formed, broke. Wept.

"When you weary of emptying your belly," he said, "come to me."

I opened my mouth to reply, then turned and staggered to the rail. Where I promptly emptied my belly.

FIVE

DEL CAME looking for me, found me: perched again upon the rope coiled back at the stern. She stopped, arching eyebrows. "Well?"

"Well what?"

"Any progress?"

"Progress at what?"

"With the captain."

"Oh. No. I mean—" With infinite care I examined a scrape across one kneecap. "—I'm not rushing it."

After a moment of silent perusal she squatted down so she could look into my face. "What's the matter?"

I hitched a shoulder. "She's not exactly what I expected."

"No—I mean, what's the matter with you?"

I eyed her warily. "What do you mean, what's the matter with me?"

"You've been ill again. I can tell. You get this greenish tinge around your mouth, and your nose turns red."

I fingered the nose, frowning, then sighed and gave up. "I'm sick of being sick. This is ridiculous!"

Her mouth twitched. "And no aqivi to blame it on, either."

I peered at her hesitantly. "Do I feel hot to you?"

She felt my forehead, slipping hands beneath flopping hair. "No. Cold." She moved out of the squat, sat down next to me on the rope. "I still say something stung you."

"Maybe so." I sat with both arms hooked over my thighs. The right wrist no longer wept fluids. The pustules

53

were gone. The only trace of what had existed was a faint ring of reddened flesh, but it was fading rapidly. "Do you know what *io* means?"

Del shook her head.

I elaborated. "He said *io*Skandi."

"Who did?"

"The blue-head. First mate."

She shook her head again. "We know Skandi is a place, and Skand*ic* might indicate a person from Skandi, but *io*?" She shrugged. "Maybe a city in Skandi?"

I sighed, absently rubbing a wrist that felt and looked perfectly normal. "Could be. That makes as much sense as anything, I suppose." I slanted her a glance. "Well?"

"Well what?"

"Any progress on your end?"

She smiled. "I'm not rushing it."

I grinned briefly, but it died. Quickly. I stared steadily at the deck. This next part was going to be hard. "Del."

She closed her eyes against the wind. "Hmmm?"

"They took no coin, no jewels, no cargo, no ship. Only you, and me, and the captain." Now I inspected a cracked toenail. "They may intend to sell us."

Her eyes snapped opened. After a moment of tense silence, she said carefully, "That would make sense." And as I went rigid from head to toe, she put a hand upon my knee. "I know, Tiger."

"Del—" I bit into the pierced cheek, bringing fresh blood. "I can't do it again."

The hand tightened. "I know."

"We have to find a way off this ship. Before—" I shut my eyes, squeezed them, then opened them. "Before."

"We will."

I pushed myself to my feet then, took two long strides to the rail and gripped it. Sea spray dampened my face as wind stripped back my hair. It was harder than I'd thought.

"Are you sick again?"

I spat blood, then spoke steadily, without excess emotion. "I will drown myself before I let anyone sell me into slavery again."

"Oh, Tiger—" A half-hearted, desultory protest.

I swung to confront her, startling her with my vehemence. "And you had better not pull me out of the water. Promise me that."

Del stared at me, weighing words, tone, expression—and began to believe. The color drained until she was white-faced, horrified, sitting stiffly upon the rope. "I can't make such a—"

"Promise me."

She shook her head decisively. "There will be a way . . . we will find a way, make a way—"

"No," I said bitterly. "Not again."

"Tiger—"

"First the Salset for sixteen or seventeen years, then Aladar and the mines. I can't do it again. I *can't.*"

She attempted reason now, still not certain, but taking nothing for granted. "You freed yourself of the Salset. And you got free of the mines. There are opportunities that—"

"Enough." I cut her off curtly. "Don't ask it, don't wish it, don't expect it, Del. I can't."

Abruptly she thrust herself from the rope and stood there rigidly, trembling. She sought to speak, could not. Then turned to walk away with none of her usual grace.

"Del—"

She spun, furious. "Don't!"

I gestured futility. "I have to do—"

"No, you don't. You don't have to do any such thing."

I clamped my jaws shut. "I can't—"

"I can't do it! Do that? I can't! *I* can't!"

"Del—"

"No." In the coldest tone I had ever heard from her. "Are you so selfish, that you can ask this of me? Are you so blind, so arrogant?"

My voice rose. "Arrogant—!"

"What are you, to ask this of me? To expect me to watch you drown?"

"I didn't mean you had to *watch*—"

We were both shouting now. "You are a fool!" she

cried, and then added something in uplander so vicious I knew better than to request a translation.

"It's not the first time," I reminded her sharply. "When Chosa Dei was in me, you agreed to kill me. This time I'm only asking you not to rescue me."

"And I couldn't do it!" she snapped. "Do you recall I had my jivatma at your throat?"

I did. Clearly.

"Do you recall how I promised then to make certain Chosa Dei would not be set free?"

I did.

"Do you recall how he very nearly took you as his own, as his body, so that he would have the means to destroy the land?"

Oh, yes. I recalled.

"I knew then I couldn't do it," Del said. "I *knew* it. I promised you then—and I couldn't do it."

"Del—"

"I will make no more such promises, Tiger. No more. Never." Tears stood in her eyes. Outrage, most likely. And maybe something else. "The only promise I shall make you is that I will die for you."

"Del, don't . . . you don't—"

"I do," she said. "Oh, I understand. I see. I *know*. And I refuse." She stepped close to me, very close, so that I felt her breath on my face. "In the name of my dead jivatma I swear this much: that I will do everything within my power to defend your life against any threat. Even one made by you." She was trembling with anger and, I thought, fear. "Don't ask anything more. Don't wish anything less. Expect *nothing*—but that I will die in your place to keep you from being a fool."

I caught her wrists, gripped them firmly. Opened my mouth to answer, to deny her this oath—and saw we had gathered a crowd of grinning onlookers. I swore, released her, and turned sharply back to the rail.

I stared blindly at the sea as I listened to her go.

N ear dawn I awoke. I don't know if it was a sound, or the lack of. But I realized I was alone.

The emptiness was abysmal.

I stretched, twisted, and shook out parts of my anatomy until sweat sheened me. It was dawn, both breezy and cool, but I'd lost myself in the rituals I'd been taught at Alimat, in training to the shodo. He had explained that even a boy of seventeen should never assume his body was fit, and that as he aged fitness would become harder to achieve.

Of course, I didn't believe him. At seventeen (or sixteen, or eighteen; no one knew for certain), after nearly two decades of labor for the Salset, I was more than certain I was fit. After all, I'd survived slavery, had killed a sandtiger for my freedom, had been taken on as a student of Alimat. After I defeated Abbu Bensir, Alimat's best apprentice, I knew my conditioning was superb. Hadn't I nearly *killed* Abbu?

Well, yes; but accidentally. Killing him wasn't the object. Defeating him was, and that I'd accomplished. Quite unexpectedly.

However, the shodo himself, with unequivocal skill despite his advanced age, soon convinced me that despite the quickness and strength of my young body, and the potential for remarkable power and true talent, I was merely a boy. Not a man. Not a sword-dancer.

It had taken me years to understand the difference. By the time my body was honed the way the rituals of Alimat required, I was nothing like that boy who'd killed the sandtiger—and nearly killed Abbu. I was nothing like the man who moved quickly through the first four levels, followed by three more. I was a child of Alimat: conditioned to codes and rituals and the requirements of the circle.

And now I stood outside of all the circles, self-exiled. But the body remembered. The mind recalled. Reflexes roused, began to seep back despite scrapes and bruises and gouges. I was more than twice the age I'd been when Alimat had accepted me, and I knew intimately the weight of the shodo's wisdom: as a man ages, fitness becomes harder to achieve.

As years in the circle are measured, I was no longer young. I bore scars from all manner of battles and circumstances, owned a knee that complained occasionally, and had noticed of late that my distance vision took a bit longer to focus.

But I was a long way from being old, fat, or slow.

Fortunately for my plan, the captain noticed that.

She leaned her back against the rail, elbows hooked there idly—which, I could not help but notice, enhanced the jut of her impressive breasts. She rode the deck easily, graceful as cat, while wind whipped the red braid across one shoulder like a loop of twisted rope. Where the sun picked out highlights, strands of hair glowed gold as wire.

She smiled. "Do you know, I believe you might match Nihko."

"Who?"

"Nihko," she answered. "My first mate."

"Oh. Blue-head."

The woman laughed. "Is that what you call him? Well, he has a name for you, too."

"He does, does he?" I bent, flattened palms against the deck. "And what would that be?"

"Something vulgar."

I grunted. "Nothing new."

"I imagine not," she agreed. "And I expect your woman calls you something equally vulgar, now."

I straightened. "What 'my woman' calls me is none of your concern. And you of all people should know better than to describe her that way."

A red brow arched in delicate surprise. "What? Is she your woman no longer, now that you have argued?"

"She isn't 'my woman' *ever*."

"No?"

"No." I paused. "Not even before we argued."

"Do you not own her?"

I shook out my arms, flexed knees; I was cooling now in the wind, and sweat dried on my flesh. "No one owns her. She isn't a slave."

"But she is bound to you, yes?"

"No."

"Then why would she stay with you?"

I scowled at her. "The reason any woman stays with a man she—admires."

"Admires!"

"Likes," I amended grudgingly.

"Even now, do you think? After you shouted at her?"

I stood at the rail. "She shouted back."

"And now she will leave you?"

"It's a little hard to leave me when we're both stuck on this boat."

"Leave you here." She touched one breast, indicating her heart.

"Ask her," I said grimly.

"Nihko says she refuses to let you die."

I didn't realize they'd overheard *quite* that much. "Del does what she pleases."

"And if she pleases to keep you alive?"

I shrugged. "A man can find ways to die."

She considered that. "And why should he wish to die?"

He doesn't. But. "There are choices a man makes about the way he lives."

"Ah." She smiled. "And now you have argued together and are in bad temper, like children, because she *likes* you enough to wish you to survive, even if you wish to die."

"No one should interfere with a personal choice."

"No?"

"No."

"And if *her* personal choice is to keep you from dying?"

I glowered at the water and offered no reply.

"Would you prevent her from dying?"

That one was easy. "I have."

"And she, you?"

I turned on her then. "What is this about?"

"So, you will not admit a woman may prevent a man from dying? Does it weaken your soul, to know a woman can?"

I set a hip against the rail and folded arms across my

chest. "What's my prize, if I answer your questions correctly? And how would you know if I did?"

She laughed at me. "On this ship, there is truth among men and women."

"Truth?"

"I tell you a truth. There is no man of my crew who was born believing a woman could save his life. But they learned it was so, when I saved theirs."

"*You* saved theirs."

"Oh, yes. I bought them."

I stiffened. "*Bought* them—"

"Out of slavery," she answered. "All save Nihko. Nihko came to me."

"Why?" I asked sharply.

"Ask Nihko."

"No—I mean, why did you buy them out of slavery?"

"I required loyalty. And that cannot be bought, or beaten into a man."

"Loyalty for what?"

"My ship."

I began to understand. "You couldn't hire a crew."

"Coin does not buy loyalty."

"No men would hire on with you as captain. So you bought yourself a crew another way." I shrugged. "Slave labor."

"I bought them. I freed them. I gave them the choice. Eight of ten sailed with me."

"And the two who did not?"

She hitched a single shoulder. "Free men choose as they will. Those two chose to go elsewhere."

"Loyalty you couldn't buy."

In the sun, her eyes were pale. "They would have left me later. It was better to lose them then."

"And the others?"

"One is dead," she said. "The others are here.

"Still."

"Still." She tilted her head slightly. "The only man who would ask his woman to let him die rather than become a slave is a man who has *been* a slave."

Anyone who had seen my back knew that. I eyed her

up and down. "You seem to have an intimate knowledge of slavery."

She lifted her chin in assent. "My father owned many."

I had been on the verge of assuming she had been one. Or a prostitute, which is, I'd been told by Delilah, a form of slavery. But this was nothing I had expected of the conversation. "And does your father know what his daughter does?"

"What she does. What she is." A strand of sun-coppered hair strayed across her face. She trapped it and pulled it back, tucking it behind a gold-weighted ear. "He is a merchant," she said, "of men. He sells, buys, trades."

"So," I said finally, "you bought these men from your father, freed them—and now you ask them to do to other men what was done to them."

She said matter-of-factly, "Booty is many things."

And the daughter of a slaver would have no trouble finding a market for me. Or Del.

I shook my head. "No."

Small teeth glinted white. Even the rim of her lips was freckled. "*She* believes you worth saving."

I shrugged. "No accounting for taste."

It startled a laugh from her. I watched her eye me up and down, assessing me; it was what I had hoped to provoke in her, an interest in imagining what might come of intimacy, but now I could not help but wonder if she assessed me as a man who might perform in her bed—or perform as a slave. The chill in my gut expanded.

"So," she said, "you are willing to die for your freedom, as you believe death is better than slavery. I ask you, then, will you live for your freedom? If you were offered the choice?"

"I saw the choice you offered our captain in the reefs."

"But there was a choice," she insisted quietly. "I did not require him to sail his ship aground. He could have surrendered to us and saved his ship, his cargo, and the lives of his men."

"Maybe *he* didn't want to become a slave either."

"But that is the final choice," she explained. "If you have the means to buy your safety, I do not insist upon selling anyone." She flicked a hand briefly and eloquently. "Find a way to buy your freedom, if you would not have me sell it. That is your choice."

I could ignore the opening, and risk not getting another. Or I could test the possibility while making no commitment. "And what," I asked steadily, "might you count as coin?"

The slaver's daughter smiled. A light came into her eyes. "There are seven intact men on board," she said, "and I doubt you may offer more than they have."

"Have offered?" I asked. "Or are forced to surrender out of loyalty?"

"You owe me no loyalty."

"No."

"You owe me escape," she said. "To prove you are better than we judge you. And that is what you plan even here and now, as we speak."

"Is it?"

She nodded once. "I do not rule my men. I *understand* them."

"And you believe you understand me."

"More than you understand me." She grinned. "I repeat: I doubt you may offer more than my crew have."

I shrugged casually. "There are men—and there are men."

She ignored that. "I have seen your hands."

"So?"

"So. I know what manner of work causes calluses such as those. Not slave labor, but skill. Practice. Dedication. Discipline."

"*I* repeat: So?"

"You seek a sword," she said calmly. "You believe that with a blade in your hand, it will prove no difficulty to overcome eight men and one woman."

"I do, do I?"

"It shouts from your eyes. From your body. In every movement you make here, returning your body to fitness." She was serious now. "There are two kinds of men in the world: fools, and those who are dangerous."

I spread my hands. "Me? Dangerous?"

"As Nihko is dangerous. You are two of a kind."

"I've got a bit more hair on my head."

"And testicles."

That startled me. "What?"

"Some men pay with more than simple coin."

I pondered that. I pondered the idea of a man surrendering himself so far as to lose that which makes him a man. But then, there was no certainty Nihko had *had* a choice.

I cleared my throat, trying to ignore the reflexive tightening of my own genitals. With effort I changed the subject—and the imagery. "And your price, captain?"

With no hesitation she answered, "The woman."

I bit down on my anger. "Why barter for what your men could take?" Del would account for a few, but in the end superior numbers would undoubtedly prevail.

"For my men?" Her smile was bittersweet as she shook her head. "Oh, but I want her for myself."

I stared at her, speechless.

"And now you know," she said, "why my father cast me out, and how I came to be a renegada."

SIX

DEL, in the tiny cabin we'd been "assigned," swung around as I shut the narrow door behind me. Her expression was pensive; that changed to studied patience as she recognized me.

I cleared my throat. "Well," I began, "it *seemed* like a good idea. I just didn't quite figure on this—minor complication."

Blue eyes narrowed; Del knows all my tones and euphemisms. "What minor complication?"

I spread a hand across my chest. "There is, after all, one woman in the world who is not overcome by my manly charms. *Only* one, mind you—but still. I am crushed. I am undone. I am destroyed. I will undoubtedly never recover."

"You made your move on her." She considered my expression. "I thought you said you weren't rushing anything."

"I didn't make any kind of move," I said. "Well—innuendo. But that's not really a *move*—"

"Depending on how such things are interpreted."

"—at least, not the sort of thing I really consider as an official move," I finished, ignoring her interruption. "There's an art to seduction, you know."

"Seduction requires subtlety," Del said. "You have none."

"None?"

"It is one of your charms," she observed, "that there

64

is no guile in you. At least, not when it comes to such base instincts as copulation."

I affected horrified shock. "Hoolies, bascha, why don't you just take all the romance right out of it!"

"You say what you want, Tiger. I respect that."

I leered at her. "Respect this!"

Del sighed. "As I said, there is no subtlety in you."

"Well, there *was*," I answered. "At least, I *thought* I was being pretty subtle. But it's lost on that woman."

" 'That woman?' " Del eyed me curiously. "My, this sounds serious."

I began again. "She wounded me. She cut me to the quick. She utterly shattered my spirit—"

"Which will recover," Delilah put in, arid as the Punja, "with liberal applications of *my* affection and attentions, I assume."

I dropped the pose, took a step forward, hooked an arm around her neck and pulled her close against my chest. Into her hair I said, "Forgive me, bascha."

Her breath was warm on my neck. "For failing to seduce the captain?"

"No. For picking a fight with you. But I couldn't think of any other way."

Del, chin resting on the top of my shoulder, held her silence.

"You did know," I said, aware of her stiffness. "You realized, didn't you, what I was doing? Out there on the deck, in front of all the crew?"

After a moment she inhaled. "A man is often the most convincing in what he says when he *means* what he says."

"Del—"

"That was no lie, Tiger, what you said. That was not for effect. You may have intended to mislead them, but you did not mislead me. I will say it again: you have no subtlety in you. You are honest in all things, even when you lie." She set the flat of her hand against my chest and stepped away so that she could look me in the eye. "You have an honest heart. And that is what you spoke from."

This was not exactly heading in the expected direction. I tried again. "Del—"

"You meant this as much as you meant it when you repudiated all the honor codes of Alimat." Her voice was oddly flat, as if it were hard for her to speak. "When you stepped out of the circle that day before Sabra, before Abbu Bensir and all the other sword-dancers, renouncing—"

"I know what I did," I said sharply, cutting her off.

"You meant that," Del declared, "and you meant this."

I exhaled noisily, expelling all the air from my lungs, then scrubbed the heel of one hand across my forehead. "Yes, well, we all do things we have to. Even if we don't want to."

Her tone now was almost gentle. "You used me, Tiger."

I didn't shirk it. "To make them believe. Yes."

Del nodded. "As I used you to buy my way back onto Staal-Ysta."

I blinked. This was an *entirely* different topic.

"I used you, manipulated you," she said. "Offered you to them, like meat on a platter. I bought my way into a place I could no longer go, because of oaths and codes I once honored."

"To see your daughter." Whom I had not at the time known existed.

"I felt it worth the price," Del agreed. "The—risk. But I was wrong. I never should have used you so poorly."

I shrugged, discomfited as much by her emotions as by such painful recollections. "That's in the past, ba-scha."

"You might have left me at any time. No doubt some people would have counseled you to. Some would have named you mad, to stay with me in such circumstances. What I did was—unconscionable. Unforgivable."

I tried to be offhand. "Well, there's no accounting for a man's folly when a woman is involved."

Del's bittersweet smile was of brief duration. "Or a woman's, when a child is involved."

"So," I said after a moment, "we're even."

"Are we?"

"We've done things to—and *for*—one another." I hitched my shoulders briefly. "And will, I assume."

"Do things to and for one another?"

"Well, yes. It seems to be our habit."

Del nodded. "And knowing that," she said, "you will perhaps forgive me."

Oh, hoolies . . . "*Now* what have you done?"

"I have undertaken my own seduction."

The first mate? But the captain had said the man lacked testicles!

Del read my expression. "No," she said, "not like that. Why do you assume the obvious?" Then she answered herself immediately and matter-of-factly. "Because you are male." She went on before I could raise a protest beyond opening my mouth. "There is the seduction of the mind as well as of the body. It requires subtlety. It requires duplicity." She pressed both hands against her breast. "And both of those live here."

"Now, bascha, I don't think that's an accurate summation of—"

"Take pride in that you were convincing," she said. "I believed you. That's what you wanted—*needed*—so the others would believe as well. And so I do believe, and now so do they."

"But it was only to make the captain think we were fighting. So that it might seem more likely I'd look to her, to make you jealous."

"That would be a logical assumption, yes," Del agreed, "but I have said she is not a stupid woman. She will not be taken in by ordinary means."

"You calling me ordinary?"

"Surely the gods would curse me if I said such of a jhihadi." She doesn't miss anything, this woman. "So of course I will never do so. Ordinary you are not." Her mouth tensed into a flat, thin line as she thought of something, then relaxed. "And I have taken pains to make certain the first mate knows it."

Alarmed now, I blurted it. "What have you done, Del?"

"Undertaken to tell him the truth of you."

"The—truth?"

"So far as we know it." Pale brows arched. "We have established that truth is much more convincing."

"*What* truth?"

"That you may be Skandic. That we believe you are. That a man appeared to believe you were, when he saw you. That we are—were—sailing to Skandi to investigate."

None of it sounded terribly fascinating. "Why would the first mate care about any of this?"

"Because he said so."

I thought that over, weighing scenarios. "In what way?"

"In the way of a man who desires coin."

"Now wait a minute, bascha. Apart from making some coin off me in the slave markets—and you'd probably bring more—there're not many options."

"He came to me, Tiger. He asked questions about you. Because I was angry, I answered them."

"Angry." One should always be careful when Del admits to anger. "In what *way* were you angry, what questions did he ask, and how did you answer them?" Better to string the whole thing together, or this might take all day. "And what did he say once you had answered them?"

"He was—unsurprised."

That made me uneasy. "Unsurprised about what? Me? You?" I raised a silencing hand. "Never mind that. Let's go back to the questions before that one. The ones about you being angry, what he asked, and what you said."

"I was angry in just the way you intended me to be, when you made that scene on the deck," she said simply. "He asked who you were, where you were from, who your parents were—"

I interrupted sharply. "And did you tell him I don't know?"

"I told him the truth, Tiger. As I had decided—but also because I had no choice."

"What do you mean, no choice?"

"It was the only way I could think of to keep you alive."

I growled frustration. "What in hoolies—"

She continued steadily. "He says there is no doubt you are indeed Skandic—*io*Skandic, he called you—and that he will speak to his captain about taking you there."

This sounded suspicious. "Just like that?"

"Well, no," she confessed. "They are renegadas, after all."

"Ah." It made more sense now. "For a price."

"But you do not have to pay it."

"Well, that's a relief! Seeing as how I have nothing to pay it with!" I scowled at her. "Spill it, bascha. What in hoolies is going on?"

Del hitched her shoulders. "He said they would make a plan, he and his captain, and then they would tell us."

"Oh, *that* sounds promising!" I caught the string of sandtiger claws tied around my neck and yanked it straight; one of the curved claws had caught in my hair. "Did he tell you her father is a slaver?"

"This has nothing to do with slavery," Del said gently. "It has to do with a boychild born in the Southron desert of parents he never knew, who grew to become a man who grew to become a jhihadi—and who apparently looks enough like a man *from* Skandi that others speak to him in that language."

"But we don't *know* that I—"

"He says you are. And I believe him."

"Why? What has he done to earn your trust?"

"I don't trust him," she explained coolly. "I said I *believed* him. And it is for what he is, rather than what he says." Del smiled a little, studying me. "You see a bald man with rings in his eyebrows and blue tattoos on his head."

"That pretty much sums him up, I'd say."

"But *I* see a man who is of the same bone, the same body, even the same eyes. With hair, Tiger, he could be you." She paused. "Though he is older than you, and the hair might show more silver."

"Oh, thanks." I glared at her, thinking about the silvering strands she'd begun finding in mine. "You think we're long-lost brothers, or something?"

She made a dismissive gesture. "No, no, of course not. That would be too much like a tale told around the fire-cairn."

"No kidding!"

She looked straight at me. "I said there was no telling who you might be related to. Kings even. Or queens."

"What, no godlings? I'm a messiah, after all."

Del smiled blandly.

"In the name of—" But I broke off as the door opened. Del looked over my shoulder. I swung in place, badly wishing I had my sword. I felt naked without it.

Blue-headed Nihko stood in the doorway. With him was the captain. "Come out," she said. "We have decided what it is we shall do with you."

"Feeding me would be nice."

"Oh, no." The red-haired woman smiled, glanced pointedly at my waist. "Best you lose the extra flesh."

I swore as Del—thank you, bascha—smothered a laugh.

"Come out," the captain repeated. "Or shall I have Nihko *fetch* you out?"

Nihko and I eyed one another. We had history now. I'd upended him on the island, he'd laid hands on me. We were, as Del and the captain had noted, similar in size, in bone, in strength. It would undoubtedly be a vicious—and very long—fight.

Or else a very short one, equally devastating.

We reached the same conclusion at the same time. And offered one another faint smiles of acknowledgment as well as unspoken promise.

The captain shot an amused glance at Del. "I might pay to see it. Would you?"

"No," Del answered promptly. "But I would collect the coin—and a portion of the wagers—for allowing others to."

"Nah," I retorted. "It would be over before anyone could pay."

Nihko smiled blandly. "Likely so. You would be too

busy losing the contents of your belly to offer a decent fight."

I scowled at him blackly, mostly because I *was* feeling a trifle queasy. Again.

"Out," the captain said crisply. "Up on deck. Now."

Up on deck, now, in the clean, salt-laden air, I could breathe again. A stiff breeze whipped hair into my eyes. I crossed my arms and leaned my spine against the rail, affecting a nonchalance I didn't really feel, especially with the deck heaving beneath us and the rail creaking a protest under my weight. But such poses are necessary; and either they believe you, or they know exactly what you're about.

Nihko and his captain knew exactly what I was about. But they let me have the moment regardless. "So?" I began. "What is it you plan to do with us?"

The woman's pale eyes glinted. "I told you to find a way to buy your freedom."

"You did."

She glanced briefly at Del, as if seeking an indication I'd told her what the captain had said about being interested in my companion rather than in me. Del, who didn't know any such thing—we hadn't gotten that far, and I wasn't certain I'd have told her anyway—merely looked back. Waiting. Which she does very well.

After a moment the captain smiled a little and met my eyes. "And so this woman has done it for you."

I didn't know if that was for my benefit, or the truth. She knew *I* knew what she meant, even if Del didn't; if Del did, well, it made for an interesting little tangle.

I refused to play. Besides, as far as she knew, Del and I weren't on friendly terms. "Whatever the woman offered was without my knowledge."

"Men do precisely that for women often enough." But the captain indicated the first mate with a tilt of her head. "Nihko says you are Skandic."

"I might be. But Nihko doesn't *know* that I am. No one does, including me."

"That does not matter. Explain it, Nihko."

Blue-head explained it.

By the time he finished, I was shaking my head. "It'll never work. It *couldn't* work. Not possible."

"Everything is possible." The captain was unperturbed by my refusal. "Certainly this is. Because it might be true." She smiled, eyes bright with laughter. "A man with no past could be anything at all."

"Or nothing." I shook my head again. "I'm not a mummer. I could never pull this off."

She captured whipping hair, pulled it forward over a shoulder and began to braid it into control. "There is no mummery involved. We are not asking you to be—or to behave as—something you are not."

"That's *exactly* what you're asking."

"You present yourself as what you are." The captain paused in her braiding to meet my eyes. "Or, rather, *we* present you as what you are."

"Your captive?"

Unprovoked, she went back to braiding hair. "I am known in the city."

I made it into an insult. "Undoubtedly."

She continued serenely. "I am known for precisely what I am. It would be accepted by all the families as truth: Prima Rhannet seeks to spit in her father's eye by parading herself, her crew, and her lifestyle throughout the city: an ungrateful, unnatural, outcast daughter who ignores custom to present herself to one of the finest families *of* the city."

"That's you," I said. "What about me?"

"Who presents herself to one of the finest families of the city in order to reap a reward of such incredible value that in one undertaking the ungrateful unnatural outcast daughter outdoes her father." She did something with the end of the braid to keep it intact—how women do that is beyond me—and waited for me to respond.

I nodded, understanding. "This is personal."

"It is many things," she—Prima—said. "It is a means to make coin; the reward would be incalculable. It is a means to spit in my father's eye; because no matter that I was so crassly rewarded, I would still be acknowledged as the woman who returned to the Stessa family something of great value: the means to continue the line."

"A line near extinction, as you have explained it." I shook my head. "It will never work" I glanced at Del. "Tell her."

"But it might," Del said mildly.

So much for help from *that* quarter.

"Nothing need 'work,' " Prima elucidated. "It need only be believed."

"For how long?"

"Long enough for us to receive the reward, accept the public gratitude of the Stessa metri, to hear of my father's resentment, to resupply the ship . . ." She made a graceful gesture with one hand. ". . . and sail away again."

"Leaving me behind?"

"Leaving you behind with a dying old woman—a dying old *rich and powerful* woman—whose only goal now is to find a legitimate way to continue the family line. If you see no advantage in that, you are truly a fool."

I shook my head definitively. "Never work. I won't do it."

Prima Rhannet arched sun-gilded brows. "No?"

"No."

Nihko promptly hooked my feet out from under me and heaved me over the rail.

Water is hard. It felt like a sheet of hardpacked dirt when I landed, smashing into it flat on my back. For a moment nothing in my brain or body worked. I was so shocked I didn't even breathe—and then I realized I couldn't.

Water is *hard*. And when you land in—or *on*—it the way I did, taken completely unaware and utterly inexperienced with such things as flying followed by swimming, you get the air knocked right out of your lungs.

Then, of course, I sank.

SEVEN

AFTER I had swallowed enough saltwater to founder a dozen ships, I felt hands touching me. Pinching me. But I'd already exhausted strength with remarkably dramatic and equally ineffective struggles, and had reached the point where it seemed much easier simply to let go. Because the lungs weren't working at all anymore, and pretty much everything had grayed to black.

Something seized my hair. It yanked. Then something else pinched my chest again, and *it* yanked.

Not breathing didn't bother me in the least—until I was hauled by rope up the side of the ship, banging dangling limbs; jerked painfully over the rail; dumped unceremoniously on the deck. Whereupon someone set about pummeling my abdomen and ribs until I felt certain the cook was simply tenderizing my hide before chopping it up and tossing it into the pot.

About this time my lungs decided they wanted to work again, and in the middle of whooping for air, my belly expelled the ocean.

This time several hands shoved me over onto my side, so I wouldn't choke. Supposedly. I'd already gagged and coughed and choked enough to die three times over. But eventually the spasms passed, air made its way back into abused lungs, and I lay there in a tangle of knotted rope, sprawled facedown on the deck with absolutely no part of me beyond those lungs capable of moving.

Someone bent over me. I felt forearms slide beneath

my armpits, then elbows hooked. I was heaved up from the deck like so much refuse and set upright on my feet with belly pressed against the rail and held firmly in place, where I was permitted to view what had very nearly been my grave. It didn't look any better from above than it had from inside.

"The ocean is large," Prima Rhannet said lightly, "and between here and Skandi there is much of it. Shall we begin again?"

I was so muddled with the aftermath of confusion, shock, and near-drowning that I could barely remember my name, let alone what we were talking about. Standing upright seemed a fair achievement. Speaking was beyond me.

"Is he always this stubborn?" she asked.

Del said, "Yes."

That raised a croak of protest from me. Where in hoolies was *she* as they heaved me into the ocean?

"Perhaps you might suggest to him that he had best do what we ask," Captain Rhannet said. "This was your idea, after all."

I realized it was Nihko who pinned me against the rail. Or held me up, depending on your point of view. I was wet. So was he. One big hand was knotted into my hair, holding my skull still. Wobbly as I was, it wouldn't take much to dump me overboard. Again.

"Stubborn," he said, "or stupid."

"Well," Prima observed, "the same has been said of you."

The first mate laughed. "But none of them has lived to repeat the calumny."

Calumny. A new word. I'd have to ask Del what it meant.

"So," the captain began, talking to me this time, "shall you count the fish for us again?"

I spat over the side. *That* for counting fish.

Of course, it was much less intended as an insult than the clearing of a throat burning from seawater and the belch that had brought it up. I did the best I could with the voice I had left. "Being rich," I managed, "has its rewards."

Nihko grunted and turned me loose. I promptly slid to the deck and collapsed into a pile of strengthless limbs and coils of prickly rope.

After a moment, Del squatted down beside me. "They're gone, Tiger."

Here. Gone. What did it matter?

"You can get up now."

I wanted to laugh. Eventually I managed to roll from belly to back. The sun was overhead; I shut my eyes and draped an arm across my face. "I think I'll just . . . lie here for a while. Dry out."

"I expected them to beat you up," she explained, "not throw you over the side."

Ah. Vast difference, that.

"But now they'll take us to Skandi, which is where we meant to go in the first place, and we can get on about our business. I think it is easier than seducing people who may not be seduceable, and trying to steal weapons from large men who wish to keep them."

I lifted my arm slightly and squinted into the face peering down from the sky. Against the sun, she was an indeterminate blob. "This was your idea of keeping me alive?"

She appeared to find no irony in the question. "Yes." A pause. "Well, not precisely *this*."

"Was that you who pulled me out of the water?"

"Nihko did."

"He was the one who flung me into it."

"Well," Del said, "I suppose it was rather like watching a bag of gold sinking out of reach."

"And where in hoolies were *you* while this was going on?"

"Watching."

"Thank you."

"You're welcome." She put her hand on my shoulder and patted it. "It takes longer than you think to drown, Tiger."

Well, *that* made all the difference in the world.

"So," I said rustily, "we scam a dying old woman who happens to be very rich, and very powerful, with no living heirs but the grandson of a distant cousin from an offshoot branch of the family she detests—and then Prima Rhannet and her Blue-Headed Boy will turn us loose."

"That is the plan," Del affirmed.

"Nothing to it," I croaked, and dropped the arm over my eyes again.

Several days later, at dawn, I stood at the bow of the ship as we sailed into Skandi's harbor. There were, I'd learned, *two* Skandis. One was the island. One was the city. To keep them straight, most people referred to the city as the City. This had moved me to ask if there was only one city on the island, because if there were more, calling one city City among several other cities struck me as unnecessarily confusing, but Nihko Blue-head and Prima Rhannet simply looked at me as if everyone in the world knew Skandi was Skandi and Skandi was City and all the other cities were cities. Period.

I then reminded them that if I were to portray myself as a long-lost relative of some old *Skandic* lady, in line to inherit all her *Skandic* wealth and holdings, it might be best if I, supposedly Skandic myself, knew a little something about Skandi and Skandi.

Whereupon Prima merely said that it would be best if I remained ignorant, because knowing a little might be more confusing than knowing nothing. Whereupon the first mate suggested I was admirably suited for the role just as I was.

So now I stood at the bow of the blue-sailed ship that had driven us into the reefs (thereby destroying our ship, our belongings, and very nearly ourselves); abducted us from an island (and from my horse!); and now planned various nefarious undertakings with some poor little old lady who wasn't long for the world. A world that was, to me, markedly alien, if only to look at. I suppose one harbor is very like another. But this one struck me as—creative.

Skandi itself was an island. But it wasn't shaped like a proper island, supposing there is such a thing; it was in fact very much a *ruin* of an island, the leavings of something once greater, rounder. This island was not like any other I'd seen on the way, because most of the island was missing.

Imagine a large round clay platter dropped on the floor. The entire center shatters into dust. Oddly, all that remains whole is the *rim* of the platter, but it's bitten through at one point. And yet Skandi's platter rim isn't flat. It juts straight up from the ocean as a curved collection of cliffs, layer upon layer of time- and wind-carved rock and soil, afloat, anchored by some unseen force far beneath the surface. And the platter, viewed from above, might better resemble a large cookpot, a massive iron cauldron, with the ocean its stew. We, a ship in the harbor, were one of the chunks of meat.

Del came up beside me. She gazed across the harbor that more closely resembled a cauldron, eyes moving swiftly as she took in the encroachment of island that opened its arms to us in a promised embrace. Our little chunk of meat floated now in the center of the giant cauldron, and I had the odd sensation that the invisible giant looming over our heads might spear us with his knife as a delicacy.

"It's a crown," Del mused. "A crown of stone, encircling a woman's head, and the water is her hair."

That sounded a lot more picturesque than my stewpot. "Not a very *attractive* crown."

"No gold? No precious stones?" Del smiled briefly. "But there is the City, Tiger. Is it not jewellike?"

Well, no. Unless Del's giantess with her crown of stone was clumsy, because it looked to me as if she'd dropped her box of pretty rocks and spilled them over the edge of her skull.

Skandi was stewpot, crown, broken platter. From the water the remains of land reared upward into the sky, ridged and humped and folded with all its bones showing. The interior of the island itself was broken, cruelly gouged away, so that the viscera of the body gleamed nakedly in the sun.

The jewels Del spoke of were clusters of dome-roofed buildings. A parade of them thronged the ragged edge of the island's summit, then tumbled over the side, clinging haphazardly to shelves and hummocks all the way down to the water's edge. There were doors in the rock walls themselves, wooden doors painted brilliant blue; there were blue doors, too, in lime-washed buildings growing out of the gouged cliff face. Against the rich and ruddy hues of soil and stone, the blue-and-white dwellings glowed.

"The vault of the heavens," Prima said, coming up on my other side. "The domes and doors are painted blue to honor the sky, where the gods live."

"I thought I wasn't supposed to know anything about Skandi."

She smiled, looking beyond me to the face of the island. "A man seeking his home may ask his captain about it."

"Ah." I nodded sagely. "And can this captain tell me what comes next?"

"Harbor fees," she said crisply. "Port fees. Inspection fees. Docking fees."

"Lot of fees, that."

Prima Rhannet's eyes laughed at me. "Nothing in this life is free. Even for renegadas."

"And after all these fees," I said, "what happens next?"

"Say what you mean," the captain admonished. "What happens to *you*."

"Us," I corrected.

Prima's brows arched. "You and me?"

"No, not you and me . . ." I jabbed a thumb in Del's direction. "Me and *her*."

The captain affected amazement. "But I thought you were having nothing to do with one another!"

"There are times," Del put in, "when we don't. Then there are times when we shouldn't, but we do."

"And times when you do because you think you

should." Prima nodded, slanting a glance at me. "I thought as much. But did you really believe it would work, that performance?"

"Stupid people fall for a variety of things," I mentioned.

"Is that to be taken as flattery?"

I cleared my throat, aware of increasing frustration and a faintly unsettled belly. "Returning to the point at hand . . ."

"Oh, yes." She nodded, bright hair aglow in the sun. "What happens to you."

"Us," Del amended.

Hazel eyes were laughing at us. "But there will be no 'us.' "

I drew myself up in what many consider a quietly menacing posture.

This time the captain laughed aloud. "Do you believe I would permit you both to go ashore? Together?" She paused. "Do you believe that *I* do not believe you would not try to escape?"

"I don't believe I care what you believe," I retorted. "The simple fact of the matter is, if Del doesn't come ashore with me, *I* don't go ashore with me. Or, for that matter, with you." I smiled at the petite woman. "And I don't think you're strong enough to throw me overboard."

As she shrugged, her blue-headed first mate appeared.

I promptly turned and latched onto the rail with both hands in the firmest grip I commanded. "If you have him try to toss me overboard again, I'll take a piece of your ship with me!"

Prima Rhannet looked worried. "No," she murmured, "we could not have that."

Whereupon Nihko closed thick arms around Del and tossed *her* overboard.

I heard the blurted cry of shock, followed by the splash. I still hung onto the rail, but not because I feared to follow her. Because, shocked, I couldn't let go. This I hadn't expected any more than she had.

I saw her head break the surface, then pale arms. She

slicked hair back from her face and squinted up at me. Whereupon I grinned in immense relief, then turned upon the captain my sunniest smile. "Del, on the other hand, can swim. And *now* we're not all that far from the shore."

That stripped the smirk from Prima's face. She glanced sharply at her first mate. "Nihko, go."

I spun in place, blocked his way, jammed a rigid elbow deeply into his abdomen just below the short ribs. As he began to bend over in helpless response, I brought the heel of my right hand up hard against the underside of his chin. Teeth clicked together, eyes glazed over, and he staggered backward.

It was beginning as much as ending. Prima was a small woman, no match for a man as big as me, but she knew it. Which is why she did not attempt to threaten me with her knife. She simply stabbed me with it, cutting into the back of my thigh.

I yelped, swore, started to swing on her—but by this time Nihko was upright again. He caught me before I could so much as see Prima's expression. I was slammed hard into the rail and bent backward over it. One broad, long-fingered hand was on my throat.

He did not squeeze. He did not crush. He did not in any way attempt to strike or overpower me. He simply put his hand on the flesh of my throat, and it began to burn.

I heard Prima say something about throwing a rope down. I heard her shout to Del, something about rejoining us if she knew what was good for me. Briefly I thought Del should just swim for it, but I doubted she would; and anyway, I had more on my mind than whether Prima would fish Del out of the water or if Del would condescend to *be* fished. My teeth were melting.

I thought my head might burst. Not from lack of air, because I had plenty of it. But from heat, and a pressure on the inside of my skull that made me sweat with it, gasping at the pain. It was if someone had set a red-hot metal collar around my neck.

Nihko murmured something. I didn't have the first idea what he said, because it was a language I didn't speak. Something muttered, something chanted. Something *said*.

Then he took his hand away, the heat died out of my head, and I fell down upon my knees.

"Io," he said.

I put one trembling, tentative hand to my neck, expecting to feel blood, fluids, charring, and curled, crusted flesh. But all I felt were the sandtiger claws upon their leather thong, and healthy flesh beneath.

"Io," he repeated, in satisfaction commingled with anticipation.

"Go to hoolies," I responded, though the voice was hoarse and tight.

"You go," Nihko suggested.

I recalled the rash around my wrist, triggered by his touch. And now the heat in my head, the blazing of my flesh. "What are you?"

The rings in his eyebrows glinted. "IoSkandic."

"And what precisely does that mean?"

He displayed white teeth. "Secret."

I got my legs under me and wobbled to my feet. "The word means secret, or it *is* a secret?"

"Nihko," Prima said, and he turned from me.

A rope hung over the side, taut against the rail. The captain glanced at me, then at Nihko; he leaned over, grasped the rope, pulled it up even as Del herself clambered over the rail. Fair hair was slick against her skull, trailing down her back in a soaked sheet. The ivory-colored leather tunic, equally soaked, stuck to her body and emphasized every muscle, every curve.

Prima Rhannet stared. Nihko Blue-head did not. That more than anything convinced me the captain had not lied: the first mate was not, as men are measured, a man anymore. And the *woman* was more than a little attracted to the woman who slept with me.

I had seen it in men before. With someone who looks like Delilah, it's a daily event. But I had never seen the reaction in a woman before. Generally the women of the South are shocked and appalled by Del's sword, her freedom of manner and dress, her predilection for saying what she thinks no matter how it sounds. Some of the younger women were vastly fascinated, even if they had to be subtle about it lest they alert or alarm their men. Or they are intensely jealous. But no woman I'd ever seen had looked at Del the way a man looks at Del.

Until now.

And I hadn't the faintest idea how to feel about it.

There were jokes about it, of course. Crude, vulgar, male jokes, men painting lurid pictures with words, suggesting activities for women *with* women designed to titillate. And of course there were men who preferred men, or boys, who also prompted jokes. But *seeing* a woman react to a woman the way a man reacts to a woman was—odd.

Should I be jealous? Angry? Insulted? Upset? Should I say something? Do something?

Did *Del* recognize it?

Maybe. Maybe not. I couldn't tell. She was wearing her blandest expression, even sheened with water. And *would* a woman be aware of another's interest? Did Del even know such things existed?

For that matter, did Del have any idea what kind of reaction she provoked in men? I mean, she knew they reacted; how could she not? Most men aren't very subtle about it when everything in them—and on them—seizes up at the sight of a beautiful woman of immense physical appeal. There'd been enough comments made about and to Del that she couldn't be oblivious. On the whole she ignored it, which didn't hurt my reputation any: the gorgeous Northern bascha was so well-served by the Sandtiger that she neither noticed nor looked at another man.

But then, for a long time I hadn't known she'd even notice or look at *me*.

The way Prima Rhannet was looking at her.

"Well," I said brightly, trying to sound casual, "just what did you have in mind, then? You and I are to go ashore and go visit this old lady?"

Prima blinked, then looked at me. "No. I will stay here, aboard ship. It is best that Nihko goes as my representative. Him the metri will see. And once she understands what I have to offer, she will see me as well."

"And why will this—metri?—see him, but not you?"

Prima smiled faintly. "I have told you what I am. The ungrateful, unnatural, outcast daughter of a slaver. I am not of the proper family for the Stessa metri."

"But she'll see him?" I jerked a thumb at Nihko. "He's an ugly son of a goat with rings in his eyebrows and a hairless head painted blue. *That's* not unnatural?"

Nihko bared his teeth in an insincere smile. The captain looked amused. "She will see him because of what he is."

I prodded. "Which is?"

The first mate grinned in genuine amusement. "Secret."

I turned on my heel and stalked away, though it was somewhat ruined by the limp; the wound in the back of my thigh *hurt*. I couldn't go very far—we were on a ship, after all—but it made my point nonetheless.

Prima raised her voice. "Get dressed."

"In what?" I flung back over a shoulder. "All I've got in this whole gods-forsaken world is what I'm wearing!" Which wasn't much, being merely a leather dhoti and the string of claws. And blood trickling down my leg.

The captain shrugged elaborate dismissal. "Nihko will have something."

Nihko wasn't wearing a whole lot more than I was at the moment. But I shut my teeth together and followed him below, wanting very much to warn Del against—whatever.

EIGHT

"**W**AIT, WAIT," Del said crossly. "Let me look first."

Accordingly, I waited, swaths of lurid crimson silk and linen clutched in one hand. Having shed the dhoti, I wore absolutely nothing. Except my string of claws.

I arched brows and tilted my head in elaborate invitation. "You have something in mind?"

She flapped a hand at me. "Turn around."

"You prefer the back view?" I paused. "Or perhaps I should say, the back*side* view?"

Del whacked me across the portion of my anatomy under discussion. "Stop being uncouth. I'm trying to see that stab wound."

"Well, *that's* not any fun." I winced. "It'll do a lot better if you keep your fingers out of it."

"I've seen worse," she said after close inspection, "but it needs bandaging. Or you'll bleed all over your clothes."

"Not my clothes. *Nihko's* clothes. Do you really think I'd be caught dead in these things?"

"You are caught," she observed, commencing to tear spare linen, "but at least you're still alive. For the time being. And anyway, I've seen you in red before. It suits you."

I had once owned a crimson burnous, it was true, for meetings with tanzeers considering hiring me, or feasting me after a victory. It had even boasted gold borders and tassels. But I had never heard Del mention anything about me being suited before. "Does it?"

"Hold still." She began wrapping my thigh.

"Ummmm . . . maybe I'd better do that."

"Why?"

"If you don't know, just wait a minute. It'll be obvious—*ouch!*"

"Not anymore," she said crisply, knotting the bandage tightly. "Now, get dressed so you can accompany Nihko to this household. The sooner you are accepted as the long-lost heir, the sooner we'll be free of the renegadas."

"You act like you think I *will* be accepted as the long-lost heir," I accused, "and you know as well as I it's a load of—"

"—potential," Del put in. "Possibility and potential. Which need have nothing to do with this dying old woman—this metri?—but rather with the opportunity to get free of the renegadas once you are accepted by this metri."

"Leaving you in Prima Rhannet's clutches? Not a chance!"

Del, noting my vehemence, looked at me curiously. "It's no worse a danger to me than any other I've been in."

I had no reasonable explanation at hand (or at tongue), and began to hastily don clothing. Eventually I rather lamely settled on: "I'd hate to have any actions on my part jeopardize your life."

"After three years, you should know better. Any actions on your part *always* jeopardize my life."

"Yes, but . . ." I jerked the sash tightly around my waist and knotted the rich silk; Nihko apparently liked to wear good cloth while running ships aground. "I'm older, and wiser, and less fond of danger than I used to be. For me *or* for you."

"We don't have much choice," she pointed out. "They are going to take you to the Stessa metri, whatever that is, and keep me here as insurance against your escape. But that is precisely what you must do as soon as you have a chance. And meanwhile I will contrive a way to escape as well."

"You make it sound so easy!"

Del shrugged. "It's merely a matter of seeing the opportunity, and taking it. Or making it."

Considering I had planned to do precisely that by seducing the captain, I couldn't very well get specific with objections. Especially since I could think of no reasonable way to explain.

"I will find a way," Del said.

Having no answer to that and equally no explanation for why her presence aboard ship with its captain unsettled me, I glumly went out of the cubbyhole masquerading as cabin and took myself up on deck.

From up close, Skandi was even more impressive. Sharp-faced cliffs appeared as if some giant's hand had broken off huge chunks of raw land, leaving behind rough folds of visible horizontal layers, bands of multihued rock, soil, and mineral. And up that cliff, zigzagging back and forth in blade-sharp angles, was a track of some kind. Even from the deck I could see colored blobs moving on the track. Some ascended, some descended. People on foot, and smaller versions of what we call danjacs in the South, long-eared horselike animals used to carry loads. I suspected horses might make a better job of it by hauling carts up and down, but one glance at the narrowness of the track, the sharpness of its turns, and the steepness of the cliff convinced me the last thing *I'd* want to do was attempt to ride the stud up that trail. Maybe it was better to trust smaller loads to animals less minded to state dissenting opinions.

About halfway up the track, pocking the cliff face like a disease, were blue-doored holes dug out of the porous stone. No trees and little vegetation clung to the sides; the soil seemed disinclined to pack itself tightly around root systems, so that nothing got a foothold strong enough to encourage vast growth. What was there was pretty scrubby, and twisted back upon itself to huddle against the cliff as if afraid of heights.

"Homes," Prima said, coming up beside me.

I glanced at her, then stared back at the track. "Why would anyone choose to live in a hole?" Let alone put doors over the holes and paint them blue. "Why not build homes like those?" A gesture indicated the squat, white-painted dwellings with their hump-backed roofs.

"This island was born of smoke," she said simply, "and when the gods decreed a place for Man was required, they made the smoke solid. But there were pockets in the smoke that became as holes in the rock. When the gods placed Man here, he was poor. He settled in the rudest shelter available." She smiled. "I was born in one of those caves."

"And did yours have a door on it?"

"Of course. We are civilized, Southroner."

"Ah. And should I assume that only the wealthy live in those?" This time I indicated the houses tumbling over the edge of the cliff like oracle bones.

"Only the wealthy live in those," she confirmed, "or those who aspire to wealth and behave as if the aspirations are already fulfilled."

"Your father?"

"My father aspired for a very long time. Eventually those aspirations *were* fulfilled."

"But not, I take it, in a line of work openly approved by the truly wealthy."

She grinned. "Oh, the truly wealthy detest my father and others like him. But they require slaves to work in the vineyards, on the ships, in the kilns. There are not enough of us who are freeborn."

"Or enough of you who wish to dirty your hands with hard work."

Prima held up both hands and displayed callused palms. "My hands are very dirty," she pronounced solemnly.

"And bloody," I said gently, "even when washed clean."

The humor faded from her eyes, but not the determination. "And how often do you wash the blood from yours?"

"I dance," I retorted. "Rarely do I kill."

"I steal," she said. "Rarely do I kill."

Impasse. I sighed and jerked my head toward the cliff. "Which one of those are we bound for, captain?"

"None of those," she answered. "The Stessa household is on top of the island, in the midst of the vineyards."

"Well," I said resignedly, "at least they'll have something to drink."

The captain laughed. "Do you take nothing seriously in this world?"

"I take you *very* seriously."

She eyed me sidelong. "No, I do not believe so. In fact, you have no idea at all what to think of me."

"You ran our ship aground and plucked us off the island like so much ripe fruit," I remonstrated, "which is not precisely easy to do, plus you had me heaved me over the side of this ship—which also is not easy to do—and nearly drowned me. Not to mention the hole you poked in the back of my leg. Why shouldn't I take you seriously?"

"Because you are a Southroner."

"Ah-hah!" I stabbed the air with a forefinger. "But I'm really Skandic, am I not?—or we would not be undertaking this deception of a dying old woman designed to gain you coin. And anyway, what do *you* know about Southroners?"

"You very probably are Skandic," she agreed, "in blood and bone, if not in mind, which is definitively Southron. As for what I know about men like you, you forget I am the daughter of a slaver. As heir, I was trained in the business from childhood."

I very nearly asked if her father had sired no sons—and checked abruptly as I realized that kind of question would back up her argument. Which was not a particularly comfortable realization on my part. I scowled.

"I saw many Southroners brought beneath my father's roof," Prima continued. "Not a man among them respected women."

As annoyed with myself as with her, I challenged sharply. "You don't even *know* me, captain. I submit that you are in no position to evaluate my mind."

"I was taught to evaluate men's minds as much as their bodies," she said serenely.

"As the daughter of a slaver," I shot back, "which somewhat limits your capacity to make a legitimate evaluation. Having been captured and made over into a slave when one was freeborn is not designed to bring out the best attitude in a man, you know?"

"*You* know," she answered. "You may be a sword-dancer now, and very likely freeborn—but sword blades do not leave the kind of scars your back bears."

"Which renders me somewhat more familiar with the experience than you. No slaver ever knows a slave's mind."

"And is that how you escaped? Because your owner did not know your mind?"

"I didn't escape. I *earned* my freedom." And bore other scars to show for it as well as a name; the sandtiger I'd killed had been devouring children of the tribe who had made me a slave.

"As my crew earned theirs," Prima said quietly. "But there is more inflexibility to a Southron man's mind than what slavery may cause. And if you are truly as free in thought as you suggest, you will admit it."

"Now *that's* a double-edged sword if I ever saw one. Cursed if I do, cursed if I don't."

She grinned. "Then you may as well answer."

I glowered at her. "You're as inflexible, captain."

"Why?"

"You said you prefer women. Isn't that inflexible?"

"*You* prefer women."

"Of course I do!"

"Then you are against men."

"I *am* a man—" I began.

"As your lovers," she clarified.

"Hoolies, yes," I said fervently.

"Then we are the same, are we not?"

"How can we be the same? You're a woman. You're supposed to sleep with men, not with other women!"

"Why?"

"Because that's how it's supposed to be!"

"Is it?"

"Yes!"

"Why?"

In frustration, I set fingers into my hairline and scratched vigorously. "Because that's just the way it is."

"For you."

"For *most* people!"

"What about the woman?"

"Which woman?"

"The one you sleep with." She paused. "The one you *currently* sleep with."

"Three years' worth," I snapped. "Don't assume I take our relationship lightly."

"But of course you do. Did you not intend to seduce me?"

I scowled. Cursed if I did, cursed if I didn't.

Her expression was impish. "And would you have pursued it had the captain been a man?"

"Hoolies, no!"

"Therefore because I was a woman I was judged fair game, and you assumed I would succumb to your charms the way so many other women have." She nodded. "An inflexible—and purely Southron—way of thinking."

She was tying me up in verbal knots. "Now, wait a minute—"

"Of course, were I a woman who desired men in her bed, I might well have allowed myself to be seduced. Because you *do* have a certain amount of charm—" Startled, I shut my mouth on an interruption. "—and you did approach the campaign with more integrity than another man might."

That made no sense. "Integrity? I thought you were accusing me of having no respect for women."

"Integrity. Because you were at pains to pick a fight with your woman so there was *reason* to look to me as an alternate bedmate, and because you did not approach me directly. It was, as I said, a campaign. And I respect that. It requires imagination and forethought."

"You yourself just said I picked a fight with Del. If you value truth, how can you respect that?"

Her eyes were steady. "You *would* rather drown than be made a slave again. A man may lie for effect, to manipulate, and while the truth served you, it was indeed truth."

"You know that, do you?"

"I am a very good judge of slaves—"

"I'm not—"

"—and you are no longer one in mind or body," she finished. "There is no need for you to lie."

It was time to take control of this discussion. "Then if you respect truth, let me offer you this." I paused, marking her calm expression and determining to alter it. "If you attempt to seduce Del, I'll take you apart. Woman or no."

Calmness indeed vanished, but was replaced by an open amusement I hadn't expected. "Male," she said, and "Southron. *So* male, and so Southron!"

"I mean it, captain."

"I know you do. Honesty, if couched as a threat. Save I wonder which frightens you more: that I will attempt to seduce her—or that she might accept."

I shook my head. "She won't."

"And so I offer to you my own truth, Southroner: I will let the woman decide what she will and will not do. It should be *her* decision, yes? Because anything else is a slavery as soul-destroying as that which you experienced."

The Southroner in me hated to admit she was right. The man who had accompanied Del for the last three years, thereby learning truths he'd never imagined, did admit it—if privately—and could muster no additional argument that contained validity.

"Well," I said finally, "at least you've got to give me credit for threatening you the same as I would a *man*."

Prima Rhannet's generous mouth twitched, but she had the good grace not to laugh aloud.

It was midmorning as Del stood at the rail by the plank, waiting silently. I saw the stillness of her body, the posture of readiness despite that stillness, and knew she, as I, missed her sword badly.

Or even *a* sword. We'd both of us lost our true swords:
I three years before, when Singlestroke had been broken;
Del to the maelstrom of angry sorcerers who considered
themselves gods. She had broken that sword, the jivatma
named Boreal, to save my life, and nearly extinguished
her own. Meanwhile, I had also lost the sword I'd made
in Staal-Ysta. It was, in fact, buried in the rubble that
covered Del's broken jivatma. We had purchased new
swords, of course—only a fool goes weaponless—but
neither of them had suited us beyond fulfilling a need.
And now we had none at all, thanks to the renegadas.

Two of those renegadas waited just behind Del, as
ready as she to move if necessary. I knew by the expression in her eyes that she would not make it necessary. Not
yet. Not until after I was off the ship and on firm ground
again, where no one could toss me into the water. She
would permit me to risk myself in a true fight, but not to
drowning.

Nihko came up behind me; behind him, his red-haired
captain, glinting of gold in her ears and around her throat.
I grimaced, thinking of the plan, our circumstances;
shook my head slightly, then stepped forward to bend my
head to Del's.

Instantly four renegadas surrounded both of us. Hands
were on Del, hands were on me. I was shoved down the
plank toward the dock and nearly tripped, catching my
balance awkwardly before I could tumble headfirst into
the sea. By the time that was avoided I was halfway down
the plank, and when I turned to look at Del they had taken
her away.

So much for good bye, good luck, or even a murmured
"Kill 'em when you get the chance."

Nihko prodded me into motion as the plank bowed
under our weight. I moved, not liking the instability over
so much water. He escorted me off the ship, off the dock,
onto the quay, and to the bottom of the track slicing its
way up the cliff. From here I could look straight up and
see the cliffside dwellings looming over my head like
white-painted, blue-doored doom. The back of my neck
prickled; the haphazard manner of construction made it

appear as though everything rimming the cliff might fall down upon my head at any given moment.

"One good shake," I muttered.

Nihko glanced at me. "And so there was."

"What?"

"The histories says once Skandi was whole, and round, not this crescent left behind."

I gazed at the cliff face of the crescent uneasily. "What happened to it?"

"This was a place built of smoke," Nihko began.

Having no patience with stories about gods, I interrupted rudely. "I know all about that. Your captain already gave me the speech."

"Then you should understand that what the gods do, they can also undo." He gestured. "What was smoke became smoke again."

Hoolies, but I hate cryptic commentary! With exaggerated patience I inquired, "And?"

He turned, gesturing into the harbor behind us. "Do you see that smoke? The small islands?"

I had marked them, yes. Two crumpled, blackened chunks of land that appeared uninhabitable, in the middle of the cauldron. Rather like burned-down coals after a light rain, exuding faint drifts of smoke into the morning air.

Nihko nodded. "They are the children of the Heart of the World."

"The—what?"

"Heart of the World. It lies now beneath the sea. But the children have risen to see whether this place is worthy of their presence once again."

I gazed at him steadily. "You do realize none of this makes any sense at all."

He grinned cheerfully, unoffended. "It will."

"Meanwhile?"

"Meanwhile, the island was turned into smoke again. The land bled. Burned. Became ash. The island shook and was split asunder. You see what remains."

Not much, if what he said was true. But it seemed unlikely that such a calamity could really happen. I mean, land bleeding? Turning to ash and smoke? Shaking itself apart? More than unlikely: impossible.

Of course, I'd said a lot of things were impossible— and then witnessed them myself.

"We have maps," he said quietly, seeing my skepticism. "Old maps, and charts, and drawings. Histories. This island was once far more than it is."

Rather like Nihko himself, if what Prima had said of his castration was true. I stared at the cliff again. "I suppose we're going up that poor excuse for a trail?"

"But on four feet," he replied.

"You want me to ride one of *those?*" "Those" being the danjaclike beasties that rather resembled something crossed with a small horse and a very large dog.

"It will save time," the first mate explained, "and keep our feet clean. Otherwise we will slip and slide in molah muck all the way up, like the lesser folk." A tilt of his shaven head indicated men and women on foot toiling up and down the cliff.

"Molah muck?"

"They are molahs." He waved at a string of the creatures waiting patiently at the bottom of the track. "And they can carry four times their weight without complaint."

"I'd just as soon carry my own weight, thanks. I'm kind of used to it."

"Molah," he said gently, and I thought again about how his grip had made my wrist weep, and my throat flesh burn. "And if you are presenting yourself to the wealthiest metri on the island as a man who may be her heir, you shall ride."

"Fine," I said glumly, surveying the drooping animals tied to a rope beside the trail, "we ride. But it looks to me like we'll be dragging our feet in the muck anyhow, all the way up."

NINE

WE DID not actually drag our feet in molah muck all the way up, though it was a close call. Initially I yearned for stirrups, since dangling long legs athwart a narrow, bony back only barely padded by a thin blanket was not particularly comfortable, but I realized soon enough that stirrups would have made it worse. Riding with legs doubled up beneath my chin isn't a favored position for a man with recalcitrant knees.

For a sailor, Nihko Blue-head rode his molah with a grace I didn't expect; but I reflected that balancing atop the beastie wasn't so much different from maintaining balance aboard a wallowing ship, and therefore he had an advantage. I was more accustomed than he to riding an animal, perhaps, but horses and molahs have vastly different ways of going. Horses basically stride, planting large hooves squarely on the ground. Molahs—mince. On something that feels disturbingly like tiptoes. Very rapidly, so that one ascends at a pace that can only be called a jiggle.

I reflected that perhaps Nihko had no testicles because he'd ridden a molah up this cliff once too often.

As we climbed, tippytoeing our way around people on foot, I cast glances back the way we'd come. From increasing height it became very clear just how round the island had once been. Despite all of this silly talk about gods and smoke turning into stone (and back again), there was no question that once there had been more to the island. And it struck me as oddly familiar to Southron-raised eyes: what Nihko and I climbed was the vertical rim of a circle. The interior below, a brilliant greenish blue, was where two men would meet in the center for a sword-dance.

If they could walk on water.

Me, I couldn't, any more than I could magic weapons out of the air. What I *could* do was change the sand to grass.

Or so the legend went that others in the South viewed as prophecy. Of course, *I* put no stock in such nonsense. Even when a handful of deep Desert dwellers, led by a holy man who claimed he could see the future, claimed I was the jhihadi of the prophecy, the man meant to save the South from the devouring sands.

Horse piss, if you ask me.

And that's precisely what gave me the idea to dig channels in the desert and bring water from where it was to places it was not. Horse piss. Thanks to the stud.

Who would have been a *lot* more comfortable to ride up this gods-cursed track than a stumpy-legged, bony-backed, mincing little molah.

Hoolies, I wouldn't even mind getting bucked off if I only had the stud!

Then I shot a quick glance down the cliff. Well, maybe not.

It struck me then, as we climbed, that this was what I had come for. To see Skandi, this place I might be from, if indirectly; I'd been born in the South, but bred of bones shaped in a different land. Here? Possibly. As Del had remarked, as Prima Rhannet, as even *I* had noticed, Nihko and I were indeed similar in the ways our bodies were built, even in coloring, which seemed typical for Skandi.

And yet not everyone toiling up and down the track had green eyes and bronze-brown hair—or shaven heads decorated by blue tattoos, come to that. It was obvious, in fact, that not everyone walking the track was even Skandic, if Nihko and I were the prevailing body type; many were shorter, slighter, or tall and quite thin, with a wide variety in hair color and flesh tones. I'd grown accustomed to certain physical similarities in the South, where folk are predominantly shorter, slighter, darker, and in the North, where folk are as predictably taller, bigger, fairer. But here upon the cliff face walked a rainbow of living flesh.

And then I recalled that Skandi's economy depended on slave labor, from the sound of it, and I realized why the variety in size and coloring was so immense.

A chill tickled my spine. Here I'd come to a place that could well have bred my parents, and yet it was peopled as well by those unfortunates who had no choice but to service others who had the wealth, the power, the willingness to own men and women.

I'd been owned twice already. Once for all of my childhood and youth among the Salset, then again in the mines of the tanzeer Aladar, whom Del had killed to free me.

The South is a harsh and frequently cruel land. But it was what I *knew*. Skandi was nothing but a name to me— and now a rim of rock afloat in the ocean—and I realized with startling and unsettling clarity that I had, with indisputably childish hope, dreamed of a place that was perfection in all things. So that I would be born of a land and people far better to its children than the South had been to me.

A sobering realization, once I got beyond the initial pinch of self-castigation for succumbing to such morbid recollection. I knew better. Dreams never come true.

I shut my eyes at that. *My* dream had come true. The one I'd harbored in my soul for as long as I could recall: to be a free man. And I had won that freedom at last, had dreamed it out of despair and desperation into truth, at the cost of Salset children.

Guilt stirred, and unease. And then I thought again what I might have been had I remained with the Salset, and what I had become since earning my freedom.

As for what I was *now*—well, who knows? Sworddancer, once. Now borjuni to some people. And, others would say; others *had* said: messiah.

Who was, just at this moment, captive to a man wearing a vast complement of rings in his eyebrows.

* * *

Eventually we reached the top of the cliff. Gratefully I began to hoist a leg across the molah's round little rump, but Nihko fixed me with a quelling look and told me to wait.

If he thought I was preparing to leap off the molah and sprint for freedom, he was wrong. I just wanted to stand on my own two feet again—and to be certain I hadn't permanently squashed my gehetties on the way up. I contemplated dismounting anyway—it was a breath-taking drop of three whole inches—but took a look around and decided I'd better not. I was barefoot, after all, and we had just arrived in a clifftop area full of molahs (and their muck), throngs of people, yelping dogs (and their muck), a handful of chickens, and a dozen or so curly-coated goats. And their muck.

All of whom saw Nihko aboard his molah and abruptly melted away.

Well, the *people* did; the chickens, goats, and dogs remained pretty much as they were. They were also a lot louder, now that every person within earshot had fallen utterly silent.

I saw widened eyes, surprise-slackened mouths, and a flurry of hand gestures. About the time I opened my mouth to ask Nihko what in hoolies was going on, he spoke. A single word only, very crisp and clipped, in a language I didn't know; I assumed it was Skandic. When a stirring ran through the crowd, he repeated it, then followed up the word with a brief sentence. Quick, furtive glances were exchanged, different hand gestures were now made close to the body so they weren't as obvious. But no one spoke. That is, except for one hoarse shout issued by someone I couldn't see.

A path was instantly cleared through the crowd. A man in a thin-woven, sun-bleached tunic came toward us. He carried a stamped metal basin in both hands. Lengths of embroidered cloth were draped across his arms, and strung over his shoulders was a wax-plugged, rope-netted clay bottle glazed blue around the lip. Puzzled, I watched as he knelt there in the dirt and muck and carefully set down the basin. He unhooked the bottle, unstoppered it, poured water into the basin, murmured something that sounded like an invocation, then dipped the cloth in, meticulously careful that no portion of the fabric slipped over the side of the basin into the dirt.

All very strange—and it got stranger. He came to Nihko, bobbed his head briefly, deftly removed Nihko's shoes, and began to wash his feet.

Astounded, I stared. When finished, the man slipped the shoes back on Nihko's feet, rinsed the cloth in the basin, set it aside into a rolled-up, draining ball, then approached me with yet another embroidered length.

"Uh—" I began.

"You will allow it," Nihko said curtly.

I considered drawing my feet away, if only to spite the first mate. I considered sliding off the molah. I considered telling the basin-man with tone if not in a language he knew that I was fine with dirty feet; he didn't need to wash them for me; I'd take care of it myself when I found a public bath.

But I was in a strange place, ignorant of customs and their potential repercussions, and self-preservation prevailed. I clamped my mouth shut and let the man wash my feet.

He said something very quietly as he worked; remarking, I thought, over the healing cuts and scrapes. His hands were unexpectedly gentle, diffident. When I didn't answer, he glanced up at me briefly, waiting expectantly; when I shook my head once, he looked away immediately and completed his task without further speech. It became clear he was perplexed by my lack of shoes.

Nihko said something to him. The man blanched, collected the balled-up, soiled cloths, basin, and clay bottle, and hastily lost himself in the crowd.

I wiggled my clean toes, shot a glance at the first mate. "Wouldn't it make more sense to wash our feet *after* we get where we're going?"

Nihko smiled, but there was nothing of humor in it. "If you touch the ground with cleansed feet, you will seal yourself as one of them."

Them. "And I take it that is not a good thing?"

"Not if you wish to be sealed as heir to the Stessa metri."

I sighed. "What, are these Stessas too good to walk the streets like everyone else?" I looked pointedly at his feet. "Are you?"

"Oh, but *I* am not expected to walk anywhere," he said casually. "I am ioSkandic, and I am expected to fly."

I blinked. "Well, that would certainly save you the ride up the cliff."

One corner of his mouth quirked, but he offered no comment.

I scowled. "You're serious."

"Am I?" His expression was privately amused. "And do you know me so well that you may judge such things?"

Ah, hoolies, it wasn't worth the breath to debate. "When exactly are we supposed to go to this infamous household?" I paused. "And do we walk, ride, or fly?"

His mouth twitched again. "Even in ignorance, you ridicule possibilities."

"No, I ridicule *you*. There's a difference."

"Ah. I am remiss in my comprehension." Without glancing around to see if anyone noticed, Nihko made a slight gesture. The crowd, which had begun to speak quietly among themselves, noticed. It fell silent once again. Once again, people flowed out of the way. This time it wasn't the man with basin and embroidered cloths who came to us, but an entirely different man, a wiry man on foot leading two dust-colored molahs hitched to a kind of bench-chair on wheels.

"What in hoolies is that contraption?"

"Transportation," Nihko answered.

"And here I thought you could fly."

"But you can't. Good manners require me to travel as you travel."

"Good manners? Or because I'm your prisoner?"

"Ah, but you are my prisoner only because you have not learned the ways to avoid such things." He gestured again. The man with the molah-cart came up to us, stopped his animals, then set about collecting a rolled mat from the underside of the cart, which he unrolled and spread upon the ground. "As my companion, you may go first." Nikho paused. "And do not soil your feet."

It was clear to me that after the ritual washing, followed by the laying out of the mat, it was vital I do as Nihko said. Despite the seeming meekness of the crowd, for all I knew any transgression would earn me a quick journey over the edge of the cliff, whereupon I would descend in a faster and more painful way than on molah-back, which was bad enough. So I got off the stumpy little beastie, making certain I ended up in the center of the woven mat, and moved toward the cart. Which, from up close, looked more like a bench-chair than ever. It was woven of twisted vine limbs, bound with thin, braided rope. The bench was padded with embroidered cushions, while the back was made of knotted limbs that once must have been green and flexible, but now were dried and tough.

The ground beneath me swayed. I reached out and caught hold of the bench, gripping tightly. I didn't feel sick, but my balance was definitely off. And yet no one around me seemed to notice that the ground beneath them was moving.

Nihko swung off his molah onto the mat with the ease of familiarity. He strode past me and stepped into the cart without hesitation, beckoning me to join him.

I clung a moment longer, still unsettled by poor balance. I saw Nihko's ring-weighted brows rise, and then he smiled. "The sea has stolen your legs," he said briefly, "but she will give them back."

Ah. Neither magic nor sickness. With an inward shrug I climbed into the cart. Good thing the molahs could carry four times their weight; Nihko and I together likely weighed close to five hundred pounds.

"Akritara," he said only, and I heard the murmuring of the crowd.

The molah-man rolled up his mat, slid it into a narrow shelf beneath the bench, and went to his animals. With a jerk and a sway the molahs began to move, and I wrapped fingers around twisted limbs. Two wheels did not make for stability; the balance was maintained by the rope-and-wood single-tree suspended between molah harness and the bench itself.

"So," I began as we jounced along, "just why *is* it we're not supposed to walk anywhere?"

"Oh, we will walk. But only on surfaces that have been blessed."

"Blessed?"

"By the priests."

"You have priests who bless your floors?"

"Priests who weave the carpets in the patterns of the heavens." He glanced skyward briefly.

I made a sound of disgust. "Let me guess: they're blue."

Nihko smiled. "Only their heads."

Of course I'd meant the rugs, but that no longer mattered in view of his comment. And his head. "Don't tell me *you're* a priest!"

His expression was serene. "If you can be a messiah, surely I can be a priest."

That shut me up. But only for a moment. "So, your Order makes a nice living supplying men to destroy ships, steal booty, and kill passengers?" I arched brows elaborately. "A rather violent priesthood, wouldn't you say?"

That earned me a baleful glance. And silence.

"So, what becomes of the mats at the end of the day? Doesn't the blessing wear out? Or does this poor man have to scrub the mat each night, before picking up passengers tomorrow?"

"He will scrub it, yes. And each first-day he will take it to the nearest priest to have the blessing renewed."

"Once a week."

"So I said."

"For a price, I assume."

"Do you know of anything in this life that bears no cost?"

"You're sidestepping," I accused, "like someone in the circle who doesn't want to start the dance. So, this man pays to have his mat blessed each week so that blue-

headed folk like you don't have to walk in the dirt." I
nodded. "Sounds like a racket to me."

Nihko scowled blackly. "You would name faith and
service to the gods a *racket?*"

"Sure I would. Because it is."

His expression was outraged. "You blaspheme."

"But only if there *are* gods. And only if they care
about such things." I shrugged. "I'm not certain they give
a sandrat's patootie about anything we do. If they exist."

"You are disrespectful, Southroner."

"I am many things, Blue-head. So far the gods haven't
bothered to complain."

"You are a fool."

"That, too."

With a mutter of disdain, he subsided into silence. I
sighed and twisted to look back the way we'd come. Already the edge of the cliff receded. Beyond it I could see
nothing but a blindingly blue sky, and wisps of steam
rising from the smoking islands in the middle of the cauldron of blue-green sea.

Oh, bascha, I wish you were here. As much to share
Skandi with me as to be free of Prima Rhannet.

After wending through the twists and turns of narrow,
packed cart- and walkways, we left Skandi-the-City behind entirely. In its place was a rumpled land of worn,
rocky hillocks made of dark, thin soil and heaps of
pocked, crumbly stone. The top of the island swelled from
the cliff toward the sunrise, crowned with a bulbous but
smooth-flanked rise that could not possibly qualify as a
mountain, and yet was paramount nonetheless. Between
the city and the soft-browed peak stretched acres of land
that had broken out in a plague of rounded, basketlike
heaps of greenery. A rash of wreaths, set out in amazingly
symmetrical rows. As we passed the field nearest the
road, I leaned somewhat precariously over the edge of the
cart to get a closer look.

Baskets. Big baskets. Big *living* baskets; the vine

limbs had literally been woven into a circle and groomed to grow that way permanently. I realized the cart-bench itself was made of the same vine.

I had seen many strange plants in my life, having been North *and* South, but never vines coiled upon the ground into gigantic wooden pots. "What in hoolies are those?"

Nihko spared the edge of the track a glance. "Grapes."

"Grapes?" It astonished me. Every vineyard I'd ever seen boasted upright vines trained to grow along the horizontal, like a man standing with arms outstretched.

"Skandi is a land of winds," Nihko answered absently. "The vines here are too tender to be grown as other vines are, lest the wind strip them away. So they are cultivated low upon the ground."

There wasn't so much wind right now as to risk the vines. A breeze blew steadily, but it wasn't hearty enough to shred vegetation. The baskets of woven grape vines, crouched upon the ground, barely stirred.

"So," I said, "just why is it we can't walk on the ground? Unless it's blessed, that is. Didn't you and I walk off the ship and across the quay to the bottom of the cliff?"

"The wind and saltwater rots the mats," Nihko explained, "or we would not be required to tolerate that soiling. Thus the custom of cleansing at the top of the cliff."

"But why would we be *soiled* just by walking?"

He glanced at me sidelong. "In your land, do your priests or kings set bare flesh to muck-laden ground?"

"We don't have kings," I said absently, "and all of the holy men I ever saw were willing to walk anywhere."

Nihko made a soft sound of disgust. "But they are foreign priests. I should not be surprised."

"You walk on the boat, priest. Or have you somehow had *it* blessed?"

"Ship," he corrected automatically. "And that is not Skandi. Nowhere is Skandi but Skandi."

"Ah. Doesn't count, then, what you do elsewhere, only what you do here." I nodded sagely. "Very convenient."

He hissed briefly. "Convenience has nothing to do with it!"

I laughed at him. "Here you are refusing to soil yourself by setting foot to ground that hasn't been properly blessed, and yet you carve open the bellies of men and spill out their innards, or lop their heads off. Isn't *that* just a little messy?"

Nihko sealed up his mouth again into a thin, retentive seam. He opened it only to say something curtly to the molah-man, whose head was turned slightly in our direction as if he listened closely. The man's head snapped back around in response to Nihko's tone. I saw him make a hand gesture, and then he tugged at the molahs to encourage a faster pace.

Something to be learned of Nihko Blue-head, it seemed. And if I got lucky, maybe it was something I could use against him.

Smiling, I relaxed against the woven-limb back and let the sun beat on my face.

TEN

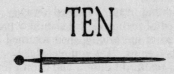

I'D THOUGHT this place called Akritara was a village, or settlement. Instead I discovered it was a collection of rooms all interconnected like a bulbous hive, sprouting multiple mounds of arching roofs and rounded domes on half-levels, like a pile of tumbled river stones. The arched roofs were painted white, the domes blue. Perched atop a hillock and surrounded by miles of ground-level wreaths of grapevine, Akritara looked precisely what it was: the preeminent household of Skandi.

So, Prima Rhannet and Nihko Blue-head didn't just intend to pass me off as a descendant of a wealthy house, but heir to *the* house.

"Never work," I murmured.

Nihko said nothing to me, though he spoke to the molah-man, directing him in a clipped, authoritative tone. On board the ship, as first mate, he'd been at ease with second-command, accepted by the crew as one of them and yet the captain's most trusted man. But ever since we'd set foot on Skandi, Nihko had behaved differently. I sensed a coiled power within him, an unspoken emotion, something akin to hostility. The people at the clifftop had clearly been afraid of him, making gestures against him—or perhaps against what he represented, with his shaven, tattooed head and silver brow rings. By admission he was a Skandic priest, and certainly he was treated as something other, something more, than merely a man. But

107

there is a vast difference between being respected for your power, and feared.

"What did that mean?" I asked abruptly. "You said if I ever got tired of feeling sick, I should come to you."

He glanced at me briefly, then returned his attention to the drive before us. "Do you feel sick?"

Startled, I realized I didn't, and hadn't for some time. "Not any more."

"Then there is no need for me to answer."

"Sure there is. There's simple curiosity—"

"Enough," he said curtly, cutting me off. "There are other concerns facing you now than the condition of your belly."

Piecing bits together, I ignored that. "There's only one thing that has ever exerted that kind of—of manifestation, had that kind of effect," I continued thoughtfully. "Except for the occasional bouts with too much aqivi, or getting kicked in the head. But all of those had cause." Which had happened with more frequency than I preferred.

Steadfastly he ignored me.

I did not ignore him. "And now you say you're a priest."

No answer.

"But priests can be many things. Men of conviction. Fools. And men of magic."

Sunlight glinted off the silver in his eyebrows.

"Are you a fool, Nihko?"

That got him. He studied me a long moment, measuring my own conviction. Then his mouth hooked down briefly. "Some would say so."

"Magic," I said, "has always disagreed with me. I have some acquaintance with it. It and I don't get along, much."

"Magic is a harsh and unforgiving master."

"And here I've always thought men desired to be *its* master."

"Fools," he said tightly. "Fools desire such things." And then he called out to the molah-man, and we passed through open gates into a sunny courtyard made less

blinding than the white-painted arches by the profusion
of vegetation.

Everything everywhere was blooming. There was no
subtlety, no careful ritual in arrangement. Things simply—grew. Many-branched, silver-gray trees; taller trees
with cloudlike crowns boasting clusters of lavender dra-
peries; long-leaved bushes bedecked by sprays of pinks
and whites and reds; a strange, twisting vinelike plant that
crawled up and over walls to display its bounty of leaves
that, changing from green, were part red and part purple
and all incandescence. The white-painted walls, the intensity of the sun, the brilliance of the skies, all combined
with the gardens to make a palette of rich color and fragrance almost dizzying to behold.

The molah-man scurried about, pulling his mat from
the shelf beneath the cart. He spread it carefully across
swept bricks, and even as he did so two men hastened
forward from the shadows of the courtyard to unroll a
narrow runner of carpet extending from the entryway. We
would not soil our feet on the bricks of the courtyard or
the stone of the steps, but be separated from the earth by
one poor mat and an exquisitely woven carpet of creamy
wool.

Nihko exited the cart-bench, then gestured for me to
follow. He led me to the shadowed, deep-set entryway,
spoke briefly to the carpet-men, then gestured me to wait.
One of the men went inside. When he appeared again, he
made way for a second man. A tall, thin, older man, gray
of eyes and hair, adorned in sheer linen kilt and a necklet
of glass and gold hanging against his bare chest. He was
too well-trained to stare at Nihko, but his quiet scrutiny
was nonetheless obvious.

Nihko spoke at length. His tone was courteous, but not
in the least deferential. The older man listened gravely,
never once glancing in my direction. When Nihko was
done making his explanations, whatever they might be—
not knowing the language placed me at a distinct disadvantage—the man said one soft word, then turned neatly
on his heel and led us into the house.

I paused theatrically at the threshold. "What about the floors? Do we dare—?"

Something glinted in Nihko's eye that was not humor. He turned from me and followed the older man. Laughing inwardly, I did the same.

We were led into a small, low-ceilinged room through which we could see another much larger room with a high arched roof. The kilted man gestured briefly to shelves set against the wall; Nihko removed his shoes and placed them there. I noted there were several other pairs of shoes as well. I wiggled bare toes again, and succeeded at last in drawing the older man's attention. He watched me gravely, measuring me in his own quiet way. That I came barefoot to the house meant something, but I had no idea of what; surely Nihko had told him I'd been properly cleansed despite being shoeless. I sensed neither disdain nor fear. He simply looked at me, expressionless.

The ground swayed again, or seemed to. I put out a hand to steady myself against the wall. With the kilted man's scrutiny so fixed, I was abruptly aware of everything about that hand: its calluses, nicks and scrapes and scars, discolorations, cracked nails, the broad palm-back ridged with tendons that flexed and rolled beneath sun-bronzed skin, the long, limber fingers that felt far more at home gripping a sword hilt than a smooth, flat, cool wall in a house called Akritara on an island named Skandi.

I thought abruptly of Del, being held on a ship as surety of my behavior.

I took my hand from the wall and stood straight with effort, trusting years of training to replace sea-stolen balance. This was a land of tall men, strong men, and nothing about me, physically, indicated I was anything unlike anyone else, save a brief, quickly hidden flicker in the older man's gray eyes. Not judgment. Curiosity. A need to *know*.

He gestured then, ushered us into the much larger room beyond. Murals adorned the walls, elaborate and brilliantly colored scenes of boys with strings of fish, of ships asail, flowers, and beasts with horned heads. The ceiling flowed overhead in a high, elegant symmetry pleasing to the eye. I followed the line up, over, and down, marking the spare, simple angles of ceiling, wall, floor, hollows like windows cut into thick walls to display adornments, the wide doors leading into other arched and domed places. Everything about the room fit, as Single-stroke had once fit my hands. Cleanly, without excess. A perfection of purity and purpose. Like a circle, and the dance.

My breath stilled in my throat. Home. I was *home*. And all of me knew it.

The back of my neck tingled. I hitched shoulders, rubbed my neck in irritation; felt again the kilted man's attention. There was a single chair in the large, airy room; neither of us was directed to sit in it. Instead, we were gestured toward large cushions on the floor. Nihko seated himself. I did not. Not even when he told me to.

"Look," I said irritably, "you brought me here. You can tell them I'm a demon or a god, and I can't protest because I don't speak the language. Right now your plan is to present me as the heir to this house, and here I am. You'll have that chance. But you can't dictate if I stand or sit." Especially since he carried neither knife nor sword, and we neither of us had established who was the stronger.

Nihko opened his mouth to answer with some heat, but shut it again as he glanced briefly at the older man. He was clearly displeased, but could say nothing now. Instead he sat stolidly on his cushion, shaven head bowed slightly, and prepared himself to wait.

Once upon a time I was good at that. An impatient man makes mistakes in the circle, dangerous and occasionally deadly mistakes. I knew very well it was best to conserve strength and energy by remaining quiet, by steadying the rhythm of my breathing, by letting my body rest. But circumstances precluded that. I was a prisoner to this man, to his captain. As much as I was a prisoner of uncertainty and self-doubt.

This moment was what I had come to Skandi for. And I was frightened of it.

Oh, bascha, lend me your strength.

But Del, as much as I, was a prisoner to people who planned unknown outcomes for equally unknown actions.

Not my choice, to be in or of this moment. But I was helpless to alter it.

The kilted man glided quietly from the room. I expected Nihko to speak to me now, but he didn't. He simply sat there, head bowed, eyes closed. Praying? Maybe. But I wasn't certain I wanted to know anything about his gods or his priesthood, or the content of his convictions.

I walked. I paced the length of the rectangular room with its arching, airy ceiling and counted my steps. Back again to the other end of the room, where the low doorway led into the entry chamber containing no more than shelves and shoes.

Beneath my bare feet lay stone, cool stone composed of tiny square tiles of similar but subtly different hues. My soles were callused from years of fighting barefoot in the Southron sand, so my flesh wasn't sensitive enough to mark pits and seams and hollows. Merely stone to me: tiles carefully cut, shaped, and laid with precise attention, grouted and fitted together into quiet, soothing patterns. The walls and ceilings, the doors and the floors formed a subtle variety of shape, and shadow, and structure. My body knew this place, knew the appeal of purity, answered seductive symmetry. It knew without knowing; there was no way it *could* know, any more than my mind could embrace the comforting familiarity of a place I had never been.

I walked. I paced. I stopped only, and at last, when the woman came into the room.

Nihko rose at once. He caught her eye briefly, then instantly fixed his gaze on the patterned floor. I, on the other hand, merely waited. I folded my arms, set a shoulder against the wall, hooked one ankle casually over the other as I leaned, and waited.

Now I could be patient. Now it mattered.

Nihko said a single word. The one I knew. Not precisely what it meant, not the infinite possibilities of semantic subtleties, but I knew as much as I needed to know.

"Metri," he said.

This, then, was the Stessa metri, the woman who would be so desperately grateful for the return of the long-lost heir that she would grant Nihko Blue-head and his impulsive, slaver-reared female captain the welcome, the status, the wealth both desired.

I looked at the woman. I marked her stature, her posture, the cool and calm smoky gray-green eyes, darker than my own, and I realized what a fool Nihko was, and Prima Rhannet, and even Del, who had told them enough of me to make them plan this plan.

She wore sheer, sleeveless linen that fell to the floor, bleached nearly white. It made her skin seem darker than the warm copper-bronze it was. Around her waist was doubled a bright green sash, and over it a soft-worked leather belt chiming with golden circlets and brilliant blue beads. Larger circlets rang softly against both arms, depended from her ears, encircled her throat. Her hair, swept back from her face and fastened into a thick tail by a series of gold-and-enamel clasps, was darker than mine. There was silver and white in it just as there were threadings of age in her face, her throat, her hands, but nothing about this woman suggested she was old. Not in body, not in bearing, nor in the clarity of expression.

"Metri," he said again.

She seated herself in the single chair. The kilted man glided silently into the room and set down upon the small table beside her a delicate crockery jar and one cup. He poured, he lifted, he offered; she accepted. And all the while she looked only at Nihko. There was no indication she was aware of me at all.

So much for desperation. So much for a dying, weak old woman badly in need of an heir. I doubted the Stessa metri would allow anything so insignificant as death to defeat her will and purpose.

The woman set down the cup, then flicked a finger in Nihko's direction. He began speaking quietly and steadily, putting little emphasis in his words. I knew nothing of what he said, what lies or truths he told, but his tone did not suggest coercion or contrived charm. Perhaps he was, after all, as aware of her strength as I.

When he was done at last, the woman retrieved the cup and drank again. Still she did not look at me. Her expression was unmoved. I've been in the circle with men less suited to hiding their thoughts. Serenity was not her gift, but she knew how to be quiet. She knew how to still her mind so her judgments were sound—and absolutely unpredictable until she declared them.

Eventually, the woman looked at me. She spoke a single accented word, and this one I knew. "Undress."

I blinked. Then bestowed upon her my most charming smile. "You first."

Nihko was on his feet instantly. Even as I came off the wall onto the balls of my feet, he struck, spewing anger and invective in a tone thick with shock. It was a blow with the flat of his hand designed to catch me across the face, the way a man strikes a slave, but I moved quickly enough to avoid the power of it. I clamped one hand around his wrist and held it.

Before I could do anything more than stop him, before I could even phrase a response, the woman rose from her chair. In three long strides she reached Nihko, and her blow, unexpected and powerful, rocked him on his feet. Shocked, he staggered back, one hand to his face. I released his wrist, wondering warily if I might be her next target.

But I was not. It was Nihko.

With timed, meticulous blows, using the flat of her rigid hand, she drove him to the ground. He knelt there, shoulders rounded in submission, tattooed head bowed before her as she spoke with quiet, vicious emphasis. When she stopped speaking, stopped striking him, when he raised his head at last, I saw the blood. The tears.

The palm of her hand was reddened from the blows. She turned to me again, and again said, "Undress."

I stared back at her, matching determination, then grinned slowly. "Hoolies, woman, all you had to do was *ask.*"

She waited.

I untied the sash, dropped it; stripped off the tunic, dropped it; undid the drawstring and let the baggy trousers fall. I stepped out of them, kicked them aside, offered a cheery smile. "I detest red anyway."

From a distance of two paces, she studied me. I've been examined before: by slavers, by sword-dancers, by enemies, by sorcerers, even by friends. Certainly by women. But her perusal of my nudity was uncannily different. There was no sense of ownership or impending purchase; no sexual hunger, no arousal, no predatory promise; no assessment to weigh my worth as a man or a sword-dancer hired to do a task. She simply looked, so intent as to be unaware of surroundings, the way an artist might study the line of bone and shadow, the play of light on flesh, the fit and function of form. To see how the body was made, how it worked, in order to recreate it—or to recognize it.

I expected her to gesture me to turn, or to demand it with a curt command. She did neither. She walked beyond me with smooth, measured strides and stood at my back.

Nihko remained on the floor. He was watching her, not me, making no effort to wipe the blood from his split lip, to erase the drying tears. He knelt there, knees doubled up beneath him, green eyes transfixed by the woman's actions.

"Getting an eyeful?" I asked lightly.

She caught a handful of hair and lifted it briefly from the back of my neck. Then let it fall as she moved from behind me. She returned to the chair and seated herself quietly. "What have you been," she asked in a cool, accented voice, "to deserve such punishment?"

"What have I been?" I hitched a shoulder, wondering what Nihko had told her. What he expected me to tell her. What *she* expected me to tell her.

I gave her the truth. Briefly, explicitly, without embellishment. Naming off the names of the tasks I had done, the dances I had won, the enemies defeated. All the truths of my past, despite the ugliness, the brutality that had driven a terrified boychild into tenacious manhood.

Her voice was uninflected. "How many years have you?"

I shook my head. "No idea." Still the truth.

Her eyes narrowed slightly. "Guess."

I laughed then, genuinely amused. "Better to throw the oracle bones. The odds are better."

She flicked a glance at Nihko, then returned it to me. "Has he told you, this man, this *renegada*, this *ikepra*, what you would gain if I accepted you?"

"Yes," I answered bluntly. "My freedom, and the freedom of the woman who travels with me."

"No more than that?"

"That's enough."

"So you say."

"So I mean."

She nodded. "Then go. This ikepra cannot prevent you. I give you your freedom. Go."

I shook my head. "Can't do that."

"Because of the woman?"

"Yes."

"There are other women."

I laughed softly. "There is no other woman like this one," I said simply, "any more than there is anyone else like you."

She studied me again. "Well," she said finally, with exquisite matter-of-factness, "of course that alters everything." A hand flicked in Nihko's direction. "Rise."

He rose.

"Do you know why I beat him?" she asked me.

I shrugged. "You don't like him?"

A spark of amusement leaped briefly in her eyes, was extinguished. "He insulted my house."

"I assumed something of the sort."

"He insulted you."

"Me?" I blinked. "Why in hoolies would anything he said of a foreigner matter to you?" Enough that she would strike him blow after blow with her own hand.

"Do you know what he is?"

I thought of any number of explicitly vulgar things I could say Nihko was, but restrained the impulse. She probably knew anyway, judging by her contempt. "Not as you mean it, no."

"Ikepra."

I shook my head. "You've said that before. I don't speak or understand the language. I have no idea what you're talking about."

"Profanation," Nihko said, hushed but not hesitant.

Startled, I looked at him. His eyes glittered, but the tears were gone. He was—ashamed. In that moment, before this woman, he detested himself.

"Well," I said, "there are a lot of things I could call you, but that's not one of them." I paused. "Why? Who are you? What did you do?" Another pause. "Besides sailing away with a slaver's daughter to rob and capture harmless Southroners like me, that is."

"Harmless?" Nihko's smile was ghastly. "A blind man sees neither power, promise, nor danger."

"And this blind man isn't hearing much either," I retorted. "Fine. You brought me here, told this woman I'm her long-lost heir. We're done. You can turn Del loose now, and we'll get on about our business."

"Nihkolara will not do so," the woman said, "until he has been rewarded. That is why he came."

"Not for me," he said sharply. A wave of color suffused his face, then faded; had he insulted the house again? "I serve Prima Rhannet."

"Oh, yes." Smoky eyes glittered coldly. "You would have me receive her. Here."

"She would have it. Yes."

"Is there a problem with that?" I asked cautiously, wondering what in hoolies I'd do if this woman refused to cooperate and Prima Rhannet decided to keep Del.

The metri was displeased. "That would seal her acceptable to the Eleven Families."

"That doesn't mean you have to *like* her, does it?"

She ignored me and spoke to Nihko, whom she'd called Nihkolara. He had never named himself in any of the words he'd said to her, or to the kilted servant. But she knew who he was. "There must be proofs."

"Name them, metri."

I frowned. The balance of control had shifted. He was ikepra, whatever that meant, self-proclaimed profanation, but the tension in the room was all hers now. He knew what he was, knew his place, and for the moment he ruled it.

She shook her head. "He is scarred all over. Had the *keraka* ever existed, it is banished now."

The—what?

"There are things from within the body," the first mate offered, "far more convincing than marks upon the flesh."

She shook her head again. Gold chimed faintly. "There are others in this world who appear to be Skandic, even those with real or falsified keraka. And many of them have been presented to me as you have presented him. Pretenders, all of them." She smiled. "I am old. I am dying. I need an heir of the house. Were I a malleable woman, I would have ten times ten the number of men standing in this room, this moment, vowing with utter conviction that they are my one true heir."

"Look," I said, exasperated, "I don't even care if I'm Skandic, let alone your long-lost heir. I mean, yes, I suspect I *am* Skandic—it's why we set out in the first place, to see—but I'm not vowing to be your heir or anything else supposedly special. I don't care about your wealth, your influence, your legacy, whatever it is that all these other men want, what Prima Rhannet wants. *I* just want my freedom." I looked at Nihko pointedly. "And Del's."

She remained unconvinced. "A clever man will deny a birthright in order to win it."

"A clever woman, an old, dying, desperate woman"—I made it an irony between us—"would discern the attempt and discount it."

"Metri," Nihko said, and then added more in Skandic.

When he was done, her face was taut and pale. She looked at me, hard, and was old abruptly, older than her age.

"What did you say?" I asked sharply. "What did you tell her?"

"About sickness," he said. "About the weeping of

your wrist"—he touched his throat—"and the burning of your flesh."

She gestured then, cutting us off. I saw the minute trembling in her hand as she stretched it toward the kilted man and spoke a single word.

He placed a small knife in her palm.

I stiffened. "Wait a moment—"

"You will see," Nihko said quietly, "and so shall she."

The woman rose. Her steps now were not so steady, though there was no less purpose in them. She walked to me, touched me briefly on the wrist as if in supplication—or apology—then raised both hands to my neck. She was a tall woman, nearly as tall as Del. I felt her touch, the coolness of her fingers, the trembling in her hands. There was no pain, only a deft cut in something I thought was hair, until she lowered her hands and I saw a strip of braided twine with a single ornament attached, a thin silver ring worked into the weave.

"What—?" I put my hand to my throat, curling fingers around the leather thong with its weight of sandtiger claws. "Where did that come from?"

"Here." Nihko brushed a finger against his left eyebrow. "When you lay on the deck after I dragged you out of the water, vomiting up the ocean, I attached it to your necklet."

"What in hoolies *for?*"

A single long step and he put a hand on my chest. "This," he answered gently.

I didn't get sick. I didn't vomit up the ocean, or the contents of my belly. I simply lost control of every working part in my body: of the eyes, the ears, the voice, the movements of my limbs, the in- and exhalation of my lungs, the beating of my heart.

And died.

ELEVEN

I JERKED bolt upright, sucking air into starving lungs in one long, loud, spasming gasp. Once I had it, I held the air so as not to let it out again, to know the horrific helplessness of simply *stopping*. I clutched both hands over my heart, blind to the world until I felt the steady, if pounding, beat, and then I became aware that I was no longer in the big, arch-roofed reception room, but in a smaller, round room with a dome huddled atop it.

And in a bed. With people around it.

I let my breath out and fixed the blue-headed first mate with a baleful glare. *"What in hoolies did you do to me?"*

Casually he replied, "Killed you."

I thought that over, reassuring myself that my heart yet beat and my lungs yet worked. "Then why am I alive now?"

"I resurrected you."

"Can you do that?"

"You are breathing, are you not?"

"*How* did you do it?"

His lip was swollen from where the woman had struck and split it. "I am ikepra," he said simply, "but there remain those things of the Order of which I do not speak."

I noticed then that the Stessa metri sat in a chair beside the bed, hands folded in her linen-swathed lap. Beyond her, leaning casually against the wall, was Prima Rhannet.

The first shock had worn off. And I knew . . . I

whipped my head to the right and saw her there, waiting. "Bascha!"

She was unsmiling, but the relief in her eyes was profound. There were many things I wished to say to her, but I offered none of them now. Not until we were alone again. But she understood. We both of us understood. It's handy when you know someone well enough, intimately enough, that many things pass between you with no need for actual words.

Relief brought with it an outward rush of released tension. Feeling wobbly, I scooched back in the bed and leaned against the headboard. A quick automatic self-inventory within a moment of waking had told me I was still unclothed, but modesty was served by a linen coverlet, which I yanked up over my lap as I noted Prima Rhannet's crooked smile and laughing eyes. And why was *she* looking, anyway? I scowled at her; was rewarded with a wide, mocking grin.

The Stessa metri sat very still in her chair. I looked at her, weighed the extreme degree of self-containment evident in her posture and expression, and sighed. "I take it you paid them."

Her gaze was steady. "Nihkolara proved beyond a doubt you are Skandic," she said. "Whether you are my grandson is as yet unknown, but I dared not take the chance."

I blinked. "Grandson?"

"It is possible," she said calmly.

"Grandson," I repeated, astonished by the complexity of emotions that single word—and its context—roused. "But—" But. There was nothing to say. I just looked at her, stunned, and shook my head.

One dark eyebrow rose a fraction. "No?"

No. Yes. Maybe. I don't know. Ask me later.

Hoolies.

I focused on something else. "You paid them, so why are they still here?" I flicked a glance beyond her to the red-haired woman in the corner. "You didn't seem too enamored of the idea of receiving a slaver's daughter in your home."

I was rewarded by the slow bloom of color in the freckled face. Prima glowered at me, all trace of mocking amusement wiped away.

"And so I am not," the metri replied. "But there is more involved in this enterprise than coin."

I glanced at Del. "Get your feet washed?"

That baffled her utterly. "My feet—?"

Prima Rhannet laughed harshly. "We were denied the honor," she said in a clipped tone, "but be certain the floors shall be cleansed when we have gone, and the carpets reblessed."

"But . . ." I looked now at Nihko. "I don't get it."

"I am ikepra," he answered steadily, "and all know it. But they had rather take no chances."

"Any more than I," the metri put in quietly.

I cleared my throat. "So. Here we are." I glanced around, marking faces one by one until I came to hers again. "What happens next?"

"You shall be accorded the hospitality of my house, you and your woman."

"And your new friends," Prima said pointedly, a certain amount of malicious glee underscoring her tone.

The metri didn't miss the point. "As well as your companions."

"Now, wait," I said. "They aren't my companions. They are my *captors*. There's a difference."

"But of course there is not," replied the woman who might—or might not—be my grandmother. "Because if it is true you are my heir, then of course your companions must be treated with honor, received as my guests before the Eleven Families of Skandi."

"Kind of a rock and a hard place, isn't it?"

The spark flickered in her eye, was gone. "Such bruises heal."

I grinned. "So they do."

"As for now . . ." She rose. "I will have your companions conducted to rooms worthy of their status, while you and your woman reassure yourselves that you are indeed both whole."

Even Nihko and his captain capitulated and followed

her out of the room. With their departure I felt the last bit of tension drain from my body. My skull thumped against the wall. "Gods, I'm tired." I stretched out my hand; Del took it. Tightly. "Was I really dead?"

She hitched a hip onto the bed and perched beside me. When I tugged insistently at her hand, she moved closer, finally matching her length to mine as she settled shoulders against the headboard. "You weren't breathing when I came here, nor was your heart beating. If both of those symptoms constitute death, then yes, you were dead."

I felt at the flesh of my chest, seeking answers. The heart continued to beat, and I was aware of steady breathing. Not dead, then. Now. "I don't understand. How did Nihko do such a thing?"

"Let us be more concerned with the fact he *un*did it," Del suggested. "It took him two days."

"Two days?" I stiffened. "You're not saying I was dead for two whole days!"

"I am."

"No."

She shrugged.

"This is impossible, bascha!"

"Be grateful it's not," she replied, "or you would likely be buried somewhere on this rock."

"Oh, no. If I'm buried anywhere, it'll be in the South."

She slanted me a sidelong glance. "You might be somewhat rank by the time we got you there."

"Too bad," I retorted. "At least *I* don't have to smell me!"

"Of course, I could have you burned," Del said consideringly, "and take you back in an urn. That would be more convenient."

"Oh? And what kind of urn would be appropriate for a man who is also messiah?"

Her expression was guileless as she looked at me. "Likely an empty aqivi jug."

"Empty!" I glared at her aggrievedly. "Hoolies, bascha, if you're going to drag my remains around in an aqivi jug, at least let it be a *full* one!"

She broke then, laughing, and turned hard against me, setting her head down into the hollow of my shoulder. I hooked an arm around her and contemplated the immensity of being alive after one has been dead. And the simple, unadorned joy of having this woman here beside me, as glad of it as I was.

"Del—"

She breathed it into my neck. "I know."

"Del—"

She put fingers across my lips. "If you say anything, you will regret it."

I extruded my tongue and licked her fingers purposefully. She removed them hastily. I grinned. "Why will I regret it?"

"Because I've seen you when you've had too much to drink. You get sad. Sappy."

"Sappy!"

"And the next day you've forgotten it entirely, which is no more flattering than you wishing you hadn't said it."

"I never wish I hadn't said what I've said to you." I reconsidered. "Well, maybe sometimes. When we have disagreements, though those are extremely rare." I was rewarded by the crimped mouth I expected to see. "But hoolies, bascha, I just came back from the dead! Doesn't that allow me some latitude to say what I want?"

"But then the Sandtiger will have divulged a portion of himself he wants no one ever to see."

"His sappiness?"

Del laughed. "You have survived by letting them think you are not soft."

I grunted. "Softness doesn't survive in the circle."

"So I have said." A strand of silken hair trapped itself against stubble and claw scars. "But I know what you are. You needn't say it where anyone else might hear."

"At the moment what I'm feeling has nothing to do with, er, softness."

Del patted my lap. "I know."

I couldn't help the startled reflexive twitch of every muscle in my body. I caught her hand, gripped it, fixed her with a forbidding scowl. "Gently, bascha!"

"No," she said. "*Fiercely.* So I know, and you know, you're very much alive."

Oh. Well, yes. I could manage that. Being brought back from the dead does give a man the motivation to make certain all the parts still work.

Some hours later, the silent, kilted servant led me out of the house to a small, private terrace tucked into one of the niches between domed room and arched. Akritara appeared to be full of such places, cobbled together over the years from a set of chambers into a sprawling assemblage of them. And here I found an array of potted plants, all blooming so that the air was rich with fragrance. I was startled to see that a rising breeze blew the hedges along the low wall into tattered fragments; this must be the wind Nihko had mentioned, forcing the people of Skandi to train their grapevines into baskets.

I squinted against the dust, then turned back toward the house as the servants touched my arm. And there was the Stessa metri, seated in a chair. The linen of her belted tunic rippled slightly, but her chair had been set back into a niche that the wind only barely reached.

Her eyes appraised me coolly. "Do you feel better?"

I ran a hand down the front of my tunic. "A bath, fresh clothing, a meal—what more could a man ask?"

"I referred to none of those things."

I blinked, then felt my face warm. Which in itself annoyed me; I haven't blushed in, well, so many years I couldn't count them.

"Well?"

"Well what?"

"Do you feel better?"

"I'm just glad I'm alive to feel anything."

Her gaze yet probed me. "Did you not release your seed in her?"

I looked around for a chair. Didn't find one. Looked around for the servant in hopes he might bring one, but he was gone. So I sat down on the nearest portion of knee-high wall, in the wind, and smiled sweetly at her. "Aren't you a little blunt for a woman of your, um, maturity? Or are you just trying to shock me?"

One brow rose slightly. "Do you shock?"

"Not often."

"I thought not." She smoothed a fold in the sheer linen of her tunic skirts with a deft hand. "Did you?"

"Did I what?"

"Release your seed in her."

I considered her. "Do you *want* me to believe you're a woman who takes pleasure in hearing bedroom tales of others?"

"Tell me," she said only.

I stood up then, left the wall, took three strides to her. Leaned down, looming, so that my face was but a thumb's length from hers. "Yes," I said. "Anything else you want to know? How many times, who was on top, how long I lasted?"

She did not recoil from my closeness, or my tone. "My heir," she said quietly, "must be capable of bedding a woman. Of what use is an heir if he can sire no children?"

I straightened, startled. "This is about children?"

Her gray-green eyes were smoky. "Do you *wish* to believe I'm a woman who finds pleasure in hearing bedroom tales of others?"

I opened my mouth, shut it. Could find no response.

"Give me your hands."

"My hands?"

"I want to examine them."

"Didn't you get a good enough look at me before?"

Her eyes locked with my own. "Who was your mother, that she taught you no manners?"

Unaccountably, it stung. "Your daughter?" I challenged.

From that, she flinched. Color moved in her face, fading. Abruptly I regretted what I had said—exactly as Del had suggested a matter of hours before. It was true this woman had taken me completely off-guard with her questions, but that didn't mean she deserved rudeness in return.

Unless she expected it. Wanted it. To make it easier for her to dismiss me as yet another pretender.

I walked away from the woman then, returning to my perch upon the low wall. I spread my legs, felt the underside of my thighs clench to grip. Tapped sandaled toes faintly against the stone beneath my feet even as the breeze whipped my hair flat against one side of my head. "What happened?"

She told me. Calmly, quietly, with no obvious pain or sorrow, but it was there in her eyes. When she was done, I watched her watching me, weighing her story even as she had weighed mine three days before.

I rose, went to her. This time I didn't loom. I knelt down and offered my hands.

She took them, held them. Turned them. Felt the sword-born calluses, the scars, two knuckles that were enlarged, a little finger left slightly crooked in the healing after a break. I could not read what was in her face, but I thought I knew. This flesh could be hers, and the blood that ran beneath it. As much as perhaps it wasn't.

She released me. "I must *know*."

Still kneeling, I shook my head. "There are no easy answers."

"Even difficult answers are answers."

"Maybe," I said. "Maybe not."

Her eyes were shocked. "You would rather not know what became of her?"

"Either way offers no comfort. If she died, knowing won't bring her back. If she gave me away voluntarily—"

"My daughter would never have done so!"

"Then maybe she wasn't your daughter. Maybe I'm not your grandson. Maybe I'm just a Southron/Skandic half-breed, or a full-blooded Skandic lost to the desert of a foreign land." I shrugged. "Or maybe I'm just the unwanted result of some man releasing his seed, and so the girl—released me." Into the Punja, where a newborn infant would die in a matter of hours, offering no proof of one night's pleasure. Or rouse the memory of rape.

"That, too, is possible."

"In which case I'll thank you for your hospitality, collect Del, and go."

"Wait." She gestured briefly as I rose, then dropped the hand to her lap. "Does it mean nothing to you that I might be your grandmother? A wealthy, powerful, dying old woman who was bred of the oldest and most respected family of the island?"

I had at some point shattered her demeanor. She was still proud, still strong, but a sere bitterness chilled her tone. I thought then of all the men who had come before her, claiming to be the grandson of a wealthy, powerful old woman bred of the oldest and most respected family of the island.

She had undoubtedly heard countless lies. I gave her none. Only honesty. "It would mean more," I told her, "just to have a grandmother. No matter who or what she is."

I left her then, as she wept.

TWELVE

AS GUESTS, we had been given the run of the place. Servants tended the household assiduously, all kilted, all quiet, all perfectly courteous. I didn't know where Nihko and his captain were, but I did know where to find Del. She intended, she'd said when I left her to see the metri, to drown herself.

She meant in a *bath,* of course. So I went to the chamber housing the tub.

It was far more than a tub, actually. The builders had dug a large, shallow, square hole in the ground, plastered it, laid out tiny tiles on the sides and bottom in an elegantly precise pattern of waves and clouds, blue on blue of every shade. Overhead arched the ceiling, very dark blue with a spray of silver and gold stars painted to mimic the night skies. Squares and slots were cut into the deep walls through to the exterior, then covered against windborn dust and debris by membranes, opaque but scraped thin enough to let in the light. The shelf around the pool itself was stone as well, pale, worked slabs fitted together into an almost seamless array. Through some builder's trick with pipes the water was warmed and let in and out from beneath the surface. I had enjoyed myself immensely earlier, forgoing a shared bath only because if Del and I *had* shared, I'd never have answered the metri's request to attend her.

Now I was finished with that, and Del was still in the pool. Alone.

Perfect.

For the second time in three days I stripped down for a woman, leaving borrowed clothing heaped upon the floor, although I confess this time the experience was much more pleasurable. Del, floating easily, challenged me to dive in, which she knew very well I couldn't and wouldn't do. Instead, the best I could manage was to bend down, catch my balance one-handed against the stone shelf, and slip over the edge.

The water came to mid-chest even in the center of the pool; I was in no danger of drowning. Unless Del had some nefarious plan to rid herself of me.

The closest she came to it was to hook a hand into the thong holding the claws and tug gently, urging me closer. "Well?"

"Well what?"

"What did the metri say?"

The metri. I sighed, dipped down to wet myself to my chin, stood up again. Soaked hair straggled down well onto my shoulders; I *really* needed to cut it. Del's was slicked back against her skull, baring all of her face. The Southron sun had not been kind to her Northern skin, incising a faint fan of lines at the corners of her eyes, but with a sheen of moisture over her face and the dissipation of habitual readiness, she also shed years. She looked maybe eighteen. At the most.

I felt a stab of some unnamed emotion: more than ten, possibly as many as fifteen years separated us. Before me there had been only Ajani, the Northern borjuni who had, with his men, slaughtered her family, save Del and her brother, and burned the caravan. Who had utterly altered her life, making a sword-singer out of the girl who would have been wife and mother, instead of living vengeance.

Before Ajani, she had been fifteen. And innocent of men.

Those days, those years were past now. She had slain her demons, the living as well as the dead. She was as much at peace as I had ever seen her. And young again. So young.

"Well?" she prodded.

The metri. "She wants to be certain."

"That's understandable."

"And she doesn't know how."

Del was silent a moment. "No," she said finally. "There is no way to be certain. It must be taken on faith."

I shook my head. "I'm not the man for it."

"To be her grandson?"

"To be trusted. To be taken on faith."

She stood before me, facing me: a tall, strong woman of immense will and purpose. Unsmiling, she put a hand on either side of my head and stripped my hair back, combing it behind my ears. "You are the most trustworthy man I have ever met."

"Not for this. This is—important." I recalled the metri's expression as she examined my hands. "This may be more important than anything in my life, because it's *her* life."

Del stared hard into my eyes. "And do you see why, now, I say you are the most trustworthy man I have ever met?"

"It's only the truth, bascha. Nothing more."

"And nothing less."

I turned my face into her hand, kissed it. "I don't know why, bascha. I think she *wants* me to be the one, but she's afraid."

"Why would she be afraid? Surely she has prayed to have her grandson returned to her."

"Returned for how long?"

Del frowned. "What do you mean?"

I shook my head. "I can't stay here. Even if I *am* this grandson. This isn't my place."

"You could make it your place."

I recalled how comfortable I was in Akritara, how very much at home I *did* feel, despite never having been here before. I had never in my life felt so at ease in an unknown place. Skandi fit me. Somehow, some way, it fit me.

"Why not?" Del asked.

I turned and pushed my way through the water. At the side I hooked arms over the edge, spreading elbows along the stone, and settled chin on wrists layered one atop the other. Frowning even as Del came up next to me and mimicked my posture, one elbow lightly touching mine.

"It . . . I'm—" I sighed, ducking my head to scrub forehead against hands. "I don't know. I guess I'm still just a Southroner at heart."

"No. Not since I taught you wiser ways."

It raised a smile, as she meant it to, but I couldn't hold it. "I think I will *always* be a Southroner. Even if I meant not to be. Too much of it is in my blood."

"And if your blood is Skandic?"

"It's more than blood that makes you of a place," I told her. "More than blood, or bone, or flesh. It's as much spirit, and heart, as anything else." I turned my head to look at her, even as I leaned my temple into my hand. "You are a Northerner, born and bred of its customs, its people. The rituals." She nodded slightly. "And no matter if you never return there for the balance of your life, it's what you will always be."

Del's expression was sober now, almost severe as she considered. I had stripped away the youth with my words. Now the woman was back, the tough-minded woman who stepped into the circle and danced.

Or killed.

"But I am who I am no matter where I am," she said at last. "As you would be."

"Bascha, I don't know—don't understand . . ." I shook my head again. "I have never *belonged* to anyone. Never been *of* anyone. Owned, yes, by the Salset. Trained, yes, at Alimat. And that was the closest thing I had to a family, those men at Alimat who learned as I learned the rituals of the dance, but there was always competition. Never friendship; we all knew one day we might meet one another in the circle. And now . . ." I set my forehead against my wrists, spoke into the stone. "Now there's—this."

"Yes," Del said quietly. And as quietly, "Would it be so bad if you became what you would have become anyway?"

I turned my head. "What do you mean?"

"If you are this woman's grandson, then what she offers is what you would have had."

"If."

"Toss the oracle bones ten times," Del said, "and you will win, and you will lose. That is the only certainty in the game."

"In other words, the odds are about as good *for* me being her grandson as against." I reached out and cupped the back of her skull in my palm. "Or is it just that *you* want to benefit from the wealth?"

"Of course," she agreed. "I am selfish."

I ruffled slick hair, disarranging it. "I wouldn't have had it, Del."

"What do you mean?"

"The metri's daughter fell in love with an unsuitable man. He was not of the Eleven Families, not even remotely acceptable. He was a molah-man, responsible for carting the Stessas around the island, making certain they never soiled themselves by touching unblessed ground." I smiled sadly at her perplexity. "The metri's daughter asked that he be adopted, raised up by the metri herself, so he would become acceptable. And her mother refused."

"They left," Del said, seeing it now. "They left Skandi together, and sailed away to a place where they could be man and wife with no concerns for such things."

"She was pregnant," I told her. "Due to give birth in a month. The metri intended to give the child away."

Del's eyes closed. I knew she remembered *her* daughter, Ajani's daughter, the child of rape. The child she gave into others' keeping, because she had a task. A vow. An obsession. And no time, no room, for a baby in her life.

I continued. "But the only daughter—and only heir—of the Stessa metri left Skandi with the molah-man, and neither were seen again."

Her eyes opened. The clear blue, strangely, had been swallowed by black pupils. "Such a woman would never expose an infant in the desert," she said. "A woman who gave up a life of privilege, leaving her mother, her people, her land, her legacy." She looked at me. "Such a woman would not have left you there, in the sand. Not by choice."

I closed my hand around the thick tail of soaked hair adhering to her spine. Squeezed. "There is no way we can ever know, bascha. None."

"You could *choose*—"

"—to believe that was my mother? That she loved a man enough to leave her homeland so near to term, and travel into the Punja? Yes, I could choose to believe it. I could also choose to believe otherwise."

Her gaze was steady. "And if it's true?"

I shook my head. "It changes nothing. Not who I am, what I am, or what I will be."

Del opened her mouth to answer, but it was someone else's voice I heard. A man's. Saying something in a language I didn't know, but the tone was clear enough.

We turned sharply as one, pushing off the side of the pool. A young man stood there on the far side, legs spread aggressively, arms loose at his sides. He was not kilted as the servants, but wore a thin-woven sleeveless linen tunic that displayed muscled, tanned arms. A copper-studded leather belt was wrapped around a slim, sashed waist.

He stared down upon us, green eyes fixed and fierce in a dark face. Brown hair sun-bleached bronze on top, not yet combed tame from the wind, tumbled carelessly around wide shoulders. His eyes narrowed a moment, and then he switched to a language we could understand despite the accent. "Are you the renegadas, who presume upon the metri's courtesy?"

He was young, big, angry, and of unmistakable presence. He was a man you couldn't ignore, especially when he stared at you. When he grew into himself, knew his body and its power as much as I knew mine, he would be formidable.

"Gods," Del breathed.

I glanced at her sidelong, saw the startled expression commingled with something else I didn't like much. She had told me once before that indeed she looked at other men, even as I looked at other women. Now I witnessed it.

I was naked, he was not. But not much was shielded by the thin linen. "Answer me!" he snapped.

I couldn't help myself: I smiled winsomely. "Guest," I declared, "presuming upon nothing we haven't been given by the metri herself."

Dark brows arched up beneath a lock of thick hair fallen across his unlined brow. "Then you must be the latest pretender."

So much for being winsome. I was none too pleased to be caught weaponless and naked in the water, arguing with a boy. "What I am is none of your concern."

He stepped to the edge of the pool. "It is," he said with surprising equanamity, "when I am the metri's only living—and acknowledged—relative." He smiled as he saw us exchange disbelieving glances. "Ask," he suggested gently, eyes alight with triumph, then turned on his heel and walked away. It was then I marked the sheath at the small of his back, and the knife riding lightly in it.

"*Now* I'm confused," I muttered as he disappeared. "And I don't like being confused. Not when I don't have a sword." Being without a blade set the fine hairs on the back of my neck to rising, now that I was challenged.

I pushed my way through water to the edge of the pool, grasped stone, and pulled myself up. Dripping, I bent down to reach for Del's hand. "Either he's a pretender, or I am, or the metri herself is conducting some kind of competition—" I broke off. "Are you getting out?"

As if it were afterthought, Del finally reached up so we could clasp wrists. I braced and pulled; she came up from the pool in one fluid motion, all ivory-silver and bleached gold as the water sheeted off her. Her expression was a combination of perplexity, disbelief, and startled comprehension.

I picked up the drying cloths left by a servant. Flung one at her even as I started rubbing myself down with the other. "All right," I said crossly, "you've proved that women look, too. But he's gone, Del . . . you can stop now."

"What?" Coming belatedly out of her reverie, she bent and began to dry off.

"The young godling here a minute ago." I tossed down my cloth, grabbed up the baggy trousers and began dragging them on one leg at a time. "*I* don't think he's that impressive, but you certainly seem to."

Del blinked at me. "Tiger—"

"He's a kid, bascha . . . barely formed. Not much character there yet—other than arrogance, of course, which he obviously has in full measure." I hitched the waist over my hips, tied off the drawstring, snatched up the tunic and tugged it on over my head. "But I suppose he's pretty enough to look at." I scowled. "So long as that's all you do."

"Yes, he's pretty enough to look at," Del declared. "He looks like *you.*"

That stopped me cold. "What?"

"Without the years. Without the scars." She pulled a long linen shift over her head, yanked folds free of hips and buttocks so that the hem settled around her ankles. "But very much *with* your ill temper." She bent over, swept her hair into some kind of complicated turban, all wrapped up in the cloth.

"My what?"

"And arrogance." She straightened, balanced the turban, snugged the woven belt around her waist with sharp jerks, stalked off.

I watched her back. It was very stiff.

"Looks like me?" I turned back to study the place where the young man had stood, recollecting my first impressions of him. "Him? Nah."

Surely not.

Scowling, I went off to find the metri and learn for myself what in hoolies was going on.

THIRTEEN

BY THE TIME I found the metri, the others already had. The kid, for one—although I confess he didn't look like much of a kid from the back. With Del's observation still foremost in my mind, I studied him with new eyes. He was broad enough, tall enough, and the coloring was the same. Aside from that, though, I didn't think there was so much resemblance.

He wasn't the only one with the metri. Prima Rhannet and her first mate were there as well. Everyone except the metri was talking loudly, trying to raise voices over one another until the room rang hollow with shouting. Dumbfounded, I stopped short in the doorway and stared. Didn't even blink as Del joined me there, wet hair combed out, saying something cross about enough noise to wake the dead.

The metri sat in a chair, hands folded into her lap. She wore the mask I associated with her so long as we were not discussing her daughter or the man her daughter had married: calmly self-contained and utterly unmoved by anything anyone said.

There was much gesticulation and tones of hissing hostility. Del's godling rounded on Prima and Nihko, seemingly accusing them of something they didn't much like, as they answered in kind. I was not surprised to see the red-haired captain so animated, because it was like her; but Nihko Blue-head only rarely showed so much emotion. As for Del's godling, well, I didn't know him at all, but he seemed extremely comfortable with shouting, so I assumed he had lots of experience.

This looked and sounded like nothing so much as a family quarrel. I began to suspect there was a lot more to the story than a renegade captain and her tattooed first mate, and a kid who looked enough like Nihko to be his son. And since Nihko himself resembled *me*, this made it a very tight-knit family indeed.

And I couldn't understand a word of what anyone was saying.

Out of patience, I drew a very large breath deep into my lungs and let loose a roar that overrode them all. *"Hey!"*

Even Del jumped.

Now that I had everyone's attention, I smiled my friendliest smile. "Hello," I said with cheerful courtesy. "Would you care to repeat all that in a language I can understand?"

"We," Del murmured.

"We," I amended. When no one said anything at all, I glanced at them one by one.

Prima Rhannet's hand was at her waist where her knife generally resided tied to her belt, but she wasn't wearing the knife, or even that particular belt. Like Del, she wore an ankle-length sleeveless tunic gathered at the waist into a woven sash. Nihko never was so blatant about his weapons, which he didn't have at the moment, either; he just stood with his head turned slightly toward me, eyes glittering. But the godling, as youth so often does, had turned to face me squarely, to challenge the unexpected, every powerful part of him poised for movement.

Hoolies, Del was right. He *could* be me. If you stripped away fifteen years and all the scars from me.

Or added them to him.

It was eerie. You don't usually recognize yourself in others. For that matter, you don't usually recognize yourself in a silver mirror or a pool of water unless you *know* it's you, and only then you know it's you because logic argues it must be: if you're peering into a mirror or water, the image staring back very likely is your own. I knew

my hands best of all because I was so accustomed to using
them, to watching them as I did things with them, even
without thinking about them. But unless one studies oneself from head to toe every day, one isn't even aware of
certain aspects of one's appearance.

But he was me. Or I was him. Del had already noted
it, and now the renegadas and the metri did as well. The
kid and I stood there staring at one another in startled
recognition and unspoken, unsubtle territorial challenge,
while Prima Rhannet began to laugh, and Nihko . . . well,
Nihko grinned widely in a highly superior and annoying
fashion, brow-rings glinting.

They had tossed the bones, the captain and her mate.
And won.

I touched the thong of sandtiger claws around my
throat. The metri had given me back the brow ring she'd
cut from the necklet, saying that so long as Nihko was
present I'd do better to wear it lest I lose most of my
meals. Since I had yet to learn a way of maintaining any
measure of decorum while spewing up the contents of my
belly, I accepted the ring, knotting it back into the thong.
One of these days I was going to find out just *why* Nihko
made me sick.

Other than for the usual reasons, of course.

The kid said something under his breath. The metri
responded with a single word that flooded his face with
the dusky color of embarrassment, or anger. As he glared
at me I began to appreciate, in a very bizarre and detached
sort of way, just why so many people gave way to me
when I employed the most ferocious of my stares.

There was no subtlety about Del's godling, but he
might learn it one day. If he lived.

"Family argument?" I asked lightly.

"They soil this household," the kid hissed, switching
languages easily. "As do you."

"Herakleio," the metri said only.

His hands were fists. "They do," he insisted. "All of
them. Prima is a disgrace to her father, her heritage—and
Nihkolara is ikepra! *This* man"—he meant me, of
course—"is a pretender." He shifted his furious glance to

Del, all fired up to make other accusations, and realized rather abruptly he knew absolutely nothing about her.

Except that she was beautiful. And, I didn't doubt, that he had seen her in the pool. Without clothing.

I watched the change in him. The anger, the touchy pride remained, but slid quietly beneath the surface as something else rose up. Color moved in his face again. He drew a breath, expelled it sharply through his nostrils, then consciously relaxed the fists into hands again.

I gave him marks for honesty: he did not try to charm the woman who had just seen his childish display of temper. He accepted that she had, was ashamed of it, but did not deny it.

The metri moved slightly forward in her chair, immediately commanding the attention of everyone in the room. She was smiling in triumphant delight, rather like a cat, as she looked first at the boy who claimed he was her kin, then at me who claimed I was not.

The woman laughed. Slowly, as if tasting something unexpected and quite delicious. "I should have both of you sheathed in plaster," she said calmly, "and placed on either side of my gate. Surely everyone in the islands would come to marvel at my new statuary."

"Naked?" Prima inquired.

Rather surprisingly, the metri did not take offense. "Oh, I believe so. Unclothed, and ambitiously male."

The kid—Herakleio?—was stunned. He turned jerkily toward her, jaw slackening. "Metri?"

"Come now, Herakleio," she said. "Admit the truth. He is you."

"He's old!" the kid announced.

Nihko grinned. Prima gulped a laugh. Del put fingers across her mouth as if to hide a treacherous response, expression elaborately bland.

I smiled, vastly unoffended. "Older than you," I agreed, "which serves me just fine, as the first one born inherits soonest."

A glint in the metri's eyes told me she understood and appreciated the provocation. Especially as it worked.

"First born!" Herakleio shouted, furious all over again. "First born of what whore?"

"Stop." This time it was the metri, all amusement wiped away. "You soil this household with such shouting, all of you."

Herakleio shot a venomous glance at Prima Rhannet. "And why do *you* care if we are naked? Men are nothing to you."

"Oh, men are a great deal to me," she replied, unperturbed. "I have no complaint of them, in general. I merely choose not to sleep with them."

He colored up again. "You slept with *me*."

Ah. More and more interesting.

Prima grinned. "It passed an otherwise long night."

"But—"

"And it served to show me my preferences were other."

I blinked. She said it so blandly, without pointed offense, and yet no man could help *but* take it as an offense.

Herakleio did, of course, and responded by hissing something of great emotion, though he said it in Skandic so I couldn't understand. Prima merely laughed at him. Nihko, perhaps wisely, kept his mouth shut.

I frowned at him. "What is your stake in this?" I asked. "Do you fit?"

It instantly diverted Herakleio. "Oh, *he* fits. Has he not told you what he was, and is?"

"I've heard a word," I said clearly. "I've even heard sort of a definition. But I haven't the slightest idea what any of it means."

"Ikepra," Herakleio sneered, glowering at Nihko. "Tell him, Nihkolara."

"Tell him yourself."

Always an impressive response. I sighed and exchanged a speaking glance with Del. She was as much at sea as I.

"Ikepra," Herakleio declared curtly, as if I should discern from tone and posture all the complexities of definition. "He should have been thrown from the cliff."

"But then I would have flown," Nihko countered mildly.

"You sailed," Herakleio gibed. "You sailed with *her.*" A finger punched air in Prima's direction.

"And have not regretted it."

This time it was Del who cut off the conversation. She looked at the metri, who was watching both Nihko and Herakleio with an unfathomable expression, and asked what undoubtedly should have been asked at the very beginning. "What do you mean to do with us?"

The woman arched one eloquent brow. "Decide."

"Decide?" Herakleio asked suspiciously, who knew this woman better than any of us.

"I have two heirs, now," she answered. "Only one may inherit."

"Two?" Herakleio exploded. "How is this possible? He is a pretender—"

"Is he?"

"Am I?" I fixed the metri with a scowl. "Is he kin to you?"

"This boy?" She smiled. "Oh, yes. He is my brother's wife's brother's grandson."

I gave up trying to work that one out. "Then you don't need me or anyone else. You've got your heir."

"Male," Herakleio pronounced darkly.

I raised my brows at him. "Is there some doubt as to that?"

"He means he descends from the male line," Prima supplied.

I shook my head. "So?"

"The *male* line," Herakleio gritted between clamped teeth.

I sighed. "In case you've forgotten, I'm not from around here."

"We are counted from the female line," Nihko explained.

Prima nodded. "And from the gods."

I stared at her. "You think you're descended from

gods?" So much for my self-description of Herakleio as a godling being effective sarcasm; irony doesn't work if you believe it's the truth. "This is ridiculous. You're people just like everyone else!"

Prima slid a veiled glance at Nihko from beneath lowered lids. "Some of us are—more."

"*Were* more," Herakleio corrected pointedly with intense scorn.

After a moment I just shook my head in disbelief and looked again at the metri. "I think it's time I left. I've got no stake in any of this, and no time to sort it out. I'm not your grandson, and I'm certainly not a godling!"

"Jhihadi," Del murmured.

As quietly I retorted, "You're not helping."

"But you may be," the metri said quietly, "and I cannot afford to lose you if it be true."

"You can't very well *keep* me," I shot back. "You bought my freedom from renegadas—"

"Precisely," the metri confirmed. "There is a debt between us now."

"Debt?" I was incredulous. "How in hoolies do you expect me to pay you back?"

Unsmiling, she looked at Herakleio. "Take this boy and make of him a man."

In the ensuing hubbub—Prima was laughing while Herakleio sputtered furious protest—I turned on my heel and walked out.

Del followed me right out into the courtyard entry. There she stopped, as if surprised I hadn't. "Where are you going?"

I swung at the gated entrance, stiff with frustration. "Away."

"Away *where?*"

"Just away. I don't belong here. I don't belong with these people. I don't want to have anything to *do* with these people!"

"Not even if they are your kin?"

"I disown them," I answered instantly.

Del examined my expression. "I think the person with no coin or property can't disown anyone."

"Then I repudiate them."

She nodded. "You can do that."

"Good. I do. I have. Let's go."

She was by all appearances stuck on one question. "Where?"

"Out of here. I've had enough of Skandi, metris, blue-headed priests, women ship captains, women ship captains who sleep with other women, and wife's brother's grandsons."

"Have you coin?"

"No. Where would I get coin?"

"Where indeed?"

I glowered at her. "Are you suggesting we *stay?*"

Del assumed her most innocent expression. "The metri did pay for your release . . . but I merely suggest we devise a plan before we go anywhere."

I opened my mouth to answer, shut it as I saw Nihko come out behind her, stepping from shadow into sunlight. "Plans are useful," he observed. "Have you one?"

I switched my scowl from Del to him. "I have done very well making a living in this world without any plans. This situation is no different."

"But it is," Nihko disagreed politely. "You don't even speak the language."

"You speak mine," I said. "So does Prima, so does the metri, so does Heraklitus."

"Herakleio," Del corrected, and I shot her a ferocious glare.

"We speak it," Nihko said, "because we have been made to. My captain and I sail to foreign ports. The metri deals with merchants and traders of other lands, and to be certain dealings are honest one must speak the language. Herakleio has learned because the metri required it of her heir."

"Then he *is* her heir."

"He is her kin," Nihko elaborated. "But male-descended. It matters."

"Why does it matter?"

"This is Skandi. Things are—as they are."

"And you?" I asked curtly, angry enough to offend on purpose. "What exactly are you, ikepra?"

Nihko did not provoke. He wasn't Herakleio. "Ikepra," he answered. "Profanation. Abomination."

"Why?" Del asked.

He did not flinch from it. "Because I failed."

"Failed what?" I asked.

"The gods," he said, "and myself."

I stared at him a long moment, matching stare to stare, then shook my head. "Let's go, bascha."

"Tiger—"

Nihko's brow rings glinted in the sunlight. "You would abuse the metri's hospitality?"

"Look, I don't want to abuse anyone's hospitality. But you certainly didn't offer us any when you destroyed our ship, and you didn't improve matters by attempting to sell me to the metri—"

"*Did* sell," he put in.

"—and she's not exactly being hospitable by ordering me to make a man of her brother's wife's brother's brother's grandson," I finished.

"That's one 'brother's' too many," Del pointed out helpfully.

"Do you not believe he needs it?" Nihko inquired.

I glared at him again, eyes narrowed. "Just where do you fit, Nihkolara? Aside from being profanation and abomination, that is. What are you to these people? What are they to you?"

"My past," he said only.

Another figure moved out of shadow into light. The boy whom the metri wanted to be a man. "Tell him, Nihkolara," Herakleio challenged, lounging against the white-painted stonework of the entryway. "Tell him the whole of it."

Nihko made a gesture. "Herak . . . let it be."

"Herakleio. Ikepra are not permitted familiarity."

Color stained the first mate's face, then flowed away so he was alabaster-pale. There was tension throughout his body; Herakleio had reached inside him somewhere, touched a private place.

Herakleio displayed white teeth in a sun-coppered face. "Tell the pretender how you *fit*, Nihkolara."

And Nihkolara told me, while the heat beat on our heads.

FOURTEEN

I FLOPPED flat on the bed and stared up at the low ceiling. "This is all too complicated. And getting worse."

Del, sitting as she so often chose to sit—on the floor against the opposite wall—shrugged. "What is complicated? There were eleven women placed upon the island by the gods, and each bore eleven daughters *of* those gods. Then the gods sent those daughters sons of other women, and so the Eleven Families took root and flowered here."

"How poetic," I observed sourly. "And of course you'd find it easy: it's all about *women.*"

"I suspect it is simpler even for gods to get babies on women."

I rolled my head and looked at her. "You're finding entirely too much amusement in this, bascha."

"Am I amused?"

"Inside. Where I can't see."

Her mouth twitched. "And from those eleven daughters came sons and daughters of the sons sent to lie with them, and so the people of first couplings may name themselves gods-descended."

"But not everyone on Skandi is gods-descended." I realized what I'd said and amended it immediately. "Not everyone *believes* they are gods-descended. I mean, they aren't gods-descended, of course, because no one is, but if they think it's possible, they might believe they aren't. Even if others are. *Believe* they are, that is." I dropped my forearm across my face and issued a strangled groan. "I *said* this was too complicated!"

Del seemed to grasp it well enough. "They believe they aren't gods-descended because certain sons came to Skandi from other islands, not from gods, and married the daughters of those first divine couplings."

From under my arm I added, "And so those who can count the generations back to those specific eleven women consider themselves superior to everyone else."

"Well," Del said judiciously, "I suspect that if I were descended of gods, and the others weren't, I might count myself superior."

I removed my arm and hiked myself up on one elbow. "*You* would? And here I thought you considered yourself no better than even the lowliest slave, bascha."

"I said 'might,' " she clarified. "And it doesn't matter, here. Here I am a woman."

"You are a woman anywhere. And I know for a fact a lot of men are convinced you *are* gods-descended."

"Thank you."

"Of course, they don't know you as well as I do." I flopped down again, pondering the information. "It seems obvious enough to me: these eleven women found themselves in the family way, and, thus disgraced, were exiled here." I shrugged against the mattress. "It's a pretty story they all made up to excuse their wanton behavior, and the eleven little outcomes of it."

"But it might be true."

"Oh, come on, bascha—gods impregnating women?"

"It would be an explanation for why there's magic in the world."

"Magic? Hah. Maybe superstition. Stories. Meant to entertain—"

"—or enlighten."

"—or to pass the night—"

"—or to keep a history alive."

"—or to simply waste time." I thrust an arm beneath my head and changed the subject. Sort of. "So Nihko and the metri are related through the now-infamous Eleven Families—"

"And Herakleio."

"—which explains why so many Skandics look alike."

"Which explains why you look like so many Skandics. You are."

"But not necessarily related to the metri, or Nihko, or your boy Herakleio."

"He's not my boy," Del declared. "He's older than I am."

"By what, one or two years?"

"That's still older, Tiger."

"While I'm just *old*."

"You should take a nap," Del advised after a moment.

"Why? Because I'm old?"

"No. Because you're cross-grained."

"Cross-grained?"

"Out of sorts."

"I know what it means, bascha. And if I am, it's because I'm tired—"

"I said you should take a nap."

"—of all these convoluted explanations," I finished with emphasis. "Hoolies, this is ludicrous! Women impregnated by gods, and men sent to marry their daughters—"

"Most history *is* a collection of stories," Del said. "It is so in the North."

"And I got my name because I killed a sandtiger I magicked up out of my dreams," I blurted in disgust. "Hoolies, do you think I really believe that? I was a kid. Younger even than Herakleio. Or you."

"You have done things," she said finally, "that are not explainable."

"There's an explanation for everything."

"And your sandtiger?"

I shut my eyes. "Coincidence. Hoolies, I just wanted a way out of slavery. I took advantage of something that happens once or twice a year. It was just the Salset's turn to be meat for a beast."

"And changing the sand to grass?"

"The sand *isn't* grass, Del. It's sand. And besides, all I did was suggest they bring the water to where it wasn't."

"Which can change the sand to grass."

I grunted. "In time, I suppose."

"Magic, Tiger, wears many guises."

"Like Nihko?"

Del was silent.

I turned my head against my arm. "Well?"

"I don't know."

"Maybe *you* should take the nap."

"I am neither tired nor cross-grained. I am, after all, younger than you." She smiled sunnily even as I scowled. "Besides . . ."

"Besides what?"

"You were dead only yesterday."

"But alive today—and lacking a sword." I swore. "I *hate* to be without a sword. I get into trouble when I don't have a sword."

"You get into trouble when you *have* a sword."

"But I can also get myself out of it. If I have a sword."

Del observed me. "You are on edge."

"Aren't you?"

"They haven't offered to harm us."

"But they haven't told us what they intend to do with us either. I don't find that comfortable."

"Especially when you lack a sword."

"If I had one, we'd be gone from here already."

"There's more to it than that."

I sighed, conceding it. "Something doesn't feel right."

Del was silent.

I glanced at her. "Well? Don't you feel it?"

She nodded.

"There. See?" I smiled triumphantly.

"All we can do," she said, "is wait. Watch. Be ready."

"I'd rather be ready with a sword in my hands."

"Well, yes." Del's smile was crooked. "But we have none, either of us, and until we can get them I think we'd best do what we can to preserve our energy." She paused. "As I said, you were dead only yesterday."

Rather than debate it any further—I *was* on edge, and tired—I took a nap.

Upon awakening alone, I went off in search of Nihkolara to clear up a few matters. It took me a while to track him down, but I found him at last seated upon one of the low perimeter walls surrounding Akritara, staring off into the distance. Beyond him, the setting sun leached the blue of the sky and transmuted it to dusty purple, streaked with ribbons of orange and gold.

As if a friendly companion, I sat down upon the wall next to him and swung both legs over, perching comfortably even as the evening breeze stripped hair out of my face. (Which was one thing the shaven-headed first mate didn't have to contend with.) "So, how did you do it?"

He made no sign he was aware of my presence, though obviously he was. I figured Nihkolara was only rarely taken by surprise.

I kept my tone light. "It's not every man who can make another appear to be dead—"

"You were."

"Dead?" I expelled air through my nose in sharp commentary. "I don't think so. But I'll admit it's an effective trick."

He continued staring into the sunset. "Believe as you will. You are an apostate."

"I?" I slapped a hand against my chest with a meaty thwack. "But I am a messiah. How can *I* be an apostate?"

He shook his head slightly. "You treat it all as a huge jest, Southron. Because you are afraid."

"Afraid of what? You? That kid?"

"Afraid of the truth." He glanced at me briefly, then looked back into the fading day. "What you do not understand, you ridicule. Because you know there is something in the heart of it that may be dangerous."

"I understand danger well enough." I swung my feet briefly, thumping heels against plastered brick. "But you're avoiding my question."

"You appeared to be dead because you were."

I sighed. "Fine. For the sake of argument, let's say I was dead. How, then, did you bring me back?"

Nihko grinned into the air. "Trickery."

"More secrets, I take it?"

The grin faded. He looked at me now, gaze intense. "Because I am ikepra does not mean I lack belief," he said, "and it is belief which rouses power. It means only that I failed in the maintenance of my oaths, in the convictions of my heart." Something moved in his face, briefly impassioned, then was diluted beneath a careful mask. "The body was weak."

"Strong enough," I commented. "We've wrestled a little, you and I."

"Flesh," he said dismissively. "I speak of the heart, the soul. But the body is a base vessel of vast impurities, and if one cannot cleanse himself of such, the vessel is soiled."

"Ikepra?"

"Broken oaths," he said, "provide a weak man with weaker underpinnings. Eventually they crumble—and so does he."

I had intended to comment, but the words died in my mouth. We were more alike than I wanted to admit, Nihkolara and I. Possibly related, though I didn't see how that would ever be settled. But certainly linked in the heart by knowledge of broken vows and shattered honor, and lives warped because of it.

"So you found Prima Rhannet, because the kind of oath she wanted was one you could serve."

"Without doubt," he confirmed. "Without hesitation. It is far easier to kill other men than to kill one's soul."

"Killing other men *does* kill the soul."

He stared at me as if weighing my intent. Brow rings glinted. In clear light I could see the hint of a scab in his left eyebrow where he had cut from his flesh the ring I wore on my necklet. "If one's soul is not already dead."

I meant to answer, to dredge up some kind of witty remark that would diffuse the tension. But Nihkolara stood up and stepped over the wall onto the cobbles of the courtyard. I smelled the perfume of the blossoms, the acrid tang of dust lifted by wind. And the sweat of fear.

"I think," he said, "you have a stronger heart than I."

"I have *what*—?" But he turned from me before I could complete the question and walked away with purposeful strides.

Realizing he had deflected my questions away without divulging answers beyond glib, unspecific replies and personal challenges, I stared scowling into the sunset, disgusted that I'd let him get away with it.

From here you couldn't see the actual edge of the cliff, or know that the world currently was little more than a crescent of wracked remains, but the heart sensed something. It knew the island was paramount upon the waters, and yet subject to them. I felt at once isolated, apart, humbled, despite the awareness that the earth stretched far beneath me as if I were a god.

God. Hoolies. Nihko and everyone else had me thinking like they did.

I shifted my weight then, an infinitesimal amount. A slight redistribution forward, leg muscles bunching, so that it would require very little effort on my part to spring up and turn, balanced for defense *or* offense. Because I knew he was there.

"You fool no one," Herakleio announced belligerently.

I smiled into the sunset. "Not anyone? Oh, I am irredeemably devastated."

"You believe you are clever, claiming to want no part of us, when it's obvious you mean only to mislead us, to convince the metri that you are the son of her daughter."

Still smiling, I said, "You are a gloriously self-indulgent, self-centered fool, Herakleio. What makes you think I *should* want any part of you?"

"Because of what we are," he shot back. "The Stessoi are gods-descended, one of the Eleven Families . . . we are wealthy and powerful beyond any man's dreams, pretender, and certainly beyond yours. You come here thinking to fool the metri—"

"I was brought here," I interrupted crisply, "against my own will. But I came because the choice was simple."

"To be poor, or rich."

"To be free, or enslaved. And there was the small matter of my companion being held onboard ship, to insure my cooperation." I shrugged. "Some choices are easy. Especially when they concern others."

"But you are free now. The metri has paid the renegadas. Your companion is here, not there. You may go."

"But the metri has reminded me of a thing called a debt." I sighed. "Unlikely as it may sound, I don't like owing anyone. I prefer to pay such debts."

"*I* will pay it!"

I turned then, swinging legs back over the wall so I might face him. "And then the debt would be yours."

He was prepared for that. "You would pay it by leaving."

I examined him, marking the look in his eyes. "Are you so very afraid that I am who the metri wants me to be?"

He denied it, of course, but his eyes told the truth. "There has been a parade of pretenders presenting themselves to the metri. You are no different."

"But I am," I replied. "And now that I have seen you, I understand why." I grinned. "Like it or not, boy, we are seeds from the same plant."

"Every islander born bears some resemblance to us," he countered quickly. "Do you think there are so many of us on Skandi that we would never intermarry?"

"But only those from the Eleven Families are permitted to intermarry," I said. "The gods-descended, naturally, wouldn't dream of marrying anyone else. Which means that descendants of those families are bound to closely resemble *one another,* but not necessarily anyone else." I raised inquisitive brows. "Do you know if any of the other metris is missing a relative?"

He hissed something at me in Skandic, stiff as an affronted cat.

I grinned at him. "Relax," I said. "There's a way out of this."

"I could kill you."

That language I understood very well. "Well, yes, that's one way, though I confess it's not the way *I* would prefer. And since the metri is not a stupid woman, she'd likely know it was you right off." I shrugged. "I don't know what the customs are like in Skandi—maybe murderers are still allowed to inherit."

Something in his expression suggested they were not. "What is your way, then? And why would you tell me it?"

"Because I suspect the metri wants you to inherit," I answered calmly.

It perplexed him. He *was* young.

"First," I said, "it's not as easy to kill another man as you might expect. And I'm not talking about the physical ability to take a life, but the will." Before he could protest, I continued. "Anyone can kill in self-defense, or to protect their kin. But to purposefully track a man and challenge him requires an entirely different part of the mind." I tapped my head. "And to carry through without getting killed yourself . . . well, it doesn't always work out the way you'd like."

"*You* are alive."

"How old are you? Twenty-three?"

The question took him aback. "Twenty-four."

I nodded contemplatively. "For every year you have been alive, I've killed a man. Or maybe two. Possibly three. I'm alive not because I wanted it more than the others, but because I learned how to find the *ways* to survive. And the ways to kill. In here—" I touched my forehead,"—as much as in here." This time my heart.

He frowned. "Why are you saying such things? Do you mean to frighten me?"

"You're twenty-four. Nothing frightens you."

It stung. He glared at me, lips tight.

"Good," I said. "It shut you up. Maybe if you listen, you'll learn something."

He stopped listening. "This is not your place. This is not your world. This is not your legacy."

"It's yours," I agreed. "But if you want it, you're going to have to learn how to deserve it."

"*Deserve* it—!"

I stood up, wiped my palms together to brush away dust, then took one long stride that put me right up against Herakleio. Before he could step away or protest, I poked fingers into his breastbone. "You're soft," I said gently. He made to move; I caught a wrist, clamped, and held him in place. "Big, broad, strong, and likely very quick, but soft. Soft up here—" I placed one forefinger against his brow and nudged. "—and soft down here." I dug stiffened fingers into his belly.

Outraged, he opened his mouth to shout but I raised my voice and overrode him.

"I suspect you spend most of your time drinking in cantinas—or whatever you call them here—hanging out with your friends—likely young men of the other ten supposedly gods-descended families about your age—and entertaining women. You repeatedly ignore the metri's requests that you learn how to do the accounting because figures are boring, and you haven't the faintest idea how the vineyards are run because you'd rather drink the results than make them." I released his wrist. "In short, you are a perfectly normal twenty-four-year-old male of a wealthy, powerful family who believes his ancestors were sired by gods."

He sputtered the beginnings of an incoherent response. I cut him off.

"She's dying," I said. "She needs you to be prepared. She needs to know everything her family has worked for will be secure in your hands."

He managed a response finally, sharp and aggressive. "Not in *yours?*"

"There is no proof I am the son of her daughter. There never can be. She may want to believe it, but she doesn't *know* it. And it matters."

"She's the metri. She can simply declare you heir."

"But she didn't," I told him. "She asked me to make a man of the boy who is."

"As if you could!"

I shrugged. "Try me."

His lip curled. "Southroner. I know what you are, you sword-dancers. Kill-for-hires. All these games about honor codes and oaths—I *know* what you are. Men of no family, no prospects. Honorless men who worship a sword, who worship death, because there is nothing in your lives otherwise, no heritage, no pride, no place with the gods when you die." He leaned into me, challenging with his body. "And *you* speak of making me a man."

He definitely had mastered scorn. Fortunately, I had mastered patience.

Well, sometimes.

I crossed my arms and grinned. "Heard of us, have you?"

"You are as bad as ikepra, you and men like you. And you dare to come here into this house, into the *metri's* house, and profane her dwelling."

"I'm sure she's capable of hiring some priest to come cleanse and rebless it once I'm gone."

"Go now," he hissed, spittle dampening my face. "Go *now,* sword-dancer."

I did not wipe my face. Softly, I said, "Make me."

He was, no doubt, accustomed to striking slaves, because he drew his right arm across his chest as if to backhand me. I, meanwhile, jammed a fist deep into his belly, and when he bent over it, I hooked an ankle around his. A quick leveraged jerk to upend him, and he was all flailing arms and awkward body.

He landed hard, as I meant him to, sprawled flat on the stone of the terrace. Taken completely unaware, he drove elbows into stone, smacked the back of his skull, scraped his forearms, all before his legs and butt landed. When they did, he bit his tongue, which bled all over his chin and fine linen tunic as he wheezed and coughed.

I stood over him, but not within range even if he'd had the wherewithal to attempt anything. "Insults don't accomplish much," I told him, "unless you're better than the other man." I flicked a spot of dust off my tunic. "And then you don't need 'em."

Spittle mixed with blood came flying out of his mouth. He missed.

"I pay my debts," I told him. "If you don't like it, take your complaints to the metri."

Rage contorted his features. Even if he had been quick enough, skilled enough, he was so angry now any attack would have been ineffective. Breathlessly he loosed a string of teeth-gritted invective that undoubtedly would have scorched my ears had I understood the language.

Then again, maybe not. I've been sworn at by the best. And she was far preferable as company than the metri's brother's wife's brother's grandson.

I waved farewell at him. "Come see me in the morning."

FIFTEEN

IT WAS conveyed to us by the kilted servant that the metri would have us all in to dinner. I got the impression this was a rare occurence; not that guests weren't hosted properly, but that two of those guests were renegadas.

Ah well. After my discussion with Herakleio, I was primed for a more interesting atmosphere.

Which is exactly what I got. Del and I were escorted into a large, airy dining chamber already peopled by Prima Rhannet, her first mate, Herakleio, and the metri herself. Who, standing quietly beside the door, greeted me courteously, then smashed the flat of her hand into the side of my face.

The shock of it drove me back a step. Instinct took over instantly, and I trapped her wrist in one hand before she could strike again, though she did not appear to intend it.

I rubbed the knuckles of my other hand against my stinging cheek. "What in hoolies was *that* for?"

"Punishment," she said crisply, "for striking Herakleio."

"Now, wait just a moment—"

"It was required. I am the metri. Discipline is dictated by me."

"And what about Herakleio trying to strike a guest in the metri's household?"

"Herakleio has been punished as well."

I glanced beyond her to the table. Herakleio glared

back at me. Yes, his left cheek bore a ruddy spot high on the bone.

I released her wrist. "If you intend me to make a man of him, it's going to require more than sweet words and soft caresses."

She inclined her head. "I give you leave to do what is required."

"At the risk of getting smacked around by you?" I shook my head. "That's not in the contract."

"We have no contract," she answered at once. "This is a debt, which you intend to discharge." Her eyes glinted. "However, the point has been made and need not be repeated. Now, seat yourselves at my table and enjoy the bounty of the house."

I turned as she moved through the door *away* from the table. "What about you?"

She paused. "There are things to be settled among you. It were better done without my presence, so you may speak freely."

And then she was gone, leaving Del and me staring in bemusement at the others.

Prima snorted, poured herself wine from a jar. "Neatly done," she said. "Why soil herself by eating in the same room as renegadas?"

"What about me?" Herakleio shot back. "*I* am left to eat in the same room as renegadas."

"But you are already hopelessly soiled," Prima retorted. "You slept with a renegada."

"You weren't one then!"

"No," she agreed. "I was the daughter of a slaver. Likely the metri believes that every bit as bad." She gulped wine, smiled through glistening droplets painting her wide mouth. "Herak, you are such a child sometimes. But pretty, I will admit."

He recoiled. "Pretty!"

She waved a hand in my direction as Del and I took our seats at the table. "All you Stessoi are pretty. Even the women."

"*You* would know," he sneered. "Though no Stessa

would ever demean herself and dishonor her family by—" A pause. "—cohabiting with such as you."

"Such as I," Prima said silkily, "come from the best families."

"Not yours."

"Oh, mine is a family of slavers. But what of the original Eleven Families? Can you swear there is no other woman such as I, nor a man who might prefer another man in his bed?" She smiled sweetly. "One such as you, perhaps."

Beneath his tan, Herakleio turned pale as bleached linen, then reddened nearly to purple. He was so shocked and outraged he couldn't summon a voice to speak with.

Prima laughed at him. "No, Herak, I do not suggest your taste runs in that direction. Be at ease. I only meant that certain men may desire you even as women do."

Clearly he had never considered that. But then, neither had I. I knew of such men, such interests, of course, but had never really contemplated how I'd feel were I the object of another man's interest.

Prima Rhannet, having plunged both Herakleio and me into mutual black scowls and deep thoughts, grinned at Del. "Men are such fools, sometimes. They think they *are* that which dangles between their legs." She lifted her cup as if in salute. "While we women know the only truly important part of the body resides within our skulls."

"Perhaps," Del agreed, dipping a chunk of bread into olive oil, "but that need not mean we are better than they."

"Women *are* better than men."

"Some women are better than some men," Del countered quietly, and filled her mouth with bread.

I had poured myself some wine. Now I stopped the cup halfway to my mouth. "That isn't what you claimed when we first met!"

Del arched brows at me and continued to chew.

"It isn't," I repeated. "You told me men were nothing but beasts driven by lust and violence."

She hitched a shoulder. "The men I knew were. I had gone South, remember?"

"What about me?"

She didn't answer, which was answer in itself.

I set the cup down with a thump. "If I'm that bad—"

"You were," Del said. "But you aren't anymore. I have leavened you—" She grinned. "—like bread."

"Thank you for that, bascha!"

"You inspire me." Prima took off a chunk of bread from the loaf in the center of the table and sopped it in olive oil. "The truth is, all men are born fools," she declared, "and if you forget, they remind you."

Nihko was being conspicuously silent. I fixed him with a hard eye. "What have you to say?"

He had bypassed the bread and was serving himself a large fish from the platter. "I? Nothing. I know better."

"He has heard it before," Prima said.

Herakleio's color was high. "And he has little to say for men, anyway. He is missing a significant portion of those parts Prima repudiates so eloquently."

It was purposely cruel. It was also a killing offense, though Nihko simply began stripping meat from the fish.

Prima wasn't smiling or laughing anymore. "He will not provoke," she said. "But I will, Herak."

Herakleio feigned fear, then looked at me. "Did Nihkolara explain why he is—without? How he came to lose that which he most adored, and wielded most assiduously?"

"Enough," Prima said.

"How he alone seemingly intended to people several islands with his byblows," Herakleio continued, "and might well have accomplished it had he kept himself to whores and unmarried women. But he did not. There was the Palomedi metri's daughter, you see—when the metri herself believed he was faithful to *her.*"

"Recall what he is!" Prima said sharply.

Herakleio filled it with scorn. "Ikepra."

I poured more wine. It was very good. Maybe it wouldn't be so difficult to remain here for a while. "This is what I enjoy most in life," I said lightly, "good food, good wine, good friends."

Del's expression was guileless. "Pity Abbu Bensir

isn't present." Before I could say yea or nay, she served me with something from a common dish.

"Who?" Herakleio asked crossly, even as I scowled at Del.

I peered at the food, frowning. It looked like leaves all rolled up into miniature sleeping bundles.

"Abbu Bensir is a sword-dancer," Del answered. "A very good sword-dancer. In fact, he claims to be the best in the South."

"Ah." Prima shot a grin at me. "Surely there are those who disagree."

"Surely there are," Del confirmed demurely.

"What is this?" I poked the rolled plant with a wary finger.

Prima leaned, plucked one bundle from my plate, paused long enough to say "stuffed grape leaves" and bit it in half.

"Stuffed with what?"

"Kill-for-hires," Herakleio said dismissively.

For one bizarre moment I thought he meant that's what was rolled up inside the grape leaves. But no.

Del turned at once to me. "Is that true? That all sword-dancers are hired murderers?"

She could answer as well as I. For some reason she didn't want to. I bestowed upon her a look that promised we'd discuss this later, then glanced at Herakleio.

"I have killed," I said. "But then most men have, in the Punja, because there is often no choice. But that has little to do with being a sword-dancer."

"How not?" Prima asked, having survived the leaf-bundle.

Herakleio snorted disdain, helping himself to the common bowl.

"I dance," I pointed out. "I am hired by tanzeers—our desert princes—to settle disputes in the circle so that men need not die." I shrugged. "Skirmishes, battles, and wars waste men in a hostile land that kills too many by itself. It's simply good sense to save lives by settling disputes in the circle."

"But you say you've killed!"

I picked up one of the leaf-bundles Del had bestowed upon me. "Bandits," I answered. "Borjuni. Slavers. Tanzeers." I bit into the bundle, contemplated its flavor, swallowed. "Sorcerers."

That shocked Herakleio. "Sorcerers!"

"Have you none here?" Del asked.

"IoSkandi," Prima said, avoiding Nihko's look.

"Who?" I asked. "What *are* they, anyway? I've heard the term before." I shot a glance at Nihko. "Though it seems to be a secret."

He smiled enigmatically. "And so it shall remain."

Herakleio turned the topic back upon itself. "This Abbu Bensir," he said. "*Is* he better than you?"

I opened my mouth to answer, shut it. Was aware of Del's attention though she hid it, and the scrutiny of the others. In the South I might have immediately confirmed my status with dramatic bravado, but I was not in the South. And for some reason, here and now, I felt like telling the truth. "I don't know."

"Have you ever danced against him?"

"Many times."

"Then you should know who is better. Or are you afraid to admit he is?"

"We were trained together, Abbu and I. We sparred many times then, and have since, to test skills and conditioning. But we have met only one time in a circle that would have determined who truly was better."

"And the result?"

I shook my head. "There was none. The dance was never finished."

"Ah." Herakleio smiled as if he knew why. "And so the true answer must wait for another time, another circle, and another dance."

"No," I said.

"What, then? Is he dead?"

"He was very much alive the last time we saw him."

"Then why will you never settle things?" Herakleio demanded. "Are you afraid?"

The food was suddenly tasteless in my mouth. "There are rituals. Honor codes, oaths, things that bind those of us who are trained by swordmasters such as I was, and Abbu. In the circle dishonor is not tolerated, nor broken oaths. Not among true sword-dancers; there are men who fancy themselves sword-dancers, who attempt to act the part, but they aren't. They just want the glory without the years, the work."

"Or the oaths," Del said softly.

I shrugged. "Abbu and I might meet again someday, but it won't be to settle who is better. It will be a death-dance, to punish a man who broke all the codes and honor of Alimat."

"Why?" Herakleio demanded.

"Elaii-ali-ma," I answered. Then phrased it in a word they'd understand, as I looked at Nihkolara. "I'm ikepra, too."

The muscles of his face stilled. His hands stopped moving. Even his eyes, fixed on me, were hard as stone.

Among dangerous men there are two kinds of quietude of the body: when he is at ease, and when he wishes to attack. The latter is not the same as being prepared to fight or to defend, though it can be mistaken as such by the inexperienced. The latter is neither bluster nor challenge, but the willingness and the wish to tear into pieces the offending party.

And not doing it.

Beside me, Del, too, stilled. Prima Rhannet had stopped breathing. Only Herakleio, blind to the tensions, was relaxed. And smiling, as if pleased by my answer. I had, after all, confessed my unworthiness in terms he understood.

Nihkolara rose. His hands at his side trembled minutely, as if he could not bear the demands of his body. He had not reacted when Herakleio disdained his manhood, but for some inexplicable reason, my casting myself into his place stirred in him some deep response.

"Nihko," Prima said softly.

He did not look at her, but only at me. With effort he moved his jaws. "A man living in darkness," he said, "has not known the light and thus may not repudiate it, nor hold common cause with one who has."

With immense self-control and no little dignity, he walked from the chamber.

Prima was unsmiling as she looked at me. "That was ill done."

"Was it?" Del inquired with a softness I recognized. "Tiger is what he is, and may confess it freely to anyone he wishes."

Prima, who did not recognize such softness, began with some heat. "Nihko is what *he* is—"

"And has the freedom to be so," Del interrupted. "So do we all: man, woman, renegada, sword-dancer. Skandic or Southron."

"But *is* he a man?" Herakleio, of course, was focused on insults. "Nihko no longer claims the part of—"

"Stop," I said, so coldly that he obeyed me. "There is more to manhood, as Captain Rhannet put it so eloquently, than that which dangles between our legs."

Herakleio laughed. "The willingness to use it?"

Prima ignored the comment, ignored Herakleio, and stared searchingly at me a long moment. Her expression was unfathomable. Then her mouth twisted, and she looked at Del. "You do have him trained."

Del neither smiled nor replied. This time, Prima recognized the softness in the Northern woman that had nothing to do with weakness of will, and everything to do with strength of purpose. And her eyes shied away.

"The metri," I said as I picked up my wine, "is a very wise woman."

"For avoiding this?" Herakleio suggested.

"For allowing it," Del answered.

Prima didn't much like what that implied. Her eyes narrowed thoughtfully as she contemplated the idea. She shook her head slightly, then downed her wine as if to gulp it might wash away her suspicion.

I looked at Herakleio. "Among the powerful," I said, "there are reasons for everything. And results wrung from those reasons."

Clearly puzzled and irritated by it, Herakleio made a curt, dismissive gesture. "That makes no sense."

"The metri knows it does," I said. "And for some

inexplicable reason, she seems to think I can teach you to understand."

Herakleio favored me with a withering glance. "A waste of time."

I grinned at him. "Yours? Or mine?"

Prima laughed. "It might be worth watching."

Herakleio glared at her. "Do you think to *live* here?"

"My ship is my home," Prima replied. "But the metri has said she will receive me here before the other families." She paused. "Formally."

At that Herakleio stood up, stiffly affronted. "You soil this household," he announced, and took himself out of the chamber with definitive eloquence.

The captain grinned a slow, malicious grin, then cut her eyes at me as she poured her cup full once again. "Good food, good wine . . . good friends."

I smiled back in kind. "Or interesting enemies."

SIXTEEN

AFTER DINNER I paid a visit to the kilted servant, whose name I learned was Simonides, and put my request before him. He agreed it could be fulfilled, and would be by morning. I thanked him and departed, wanting very much to ask him how he'd become a slave, how he bore it, and if he hoped for freedom one day. But I did not ask him those questions, because I knew that a hard-won tolerance of certain circumstances, the kind of toleration that allows you to survive when you might otherwise give up, was fragile and easily destroyed. It was not my place to destroy his.

From Simonides I went in search of Prima Rhannet, whom I found alone in the chamber she shared with Nihkolara. The metri's hospitality had not, apparently, extended to *two* rooms for such people as renegadas.

Or else she believed the captain and her first mate were lovers.

"What?" Prima asked crossly as I grinned at the thought.

"Never mind." I didn't enter, just lounged against the doorframe. "Where's Nihko?"

She was drinking more of the red Stessa wine, sitting on the bed against the wall with her legs drawn up beneath her skirts, tenting linen over her knees. A glazed winejar was nested in the mattress beside her hip. "He has gone back to the ship."

"Upset with the dinner conversation?"

"It is his task," she said lugubriously, "to be certain all is well with my crew and vessel."

"Oh, of course."

Her tone was level. "What have you come here for?"

"Explanation. Introduction. Education."

She frowned. "About what?"

"Herakleio," I answered. "You share a past. I want to know about it."

Coppery brows leaped upward on her forehead. "You want to hear *gossip?*"

"Truth," I said. "It seems you know it."

She studied me, assessing my expression. After a moment she hooked a hand over the lip of the winejar and suspended it in midair. "I have only the one cup," she said, "but you may have the jar."

I remained where I was. "Is it so difficult for you to be in this household that you seek courage in liquor?"

Her chin came up sharply even as she lowered the jar. "Who are you to say such a thing?"

I moved then, entered the room, did as Del so often did and took a seat upon the floor, spine set into plaster. I stretched out long legs, crossed them at the ankles, folded arms against my ribs. "Someone who knows as well as you how to read others."

She smiled at that, although it was shaped of irony and was of brief duration. "So."

"The daughter of a slaver hosted in the house of the Stessa metri, *the* metri of Skandi—and a woman who once shared a bed with the heir. You must admit it has implications."

Bright hair glowed in lamplight. "Herakleio," she said dryly, "has slept with any woman willing to share his bed."

"And you were willing."

"I was."

"Even—" But I let it go, uncertain of how to phrase it.

She knew. "Even. But you see, it was many years ago.

Before I understood what was in me. And I fancied myself in love with him."

"What about him," I asked, "is even remotely loveable?"

Prima laughed. "Oh, you have seen him at his worst. You inspire it in him. But Herak is more than merely a spoiled pet of a boy. There is stone in him, and sunlight as well."

"And so you slept with him."

She got up then, climbed out of the bed and came across to me, winecup in one hand and winejar in the other. She sat down next to me, set her spine against the wall even as I had, and handed me the jar. "Have you never done a thing that took you at the moment as a good thing, a thing that needed doing, only to regret it in the morning?"

"I never slept with another man." I lifted the pottery jar, set lip against mine, drank. "Nor ever want to."

"Oh no, that is not in you." She said it so casually. "But what of women? Surely there have been women you regretted in the morning."

"There have been *mornings* I regretted in the morning."

She laughed deep in her throat: she understood. "But it is true, is it not, that we too often do what we wish we had not?"

"You regret sleeping with Herakleio."

"Yes. And no."

"Oh?"

She drank her cup dry, then stared blindly at the opposite wall. In the ocher-gilt wash of lamplight, her many freckles merged. "He was my first man," she said, "and my last." She saw my frown of incomprehension. "Oh, there were other men in between. But I realized they offered nothing I wanted, not in my heart. It was women . . ." She let it go, shrugging. "But I was afraid of myself, of the truth, and so I sought out Herak again to prove to myself that I was like other women."

"And instead—?"

"He was drunk, was Herak. He did not even know me.

I was merely a woman, and likely his second of the night. He slept hard when we were done, and did not awaken even as I withdrew." She swirled the lees in her cup. "By morning I understood the truth of what I was, what I wanted; what I was not, and did not want. So Herak twice had the awakening of me."

"*You* are drunk, captain."

Prima smiled, blurry eyes alight. "Of course I am."

"Why?"

"Because I am here. Because Herak is. Because Nihko is not." She recaptured the jar from me and poured her cup full. "Because I want your woman, and she will not have me."

It startled me because I had not been thinking of Del, or of Del in those terms. And then it lit a warmth deep in my belly that had nothing to do with lust.

Prima Rhannet turned her head to stare hard at me. "And that is what you *truly* came to me for."

"It is?"

She was drunk, but for the moment a smoldering anger burned away the liquor. "You wanted to know if I bedded your woman while I kept her on my ship."

"That isn't why I came."

"Why else?"

"To ask about Herakleio."

"Hah." She drank deeply, wiped her upper lip with the back of her hand, then tipped her skull against the wall. "It must be in your mind. A woman who sleeps with women. Others find it perverse. Disgusting. Frightening. Impossible. Unbelievable. Or at the very least, awkward."

"Well," I said consideringly, "you must admit it's a bit out of the ordinary when compared to most people."

"As is being a woman who captains her own ship when compared to most women."

"So instead of limiting yourself to only *one* extraordinary achievement, you accomplish two."

After a moment she said, "I had not thought of it that way."

"Which means you're doubly blessed—"

"—or doubly cursed."

"Depending on who you talk to." I gestured. "Then again, you're also a renegada. A *woman* renegada."

"Thrice cursed!" She sighed dramatically, then glanced sidelong at me. "I enjoy being—unpredictable."

"I figured you did."

"But that is not why I do what I do, or am what I am."

"I figured it wasn't."

She contemplated me further. "She told me you were, once, everything she detests in a man."

I drank deeply of my cup, then hitched a shoulder. "Depending on who you talk to."

"I talked to her."

"Then I was. If she says so. To her."

"She no longer detests you."

I grunted. "That is something of a relief."

"She told me you still have some rough edges, but she is rubbing them off."

I grinned into the winejar as I tipped it toward my face. "I enjoy having Del rub me off."

"That is disgusting!" Prima Rhannet jabbed a sharp elbow in my short ribs, which succeeded in startling me into a recoil and coughing spasm that slopped wine down my chin and the front of my tunic. "But amusing," she conceded.

I caught my breath, wiped my chin, plucked the wet tunic away from my skin. I reeked of rich red wine.

The captain hiccoughed. Or so I thought initially. Then I realized it was laughter she attempted to suppress. I scowled at her sidelong. "What's so funny?"

"You want to know how, and why," she said. "Every man does, except those who understand what it is to desire in a way others declare is wrong. They wish to know about mechanics, and motivation."

I opened my mouth to respond, shut it. Converted images in my head, and realized with abrupt and unsettling clarity that she was no different than I. I had been, after all, a slave, someone vilified, excoriated, for something I could not help. For being what I was, had no choice in being.

And I recalled so many nights when I cried myself to

sleep, or when I hadn't slept at all because the beaten body had hurt so much. And how I had longed for, had dreamed of a world in which I had value beyond doing what others told me. What others *expected* of me, and punished to enforce it.

"I think," I said slowly, "that it shouldn't matter what others think."

"But it does."

"It does," I agreed bleakly. "But maybe it shouldn't. Maybe . . . maybe what's important is how we feel about ourselves."

I, of course, had believed I deserved slavery. Because I had been told so. Because I knew nothing else. Thus even the wishes, the dreams, had worsened the guilt.

"And if she thought of you now as she thought of you originally?" Prima asked. "Your Northern bascha?"

I stared into the darkness of the winejar, unable to find an answer. Not one that made any sense, nor *could* make sense to her.

"It matters," she said. "One can justify that it does not, that the opinions of others are without validity, but if the one person you care for more than yourself believes you are beneath contempt, then your life has no worth."

I stirred then. "I disagree."

"Why?"

"Because true freedom is when the only person whose opinion matters is your own. When you know your own worth."

Prima smiled. "But so often it is difficult to be comfortable in your own skin."

"Well, mine's a little battered," I said, "but on the whole I'm pretty comfortable in it."

Now.

"While hers no longer fits the way it used to."

I looked at Prima sharply. "What do you mean? And how in hoolies do you know anything about it?"

"We spoke," she answered, "as one woman to another. Women who have made a life among men no matter how difficult the task, no matter how vilified we were— and are—for it. As sisters of the soul."

"And?"

"And," the captain echoed, "she admitted to me that she has lost herself."

"Del?"

"Her song is finished," Prima said. "So she told me. She found her brother. Found the man who destroyed her family, her past, the future she expected to have. And she killed that man." Her eyes were smoky in the light. "Her song is finished, and now she hears yours."

It startled me. "Mine?"

"Of course. She came here with you, did she not?"

"You made certain of that, captain."

Prima laughed. "But you were bound here regardless of my actions."

I conceded that yes, we had been.

"But Skandi had nothing to do with her life," she continued. "It played no role."

"I don't know that Skandi plays much of a role in anyone's life," I pointed out, "except to people who live here."

"You are avoiding the truth."

I sighed. "All right. Fine. Yes, Del came with me to Skandi. In fact, it was Del who suggested it." I brightened. "Which means it does *too* have something to do with her life!"

The captain laughed and lifted her cup in salute. "But my point is that her song now is yours, not her own."

"And are you suggesting she'd be wiser to hear *your* song?"

The smile fled Prima Rhannet's mouth. "I might wish it," she said softly, "but no. She is a woman for men. For *a* man," she amended, "since no other man but you has taken her without force."

I was not comfortable with this line of conversation. I knew well enough of Del's past, but saw no need to discuss it with anyone other than Del. Who never did.

At least, with me. Seems she had with the renegada.

Prima saw my expression, interpreted it accurately. "I only mean you to realize what it is to have a woman such as she with you," she said. "A woman who *chooses* to be

with you, because it is what she wants. There is honor in
making such a choice, if that choice agrees with your
soul. It is no diminishment for a woman to be with a man,
to *want* to be with a man—but neither is it diminishment
for a woman to want to be with a woman."

Put that way, well, I guess not. It was the other side of
the mirror, the reflection reversed. So long as both sides
of the couple were happy, with needs met, honor respected, no one forced or harmed, did it matter if the couple was comprised of two women, or two men?

Maybe not. Probably not. But it was hard to think of
it in those terms. It made me uncomfortable. It was too
new, too *different*.

More questions occurred. Should a woman be with a
man because she was expected to? Because she was made
to? Was it not akin to slavery to be forced to do and be
what others insisted you do and be?

I had been what the Salset had made me. Prima Rhannet had apparently tried to be what she was expected to
be, and found it slavery of the soul. For Del, raped repeatedly by a man who murdered her family, it might be simpler to avoid men altogether. She hadn't. She'd sought
and found me, because she needed my help. But that time
was long past, that life concluded.

The captain was right: Del had *chosen* to be with me.
Such choices, freely made, were framed on personal integrity, not on expectations. That satisfaction of the soul
was paramount.

With quiet fierceness Prima went on. "Men do not believe women have honor. They are threatened by such
things in us, because they fear our strength. Better to discount it, to ridicule it, to diminish it, before we recognize
and acknowledge our worth. Because then their lives
would change. They would no longer be comfortable in
their own hearts, and skins."

I knew that in the South, what she said was true. "And
yet here in Skandi, *women* rule the households, the family
business ventures." I paused. "Even the lines of inheritance."

"But such things are expected of women," Prima

countered. "I speak of the things women are not believed capable of doing."

I couldn't help it: I was relieved to be back on ground made familiar by discussions with Del. Many discussions with Del. "Such as captaining a ship?"

"Women," she said, "should be permitted to do anything. And accorded honor for it."

I smiled. "Even if they choose to remain in the household doing those very things *expected* of women."

Prima opened her mouth to argue. Shut it. Glared into her cup.

I provoked intentionally. "Women should be accorded the same choices, no?"

She was crisp and concise. "Yes."

"But not every woman wishes to captain a ship."

"No."

"And if she chooses not to do so, women who choose *to* do so should not discount it, ridicule them for it, or diminish it."

She continued to glare, mouth hard and taut.

"The blade cuts two ways, captain."

"Yes," she said finally. "But there should be a choice. Too often there is not." Then, challenging me, "And would you have argued that before you met your Delilah?"

I smiled. "It's Del who put the other edge on that blade, captain. Before then I would have vowed no blade had more than one."

"So."

"So."

"You are a better man because of her."

"I am a better man because of her."

She nodded. "So."

"So."

Prima drank long and deeply, stared broodingly at the wall, then abruptly changed topics. "Herak," she said, "has ambitions to exceed Nihko's legend."

"Nihko's?" In the sudden switch, all I could think of was what he now lacked.

She waved a hand. "Not because of that. Because of

what he was. Before." Prima drank. "Nihko was the son of the Lasos metri's sister. And women wanted him."

"I take it he wanted them back."

"Oh, indeed. And got them."

"And paid the price."

"Oh, indeed. He paid it." Prima sounded tired. "Herak, at least, keeps himself from married women, and metris, and metris' daughters."

I shifted my legs a little, cleared my throat, tried to wipe out of my mind the vivid imagery. The ultimate punishment for a man who loved women too much, as well as the wrong ones.

"Why do you care?" she asked. "Why ask me about Herak?"

I smiled. "A dance is undertaken inside the head as much as with the body."

It mystified her.

"Tomorrow I invite Herakleio into his first circle. I like to know a man's vices before I use them against him."

Prima Rhannet pondered that. Then she smiled in delight. "You think like a woman."

"Flattery," I said comfortably, and grabbed the wine-jar back.

Del awoke in the darkness as I slipped into bed beside her. She didn't turn to me even as I fit my body to hers, snugging one arm over and around her waist. "Wine," she said disapprovingly.

It was, I thought, self-evident. I buried my face in her hair, inhaling the clean scent.

"Who with?" she asked. Then, thinking she knew, "Did you drink the boy insensible?"

I bestirred myself to answer. "Not the boy. The captain."

Del went stiff.

"What's wrong, bascha?"

"Why her?"

"She had the wine."

"Why *her*?"

"I had questions."

Del did not relax. "And curiosity?"

Yawning, I offered, "Curiosity is generally the father of questions."

"Did she answer them?"

"Those she could. And raised some others." I tightened my arm at her waist, settled closer. "Go back to sleep, bascha."

"Why?" she asked. "Are you sated?"

My eyes sprang open. I lifted my face from her hair. "Am I *what?*"

"In curiosity. In body."

"Hoolies, Del, you think I slept with her?"

For a moment there was silence. "I think you might want to."

"What in hoolies *for?* She doesn't like men, remember?"

"To prove to her she's wrong."

I was so muddled by then I couldn't even dredge up a comment.

"To change her mind."

I snorted. "As if I could!"

"But wouldn't you wish to try?" Del's tone went dry. "Surely you could rise to the challenge, Tiger."

I laughed then, letting the wine overrule my better judgment. My breath stirred her hair.

In the voice of confession, she said, "I don't understand men."

I was fading. "Oh, I think you understand men all too well, bascha." I yawned again. "Beasts driven by lust and violence."

"I was driven," she said, "by lust *for* violence."

I wanted to understand, to tell her I understood, but I was too sleepy. "I'd rather you were driven by lust for me."

She relaxed then, utterly. The tension drained out of her on a resigned sigh. I knew better than to believe she'd never come back to the topic, but at least for tonight I was to be allowed respite.

Maybe I was getting old. (Well, old*er*.) But at that moment I was content merely to hold her, to share the warmth of this woman in my bed, and slide gently over the edge of sleep undisturbed by self-doubts or complex questions.

SEVENTEEN

I STOOD THERE on the summit, poised to fall. Except I wouldn't, couldn't fall, because I could fly. Was expected to fly.

Needed to fly.

The wind beat at me. It whipped moisture from my eyes and sucked them dry. Stripped hair back from my face. Threatened the breath in my nostrils and thus the breath in my lungs. Plucked at my clothes like a woman desiring intimacy, until the fabric tore, shredded; was ripped from my body. And I stood naked upon the precipice, bound to fly. Or die.

Toes curled into stone. Calluses opened and bled. I lifted my arms, stretched out my arms, extended them as wings, fingers spread and rigid. Wind buffeted palms, curled into armpits. I swayed against it, fragile upon the mountain. Poised atop the pillar of the gods.

"I can," I said. "I will."

Wind wailed around me. Caressed me. Caught me.

"I can. I must. I will."

Wind filled me, broke through my lips and came into my mouth, into my throat, into my body. It was no gentle lover, no kind and thoughtful woman, but a force that threatened, that promised release and relief like none other known to man.

Arms spread, I leaned. And then the wind abated. Died away, departed the mountain, left me free to choose.

I leaned, seeking the wind. Waiting for it to lift me.

Soared.

Plummeted—

—and crashed into the ground.

"Tiger?" Del sat up, leaned over the side of the bed. "Are you all right?"

I lay in a heap on the stone floor. Groggily I asked, "What happened?"

"You fell out of bed."

Groaning, I sat up. Felt elbows, knees. Peered through the darkness. "Did you push me?"

"No, I did not push you! You woke me up trying to shout something, then lunged over the edge."

"Lunged."

"Lunged," she repeated firmly.

I felt at my forehead, aware of a sore spot. Likely a lump would sprout by morning. "Why would I *lunge* over the side of my bed?"

"I don't know," Del said. "I have no idea what makes you do anything. Including drinking too much."

Back to that, were we? I stood up, tugged tunic straight, twisted one way, then the other to pop my spine. The noise was loud in the darkness.

"A dream?" she asked.

I thought about it. "I don't remember one. I don't remember dreaming at all." I rubbed briefly at stubbled jaw. "Probably because I feel so helpless without a sword. Kind of—itchy."

"Itchy?"

"Like something bad is going to happen."

Del made a sound of dismissal. "Too much wine." And lay back down again.

"Here," I said, "at least let me get between you and the wall. That way if I lunge out of bed again, I'll have you to land on."

Del moved over. *To* the wall. Leaving me the open edge, and below it the stone floor.

"Thanks, bascha."

"You're welcome."

I climbed back into bed, examined the side with a careful hand, found nothing to suggest a structural weakness. Likely I'd rolled too far, overbalanced, and just tipped over the edge. No matter what Del said about lunging.

Since she wouldn't cooperate and give me the wall side, I compensated by wrapping both arms around her. If I went, *she* went.

Smiling my revenge, I fell into sleep again.

In the morning I had indeed sprouted a lump, though not a bad one. Del caught me fingering it, pulled hair aside to look, then made a waving gesture. "You smell like a winery."

I grinned. "Not inappropriate, since we're *living* in one at the moment."

"Look at you." In tones of accusation.

I didn't have to. I knew what she referred to. A tunic stained red with spilled wine the color of old blood. I grasped the hem cross-armed and yanked the tunic off over my head. "There," I said. "All gone."

She eyed me askance, sorting out the spill of fair hair. She was rumpled, creased, and sleepy-eyed in a sleeveless, short-cut tunic that displayed nearly all of her exceptionally long and lovely limbs, incontestably magnificent despite her morning mood. I leered and made as if to swoop down upon her.

Del ducked away. "Not until after you've had a bath!"

"That'll have to wait," I said. "And so will you, if you think you can stand it."

She frowned, finger-combing her hair. "What are you talking about?"

"Today I begin transforming Herakleio into a man. It's dirty, sweaty business, that. The bath will come later."

Warily she asked, "How are you intending to transform him into a man? By outdrinking him?"

"Oh, I have no doubt I can outdrink him. I expect I can outdo him in most things, frankly." I recalled Prima Rhannet's comment about Herakleio's appetite for women. "Though I have learned some self-restraint over the years."

"*Have* you?"

"At knife- and sword-point, maybe, but self-restraint

all the same." I stretched long and hard, waiting for the bones to settle themselves back into place. Some mornings they were slower to do so than others.

"You," she said dubiously. "You, transforming him into a man."

I twisted my torso in one direction, then back again. "You think I can't?"

Del considered her answer. "I think there are indeed things you can teach anyone," she said finally. "But— . you know nothing about Skandi."

"I know a little something about being a man."

She contemplated my expression, made the decision not to allow me any more rope lest I take it and hang her with it. "Can I watch?"

I bent over to touch my toes, gripped them. "Later," I said tightly. "There's something I need you to do, first."

"Me?"

"Go see Simonides, the metri's servant. He's got a few things for you."

"For me."

"Well, for me and Herakleio, actually, but we'll be busy first thing. When you see what Simonides has assembled, you'll know."

"Will *he* know I know?"

I clasped palms behind my skull and pushed it forward, twisting, letting the knots in my neck pop loose. "Probably not."

"You're being obscure, Tiger."

"No, I'm not." I shook out my arms, let my hands flop like fish fresh off the hook. "I'm being *entertaining*."

In a severe tone, she said, "You're not going out like that."

"I'm not?" I wore lightweight, baggy trousers held up by the drawstring pulled tight across my hipbones. No shirt, no shoes; I was free of encumbrances, which is the way I preferred it. "Why not?"

"You'll frighten the poor boy half to death."

The "poor boy" was one year older than Del. "Good." I displayed my teeth in a ferocious grin. "Now, come here."

"Why?" Warily.

"Don't trust me, bascha?"

"Sometimes."

"Come here." I paused. "Please?"

Somewhat mollified, Del got up and approached.

"Here." I grasped her arms, lifted them, urged them around me. "Tight."

"Tiger—you *stink* of wine!"

"Would you, please?"

She sighed and wrapped her arms around me.

"Squeeze," I directed. "Tight."

She squeezed.

"Tighter."

"Tighter than this?"

We were plastered together. "Tight as you can, bascha."

She squeezed, and several of my spinal bones decided to pop back into place. Noisily.

"Gods," she said, and let go in shock.

"Better," I sighed, then grinned at her. "Now *you* smell of wine."

"Which was likely your intent all along."

"Oh, no. At least, not my *sole* intent." I leaned forward, smacked her a kiss that landed half on her mouth, half on her chin, and headed out the door. "Don't forget to go see Simonides."

"After my bath," she muttered.

Herakleio was spoiled. Soft. I opened the door to his room and walked in, with nary a blink from him. Probably because his eyes were sealed shut in a sleep so heavy as to verge on unconsciousness.

He was sprawled all over the bed, limbs tangled in linen. Apparently he had gone out on the town after dinner; I smelled wine and harsher liquors as well as a tracery of smoke. It wasn't huva weed—I doubted that grew in Skandi—but something similar, very rank even in a small amount when mixed with the traditional *perfume of cantina,* as Del had once described it.

The first test: failed.

"Up," I said quietly.

Not a flicker of response. Second test: failed.

The nearest foot stuck out from the side of the bed. I clamped hands around the ankle and headed toward the door, dragging the slack body out of bed entirely so that he flopped to the floor.

That woke him up.

Most of the bedclothes had accompanied him, so that he remained tangled even on the floor. In a flurry of linen and curses, Herakleio finally dug himself out from under and recognized me.

"You!"

"Me."

"What do you *want?*"

"You."

"Me?"

It was quickly becoming a repetitive conversation. "You."

"Why?"

Well, at least it was a change. "Orders."

"Orders? Orders? Whose?"

Maybe after a night out all he could think in were single words of single syllables. "The metri's," I answered. "Remember? I'm supposed to make a man of you."

He sat rigidly upright in a tangle of bedclothes and naked brown skin. "*This* is supposed to make me a man? Dragging me out of bed and dumping me on the floor?"

"It's a start. Not much of one, I'll admit, but a start."

He was beginning to wake up. He blinked outrage from his eyes and focused properly, brows lancing down to knit over his nose. He looked at me, and then the expression changed. "Gods," he murmured, staring fixedly at my abdomen.

Ah. The infamous scar.

"Up," I said, waggling fingers at him.

"Who did that to you?"

"A woman. Now, get up."

He didn't move. "A *woman* did that to you?"

"She did have a sword," I clarified. "Up, Herakleio."

"*A woman* cut you? With a sword?"

"A woman. With a sword."

"Gods," he said again.

"I'm just full of little mementos," I told him. "Nihko wears tattoos, I've got scars." I bent down to grab a wrist, but he scrabbled back. "Then get *up*," I said. "You can't learn much sitting on the floor."

"Much about what?" he asked warily.

"Anything. Look, this wasn't my idea, remember? I owe the metri a debt, and this is how she wants me to repay it."

He stood up then, letting the bedclothes drop entirely. He wore nothing but a sullen, smoldering resentment. "And just what is it *you* are supposed to teach me about being a man?"

"Come along and find out."

"Come along where?"

"Out."

"Out where?"

"Hoolies, Herakleio, is there anything in your mouth besides questions? Why don't you come along and see for yourself?"

"Breakfast," he challenged.

"After. If you've still got the belly for it."

That stung. "I've got the belly for it now."

"Maybe so, but we're not going to put anything in it now. Now we are going to introduce you to the dance."

"The what?"

"The dance."

"With *you?*"

"Not that kind of dance."

"I don't want an introduction to *any* kind of dance with you." He paused, then in tones of discovery, "You mean a sword-dance."

"Yes, I mean a sword-dance." I gestured. "Come on."

More outrage. "I have no clothes on!"

"Not willing to risk the valuable parts to a sword blade?" I grinned. "Why not, Herakleio? Too slow after last night?"

He glared. "I know nothing about using a sword, or dancing with men."

"That's right—you prefer to dance with women. So I've heard." I indicated the door. "Put some pants on, then, if it makes you feel better."

He swatted tangled hair out of his eyes. "Going back to bed would make me feel better."

"Undoubtedly, after all that you drank—and smoked?—last night. But you've mastered that already. Now it's time to master something else."

"A sword?" Asked with contempt.

"Among other things." I picked up a soiled tunic from a bench beside the door. "This ought to be enough."

He caught it as I flung it, curled his lip at me.

"Be a good little heir," I suggested. "Do as the metri wants."

It was reminder enough that another potential heir was in the metri's household. He shook out the tunic and tugged it on over his head. With grand scorn, he said, "Can I take a piss first?"

"You'd better," I suggested, "or otherwise you'll have soiled yourself before the morning is over."

Then I told him where to meet me and left him to his nightjar.

The house itself was built upon a lumpy pile of rumpled, porous, windblasted stone. It wasn't *much* of a rise— except for the cliff face, none of the crescent-shaped island was sharply cut or dramatically taller than the rest—but it was somewhat higher than the land surrounding it. Akritara was encircled by outgrowth pockets of stone-tiled courtyards and terraces delineated by low, slick-blocked walls painted white. Imagine a series of spreading puddles joining up here and there with one interlocking series of rooms plopped down in the middle, on different half-levels interconnected by sloping stone staircases, and you have an idea. Despite the hand-smoothed, rounded exterior corners of the rooms, the house was in no way strictly curved, in no way cleanly defined by a square room here, a square room there. It was a whole bunch of rooms clumped and mortared together, somehow forming a whole.

Having grown up in the hyorts of the Salset, individual roundish tents set in a series of ranked circles around the headman's larger hyort, I decided Akritara wasn't all that different than a tribal village. But it was made of stone because, I'd been told, there was no wood on the island except what was brought in from other lands, and none of the domed, arched rooflines followed the rules of precedence or symmetry.

But one low-walled, stone-tiled terrace on the side of the house was larger than the rest, and overlooked the part of the island that led to the city, and then to the rim of the caldera. It was here I went, here I groomed the tiles free of larger pebbles, grit, of shrubbery deadfall blown inside the wall. Barefoot, I walked the stone, feeling with the soles of my feet how the tiles were fit together, how the mortar joined them into permanence. I walked the terrace slowly, carefully, letting my feet come to know the place. I searched the surface with eyes as well, and fingertips. Some of the tiles were chipped at the corners, pitted by time and water. Hairline cracks ran through many of the squares, formed larger seams in others. But it was good stone well fit together. There were no significantly loose tiles, no broken or shattered pieces, nothing that could cause a foot to catch and falter, to betray the balance.

In Alimat, shodo-trained, we learned to dance on all surfaces. The Punja, the deep desert, was composed mostly of sand, but the South was also made of other blood and bone. The shodo had samplings of these other surfaces brought in from the borders of the South, and circles were made of each. Sand, pebbles, gravel, hardpan, cracked and sunbaked mudflats, the crumbly border soil, the shell-seasoned sand of the coast near Haziz, hand-smoothed slabs of mud brick slick in the coating of water poured across it to simulate rain. On all these surfaces, in all these circles, we learned to stand, to wait, to move, to *dance*—long before a sword was ever put into our hands.

There was a faint tracery of windblown powdered grit across the tiles. I would ask Simonides about having the surface washed daily, to strip the face of the tiles of obstruction that could cause a bootsole, sandal, or callused foot to slide, but for now there was nothing to do for it but bear it. And we wouldn't be moving all that much. Not at first.

When Herakleio came at last, he found me walking the wall. It was perhaps knee-high, two handspans wide. I followed its curving spine surrounding the terrace, from the corner of one room to the corner of another, and all the distance between.

Bemused, he watched me. His posture was impatient, stiff, all hard bone and angles. There was no grace in him as he stood there, no interior balance. There is harmony in the body required by the dance. For the moment he had none.

He had, I was certain, gotten his height early. I suspected his hands and feet had seemed larger than life; he tripped over things, dropped things. Elbows were knocked against lintels, thighs scored by table corners, shins mottled by bruises. He'd outgrown that at last and now was in control of hands and feet, comfortable in the way his bones fit together, the angles of the joints, the smooth flow of tendon and sinew beneath the brown skin, the distribution of his weight. But there is spirit in bones and flesh that has nothing to do with how a man is made, only in how he thinks.

I walked the wall. Heel to toe and back again, then stood sideways across it and marked my way by instep one pace at a time. Eventually he grew bored, irritable, not even remotely curious.

As he opened his mouth to speak I stepped down off the wall. "Hop up, Herakleio."

"Up," he echoed in disbelief. Then, condescendingly, "I think not. I can conceive of better ways to waste my time."

I jerked a thumb. "Up."

"I am no longer a child, pretender, to play at such things."

"Well, the metri seems to think you are." I shrugged. "Indulge her by indulging me."

A parade of emotions flowed across his face. Resentment, realization, annoyance, impatience. But he moved. He stepped up onto the wall in one easy movement, muscles flexing smoothly beneath the flesh of his thighs below the hem of his tunic, and stood there.

"Well?" he inquired with elaborate contempt.

I pushed him off.

He didn't fall. Didn't wobble. Didn't flail with arms. Overbalanced, he simply stepped off. Now the wall lay between us.

"What—?" he began hotly.

"Get back up," I said, gesturing. "This time, stay up there."

He glared at me. "You're only going to try to knock me off again."

"Yes," I agreed. "And you're going to try *not* to be knocked off."

"This is a waste of time!"

"I thought so, at first." I shrugged. "I learned."

"Learned?"

"Many things," I told him. "Among them how to fall . . . and how not to fall."

"But this is—"

I stepped across the low wall, placed the flat of my hand against his spine, and shoved.

Herakleio, as expected, as intended, took one long pace in an attempt to reclaim his balance, smashed his toes into the wall, and saved himself from a nasty fall only by jerking a leg up and over, planting the foot. He barked his shin on the way, straddled the wall with a rather ungainly posture once he'd caught himself, but didn't fall.

"There," I said. "Not so hard, is it?"

He had three choices. He could pull one leg up and over on the far side of the wall, moving away from me; he could pull the other leg up and over, moving toward me; or he could stay exactly where he was, one leg on either side of the wall.

Herakleio stayed put.

"Good," I commented. "Keep both feet on the ground whenever possible."

He was furious. He told me so using clipped, hissing words in a language I assumed was Skandic.

"Hop up," I said. "Walk the wall, Herak. Imagine you'll die if you step down on either side." I paused. "That is, if you have any imagination."

"What, with you waiting to push me off?"

Mildly I suggested, "So don't let me."

He sucked in wind enough to blister me with all manner of vulgar commentary, but just then Del came around the corner into view and he shut his teeth with a click.

She carried two four-foot sticks in her hands—Simonides had donated precious broom handles—plus a couple of shorter, narrower pieces of wood, leather strips, a fruit knife, cloth, and a waterskin. She wore, as she had since arriving at Akritara, a long sleeveless linen tunic, very sheer, bound at the waist by a sash of crimson cloth. Flat rings of hammered brass were stitched into the fabric. They glinted in the sunlight.

She took in the sight of Herakleio straddling the wall, me waiting at ease very nearby, and chose to perch upon the wall at some distance from us both. She laid out the makings and without saying a word set about her task.

"Walk the wall," I said.

Herakleio shot me a glance of smoldering fury. But Del was within earshot. Del could see what he did or did not do. Del was a woman; Del was a beautiful woman; Del was the kind of woman for whom a man would fall down and eat dirt until he choked if she so much as indicated an interest in seeing him do so.

He stepped up onto the wall and began to walk it.

EIGHTEEN

EVENTUALLY I let Herakleio off the wall to stand on the ground again. He was hot, dusty, sweaty, and immensely frustrated. From time to time he'd muttered to himself, but it was quietly done, and only when he had made certain Del's attention was focused on her work. When she did glance our way, he stood very straight, shoulders level, arms loose at his sides, head put up with a proud lift.

Oh, he was a good-looking young buck, no question. A veritable godling, as I'd noted before. He was gifted with the tools that could make an expert sword-dancer: the balance, the reach, the grace, the power, the explosive quickness. His body was not built for elegance, for litheness, but it nonetheless understood how to compensate. And it wanted badly to win. The reason it didn't win was because *my* body knew how to defeat it.

Looking at Herakleio, understanding completely the needs of a young and vital body hungry for activity and proper focus, I understood at last why the shodo of Alimat, petitioned weekly by anxious boys, had unaccountably accepted as student a former slave in the year he refused to accept anyone else.

Fifteen years, give or take, and the desire to learn. That was what lay between us, the metri's heir and me. A thin line, I thought, albeit built of tension.

I looked beyond him to Del, raising eyebrows in a silent question. In answer, she came to us and presented me with two practice swords cobbled together from broomsticks, vinewood, and leather. One I handed to Herakleio.

"Now's your chance," I said. "Have at it."

He stared blankly at the sword, then looked at me. "What?"

"Hit me," I invited. "Beat the hoolies out of me."

"I would *like* to," he said with cold viciousness, "but—" And broke it off abruptly.

"But?" I prompted.

He slid a glance at Del, firmed his chin, glared back at me. "I am not a fool. I know what you are. I know what you will do."

"And what am I?—besides all the vulgar things you are no doubt calling me inside your head."

"Sword-dancer," he said bitterly.

"Ah." I smiled. "Is that an admission that I might know what I'm doing?"

"That you know how to kill people, yes."

"But killing people, as I explained at dinner, is not what the dance is about."

He sneered. "What *else* might it be?"

Gently I shook my head. "Some questions are better answered by the student, when he has learned them."

He wanted very badly to throw down the wooden sword. He probably wanted worse to smash it across my face. But Del was with us—and his eyes told me he knew I would win the argument, be it verbal or physical.

"Try," I suggested. "You might get lucky."

He tried for a long time.

He did not get lucky.

Later, much, much later, I soaked the sweat and grit and soreness—and the residual taint of wine—out of a filthy body. I'd excused Herakleio around midday, watched him consider breaking the broomstick "sword" over his knee, watched him eventually decide to simply stomp away. But he took the sword, as I'd told him to.

Now, with Del sitting beside the pool resetting the leather wrappings on my wooden weapon, I dawdled in the water. It was warm, relaxing, and I felt the muscles ease themselves out of knots and stiffness.

Del, hearing my noisy sigh of satisfaction, glanced up from her work. "Tired?"

"He's strong."

"He never touched you."

"*Keeping* him from touching me took some effort." I sloshed arms through the water. "And I'm out of shape. Out of practice."

Del was startled. "You admit it?"

"Hoolies, I'll admit a lot of things, bascha. You just have to make sure I'm either drunk, or wrung out like I am now."

"I will remember that." She paused. "Why did you let him try you so early?"

"Everyone who ever wants to learn a skill wants to learn it yesterday," I explained. "They're not interested in what comes before. I remember how frustrated I was that I wasn't even allowed to *hold* a sword for so many weeks, while I learned footwork. Not even a practice sword."

"So?"

"So I let him hold it. Let him try it, and me. Let him see it's not so easy as he might think."

"I doubt he thinks it's easy."

"Kids his age always think it's easy."

Del averted her gaze. "Sometimes, it is."

"Sometimes. For some people. For specific reasons." I knew what she meant. She'd been an apt pupil of the sword, surpassing most if not all of the *ishtoya* on Staal-Ysta who had begun before she had. Because she was gifted with the body to be so, but also because she had needed to be better so very badly, to achieve her goal—and to be considered good enough. "Now he understands the fundamentals are imperative. You'd better know how to *avoid* a blade before you try to use one."

"Defense is much more difficult to learn than offense," Del agreed. "And far more vital in the circle."

I ducked beneath the surface of the water, came up with my head tilted back. Water ran down from my hair.

"So, bascha, who do you think is better? Me, or Abbu Bensir?"

She blinked in surprise. "That is not something I can answer."

"Why not? You know what I'm capable of. You've sparred *and* danced with Abbu. And you saw us dance in Sabra's circle."

She shook her head. "I can make no answer, Tiger. I think only a dance could settle this."

"But there won't ever be a dance. Not a proper one." I worked at a tight shoulder, schooling my voice into a bland matter-of-factness I didn't feel. "No proper dances ever with anyone, only excuses for killing."

She set the sword beside her and turned all her attention to me. "It's what the metri expects of you, isn't it? Having to train Herakleio has put you in this mood."

"He could be good."

"But he won't be."

"He doesn't want it. Doesn't *need* it. But then that's not the metri's point."

"No," Del agreed.

"Discipline," I said crisply, lending to my words the tone and enunciation of lecture. "Adherence to the requirements of responsibility. A mature understanding of how mind and body is bent to the will of the task. I am to teach him what she can't, so he will be what she needs. What the family needs." I grinned at Del. "Isn't that about the stupidest thing you ever heard? *Me* teaching this kid about responsibility?"

Del didn't smile. "I think it's very wise."

"Come now, bascha. You've spent three years chiding me about things I've said and done, my refusal to accept responsibility . . . my affection for aqivi."

She tilted her head in acquiescence. "If I felt explanation was appropriate, so you might better understand how such ideas can offend, or when I felt you should accept responsibility. Yes. I've chided."

Clutching a ball of soap, I lathered my chest vigorously. "I'm always offending someone."

"Sometimes intentionally. But it is those times when

it is not intentional, when it is merely a reflection of ignorance—"

"Like believing women are mostly suited for bedding?"

"That," Del confirmed. "And other things."

"Like believing a woman can't handle a sword the way a man can?"

"And other things."

"Like believing—"

"Tiger, if it has taken three years to train you out of such things, it will surely take three *additional* years to declare them!"

I grinned. "This seems a good place to spend three years."

She went very still. "Do you want that? To stay?"

"Don't you mean do I want to knock Herakleio out of the running and let the metri name me heir?" I scratched at the skin beneath chest hair. "It's an idea."

Del clearly did not know how to answer.

"But then there's you," I said.

"Me?"

"What do you want to do?"

"Me," she said again.

I waited.

"I don't know," she answered eventually.

"Stay?" I asked. "Go?"

"I don't know."

"But you have that choice, Del."

"Yes," she said, frowning.

"You don't have to stay if you don't want to."

"I know that."

"Which means you could go down to the dock and take ship today, if you wanted to."

"I have no coin."

"Oh, let's not be *practical,*" I said severely. "We're discussing the heart, here, not the head."

"We are?"

"And the heart is never practical."

"It isn't."

"The heart, in fact, is a rather perverse part of the

body, when you think about it. A heart wants to do all manner of things the head doesn't want any part of."

"It does."

"My heart, just now, isn't sure what it wants. It's in conflict."

"It is?"

"In fact, it's very curious as to what *your* heart wants."

"My heart," she said faintly.

I very nearly laughed at the expression on her face. "Del, what do you want to do?"

"Until we know—"

"Not 'we,' " I interrupted. "You."

She was getting exasperated. "What do you want me to say?"

"No, no." I waved a finger at her. "That's not it, bascha. This is about what you want. This is not about what I want, or what I want you to say—which, for the sake of argument, is to decide for yourself."

Del's brows locked together. "Who have you been talking to?"

"Are you suggesting I can't come up with such questions on my own?"

"The captain," she said suspiciously. "You drank wine together, and discussed—me?"

"We discussed all manner of things, the captain and I. Men, women, you, me, Nihko, Herakleio." I gestured. "She mentioned you were sisters of the soul."

"In some things, yes. We believe in freedom of choice, regardless of whether we are male or female. The freedom to follow our hearts."

"Yes!" I nodded vigorously. "That's what *I'm* talking about. And I want to know what your choice is. What your heart wants."

Del eyed me closely. "Did Herakleio hit you in the head when I wasn't looking?"

"Can't you just answer the question?"

She opened her mouth. Shut it. Scowled at me and mutinously held her silence.

"Del," I said gently, "you're different now."

The flesh of her face startled into hardness. "What do you mean?"

"You're not the same woman I met three years ago."

"Nor are you the same man."

"But we're not talking about me."

She thought about not responding. But did it anyway. "I do feel—different. But what do *you* mean by it?"

"Not as driven." I raised my hand. "I don't mean you've gotten soft, bascha. The edge is there when you need it, when you summon it . . . I only mean that you seem less—" I hesitated, said it anyway. "—obsessed. Than you were even two months ago."

Del looked into the depths of the water. "My song is done."

So the captain had said. "All of it?"

"Oh, there is more song yet to be sung. The undiscovered song, made as we move. But—what I *was,* the song I sang all those years I honed my body and mind and swordskill, is finished."

"And?"

"And," she said, "I am learning what it is I am to be. Who I am to be."

"You are you, Delilah. Always."

"More," she said. "And less. Depending on the day."

"Today?"

"Today," she said tartly, "I am somewhat confused by your mood."

I grinned. Then asked, "Why is it that you can admit to Prima Rhannet how you feel and what you want, but you can't admit it to me?"

Color crept into her face. When she is angry or embarrassed, her fair skin often betrays her, despite her best efforts to lock away her feelings so no one else can read them.

Eventually Del said, "Sisters of the soul."

"Is that different from being bedmates?"

"Oh, yes," she answered at once, so easily that I knew it was the unadorned truth. "Women can—talk."

"And men and women can't? Isn't that a bit unfair, telling things to women you won't tell to men?"

"Don't men tell men things they won't tell women?"

"Almost never, bascha. But that's because men don't generally talk much to one another about anything serious."

Now she was perplexed. "Why?"

"Men just don't."

"But they could."

"Sure they could. They don't." I shrugged. "Usually."

"Sometimes?"

"Maybe a little. But not very much. Not very often."

"But—you talk to me, Tiger."

This time it was my truth, and as unadorned. "You make me want to."

Del understood that truth, the emotion that prompted it. I saw the quick-springing sheen of tears in her eyes, though they were hastily blinked away. "It should be so," she said firmly. "Between men and women. Always the truth. Always the wanting to say what is in the heart."

I stood now at the side of the pool, hands gripping the lip of stone. "Then let me tell you what's in mine."

"Wait—" she blurted, as if abruptly afraid to hear such honesty.

"I want you with me," I said simply, "wherever I go. But not if the cost is the loss of your freedom."

"Tiger—"

"Do what you wish to do. Go where you wish to go. Be what you wish to be."

"With you," she said quietly. "With you, *of* you. As much as I have ever wanted anything."

It was more than I expected to hear from her. Ever. It shocked me. Shook me.

"That," I said lightly, unable to show her how profound the relief, "doesn't sound very practical to me."

"Practicality has nothing to do with the heart," she countered loftily, taking up the wooden sword. Del's eyes were bright as she smacked me lightly atop the skull. "And now you will tell me what prompted such serious talk."

"Herakleio."

"*Herakleio?*"

"And vanity. Age." I shrugged as she rested the blade on my shoulder. "I look at him and see what I was. What I can never be again."

"Tiger, you are hardly old!"

"Old*er*," I said. "In horse parlance, I've been ridden hard and put away wet."

Del stared searchingly at my face, into my eyes. Then in one smooth motion she flipped the wooden sword aside and stretched out upon the stone, fingers curled over the edge. I could feel her breath upon my face. "*I'll* ride you hard," she declared, and pulled herself off the stone into my arms.

Air-billowed linen skirts floated to the surface and proved to be no impediment.

When Herakleio came into the bathing chamber, Del—fortunately—had gone. I was out of the pool but not yet dry, dripping onto pale stone. I slicked hair back out of my eyes and over my skull, paused to note the intensity of his interest in my body. After talking with Prima Rhannet about such things, I couldn't help the question. "Is there something you'd like to tell me?"

He put his chin up, eyes glittering. "She said you have no keraka."

It took me a moment to sort out the who and the what: the metri and her examination of me the first night of my arrival. "No, no keraka. Whatever this keraka is."

"We have it, each of us." He paused pointedly. "Those who are Stessoi, and thus gods-descended. From the gods'—" he paused, translating. "—*caress,* bestowed upon us before birth."

I sighed. "Herak, I don't even know what this mark is supposed to look like—"

"A stain in the flesh," he answered. "As of old blood, or very old wine. But it never washes away."

I grinned. "Well, my flesh has been stained plenty of times with blood *and* wine, but it always washes away." I bent to grab a towel.

"Wait." His tone was a snap of sound, so evocative of

the Salset that I did as he commanded. Before I could banish the response, he was beside me. "This," he said, and displayed the back of his left elbow.

It did indeed resemble a stain, of wine or old blood. Ruddy as a new bruise, and the size of a thumbnail. A keraka, "caress"—which I supposed was as good a description as any.

I shook my head. "Nope."

"It need not be where mine is, nor shaped like this."

"Nope. Nothing. Not anywhere."

Triumph lighted his eyes. "*All* Stessoi have it."

"Then I guess I'm not a Stessa." I caught up the towel.

"Wait," he said again.

"I'm done waiting, Herak."

"She said—she said it could be that a scar has removed the keraka."

I said nothing, simply began toweling myself off. I'm not modest; nudity doesn't bother me. Though I confess I wasn't much on close scrutiny such as this: front, back, and sideways. I considered inviting him to inspect that portion of my anatomy men value above all others, but restrained myself. No matter what Prima said about his taste for women, I didn't know Herakleio. He might do it.

Abruptly Herakleio turned and strode away. Then stopped and swung back awkwardly. I was dry. Had donned the baggy trousers. Half of me was covered. Half of me was not. He was looking again at the big fist-sized pile of scar tissue that surrounded the hollowed flesh below the ribs on the left side of my chest.

"Why didn't you die?" he asked.

That I hadn't expected. After a moment I hitched a shoulder. "Too far from my heart to kill me."

"The others—the whip weals, the blade cuts . . ." He shook his head. "None of them is enough to kill a man. But that one . . . that one was. It should have."

"Why does it matter to you?"

Though he didn't avoid my eyes, his odd manner was lacking in belligerence or confrontation. "Because of Nihko. What he said."

"What did Nihko say?"

Now his eyes slid away. "IoSkandic."

I grunted. "Nihko says that a lot." I flung the damp towel over my shoulder and proceeded past Herak.

The belligerence was back. His raised voice echoed in the chamber. "What did you do to the woman?"

It brought me up short. I turned. "What?"

"You said a woman did that."

"One did."

"What did you do to her? To make her take up a sword against you? To make her do *that?*"

"Danced," I told him simply, and walked out of the chamber.

NINETEEN

SUNSET WAS glorious. Even as I prepared to go through the conditioning rituals, I paused to look. From deep in the caldera rose the plume of smoke issued of living islands, the faintest of drifting veils. Wind lifted, bore it, dissipated it with the dying of the day. I felt the sighing against my face, the prickle of it in the hair of my forearms and naked torso. Only the scar from Del's blooding-blade was unaware of its touch.

Born and bred of the South, of the desert and its sands, of relentless heat and merciless sun . . . and yet something in me answered to this place. To the wind of the afternoon, dying now into night. To the lushness of vegetation fed by ocean moisture, not sucked dry into dessication. To the smell of the soil, the sea, the blossoms; the blinding white of painted dwellings and the brilliance of blue domes, the endless clean horizons that stretched beyond the island to places unknown to me.

I smiled into the sunset, watching the colors change, then bent my mind and focus upon the slow, graceful, meticulous positioning of flesh and bone and muscle, answering with a contentment verging on bliss the blessed familiarity of ritualized movements I'd learned so many years before from the shodo of Alimat, who understood the needs of the soul as well as of the body.

The metri's servant found me there some while later. Sweat sheened me, but did not run my flesh; the breath moved freely in my lungs and did not catch; the protest of muscles left too long to ships and happenstance was fading. It would require dedicated daily practice before true fitness returned, but I was already looser than I had been since we'd left the South.

Simonides waited until I broke the pattern of the ritual. Diffidently he took up the cloth I'd draped over the courtyard wall and handed it to me. I patted myself dry even as he spoke. "The metri sends to say Herakleio has gone into the city."

It was the longest sentence I'd heard from him. His words were heavily accented, but decipherable. Still, the topic baffled me. "And?" I prompted.

"The metri sends to say this is your responsibility."

"Is it?"

"The metri sends to say you will find him in a wine-house with other young men of his age, consorting with women."

"Ah." Of course.

"The metri sends to say this is your responsibility."

"That he drinks and consorts with women?"

"The metri sends to say—"

I cut him off with a gesture. "And what do *you* say?" It startled him. He blinked. "I?"

"You."

"I say?"

"You say."

He opened his mouth. Shut it. Thought thoughts. Eventually opened his mouth again. "I say the metri expects you to bring him home."

"That's obvious, Simonides. What I'm wondering is, why?"

"Your debt."

"My debt doesn't include playing nursemaid."

For the briefest of moments a hint of amusement seasoned the quiet courtesy of his eyes. "The metri sends to say it does."

"How can the metri send to say something in answer to a statement she hasn't heard me make?"

"The metri sends to say I am, in her absence, her eyes and ears."

"And what do *you* say, O Eyes and Ears?"

Simonides folded his hands together primly at the belt atop his kilt. "I, who as the eyes and ears of the Stessoi have seen and heard this before, say he will make a drunken fool of himself at the winehouses, provoke battles of wit and words and, eventually, provoke battles of the body as well, which other men will answer. Many songs will be sung. Much damage will be done. Much coin will be spent to set the winehouse to rights."

I grinned. "The metri's coin."

"Herakleio has only what the metri gives him."

That explained a lot. "She treats him like a child, yet expects me to make him a man?"

"Here in Skandi," he said, "the mother raises the child. When the child is of age, the father raises him. The infant becomes a man. But Herakleio has only the metri, who is not his mother."

"And I'm not his father, Simonides. Send to say to the metri that *I* say that."

"But kinsman," he rebuked gently.

I looked at him sharply. His expression was guileless, arranged in the bland mask of trusted servants. There was no fear, only acceptance. This was his place. He would do it no harm, nor his people. "You truly believe that?"

His gaze was level. "I have seen all of the pretenders come before the metri. And I have seen you."

"I didn't come," I countered. "I was brought. And I had no choice."

"I have seen all of the pretenders come before the metri. And I have seen you."

I understood him then. He made a clear delineation between pretenders, and me. For some inexplicable reason, it sent an icy prickle down my spine. As if such belief were a harbinger of—something. Something dangerous.

To be someone's heir.

I sat down abruptly upon the wall. Simonides smiled. "How old are you?" I asked.

"I have sixty-two years."

"How long have you served the Stessas?"

"Sixty-two years."

"Since *birth?*"

He had the grace to gesture acknowledgment of my incredulity. "It is true I did not begin to serve until I had five years. But I was born into this household."

Five years. And every year since in service to the Stessas—Stess*oi*—to the metri. I said, "You know what I was."

He inclined his head slightly; a slave always knows another.

"And that I am free now, and have been."

Another slight nod.

"And yet you believe I am not a pretender hoping to gain wealth?"

"What you pretend," he replied simply, "is that you can be nothing others expect of you."

After a lengthy moment I managed an answer. "That is about the most convoluted piece of nonsense I've ever heard."

With utmost sincerity he demurred. "Surely you have heard better."

I eyed the metri's servant. Simonides had a sense of humor after all. "You're being obscure. On purpose."

His expression betrayed no inkling of his thoughts. "The expectations of others," he said quietly, "can cause the bravest men to tremble."

I assessed his overly bland expression. "And what do *you* expect of me?"

Simonides smiled. "To go and fetch Herakleio home before he embarrasses the metri's name—and the metri's purse."

"I'm trembling," I said dryly.

Simonides bowed.

I looked down at myself. Baggy trousers, barefoot. "It would probably be better if I had a shirt, then, yes? And shoes?"

Simonides bowed again, then took himself away.

Well, hoolies. I wasn't ready for bed yet anyway.

Del was more than a little surprised when I stopped by our room to tell her where I was bound. "You?"

"Me."

"Tiger . . ." She sat up from an ungainly sprawl across the bed. "Sending you to retrieve Herakleio from a wine-house is not unlike asking the hawk to ward the rabbit."

"But hawks know all the secret ways into the hutch." I now wore a tunic over my trousers, and sandals. "Want to come along?"

She frowned. "You don't know these people, Tiger . . . what if it's a trap?"

My eyebrows shot up. "Why would it be a trap?"

"Why wouldn't it be?"

I eyed her narrowly. "What are you suggesting?"

"I don't know." Del sounded as frustrated as I. "Maybe it's only because we're stuck here in this house, bound by its rules without knowing what they are. It makes me uneasy."

"So does not having a sword."

A muscle jumped briefly in her jaw. "Yes."

"I know, bascha. Trust me, I know." I sighed. If *both* of us suspected the metri's motivations, or intentions . . . I shook it off. "Meanwhile, you coming?"

She considered. Then stood up. "But only to be certain the hawk does not overset the hutch."

"Of course." I bared teeth. "Little rabbit."

Del tugged at the rucked up folds of her long tunic, sorting out her clothing. "This little rabbit feels somewhat naked without a sword to hand."

"This little rabbit has teeth," I reminded her.

"And the hawk?"

"The hawk has talons. But yes, he isn't pleased to be without a sword either."

"We should remedy that."

"We should. Maybe tomorrow." I stopped in the doorway, turning back. "Do you suppose they even *have* swords on Skandi?"

Del thought about it. "I haven't seen anyone with one."

"Me neither." I scowled. "What's a self-respecting man to do for a weapon?"

Del slid past me. "Use his teeth and talons."

We did not, of course, have any idea which winehouse Herakleio habituated. We didn't even know how many there were in Skandi, *on* Skandi, nor even what they looked like. Simonides, however, met us at the front door.

He arched a single eyebrow as he saw Del.

"She's the rabbit," I explained. "Also known as bait."

His face cleared even as Del glowered at me. "The molah-man will take you both into the city. As he has taken Herakleio into the city on many similar occasions, he knows which winehouses to try."

"Winehous*es*," I stressed—winehouseoi?—getting a better idea of the task. "Ah. And just how many are we to root around in?"

"Why, as many as are required to find him."

"And how many might that be?"

"We are an island," he answered. "The first in a chain of islands. We import goods and export goods."

"He means," Del translated, "that many ships come here with many men aboard them and likely every other building in the city *is* a winehouse."

"Even so." Simonides didn't smile, but I detected a faint glint of amusement in his eyes before he turned them to the ground.

I nodded. "And might this molah-man be the same molah-man who took Herakleio into the city tonight?"

"The metri employs many."

Del sighed. "Is Herakleio in the habit of sending his molah-man home before he's done drinking?"

"Sometimes. Sometimes not." He flicked a glance at me. "Sometimes he does not return home at all."

We were men. We both knew what that meant.

So did Del. "And is there a favorite woman?"

Simonides cleared his throat faintly. "Herakleio consorts with many."

"In other words, this could take us all night."

The servant inclined his head. "And even part of the day."

I glanced at Del. "Care to change your mind about coming along?"

Her expression was elaborately incredulous. "And permit the hawk to overset *all* the hutches?" She went on before I could answer. "If I stay, I won't be able to sleep until you're back. So I'll come."

"Why won't you be able to sleep?"

"Because I can't when you're gone. Not well." She shrugged. "I'll wake up every time I turn over, wondering how near dawn it is and if your dead body is lying in some rank alley somewhere in the middle of a puddle of horse piss."

The imagery was vivid. "Gods of valhail, why?"

"Because," she said matter-of-factly, "it's what women do."

"Imagine men dead and lying in horse piss?" I shook my head. "It's foolish to paint such pictures, bascha. A waste of time."

"Undoubtedly," she agreed dryly. "But it is our nature."

"To worry."

"To wonder."

"To imagine things that aren't true and won't come true?" I shook my head again, more definitively. "I always said an imagination could get women into trouble."

"But occasionally these things *are* true and they *do* come true, and dead bodies *are* found lying in rank alleys in the middle of puddles of horse piss." She paused. "Which is why women the world over began worrying in the first place."

"But it's never come true with me."

Her expression was as bland as only Del could manage. "Yet."

I scoffed. "I could also live to be an old man and die in bed with no teeth left in my head."

"You could also die in a puddle of horse piss with no teeth left in your head." She paused. "Tonight."

"And you'd rather *see* it happen than simply imagine it."

"Yes."

"Why?"

"Because perhaps I could stop it." She shrugged. "Or, if not, I could at least go home to bed *knowing* you were lying dead in a puddle of horse piss, and not merely imagine it."

Simonides, apparently recognizing where this discussion might lead—and how long it would take to get there—cleared his throat again. "The molah-man awaits."

So he did. So did Herakleio. Somewhere on an island that was full of winehouses and puddles of horse piss.

If they *had* horses on Skandi. Which I don't think they did.

The moon was nearly full. Feeling virtuous—and oddly relieved—because I'd taken the first serious steps toward regaining fitness, I relaxed against the back of the molah-cart, one arm slung around Del's shoulders as we drew closer to the city on the rim of the caldera. Now that I had my land-legs back, I didn't mind the joggle of the cart. It was soothing in a way. "Too bad we have to waste the night on finding Herakleio."

Del doesn't cuddle in public, but she did lean. With pale hair and in paler linen, she was aglow in the moonlight. "We could perhaps find him immediately," she said, "or find him very, very late."

I laughed and set my chin atop her tilted head. "You don't think *he's* lying dead somewhere in a puddle of horse piss, then?"

"He would not be so foolish as to put himself in the position to end up so."

"Why not? And why would I?"

"Because he is the heir of the Stessa metri. Heirs of wealthy, powerful people only rarely go into rank alleys with puddles of horse piss in them so that they can be killed."

"But I would? And I'm not?"

"You have. And I think even if you are the metri's grandson, she prefers Herakleio in the role."

"Thank you very much."

"You're the jhihadi, Tiger; isn't that enough? Or must you be wealthy, too?"

"Isn't it a rule that the jhidadi should be rich? I mean, what's good about being a messiah if you can't afford to enjoy it?" I patted her head. "Not that you believe I *am* the jhihadi, mind you."

"Well," she said thoughtfully, "I doubt very many jhihadis end up dead in puddles of horse piss."

"Lo, I am saved." Something occurred to me then. "Um."

Del, having heard that opening before, lifted her head and looked at me warily. "Yes?"

"We don't exactly speak the language of the locals."

"Not exactly, no. Not even *in*exactly."

"Then how are we supposed to tell the molah-man where to go?"

"Tiger," she chided, "you've never had any trouble telling people where to go."

"Hah," I said dutifully. "You don't suppose he's just going to stop at every one, do you?"

"Well, that would be a way of making sure we found the proper winehouse."

I eyed her sidelong. "You surprise me, bascha. I never thought I'd hear you describe any cantina—or winehouse—as 'proper.' "

Her turn to say "hah," which she did. Then, "We could split up."

That jerked my head around. "You expect me to let you go into a slew of winehouses in a strange land *by yourself?*"

Del arched pale brows eloquently. "And just what do you think I did when I first began looking for the sword-dancer known as the Sandtiger?"

Since Del had in fact eventually *found* me in a cantina, I couldn't exactly come up with a good retort. So I scowled ferociously.

"Besides," she went on ominously, "I don't expect you to 'let' me do anything."

"Well, no . . ." I knew better than to argue that point. "But think about it, bascha. You don't even speak the language."

"The language of the sword is known in all lands—" she began. And stopped. "Oh."

"Oh," I agreed; neither of us had one. "Look, I know the 'little rabbit' can bite—"

" 'Little,' " she muttered derisively; because, of course, she isn't.

"—but it's not exactly wise for the rabbit to walk right into the mews when the hawks are very hungry. There's only so much teeth can do against talons."

"But Skandi is not the South. It may well be that Skandic hawks would treat a Northern rabbit with honor and decorum."

"Male hawks full of liquor, and a lone female rabbit?"

"Why, Tiger . . ." Blue eyes were stretched very wide. "Are you suggesting men full of liquor might behave toward a woman in ways less than kind?"

I sniffed audibly. "Kinder than a gaggle of women gathering together after the men have left."

Del batted her eyes. "But we're only rabbits, Tiger. What can rabbits do?"

"Precisely my point," I declared firmly. "Which I guess means we aren't splitting up to look for Herakleio."

Del, who doesn't lose as often—or as well—as she wins, subsided into glowering silence the rest of the way to town.

TWENTY

WINEHOUSES the world
over, whatever they may be called, bear a striking resemblance to one another. There are almost never any windows, no source of natural light; illumination is left to
lamps, lanterns, candles fueled by bad oil, worse tallow,
and cheap wicks. Each winehouse smells the same, too:
of whatever liquor is served, of oil, smoke, grease, the
tang of unwashed bodies, cheap perfume, and bad food,
be it on the table, in the body, or issuing therefrom at
either end.

As Del had predicted, this portion of the city was indeed pretty much comprised of winehouses every other
building. The molah-man deposited us at the end of a
beaten, stony pathway that wound its way through the
moon-washed buildings, possibly even leading into alleys
full of horse piss. From there we walked.

"Pick a place, any place," I muttered.

Del obliged. "This one."

In we went. And to a man—and even to the women—
everyone stared.

In the South, in the Desert, it would have been me
they stared at. But here in Skandi I looked very much like
everyone else. It was Del they stared at.

But then, everyone stares at Del every chance they
get.

"Hawks," I muttered, "weighing out the flesh."

I felt Del's amusement. "Enough flesh on *this* rabbit."

"But tough," I said disparagingly.

She grinned. "Do you see him?"

"No. But let's ask around." I eyed the crowd and raised my voice. I knew next to nothing of Skandic, save three important words. "Herakleio," I announced. "Stessa. Metri."

Nothing. Except for stares. Only eventually did the discussions began, low-voiced, curious and suspicious. But none of them was addressed to us, and no answers were forthcoming.

"Next?" Del murmured.

Next indeed. And the next after that, and the next after that.

"Why," I complained as we headed to Winehouse Number Five, "did we not bring Simonides with us? He speaks the lingo."

"Or the captain."

"Or even the metri."

Del laughed. "I doubt she would have come!"

"Maybe what she needs is a night out on the town."

"You're talking about the woman who may well be your grandmother, Tiger."

"Well, who says she wouldn't enjoy it? Especially if she's *my* grandmother."

"Here." She gestured to another deep-set door. "Shall we ask—"

Del never got to finish her question because a body came flying out of the winehouse.

"This could be the place," I murmured, as the body picked itself up off the ground. Since it was right there, convenient to queries, I took advantage of the moment. "Herakleio," I said, "Stessa metri."

The body staggered, stared at me blearily, wobbled its way back into the winehouse. Sounds of renewed fighting issued from the place.

"Could be," I muttered, and stepped up close to the open doorway.

Del cleverly used me as a shield against anything else the doorway might disgorge. "Do you see him?"

"Not yet. He could be in the middle of it, or else not here at all."

"Do you want to go in?"

"Not until the bodies and furniture stop flying around."

They did, and it did, and eventually I poked my head in warily.

"Well?" Del asked.

"Not that I can tell. Just the usual mess." I withdrew my head. "I don't know that he'd be here in the dregs of the town, anyway."

"The molah-man was told to bring us to the places Herakleio habituates."

"Well, it could be that he likes to rub rump and shoulders with the scum of the world—" I stepped back quickly as someone punctuated the end of the fight by hurling a broken piece of chair in my direction. Or possibly part of a table. "—or not," I finished hastily, picking splinters out of my hair. "Let's move on. I don't see him in here."

A little later as we walked the circuitous tracks throughout the city, poking our heads inside various winehouse doors, Del made the observation that perhaps I was not feeling myself. After assuring her I did indeed feel very much myself, I inquired as to what prompted that observation.

"Because you're not drinking in any of these winehouses."

"Possibly because I don't know enough of the language to ask for a drink."

"Oh, surely not," Del retorted. "No man I ever knew needed to speak the language to ask for liquor."

"And how many men is that?"

"No man I ever *saw*," she amended.

"It takes less time to look and ask if I don't drink."

"That is true—but truth never stopped you before." She picked her way around a pile of broken pottery. "Could it be that you're taking your task seriously?"

"Which task is that?"

"To teach Herakleio."

I ruminated over that a moment. "I don't really care about Herakleio. But the metri . . . well, I do owe her a debt."

"Especially if she is your grandmother."

"Of course I could argue that *you* owe her the coin."

"Why?"

"It was you her coin bought free."

"I thought it was *you* her coin bought free."

"She could have refused to pay Captain Rhannet and her first mate anything. I'd have still been a guest in the household—or perhaps a despicable interloper sent swiftly on my way—but you would have remained a prisoner on the boat."

"Ship. And since the captain asked me to join her crew, I'm not so certain I'd have continued being a prisoner."

"You? A pirate?"

"Certain of my skills appear to be better suited for such a role than, say, a wife."

"Stealing from innocent people?"

"They stole from us," Del observed. "Coin, swords, the wherewithal to earn and buy more. There are those in this world who would claim we lost our innocence many years ago."

I would not debate that. "But you don't steal, Del."

"There are those in this world who would claim I steal lives from others."

"You don't steal anything but men's peace of mind."

"I refuse to accept responsibility for what you say I do to men's minds," she declared testily. "And if men thought with their minds more often than that—"

"—which dangles between our legs," I finished for her. "But I'm not talking about that. I'm talking about how you challenge entrenched customs, ways of thinking. I was perfectly content to go on about my business as a Southron man before you came along."

"And now?"

"Now I can't help but think about how unfair a lot of Southron men are where women are concerned."

"Oh, truly you are ruined," she mourned dolefully.

"Surely the men of the South will exile you from the ranks of manhood for thinking fair and decent thoughts about women."

"Surely they will," I agreed gloomily. "It's hard to be good when everyone else is bad."

"Good is relative," she returned. "But you are *better*."

"And what about you?"

"What about me?"

"You don't often have anything good to say about men in general, or me specifically."

"There could be a reason for that."

"See? That's what I'm talking about."

She considered it. "You may be right," she said at last, if grudgingly. "It's very easy to say things about men."

"Unfair things," I specified. "And you do."

"I suppose that yes, it could be said I am occasionally unfair. Occasionally."

"Does that make unfairness fair?"

"When the tally-sticks are counted, it's obvious who wins the unfairness competition. By a very *large* margin."

"Does that make it right?"

Del cast me a sidelong scowl, mouth sealed shut.

"Point made," I announced cheerfully; another notch in my favor for the tally-stick. Then, "Would you really consider being a renegada?"

"When one has no coin, and no obvious means to make any, one considers many opportunities."

"Ah-hah!" I stopped so short Del had to step back to avoid running into me. "That's the first sign of sense you've shown, bascha."

"It is?"

"You always were so hoolies-bent on doing things your way *no matter what* that you never stopped to consider the reason a lot of people do things in this world is because they have no other choice."

"What are you talking about, Tiger?"

"I'm talking about how often you suggest my plans and ideas are not the best alternatives to the plans and ideas *you* believe are best."

"Because mine are."

"Sometimes."

"Usually."

"Occasionally."

"Frequently."

"You are a mere child," I explained with pronounced precision, "when it comes to judging opportunities and alternatives."

"I am?"

"You are."

"Why is that?"

"You're twenty-two, bascha—"

"Twenty-three."

"—and for most of those twenty-*three* years you never had to think even once about how best to win a sword-dance, or beat off a Punja beast, survive simooms, droughts, assassins—"

"Kill a man?"

"—kill a man, and so forth." I shrugged. "Whereas I, on the other hand, have pretty much done everything in this world there is to do."

"But that's not because you're better, Tiger."

"No?"

"It's because you're old."

Even as I turned to face her, to explain in eloquent terms that being old*er* was not necessarily old, a body came flying out of the nearest winehouse door. It collided with me, carried me into the track, flattened me there. With effort I heaved the sprawled body off me and sat up, spitting grit from my mouth even as I became aware that most of my clothes were now soaked. Even my face was damp; I wiped it off, grimacing, then caught a good whiff of the offending substance.

"Horse piss?" Del inquired, noting my expression.

No. Molah. I got up from the puddle, grabbed hold of the body that had knocked me into it, proceeded to introduce *his* face to the puddle.

Of course, he wasn't conscious, so he didn't notice.

"Oh, hello," Del said brightly. "We were looking for you."

I turned then, straightened, saw him standing there in the doorway, looking big, young, strong, insufferably arrogant, and only the tiniest bit wrinkled.

"Ah," I said. "About time. Come along home, Herakleio, like a good little boy."

The good little boy displayed an impressive array of teeth. "Make me," he invited.

"Uh-oh," Del murmured, and moved.

"Feeble," I retorted.

Herakleio raised eyebrows. "Yes. You are."

"Oh, my." Del again.

"No," I said. "Your attempt at banter. And unoriginal to boot."

"Unoriginal?"

"It's my line."

"Well? Are you even going to try?"

"I never try, Herakleio."

"No?"

"I only *do*."

He laughed. "Then let's see you *do* it."

So I waded into the middle of him.

Oh, yes: big, young, strong. But completely unversed in the ultimate truth of a street fight.

Survival. No matter the means.

He expected to punch. He *did* punch. One or two blows even landed—I think—but after that it was all me swarming him, using the tricks I knew. I caught him in the doorway, trapped him, lifted him, upended him over a shoulder using all the leverage I had, and dumped him on top of the body in the puddle.

The body meanwhile was attempting to get up and wasn't completely prepared for the addition of two hundred pounds-plus. Both of them went sprawling.

"Well," Del commented as, fight over, I nursed a strained thumb.

Herakleio was not unconscious, though I wasn't sure the same could be said of the body beneath him. He was, however, now somewhat more wrinkled—and furious.

"Shall we go?" I asked. "The molah-man awaits."

He stopped swearing. The sound issuing from his

mouth went from growl to roar. He lunged to his feet and hurled himself at me. All two hundred pounds-plus of him.

I expected to collide with the wall even as he smashed into me. But either Herakleio was a smarter fighter than I'd given him credit for, or he was lucky. Whatever the answer, I missed the wall entirely, which would have provided some measure of support, and flew backward into the deep-set doorway.

The door was open. Thus unimpeded, Herakleio carried me on through and into the winehouse. Somewhere along the line we made close acquaintanceship with a table, which collapsed beneath our combined weights, and landed on beaten earth hard as stone.

From there it devolved into mass confusion, as cantina battles usually do. I was no longer concerned with making Herakleio accompany us back to Akritara and the metri, but with keeping breath in my lungs, teeth in my mouth, eyes in their sockets, brains in my skull, and dinner in my belly.

Out in the street it had been just me and Herakleio. Inside the winehouse it was me and Herakleio—and all of Herakleio's friends.

Like I said, smarter than I'd given him credit for.

From inside a fight, it's difficult to describe it. I can sing songs of ritualized sword-dances—or would, if I had the taste for such things *and* could carry a tune—but explaining the physical responsibilities and responses of a body in the midst of a winehouse altercation is impossible. The best you can do is say it hurt. Which it did.

I was vaguely aware of the usual sorts of bodily insults—fists bashing, fingers gouging, feet kicking, knees thrusting, teeth biting, heads banging—and the additional less circumspect tactics, such as tables being upended, and chairs, stools, and winejars being pitched in my direction. Some of them made contact. Some of them did not.

The same could be said of *my* tactics, come to think of it.

From time to time Herakleio and I actually got near

one another, though usually something interfered, be it a bench, bottle, or body. By now I was not the sole target: a good cantina fight requires multiple participants, or it's downright boring. I doubt many of the men even realized I was Herakleio's target. They just started swinging. Whoever was closest got hit. Some of them went down. Others of them did not and returned the favor.

At some point, however, a pocket of Herakleio's friends did put together a united front, and I realized it was only a matter of time before I lost the fight. I'm big, quick, strong, well-versed in street tactics, but I *am* only one man. And here in Skandi pretty much everyone is my size and weight, give or take a couple of inches and ten or twenty pounds.

It was about this time, I was given to understand later, that Del decided to end it. Or rescue me, whichever method worked. All I saw, in between hostilities, was a pale smear of woman-shaped linen coming in through the doorway—head, shoulders, and breasts shrouded with fair hair.

My subconscious registered that it must be Del, but the forefront of my brain, occupied with survival, remarked with some amazement that walking into the midst of a winehouse fight was a pretty stupid move for a woman.

Then, of course, that woman, after observing the activities, took up a guttering lamp from an incised window beside the door, selected her target, blew out the dancing flame, and smashed said lamp over said target's head.

The target snarled something in response, no doubt thinking it was yet another tactic undertaken by an enemy. But he did glance back, smearing hair out of his face, and stopped what he was doing to stare in astonishment.

Del picked up a second lamp, its flame strong and bright, and simply held it out at the end of her arm.

The target, soaked in lamp oil, lunged away from her with a shriek. The move took the legs out from under another man, who fell over and atop him.

Now two men were soaked with lamp oil. And two

men were less than enamored of the idea of seeing the
woman toss a lighted lamp into the middle of the winehouse.

Fights don't end at once. But when enough men—
those who are still among the conscious—realize everyone else has frozen into utter stillness lest even a breath
cause the woman with the flame to lose control, fights die
a natural death.

As this one did.

Being intimately acquainted with Del's control, I sat
up. It required me to kick a shattered bench out of the
way and jerk a miraculously unbroken winecup from
under my butt, but I managed. And sat there, knees bent,
arms draped over them. Watching the woman.

"Herakleio," she said in her cool Northern voice.

Curious, I looked around. I had no idea where Herakleio might be. The body closest to me, groaning pite-
ously into the floor, was not his.

Someone obligingly found him for Del. He was in a
corner trying to get up from the floor. I didn't think I'd
done the damage; I hadn't seen him for quite a while. At
some point the man with friends had simply become another target of opportunity.

Herakleio sat up at last, slumping against the wall.
One side of his face was marred by a streak of blood;
wine-soaked hair adhered stickily to the other cheek. He
peeled it off gingerly, as if afraid skin might accompany
it. His eyes found me, glowered angrily. I acknowledged
him with a friendly wave. He spat blood from a cut lip,
then managed to notice Del standing inside the winehouse
door with the lamp in her hand.

That got him off the floor. He rose, stood against the
wall, stared at her uncomprehendingly.

He must have missed her entrance. And the smashing
of the first lamp over the man's head. Now he saw her
standing straight and tall in the midst of chaos, pure and
pristine against the backdrop of unlighted night. Lamp-
glow feasted on her hair, the bleached linen tunic, pale
arms, glinted off brass rings adorning the sash that belted
her waist. It painted her face into the hard and splendid

serenity of a woman unafraid to walk the edge of the blade, to step inside the fire.

Ah, well, she has that effect on me, too.

"Herakleio," she said again.

He seemed oddly dazed. "Yes?"

"You are to come home."

There was no man alive in that winehouse who would not have answered that cool command, could he understand it; nor any who blamed Herakleio for answering. They were silent as he picked his way across the debris, paused before her briefly, then walked out of the winehouse. I had no doubt we would find him waiting in the molah-cart once we got there.

I stood up, shook out my clothing, brushed off my hands, followed Herakleio outside. What Del did with the lamp I couldn't say, but when she came out the light remained behind.

Except for the wash of it still caught in silken hair.

TWENTY-ONE

IMONIDES, WHO had not spent most of the night seeking, finding, and fighting Herakleio, rousted me from bed at dawn. I expected a murmured protest from Del, for her to burrow back under the light covers, until I realized I was alone. Which made me even grumpier.

I sat up and bestowed upon Simonides my most disgruntled scowl. "What?"

"The metri sends to say you are to attend her at once."

"Of course she does," I muttered. "She got a full night's sleep."

"At once," Simonides repeated.

I reflected there likely were two meanings for "at once" in the world: the metri's, and mine. Rich, powerful people concerned with appearances generally believe the rest of us are as concerned and will thus take time to take appropriate actions—which means their version of "at once" is different from everyone else's. But since I wasn't rich or powerful, I didn't feel bound to abide by her expectations. Which meant she'd see me as I was.

"Fine," I said, and climbed out from under the covers.

Simonides opened his mouth to say more—probably something to do with my general dishevelment in mood and person—but I brushed by him and stomped into the corridor.

The metri received me in the domed hall. I found my senses marveling again, albeit distractedly, at the fit of stone to stone, tile to tile, the flow of arches and angles, the splendid murals. Then I fastened my attention on the woman who was, or was not, my grandmother. And realized that she as much as the house was made of stone and arches and angles, and the mortar of self-control.

If she was offended by my appearance—wrinkled, stained, slept-in trousers; the string of claws around my neck; nothing else but uncombed hair, bruises, and stubble—she offered no reaction. She merely sat quietly in the single chair with her hands folded in her lap.

"There has been an accounting," she said.

As I'm sure she knew, there are many types of accountings in this world. I waited for her to explain which one this was.

"The winehouse sent it up this morning."

Ah. *That* kind of accounting. The owner was fast with his figures. Then again, he'd probably started tallying costs the minute the first winejar was flung.

I waited longer, anticipating a discussion of Herakleio's continued failings and her expectations of my plans to correct them as soon as humanly possible.

Instead she said, "I shall be extending your term of service."

There are times I can be as cool and calm as Del. Or the metri. This was not one of them.

Alarm bells went off. Noisily.

I hate alarm bells. And so I told her explicitly that I was under no "term of service," nor had any intention of being held accountable for the damage done to the winehouse by her relative, nor would pay a single whatever-the-lowest-coin-of-the-island-was when I had been on her business in the first place bringing her errant heir home. At her request.

"I shall be extending your term of service," she repeated, "to cover the cost of the damages for which you are responsible—"

"How in hoolies am *I* responsible?"

"—and to further educate Herakleio in the proper ways of manhood." She fixed me with a cold stare. "That was neither proper manhood nor acceptable behavior."

"Well, then I guess I'm not the man for the job," I shot back. "We might as well just call it off right now. And you can find someone else."

She arched expressive brows. "And how then shall you discharge your debt to me?"

"In the South," I began with careful precision, "such things are often settled in the circle. If you would care to hire a sword-dancer to contest this debt, I will be more than happy to meet him in the circle."

"Her," she said.

"What?"

"Her," she repeated.

"*Who* her—?" And then I understood.

I don't know how much of what I said the metri understood—likely none of it, since it was a polyglot of languages and none of it polite—but the tone was clear enough.

Finally I ran out of breath. "No," I said simply.

"She has already agreed."

"*Del* agreed to this?"

"She explained that sword-dancers dance for coin and debt dischargement as well as for honor."

"Doesn't matter," I said crisply, refusing to acknowledge her accuracy. "I'm not going into the circle against Del."

Not ever again. Never.

"She has agreed."

"I don't care."

"You yourself suggested I hire a sword-dancer to contest the debt. So I have done. And now your part is to meet her." She smiled faintly. "Happily, I believe you said."

"I won't do it."

"Then you have no choice but to agree to my extension of the term of your service."

"I have every choice," I retorted. "I refute your reasoning, to begin with—I did not personally, as far as I know, break a single table, or even a lamp; fingers, maybe, and a jaw or two, but the winehouse owner can't exactly charge me for that, now, can he?"

"Discharge the debt in coin, or accept additional service with me." She gestured regret and helplessness. "What I ask is not unfair. It does not approach usury."

"Maybe slavery."

She disapproved. "Hardly that."

I shook my head. "I could walk out of here today, right this minute, and get the hoolies off this gods-cursed island." Which was beginning to sound like the only possible course of action.

"And have you learned to swim?"

I frowned. "What has swimming to do with it?"

"How do you propose to get off this gods-cursed island if you cannot swim?"

"Little matter of boats," I answered. "You know—things that float."

"But none of them will float for you."

"Unless you have somehow contrived to sink all of them, I suspect I'll find one that'll float for me."

"You have no coin."

"I'll work for my passage."

"For whom? No captain will hire you on."

"No?"

The metri smoothed a nonexistent crease from her tunic skirts. "Have you not yet come to realize that the very reason people *desire* power is so they may use it?"

"And?"

"And," she continued, "I have sent to have your description carried to the owners of every ship, every boat, every raft on the island. You are an easy man to describe; one need only tell about the scars on your face."

There were things a man might do to disguise himself, but peeling the skin of my face off was not one of them. "And?"

The metri smiled. "I have power."

It took effort to remain calm, with the ice of apprehension spilling down my spine again. "The Stessoi are one of eleven of the so-called gods-descended families," I said. "Of those ten others, I have no doubt one among them will be pleased to put me on a ship. Because when you have power, you also have enemies."

Her smile was gone. "They will not aid you."

"No?"

"I own every grapevine on the island," she said simply.

"So?"

"Would you have them denied wine—or the income from its trade—because of so little a thing?"

We locked glances for a long moment, weighing the quality of mutual determination. Neither of us so much as blinked.

"So," she said eventually, "you have found me out."

"And you me."

"And I you." She relaxed in her chair, loosening only slightly the rigidity of her spine. "I should be grateful that you are as willing as I to stand your ground simply for the sheer ability to do so, no matter the consequences, because such men are occasionally valuable, but . . ."

It wasn't like her to not finish a sentence. "But?"

"But it makes our situation more difficult."

"In what way?"

The metri's cool glance appraised me. "In the matter of honor, a man may choose to be manipulated. Through custom, if nothing else; or perhaps he has no temperament for finding the way to win if it entails hardship in his house."

"A woman is indeed capable of causing hardship in a house," I said dryly.

"But a man who makes a rock of himself, a mountain of himself to stand against the wishes of the wind for the sake of honor *or* intransigence can only be moved when the gods decree it. As they decreed Skandi should break itself apart so many years ago."

"I rather like the idea of being a mountain."

"You promise to make a substantial one," she agreed with irony. "But you forget one important thing."

"And what's that?"

"I am gods-descended," she said with startling matter-of-factness, "and I can break apart even the largest of mountains into so much powder and ash."

"You," I said finally, "are one tough old woman."

"So old?"

I displayed teeth. "Older than the rocks."

It did not displease her. She was beyond the flatteries of youth and the needs of middle age. "So old," she agreed serenely. "It is well you recognize it."

"Herakleio doesn't stand much of a chance."

"Herakleio stands *no* chance," she corrected. "No more than you."

"Ah, but I'm the mountain."

"Mountains fall."

I smiled back. "And become rocks."

"But I am the island," she said, "and the island shall always prevail, even in catastrophe."

"Is Herakleio a catastrophe?"

"He has it in him to become one," she said, amused, "but I think he will not. He claims the stubborn fickleness of a child trying to make a path where no one has gone before, but lacks the werewithal to *insist*. He will turn back."

"Then you don't need me at all."

"I need you," she told me, "for things you cannot imagine."

I went very still. "And is that supposed to make me feel better?"

"What it isn't," she said, "is to make you afraid." She smiled faintly. "Do you think I intend to draw you into deadly and dangerous plots?"

"I think," I said, "you would. If you felt it would benefit you. Now, as for me—"

"I need you," she repeated, "for things that will strengthen this household."

"What *I* need," I said, "is to get off this island."

"What?" It was false amazement, dry as dust. "And not take your place as heir to Akritara?"

I scoffed. "I am no more your grandson than you are gods-descended."

Her eyes gleamed. "Truth means nothing," she said. "Perception is all."

"And since you *are* accepted as gods-descended . . ."

"If you would be accepted as my heir," she said quietly, "you might consider behaving as one worthy of the place. I have requested you teach Herakleio the responsibilities of a man, not to encourage him to behave as a boy by behaving as one yourself."

"For what it's worth," I declared, "I didn't start the fight."

"Perhaps not. But neither did you end it."

No. That had been Del.

"Maybe you should hire *her*," I muttered between my teeth.

For the first time since I'd met her, the metri laughed. "But I have. Should you not go meet her now? She is waiting in the circle."

I found Del on the terrace where I'd begun teaching Herakleio. As requested of Simonides, the stones were swept and scrubbed clean. My bare feet, trained to such things, appreciated the surface. I was callused from years of dancing on all sorts of footing, but nonetheless my body responded. It felt *right*.

She sat upon the low wall encircling the terrace. Wind rippled linen, set hair to streaming. Her face was bared, unobscured by stray locks or scowls, or even the mask she wears when uncertain of surroundings; she was at ease, and her expression reflected it. She was lovely in the sunlight, laughing at something her companion was saying.

He, unlike me, had taken time to set himself to rights. Freshly bathed, clothed, shaved, and showing few signs of the fight the night before, save for one modest bruise beginning to darken a cheekbone and a slightly swollen lip.

Hoolies, maybe I *should* have taken the time to clean myself up. "Excuse—"

But Herakleio was up and taking his leave of Del before I could finish the sentence, thereby depriving me of the opportunity to *send* him on his way. I stared after him sourly as he strode smoothly away. Then recalled why I was here, and why Del was here.

I rounded on her. "What in hoolies do you mean by hiring on with the metri?"

"Work," she replied matter-of-factly, unperturbed by my thunderous expression. But then, she's seen it before.

"But a sword-dance? With me?" I paused. "*Against* me? Why? Why would you? What do you hope to gain, Del—some bizarre form of reparation for something I've done that I've forgotten I've done? Or something you expect me to do, today or ten years from now?" I glared down at her, locking fists onto my hips. "If you think for one moment I intend to step into a circle with you, you've gone loki. You *know* I won't. You know why. You know why I *can't.* I refuse. I told the metri I refuse. You *knew* I'd refuse; so, what?—is this a plot hatched by you and the metri, women both, to manipulate me into staying here longer? Some kind of wager? An idle whim? A trick to *make* me step into a circle with you?" I sucked in a noisy breath. "Just what is it you hope to gain?"

"Swords," she replied.

"Of course, swords," I said testily. "That's why it's called a sword-dance. Swords are required. It's not a knife-dance, or a *fist*-dance, now, is it? It's a sword-dance. Which I've vowed never to undertake against you. Again. Ever."

"Well," she said musingly, "I thought this might be the easiest way to *get* swords. On an island where there don't appear to be any."

"Which makes a whole lot of sense! It's a little difficult to undertake a sword-dance when there are no swords."

"Exactly," Del said.

"Then we can't dance."

"That's true."

"Which means nothing can be settled."

"That's also true."

"So why did you accept when the metri offered the dance?"

"She didn't offer the dance. I suggested it to her as a means of settling the question of extended service."

"You suggested it? Why?"

Del smiled a little. "Swords."

"Yes, but we don't *have* any . . ." And then I ran out of fuel altogether. My face got warm all at once and, I didn't doubt, red as a Southron sunset. I said something self-castigatory in succinct and vulgar Desert, the tongue of my youth, and plopped myself down on the wall. After a moment I cleared my throat. "Was there any particular reason you allowed me to make such a fool of myself?"

"You were having such a grand time getting all hot and bothered that I didn't dare stop you." She paused. "Besides, you do it so well."

"And did you find it amusing?"

Del grinned. "Yes."

I sighed, shuffled callused feet against grit-free stone. "So."

"So."

"So the metri will find us swords."

"So the metri will."

"Thereby saving us coin we don't have."

"And time, and effort."

I squinted into the morning sun. "I knew there was a reason for keeping you around."

Del made an exceptionally noncommittal noise.

"So," I said again, "now that we've figured out how we're to get ourselves swords—" As expected, she cast me a pointed sidelong glance. "—there's something else we have to do."

"What is that?"

I caught her hand, pulled her up from the wall. "Go see a man about a horse. Or, in this case, a woman about a ship."

"Why?"

"To test a theory."

"What theory?"

"The one that says the metri can't sink every ship." I tugged. "Come on."

Del resisted. "What are you talking about? Why would she sink every ship? Why would she sink *any* ship?"

"It's a figure of speech," I said. "Will you come?"

"I've already been aboard one ship that sank out from under me," Del said darkly, arm tensed against my grasp. "I'm not interested in repeating the experience."

"Our ship is fine. It's Herakleio's that's sinking. Bascha—will you *come on?*"

Reluctantly she allowed me to pull her up and toward the nearest narrow stairway leading into the house. "Tiger, whenever you get cryptic, it means there's trouble on the horizon."

"Not this time. I just want to see if there's a *ship* on the horizon."

"And if there is?"

"See what it would cost to sail on it."

"Last time it cost us everything we had."

"She owes me," I explained, "for that and other things. It's her fault I'm in this mess."

"*That* won't convince her to do anything."

"Oh, I'll think of something."

Whatever Del said by way of observation was declared in idiomatic Northern, and I didn't understand a word. Which was probably for the best, being as how the bascha has as great a gift for malediction and vilification as I do.

TWENTY-TWO

WHEN IT became clear
Prima Rhannet was not in the household, I dug up Simonides and asked where she was. He responded by asking what I wanted her for; possibly he could help me instead.

Since I knew very well he could not and *would* not give me any kind of answer that might permit Del and me to hire the renegada captain to sail us away from Skandi—and by default away from the metri and her spoiled godling—I simply said I needed to ask Prima Rhannet a question.

Whereupon Simonides, with unctuous courtesy, said perhaps I might ask him the question, as perhaps he might know the answer.

Impasse. We exchanged a long, speaking look, measuring one another's determination not to say what each of us wanted to say, and our respective experiences with outwaiting others in identical situations. Whereupon Del sighed dramatically and inquired as to how old we were to be before the verbal dance was settled. Which reminded me all over again that the metri expected Del and me to dance with *swords* to settle the question of my "term of service," which in turn made me anxious to be going.

"Never mind," I said. "We can walk."

Simonides' expression transformed itself from confident servitude to startlement, followed rapidly by mounting alarm. "Walk?"

"One step after another all strung together until you

get somewhere else," I clarified. Then added, "Somewhere you *want* to be."

"You cannot walk," he said severely.

I smiled cheerfully. "Actually, I learned a long time ago."

He waved a hand dismissively, familiarly; clearly he had accepted me as someone who required his very special attention and personal guidence. His version of Herakleio, maybe. "You cannot walk," he repeated. "That is what molah-men are for."

"Fine. Can we borrow one?"

His expression was infinitely bland. "In order for me to summon a molah-man and his cart, I must know where you are going."

"Nice try," I said dryly. "But all you *really* have to do is summon him. You don't have to tell him a thing. Which means you don't have to know where we're going, and I don't have to tell you."

Simonides inclined his head the tiniest degree. "You do not speak Skandic." Clearly he believed he'd won.

"I speak enough," I said, dashing his hopes. "All I have to do is say 'Skandi.' I think he'll catch my drift."

"*Where* in Skandi?" Simonides inquired diffidently.

"We could be there and back by now," Del observed.

Simonides switched his attention to her. "Be where and back again?"

Exasperated, I permitted my voice to rise. "What does it *matter,* Simonides? We're not prisoners here—" I paused with great elaboration, letting the implication hang itself upon the air in glowing letters of fire. "—are we?"

I had succeeded in horrifying him. He said something quickly and breathlessly in Skandic, which eluded both of us, then clasped both hands over his heart in a gesture of supplication. His breathing came fast and noisy, as if he were overcome.

"I'll take that as a 'no,' " I said dryly. "Now can we have our cart?"

His facial muscles twitched out of horror into subtle

triumph. "The metri sends to say you must tutor Herakleio."

"What, the metri sends to say *right now* that I am to tutor Herakleio?"

"Indeed."

I raised a skeptical brow. "And when exactly, at what precise moment, did she send to say this? Just now, while we're standing here? If so, I didn't see her. And surely not *before* I found you to ask about a cart. Because surely you would have told me then the metri had sent to say I was to tutor Herakleio—except she hadn't sent to say anything, because *I* found *you,* you didn't come find me."

"Tiger," Del said, "I'm getting gray hair."

"Trust me, I have a lot more than you do, bascha . . ." I smiled in a kindly manner at Simonides. "Well?"

He drew himself up. "I am the eyes and ears of the metri."

"So, I'm assuming one of your tasks is to *guess* what she might or might not like, and thus control the issue?"

"I do not guess," he said with some asperity, "I *anticipate.*" Then, lowering head, eyes, and shoulders, he said, with a shift to dolorous dignity, "I am the metri's slave. There is so little choice in my life—"

"*Oh,* no." I cut him off abruptly. "You're not using that line—or that expression!—on me. I know you, Simonides: you're a master manipulator. You'd have to be to serve the metri so devotedly for all these years." I gifted him with an overfriendly smile. "Now, where were we?"

"Walking," Del said.

Whereupon Herakleio wandered into the room and, through a mouthful of some kind of sticky confection, which also filled his hand, asked what we were talking about.

"Going into Skandi," Del answered.

He blinked. "Is this a difficulty?"

"We seem to be having a difficulty convincing Simonides, here, that we need a molah-man and his cart," I explained.

Herakleio shrugged. "Walk," he suggested, and wandered out again.

I bent a brief but sulfurous glare on Simonides, who was looking rather deflated, then turned on my heel. And walked.

It was a long walk, and hot, but the breeze cut much of the heat and made it bearable. Then again, I'm so accustomed to the sun and the dryness of the desert that I found Skandi a gentle country, though with more moisture in the air. I think had there not been the breeze I might have been less enthralled; better the dry if searing heat than the wet thickness of moist air. People could choke in that.

Del and I, from habit, matched paces—not many men can do that with me, and no other women—and fell into a companionable, long-striding rhythm. The air was laden with the scent of grapevines, a tracery of cooksmoke, the taste of the sea. I realized it felt incontestably good simply to be out from under roofs, with the sun shining on my head. Which made me smile; *May the sun shine on your head* is one of the ritual blessings of the South.

"What are you grinning about?" Del asked.

I shrugged. "I don't know. Just glad to be alive, I guess." And free, for the moment, of the nagging apprehension.

"And glad to be alive to *be* glad you're alive." She nodded vigorously. "I feel it, too. We are free of—encumbrances."

I glanced at her as we walked. "Encumbrances?"

She thought about how best to explain. "We have chased," she said finally, "and have *been* chased without true respite for too long."

"What have we chased, bascha?"

"My brother," she replied somberly. "Poor lost Jamail, who, by the time we found him, wasn't truly my brother anymore, nor—" She broke it off abruptly as tears filled her eyes.

"Nor?" I prompted gently, though I had an idea where she was headed.

She blinked furiously; Del hates to cry. "Nor had any wish to be."

I couldn't adequately comprehend the loss, the sense of failure and guilt that had driven her so mercilessly and now seemed merely futile. I had no brother, no sister, nor ever had. But one thing that had come clear to me in three years with Del was that family, kinship, was part of the heart of the North.

"But you couldn't have known that," I said. "There is no way you might have predicted he would be so drastically changed by his experiences that he could bear no part of his past."

"He wasn't—normal, anymore," she said with difficulty. "I don't mean because of what they did to him physically, but in his mind. He wasn't my brother anymore."

Jamail had, I felt, fallen off the edge of the known world even as his sister shaped a new one. Made mute by the loss of his tongue, rendered castrate by the slavers, it did not in the least surprise me that he had sought relief as best he could, even if it meant surrendering sanity as we knew it. I had come close myself in the mines of Aladar.

"He could never be what he was, Del. But he found respect among the Vashni, and a measure of affection after the hoolies he inhabited. In like circumstances, I don't know that I'd have left them either."

She shook her head. "You have been changed by your experiences, yet you do not turn your back on your past. You've let it shape you into a stronger man instead of . . . instead of what Jamail became."

"Maybe. But I was older than Jamail. For me it wasn't a question of having had stolen the means to return to my past, because my past was nothing any sane person would want. I understood that much, at least, and why I had to use the past to shape my future, and that I had to learn *how* to do it. That wouldn't come naturally." I shook my head. "You can't compare him to me, bascha. It isn't fair to Jamail."

"But you became stronger because of what happened."

"Not for a long time." I scuffed through the cart-track, head bent as I watched dust fly. "When I was free of the Salset at last, I didn't know what I wanted to do. Just—be free. But no part of life *is* free; it costs. Always. And I had to find a way to pay for it."

"Sword-dancing."

"Eventually. Once I'd seen a few matches in the circle, realized what a man alone in the world might accomplish. It seemed far more fair than anything I'd encountered with the Salset. So I found out what I could, and pursued it. But . . ."

"But?"

"But it was the shodo at Alimat who took the former slave—the angry, ignorant, terrified former slave—and made him truly free."

She nodded. "Because you were good."

"No. Because I might *become* good. Might. If I worked very hard at it."

"You are the single most physically gifted man I have ever seen," she argued vehemently, who had trained as rigorously on Staal-Ysta. "You are completely at ease in your body, and *with* your body; I think there is nothing you could not accomplish if you wished to."

"Sheer physical ability is one thing," I said, then tapped my skull. "There is the dance up here as well."

"That is what Alimat and the shodo taught you," Del said. "You had the body: quickness, stamina, size, power—"

"But no discipline. No patience. No comprehension of what the rituals meant, and were meant to instill. What I wanted most was to prove I was free, was no man's chula, no matter what was said, or implied, or rumored, or believed about me . . ." I let it go with a hitch of one shoulder. "Let's just say I wasn't the most popular student."

"You bested Abbu Bensir." She touched her throat. "You gave him the broken voice he has even to this day."

"I got lucky."

"He underestimated you."

"That's what I mean: I got lucky."

She smiled. "But did you believe so then?"

"Of course not. I felt it was my due; how could I *not* best a man older, smaller, and slower than I?"

"And now it is your due."

"But look how many years it took me to get here."

"And here we are," Del said quietly. "On Skandi, without encumbrances. No brother to find, no sword-dancers to defeat, no sorcerers after our swords or our bodies. No prophecies to fulfill."

"I'm pretty sick of prophecies, myself. They come in handy now and again, I suppose, to keep things from getting too boring, but mostly they just stir up trouble."

Her smile was hooked down, ironic. "But you are the jhihadi."

"Maybe." I knew she didn't believe it. Me, a messiah? The deliverer of the desert? Right. As for me, well, I'd decided it depended on interpretation; I *had* come up with an idea that could eventually change the sand to grass, albeit it had nothing to do with magic, and thus lent an infinitely banal culmination to a mysterious and mythic prophecy. Which many found disappointing for its utter lack of drama; but then, real life is comprised of such banalities. "Or maybe I just got lucky. Whatever the answer, I think this jhihadi's job is done."

"Leaving him with the balance of his life to live."

"With and without encumbrances."

"What encumbrances do you have now? The metri? Herakleio?"

"Oh, I was thinking more along the lines of you."

"Me!"

"What am I to do with you?"

"*Do* with me? What do you mean, *do* with me? What is there *to* do with me?"

I couldn't help myself: I had to laugh out loud. Which resulted in Del swinging around in front of me and stopping dead in her tracks, which also were mine, so I stopped, too. As she intended.

She poked me hard in the breastbone. "Tell me."

"Oh, bascha, here you say you've changed me over

the past three years, but what you don't realize is I've changed you every bit as much."

"*You* have! Me?" Her chin went up. "What do you mean?"

"You argue like me, now."

"Like you? In what way? *How* do I argue with you?"

"You slather a poor soul with questions. The kind of questions that are phrased as challenges."

She opened her mouth, shut it. Then opened it again. "In what way," she began with deceptive quietude, "do I do this?"

"That's better," I soothed. "That's more like the old Delilah."

"And that is?"

"You as you are just now. Cool and calm." I dropped into a dramatic whisper. "Dangerous."

She thought about it.

"It's not the end of the world if you lose a little of that icy demeanor and loosen up, you know," I consoled. "I was just making an observation, is all."

She thought about it more, frowning fiercely. "But you're right."

"It's not necessarily a bad thing, Del." I paused. "Loosening up, I mean, not me being right. Though that isn't a bad thing either."

"By acquiring some of your mannerisms, your sayings?" She twisted her mouth. "Perhaps not; I suppose that is bound to happen. But . . ."

"But?"

"But I am not pleased to be told my self-control has frayed so much."

"What self-control? Self-control in that you sound like me? Self-control in that I don't have any? Is that what you mean?"

Del abruptly shed the icy demeanor and grinned triumphantly. "Got you."

"You did not."

"I did."

"You can't '*get*' somebody if they know what you're doing."

"You're saying you knew?"

"I did know. That's why I answered the way I did."

"Slathering a poor soul—in this case, me—with questions? The kind of questions phrased as challenges?"

"Now you're doing it again."

"Tiger—"

I caught her arm in mine, swung her around. "Let's just go," I suggested. "We can continue this argument as we walk. Otherwise we'll never reach the harbor by sundown."

"I don't think I'm anything like you."

"I believe there are a whole lot of men who would agree, and be joyously thankful for it unto whatever gods they worship."

"You were such a *pig* when I met you!"

Our strides matched again as we moved smoothly down the cart-road leading to the city. "Why, because I thought you were attractive? Desirable? All woman? And let you know about it?"

"You let the whole world know about it, Tiger."

"Nobody disagreed, did they?"

"But it was the *way* you did it."

"Where I come from, leering at a woman suggests the man finds her attractive. Is that bad?"

"That's the point," she said. "Where you come from . . . every male in the South leers at women."

"Not all women."

"Some women," she amended. "Which really isn't fair either, Tiger; if you're going to be rude to women, you ought to be rude to *all* women, not just the ones you'd like in your bed. Or the ones you *think* you'd like in your bed. Or the ones you think would *like* to be in your bed."

"Leer indiscriminately?"

"If you're going to, yes."

"This may come as a surprise, bascha, but I don't want to sleep with all women."

"We're not discussing sleeping with. We're discussing leering at."

"What, and have every woman alive mad at me?"

"But there are less vulgar ways of indicating interest and appreciation."

"Of course there are."

She blinked. "You *agree* with me?"

"Sure I agree with you. I'm not arguing that point. I'm trying to explain the code of men, here."

That startled as well as made her suspicious. "Code of men?"

"When a man leers at a woman, or whistles, or shouts—"

"Or invites her into his bed?"

"—or invites her into his bed—"

"—with very vulgar language?"

"—with or without very vulgar language—"

"*Insulting* and vulgar language!"

"—it's because of two things," I finished at last.

"What two things?"

"One, it lets all the other men know you've got first dibs—"

"First dibs!"

"—which is what I meant about the code of men; first dibs and rite—and right—of ownership—"

"*What?*"

"Well, so to speak."

"It shouldn't be part of what anyone speaks."

"Look, I've already told you about the code of men, which is never to be divulged—"

"And do you believe in this code?"

I hesitated.

"Well?"

"I can't tell you that."

"Why not?"

I chewed at my lip. "The code."

"The code won't let you tell me about the code?"

"That's about it."

"Then why did you?"

"Because I tell you everything. That's a code, too."

"It is? What's this one called?"

"The code of survival."

Del shot me a look that said she'd punish me for all

of this one day. "Getting back to this 'because of two things' issue . . ."

"What two things?"

"First was first dibs. You know, the reason men leer and say vulgar things to women."

"Oh." I took it up again. "—and two, it certainly saves time."

"Saves time?"

"Well, yes. I mean, what if the woman's interested?"

"What if the woman isn't?"

"Then she lets you know. But if she is, you sure get to bed a lot faster if you don't waste time on boring preliminaries."

Del stopped short and treated me to several minutes of precise and cogent commentary.

When she was done, I waved a forefinger in her face. "Vulgar language, bascha. *Insulting* and vulgar language."

She bared her teeth in a smile reminiscent of my own. "And I suppose you want to go to bed with me now. Right here in the middle of the road where anyone might come along."

I brightened. "Would you?"

Del raked me up and down with her most glacial stare. Then she put up her chin and arched brows suggestively. "Not until after we waste a lot of time on boring preliminaries."

"Oh, well, all right." Whereupon I caught her to me, arranged my arms and hers, and proceeded to dance her down the road toward the distant city.

TWENTY-THREE

"OH, HOOLIES," I said with feeling.

We stood at the top of the cliff face, overlooking the switchback trail leading down to the cauldron of water. Steam rose gently from the living islands in the center.

"What?" Del asked, as the breeze took possession of her hair.

I pointed. "The ships are all down there."

"Yes, Tiger. That's where the water is."

"It means we have to ride those molahs down."

She shrugged. "Or walk."

Uneasily I eyed the individuals who were on foot. Obviously they were laborors, or slaves, or people not of the Eleven Families. "Maybe this wasn't such a good idea. Maybe what we've already done—walking to and through town—is unconscionable, or something. Maybe that's why Simonides was upset—and why, come to think of it, Herakleio would suggest we walk, if only to get my goat."

Del was perplexed. "Why?"

I chewed at my lip, marking the commerce at the trail-head. The place thronged with people and animals, not to mention the smalltime merchants who laid out their wares on tattered cloths spread along the walls. There were cheap necklaces, bracelets, earrings; sash belts, leather belts, single blue pottery beads hung on leather thongs or multicolored cord—maybe some kind of charm; sun-baked pots, painted bowls, multitudinous other items. Del and I were in the middle of it all, bumping shoulders with people and trying not to be run into by loose goats and dogs, not to mention chickens. I occasioned little more than incurious glances, but Del, as usual, reaped the benefit of her height and coloring.

I sighed. "When Nihko brought me up, he made it clear I was not to, as he put it, *soil* myself by standing on the ground."

Del's irony was delicate. "Were you supposed to hover?"

"Mats," I explained. "First we had our feet washed, and then we stood on mats."

She shrugged, catching and separating her hair into three sections preparatory to braiding. "When Prima Rhannet brought me up, nothing was said of that. We rode up, then she rented a cart to take us to the metri's home."

"Nihko was pretty plain about it all." I glanced around. "But no one seems to be taking much notice."

Del began to braid the sections of hair, something I've always enjoyed watching for the deftness of her hands. "We walked while touring the winehouses looking for Herakleio."

"But we went right to the bathing pool, remember?" I leaned forward a little, enough to see a few more of the hard angles of the cliff track as I peered over the low wall. "Well, I suspect it's too late even if there is something to all this foot-washing. Guess we may as well head down."

Finished with the single plait, she did something with a strand that captured and held the braid, tucking and looping it into itself. "Walking, or riding?"

Neither appealed to me. Walking meant dodging molahs and their muck. Riding meant sitting atop a jouncing beast heading downward at a rate of speed I considered breakneck, when you took into account the pitch of the track.

Resolution presented itself. I looked around at the ground, saw a stone, scooped it up. "Stone wins," I said, and stealthily passed it from hand to hand several times. Eventually I held both fists out, knuckles up. "Choose."

"Stone, we walk." Del flipped the braid behind her back and tapped one of my fists.

I opened it, displayed the empty palm. "Wrong choice, bascha." And tipped the stone from the other hand, dropping it back to earth.

"Well," she said with limp cheeriness, "it's a pretty day for a ride."

"Can't say as it'll be pretty by the time I get to the bottom," I declared sourly. "It's not *your* gehetties at risk!"

"That's why I've never understood why men are almost uniformly considered superior," Del opined seriously. "The easiest way to put a man out of action is to plant a knee in his gehetties, or threaten them with a knife, or—"

"All right, bascha, you've made your point," I said hastily, cutting her off before she got more detailed about threatened gehetties. "Let's find us a couple of molahs."

Del pointed. "There."

"There" constituted a congregation of molah-men hanging about the trailhead. Their molahs were tied some distance away, dozing in the sun, but the men themselves competed enthusiastically for space and custom, calling out imploringly to each passerby something I assumed was an advertisement of their services—although how one molah might be considered particularly better than another was beyond me; they weren't horses, after all. As Del and I approached, it was no different: we were accosted, surrounded, swarmed by all the men as they competed for our coin.

"Might be a problem," I muttered to Del.

"What's that?"

"Coin to pay them with."

"Ah." It had occured to neither of us; we're used to having coin of some sort, and since our arrival such things as transport and comestibles had been provided. "I have nothing. Maybe we should walk after all."

From close up, the trail was a mass of puddles and droppings mashed by feet into a slimy, odoriferous layer of something approaching mud, or heaped cairns of fresh, as yet unmashed muck. Slaves and laborers stolidly stomped their way up and down the track, feet and ankles smeared, as they followed the beasts. No wonder Nihko had been so picky about us getting washed.

"Nah, let's ride," I said.

"What about coin?"

"Maybe this . . ." I untied the knot in my necklet, pulled it free of my neck.

"Tiger! You wouldn't!"

"Not the claws . . ." I worked at thread, finally slid the silver ring free of thong. "Nihko's little gift." I held it up so the molah-men could see it clearly in the sunlight, then pointed over the wall. "Down," I said, though I doubted any of them understood the word. Shouldn't need to; it seemed pretty obvious what we wanted.

Some of the men shrugged, shook their heads, stepped back, indicating they worked for coin, not barter. A few others stepped forward to inspect the ring more closely—and then surged as one backward into the others, crying out something I couldn't understand. Hands flashed up and made the warding away gestures I'd seen before with the first mate. Gazes were averted, heads lowered, palms put up into the air in unmistakable intent: we were not to come any closer.

Such an innocuous little thing glinting in my fingers. And yet it appeared to mean so much. "Are you sure?" I asked. "It's good silver."

More gestures, more whispered, hissing comments made to one another, and the cluster of molah-men melted away to their animals until Del and I stood in the open with no one near us at all but a single ignorant chicken, pecking in the dirt.

I let the ring slide down out of my fingers into my cupped palm. A small, plain ring about as big around as my forefinger. It wasn't whole, but cut at one point so the filed ends could pierce and be fastened into flesh. No different from what a woman might wear through her ear-lobes, though Nihko wore his—and many more of them—in his eyebrows.

And then I recalled that he'd put it on my necklet to keep me, he'd said, immune to his magic. Or whatever you wanted to call whatever it was about him that made me feel ill.

IoSkandi. I'd heard—and still heard—that word said by the men who now stood away from us. I'd heard it used by Nihko, Prima, Herakleio, the metri.

Silently I hooked the brow ring back onto my thong, looped leather around my neck again and knotted it. "Let's go," I said curtly to Del. "We're burning daylight."

"Wait." She caught my wrist and halted my forward momentum. "What is it?"

I stopped short. "What's what?"

"Something's made you angry."

"I'm not angry. I'm *irritated.*"

"Fine." She had immense patience, did the Northern bascha. "Why are you irritated?"

"Let's just say I don't like mysteries."

"And you want to know why they won't take the ring."

"I know why they won't take the ring. At least, I have an idea."

"And?"

"Nihko." I made the sound of it a curse. "I want to know what all this ioSkandi nonsense is, and what this ring is *really* supposed to do and mean."

"Perhaps we should ask him."

"I intend to—if I can ever get down to the boat."

She removed her hand from my wrist with alacrity. "By all means, go."

I sighed. "All right . . . look, bascha, I'm sorry. It's not your fault. But I've had it up to here—" I indicated my eyebrows. "—with all this magical mythical mystery stuff. I don't speak the language, so I haven't got the faintest idea what these people are saying about us; an arrogant old woman who may or may not be my grandmother is pretty much keeping me a prisoner in her house; and a young buck who may or may not be my kinsman, albeit removed umpteen hundred times, is trying to move in on my woman." I paused, rephrased immediately. "In on *a* woman. Whom I happen to care about a great deal."

"Thank you," she said gravely. "But why do you think Herakleio is, as you put it, trying to move in on me?"

"I just know," I said darkly.

Del is accustomed to my moods. Sometimes she ignores them, other times she provokes them. This was one of the times she wanted an explanation. "How is it that you know?"

I shook my head. "I just do."

"Is it something to do with the code of men?"

"No, it isn't something to do with the code of men. It's something to do with him being young, and you being young, and me being—well, old*er*."

"I could make a joke of this—" she began.

"You could."

"—but I won't," she finished. "I think this is something you must sort out for yourself."

Startled, I watched as she strode the last few paces to the head of the trail and took the first step downward. "Sort out for myself? What do you mean, sort out for myself?" I went after her. "Can't you at least tell me you don't think I'm old, and that I'm being a fool? Couldn't you even *lie*, just to make me feel better?"

She slanted me a sidelong glance as she strode down the track. "Would it be a lie if I said you were being a fool?"

"Oh, Del, come on. Humor me."

"You're going to believe whatever you decide to believe, no matter what I say."

"Well, that may be true," I conceded, "but you could say it anyway."

"I'm saving my breath."

"For what?"

"Getting to the bottom."

"He *is* young."

"Yes."

"He *is* good looking."

"A veritable godling."

"And I suppose some women might even find his attitude appealing."

"Some would."

"He's even rich—or he will be."

"So he is, and so he shall be."

"So why would you remain with me if you had a chance to be with him?"

"Possibly because you've never given me an action-able reason to leave you."

This was a new phrase. " 'Actionable reason' ?"

"You give me reasons to leave all the time. None of them has been of such magnitude that I acted on it."

"Oh." We walked quickly, steadily downcliff, leaving the trailhead behind. "So, reasons, but no 'actionable' reasons."

"Until now," she said with bland clarity.

"Oh, come on. Do you blame me?" I dodged a molah and rider making their jouncing way up the track. "Hoo-lies, I'm not exactly what I was at seventeen, or even what he is at twenty-four."

"More."

"More? More what?"

"More than you were at seventeen. More than he is at twenty-four."

"In what way?"

"For one thing," she said, "he doesn't doubt himself."

"That's one way of putting it!"

"And I doubt he questions his appeal to women."

"I'll go that."

"And I don't doubt he *thinks* he could have me if he wanted me."

"No kidding!"

"But it really doesn't matter what he thinks, Tiger. About me or anything else."

"No?"

"What matters is what *I* think."

"Well, of course it does—" I stopped short to avoid a laborer whose load was tipping precariously, made my way carefully around him.

Del marched on. "And if I were attracted to him to the degree that you seem to think I could be, or should be, enough that I'd rather be with him than with you, I would make it plain to you."

I caught up. "You would."

She stopped and turned to me, which necessitated *me* stopping. Again. "I promise," Del said. "I vow to you here and now, on this filthy trail with muck nearly to my knees, that if I decide to leave you, if the day comes when I feel I must leave you, for another man or simply to go, you will be the first to know."

Transfixed, I stared back at her. "Is that in the code of women?"

Del's mouth twitched. "I can't tell you."

"Oh, well, all right. I understand about codes." I looked down at my muck-splashed legs. "This is disgusting."

"Yes," she agreed, "it is. And the sooner we get to the bottom, the sooner we can wash everything off."

"Race you," I offered.

But Del was not sufficiently intrigued by that suggestion to agree, so we proceeded to traverse the balance of the track at a much more decorous pace.

Which meant we were even more disgusting by the time we reached the bottom.

As might be expected, Del and I headed straight toward the harbor once we hit the docks, intending to dunk ourselves up to the knees in seawater. I was thinking about finding a good stout rope to hang onto since too deep a dunk might result in me drowning, and was thus more than a little startled when a cluster of shouting men came running up to us. Not for the one hundredth time I wished I had a sword; by Del's posture, so did she. But we had no weapons, not even a knife between us. Which reminded me all over again that Del's suggestion to the metri that she hire her to dance with me in the circle was done for a purpose, not to upset me.

Meanwhile, we found ourselves as surrounded by men vying for our attention and custom as we had been at the trailhead. Except this time what they wanted us to buy was water from pottery bottles hung over their shoulders on rope, and their washing services. Rainwater, I was assuming, gathered in the many rooftop cisterns, tubs, and bowls, since Skandi, I'd been told, had no springs, lakes, or rivers. And even the rain was scarce, and thus hoarded, and thus worth selling to people who wanted to wash molah muck off legs and feet.

I glanced around. None of the laborers and slaves and others afoot were cleaning themselves off in the harbor. In fact, none of them were cleaning themselves off at all. Apparently they figured they'd just get filthy again walking back up the track, so they didn't bother. I guess Del and I looked like strangers. Soft touches.

They weren't wrong, either. I *would* have paid for the rainwater and the drying cloths draped over their arms, had I any coin.

Inspiration mingled with curiosity. I untied the thong, pinched the silver ring between precise fingers, and held it toward the nearest man.

He looked, examined, then backed off jerkily. I saw the now-familiar gesture, heard the now-familiar hissing and whispering commingled with blurted invocations against—something. To a man they stumbled over one another to distance themselves from us.

I knotted the claw-weighted thong around my neck again. "Let's find us a ship with a blue-headed first mate, shall we?"

This time was different. Instead of wobbling my way down the plank from ship to shore, I marched *up* the plank and planted my feet at the top of it. Yes, it was a precarious position; all anyone had to do to knock me off into the water was to tip me over the edge, but I was angry enough that I didn't care.

Besides, Del was there to make sure that if I got knocked in, she'd fish me out again.

A familiar face—and the body to go with it—met me there. Not the first mate, but one of the crew. He was mildly startled to see us. But his expression smoothed into cool assessment when I said a single word: "Nihkolara."

Nihko was fetched. His expression also reflected surprise, though it was replaced a moment later by a mask of blandness. He folded his arms against his chest and neither invited us aboard, nor told us to leave.

"All right," I said, "I give up. You said something to me once about when I got tired of heaving my belly up, I was to come see you. Well, I haven't heaved my belly up ever since you put this ring on my necklet, and I want to know why."

Nihko Blue-head smiled.

"I also want to know why it is that every time I try to use this ring as payment, they all break out in a rash of warding signs, babbling to one another words I can only assume are prayers, or curses; or, for all I know, proposals of marriage."

Nihko Blue-head stopped smiling. "You used the ring as *coin?*"

"Attempted to," I clarified. "We've got nothing else. It's good silver; where I come from, silver in any shape is worth something."

"Oh, that brow ring is worth a lot more than *something,*" he retorted. "No one on this island will accept it in payment, or as promise of payment, or anything at all other than what it is."

"And what *is* that, Nihkolara?"

"Mine," he said crisply.

"Cut the mystery," I snapped. "We're sick of it. Give me some straight answers."

"You have your answer, be it straight, crooked, or tied in knots. That is not coin. It buys nothing any man or woman on Skandi will give you. It buys only a degree of peace for you, in your body and your mind."

I jerked the ring from the thong and held it up. It glinted in the sunlight. "And if I gave it back?"

"You are certainly free to do so," Nihko answered evenly.

"And?"

He was guileless. "Your luck will turn bad."

I flicked it in a flashing arc toward the water. "Really?"

Nihko flung out a hand and snatched the ring from the air—"Fool!" —then mimicked my flicking gesture with deft fingers.

Something slammed into my breastbone. I folded, empty of breath, of sense, and tumbled backward into Del. She yelped once as I came down on a foot, grabbed for air, caught me, and then somehow the plank was no longer beneath either of us.

Not *again* . . . I twisted in midair, grabbed for the edge, caught. Clutched wood, digging fingers in so deep the pads of my fingertips flattened until nails cracked to the quick. I hung a moment, dangling over water; heard the splash as Del went in. Then I jerked myself up even as Nihko set foot on the plank to check his handiwork.

Breath screamed in my lungs. It wasn't fear of drowning; I had no time for that. It was pain, it was burning, it was absence of self-control over that most primitive function: the ability to breathe without conscious effort.

My chin was even with the plank. I caught movement from the corner of my eye. Nihko realized now I hadn't gone in with Del. His hand came up; would a second gesture peel my fingers from the edge?

Not this time, you bastard.

I swung under, released, twisted and caught plank again, this time on the other side. Shoulder tensed briefly, then I thrust myself upward even as I swung a leg up and over. Toes caught, then the ball of my foot. I used the momentum. Came up, reached, grabbed the closest ankle, and jerked as hard as I could.

Nihko fell. He landed hard on the planking, rolled from his back to his side, then scrabbled wildly as he overbalanced. I thought briefly what might happen if he ended up dangling from his side of the plank while I dangled opposite him. Decided I didn't like that much.

So as he swung down, I dropped from the edge again and kicked him in the gut. His entire body spasmed as his lungs expelled air, and his hands released the plank. The impact of his body flat upon the water soaked me thoroughly. But it was the best bath I'd ever had.

I hung there a moment, enjoying the view of Nihko

floundering his way to the surface, then became aware of Del's sea-slick head not so far away. "You all right?" I called.

She waved an assenting hand, treading water.

Relief. I clenched my teeth, hoisted myself up to the edge of the plank again, and hooked the foot on wood. A kick with my free leg gave me a little added momentum, and I thrust myself up the rest of the way. It was an ungainly maneuver that left me sprawled facedown on the trembling plank, but at least I was above the water instead of in it.

Then I saw the foot all of inches from my nose. And the glinting tip of a swordblade gesturing me to rise.

I looked up. Saw the wide smile in the freckled face, the wind-tangled swath of red hair, the gold and glass in her ears and wrapped around her throat.

"Someday," Prima Rhannet said, "you will have to learn how to swim. It might save you some little trouble."

Since she seemed to want it, I climbed to my feet. "Maybe."

The sword was lifted. I saw the flash of light on the blade, the tip brought up to skewer, knew what she meant to do. I would leap back, of course, to preserve my skin, and by doing it I'd take myself off the plank and into the water.

Not this time, you bitch.

I smashed the blade down with a forearm, stepped into her, tossed her over the edge, caught the sword as it flew from her grasp.

About damn *time* I had one of these suckers in my hands again.

TWENTY-FOUR

THEY CAME for me, of course, the members of Prima's crew. But I was ready for them. I waited at the head of the plank where it was lashed to the ship. It was steadier here, not so vulnerable to the motion of the ocean or the weight of men upon the wood. I'd chosen my ground, and now I stood it.

It felt gloriously invigorating to hold a sword in my hands again. "Come on," I invited, laughing for the sheer joy of empowerment and the promise of engagement. "Come ahead."

They did.

Maybe some day they'll write about it, how a lone man took on seven others. The advantage, it might be argued, was theirs; they knew the ship, knew one another, understood better the mechanics of planks between ships and docks. But they were none of them sword-dancers, none of them trained by the shodo of Alimat, none of them born to the sword.

I hope they do write about it, because from inside the engagement I couldn't see what happened. I knew only that I took them on one at a time, trapping guards, smashing blades, cutting into flesh that wandered too near my sword. It was Prima Rhannet's blade and thus the balance, for me, was decidedly off, but that's purely technical; the weapon was more than adequate to the purpose, to my needs of the moment.

By the time I'd disarmed three of them, the others drew back to reconsider options.

I laughed at them, still poised at the brink. "Come on!" I exulted, inexpressibly relieved to be rid of the prickle of apprehension engendered by our presence at Akritara, and focus strictly on the physical fight. I'd needed this. "I'm one man, right? I can't swim, this isn't my sword, I'm not really in proper condition—what's stopping you? *Come ahead!*"

It was enough to lure one of them in. Three of his crewmates bled upon the deck, though none of them would die of it. Within a matter of moments he had joined them, nursing a wounded wrist. His sword, like the others, had been slung by my own over the rail into the water.

"It's only me." I was grinning like a sandsick fool. "Of course, this is what I do for a living . . . in fact, what I've been doing for a living for nearly twenty years. Probably I'm a *little* better at it than you. Maybe. You think?" I gestured expansively. "Why not find out? Three against one? Surely that's enough to take me. Isn't it?" I waggled fingers, inviting them closer. "You're all strong men . . . you're enough, aren't you? Dreaded renegadas, cutting throats with the best—or worst!—of 'em. What's to stop you? What's to keep you from taking me?" Another came in, came close. "There, now, *that's* better!"

The remaining two fanned out, approached obliquely from the sides. I had hoped to entice them to rush me. Three against one can be a little tricky, but I did have the advantage. They could undoubtedly sail a ship far better than I, but there are not many, if any, better with a sword.

We danced. Oh, it wasn't a proper dance; there was no circle, no ritual, no comprehension of the beauty of the patterns, the movements, but the intent was the same: to defeat the opponent. In this case they had one and I had three, but the desired end was identical.

They came on. I took them one at a time, cutting, nicking, piercing, slashing, driving each of them back. They stumbled over themselves, one another, over their brethren already sprawled on the deck, discovering that a man born to the sword understands it implicitly, how it demands to be employed. A sword is not just a weapon, not just a means of killing a man, but has a soul and needs of its own. It isn't made to be looked at, nor to be used by incompetents. A sword is dead in the hands of an inferior wielder, it will hurt him as often as it will aid. But it comes alive in the hands of a man who understands it, who shares its desires.

I felt the plank thump and tremble beneath my feet. I'd expected it for a while; Nihko and his captain had had more than enough time to pull themselves from the water. So I completed my chore with alacrity, adding three more bleeding men to the pile upon the deck even as I disposed of their swords, and spun, poised and ready. Prima Rhannet stopped short, lurched backward out of range. She stood there, furious, two long paces away.

"He will kill her," she promised.

I looked beyond her, as she intended. Nihkolara stood on the dock at the end of the plank. His left hand rested on the back of Del's neck. Pretty much as I'd expected; I'd known I could take the crew—well, *believed* I could—but was not foolish enough to assume victory would be all-encompassing. Not when Del was at risk. But it takes small things as well as large to win, outside the circle as much as within.

Del's clothing, soaked and dripping, was wrapped closely around her body, more like shroud than tunic. Fair hair, now unbraided, was slicked severely back from her face, baring the bones of her skull, the bitter acknowledgment that she was surety of my behavior once again. I thought of what his touch had done to me: set a weeping rash around my wrist, burned the flesh of my throat, stopped the heart in my chest. Thought of what else—and to whom—that touch might do.

I grounded the swordtip in the wood of the plank. "All I wanted," I told Prima truthfully, "was an explanation."

Sopping hair, stripped of coils and curls and darkened to the color of old blood, streamed over her shoulders. The thin fabric of her clothing, plastered against flesh, underscored how lush her compact body was. "About what?"

"IoSkandi, ioSkand*ic*," I said. "What it is, what it

means—and why the touch of his hand upon a person can do things to him." Or to her.

Prima's lips peeled back from her teeth. With great disdain, she said, "Have you never heard of magic?"

I arched brows. "Your implication being that Nihko has it."

"Nihko *is* it," she hissed between clamped jaws.

"I thought Nihko is—or was—a priest."

"IoSkandic," she said. "Priests. Mages."

"Both?"

Prima Rhannet laughed. "He'll pray for you," she promised, "even as he kills you."

"How economical. Priest *and* mage for the price of one." Smiling, I tossed the blade aside before she could demand its return; steel flashed on its way to the water. As expected, the action enraged her. "Now, captain. Suppose you and I discuss how it is we can all of us get new swords."

Back aboard a ship I'd hoped never to see again, let alone revisit, Prima and her first mate were coldly angry that I had accomplished so much in so little time, even if they'd regained the upper hand eventually. I'd cost them the pride and self-confidence of their crew, which had survived the encounter even if the decks were now stained with their blood; had cost them every blade they had on board; and had proven the only way they could truly defeat me was to use coercion or magic. Not a pleasant realization or prospect for people who believed they were naturally superior at everything.

I leaned against the rail, arms folded, more relaxed than I'd been in weeks. There are people in the world who want to win at any cost, who will use any means to win. But Prima Rhannet and Nihkolara were not so ruthless as they might prefer me to believe. She'd said more than once they only killed people if there were no other way. Now I knew, and they knew, and they knew *I* knew that *they* knew I was not so easily dealt with as they'd believed—and that unless they truly did mean to kill me they'd better not dismiss me quite so easily.

Prima scowled at me as she paced the deck. She was damp, but drying, and her wiry hair, wind-tossed, had begun to curl again.

"So," I said cheerfully, "what comes next?"

She stopped pacing. "You go back to Akritara."

"Won't you even consider giving us passage elsewhere?"

"I will not."

"*Why* not?"

"Business," she said coolly, "with the metri."

"Still?"

"Still."

I swore briefly, which amused Prima and her first mate.

"Back," the captain said, "to Akritara."

I feigned shock. "May we do that? After all, we walked all the way down here—"

Nihkolara made a sound of disgust. "And after what you were told about soiling, and cleansing—"

"And having no coin, I attempted to barter with that ring you've got in your hand," I continued with blithe disregard for his comment. "But no one would permit us to go near them, let alone take us down on molah-back, or wash our feet at the bottom."

Nihko inhaled a long, hissing breath of intense displeasure.

"Fool," his captain said coldly. "You may have ruined everything."

"How is that, exactly?" I inquired. "Just what is it you and the priest-mage are after?"

"Swords," she said sharply. "Thanks to you."

"Ah. Well, then, speaking of swords—"

Prima cut me off. "The metri has sent to say she will hire me to supply a sword to you, and to her." The direction of her eyes flicked to Del. "But this will cost the metri far more, now, than before, because she must make good our losses—due to your folly—and you will then owe her even *more* of your time." Her blazing smile was unexpected and maliciously sweet. "Is that what you hoped for?"

Cheerfulness dissipated. I glared.

It pleased her; her mood shifted to crisp competence tinged with victory. "You will be escorted back to Akritara, where the metri will be told of your behavior. Punishment lies within her purview—"

"Wait," I interrupted sharply. "Punishment is not part of the plan."

"What *is* the plan?" Prima asked with poisonous clarity. "Have you one? Or are you hoping merely to take advantage of a dying old woman who so desperately wants a proper heir?"

"*You're* the ones who took advantage of *us!*" I shot back.

"Yes," the captain agreed with elaborate precision. "We are pirates. That is what we do."

When I could not immediately come up with a properly devastating retort, Prima turned away. To Nihko, she said, "Is he soiled beyond redemption?"

He looked at Del briefly, then at me. For a long time. "No," he said finally. "But it will prove costly to have him cleansed appropriately so he may walk among the Houses again. The metri will not be pleased."

"Will the priests do it?"

He shrugged. "She is the Stessa metri, and they will accept her petition—"

"And coin?" I inquired sweetly.

"—with the proper rituals invoked and completed." Nihko's gaze flicked to me. "Provided he does no more damage to her Name and House than has already been done."

"Look," I said, "I'm getting pretty tired of—" And was slammed to my knees, though no one touched me.

"Enough," Nihkolara hissed, so stiff he trembled with it. "If you will not hold your silence when it serves us, I will seal your mouth permanently."

My knees, mashed against hard wood, were most unhappy. But I didn't have the time or inclination to listen to their complaints. I cleared my throat experimentally, making sure nothing had been permanently sealed quite yet. "You can do that, huh?"

"What I can do," he said, "you cannot begin to comprehend."

"*That's* encouraging."

He flipped something at me. Wary now of what he next planned, I ducked, squeezing my eyes closed. Whatever it was struck my forehead, bounced off, rolled briefly against the deck. I opened my eyes and saw it then, clearly: the discarded brow ring, glinting in sunlight.

"Priests in general have a facility for mercy," Nihko observed coolly. "But be wary of mine."

"You know," I said conversationally, "I'm right here with you, and I don't feel sick at all."

"That may be remedied," he suggested. "Shall I have you spew your guts here and now?"

"Magic," Del said intently, and put up a hand to forestall question or comment. "Magic, Tiger. It has always affected you."

I arched brows. "Magic affects a lot of people. That's sort of the point."

"No. I mean *how* it affects you, much of it. You have said many times it makes you feel odd, as if your bones itch." She paused delicately. "And we know how it affects your belly."

I scowled at her briefly, then shrugged. "I notice it, one way or another."

"It means nothing," Nihko said lightly.

Del looked at him. "No?"

"Magic simply *is*," he declared. "Some people are sensitive to its existence."

"How is that?" I asked.

"The way some are made ill by certain foods," he explained matter-of-factly. "Or those poor souls who cannot ride the ocean without emptying their bellies."

"Or keep cats," Prima Rhannet contributed with an ingenuous glance at Del; her expression suggested a subtext I decided not to pursue.

"It's different with Tiger," Del said. "Magic puts him seriously out of sorts. As if it argues with him."

Nihko shook his head. "There is no significance in that."

"Indeed," the captain said, "no more than in a man claiming a woman is out of sorts once a month because she *is* a woman."

I knew better than to get into that. "And I'm supposed to believe you?"

"I am a priest-mage," Nihkolara said with devastating modesty. "I have a measure of experience with such things."

"And we have a measure of experience with *you*," I pointed out. "Why should we believe anything you say?"

"Because of the alternative," Prima replied.

"What, you'll kill us?"

"No," she said seriously, "because in Skandi, being a priest-mage means you are mad—"

I gaped inelegantly. *"What—?"*

"—and madness is not tolerated in Skandi." Her gaze was steady; she avoided looking at her first mate. "Such people are too feared to be killed outright, so they are sent away. Just as Nihko was."

"And here I thought he got in trouble over bedding the wrong woman." Nihko was not amused by my amusement at his expense. "Sent away where?" I asked, enjoying his expression.

"IoSkandi," the first mate answered with a vast contempt for ignorance.

"IoSkandi is a lazaret," Prima Rhannet explained gently to my incomprehension, as if taking pity on a child. "It's where madmen are sent to live until they cease to do so."

I looked at Nihko. "For someone who's supposed to be mad or dead, you're very calm about all of this."

Del spoke before he could answer. "Why?" she asked him intently. "Why didn't you die?"

Nihkolara said only: "I am ikepra."

"I thought you said that meant you were abomination," I put in sharply. "Profanation."

"Those with power are known to be so because they go mad," he said, "and are sent to ioSkandi. There they survive to purposely rouse the power, if it may be done, so they may control it for the needs of their own salvation;

if they cannot, they die of it. Those who survive learn what the true nature of magic is, and how to cohabit with it."

"And?"

"Those who reject it, those who leave ioSkandi and the priest brothers, are abominations."

"Yet you left."

"And thus I am adjudged apostate by my priest-brothers, the mages. As I am adjudged *io*—mad—by the people of the island."

"And feared even more because you are not in your proper place." Del nodded. "You do not fit. You live *outside*, without rules, without rituals." She glanced at me briefly, using the Southron word. "Borjuni."

He shrugged. "Ikepra."

But borjuni were simply men without morals. None of them had any magic, any priestly trappings. In Skandi, where eleven specific families were considered gods-descended, what Nihko represented as a member of one of those families—as madman, priest-mage, *and* ikepra—was far more fearsome than mere Southron bandits.

I understood now the intent of the warding gestures, the whispered comments, the rejection and outright abhorrence of the concept of the brow ring as barter. And yet the solution seemed obvious. "You could leave, you know. Avoid all kinds of unpleasantness."

Nihkolara hitched a shoulder. "And so I do leave. Every time my captain's ship sails."

"But you come back. I meant leave *permanently*," I clarified. "Only a fool would remain."

"A fool." Nihko smiled. "Or a madman."

I shook my head. "So, you'd have us believe you still have this power, even though you're exiled from the brotherhood." Even as I was exiled from the oaths and rituals of the sword-dance.

"He has power," Prima said sharply. "You have experienced it. Exile need not strip one of one's gift."

Any more than being denied the circle stripped me of *my* gift.

"But he rejected it," I maintained, which was entirely

different; I'd never reject my sword-skill. Then I looked piercingly at Nihko. "Or did it reject you?"

Something flared briefly in his eyes, some deep and abiding emotion so complex I could not begin to define the elements that comprised it.

"Tell him," Del commanded the first mate, as if she had acquired the pieces of an invisible puzzle and put them together even as we stood here. "You have used this magic on him more than once, and have provided him the means to control his sensitivity to it when in your presence." She nodded at the brow ring glinting on the deck. "If you are—or were—a priest in service to the gods, whatever gods they may be, it is your duty to inform those who are at risk what it *is* they risk."

Prima Rhannet inhaled a quiet, but hissing breath. "You see too much."

"Well, I'm blind," I said curtly. "Why not explain it to me?"

Nihkolara did. "The power, once understood, once acknowledged, once invoked, will never reject its vessel. But that vessel may reject *it.*"

"And?"

"Tie a string around your finger as tightly as you may, and leave it so," he said, "without respite. What is the result?"

Del said, "It withers."

Prima said, "It dies."

I looked at Nihko. "And you're not dead."

"Nor ever will be," he agreed, "until such a time as the gods decree I have lived out my allotment."

"So, if I broke your neck even as we stand here, you wouldn't die?"

The contempt was back in his eyes. "I am not immortal," he said. "But I will not intentionally tie a string around my finger so that it may wither and die." He paused. "And you would not be permitted close enough to break my neck."

"Really?" I grinned toothily at him. "Is that why I've dumped you on your rump more than once?" I made a show of examining his soaked but drying person. "And knocked you into the water?"

Del's posture was suddenly such that we all became aware of the sheer power of her presence simultaneously. It was a subtle magic she had in good measure, and a power I understood and admired.

To Nihkolara she said, "You have relied on magic to defeat this man, always. What are you without it?"

Prima's sun-coppered brows slid up in startlement. "My, my," she murmured with elegant implication. "So the tiger's mate defends her male. He *has* trained you well."

"Oh, stop," Del said coldly. "You invoke such imagery to provoke, and without cause. You would do precisely the same for Nihkolara, with nothing in it of men and women beyond coincidence of gender. You don't sleep with him. He *can't* sleep with you. Do you then count the binding between captain and first mate, friend and friend, as the lesser because bedding is not involved?"

Color flared in Prima Rhannet's face, filling in the spaces between freckles, then ebbed away so thoroughly all one could see *were* freckles, the angry glitter of her eyes. And yet she offered no answer because there was none that gained the victory.

Oh, yes. She would defend Nihkolara with her life, and he her with his.

Nihko recognized challenge no matter the gender. "But I *have* the magic," he said coolly in answer to Del's original question, "and only a fool refuses to use an advantage."

"A fool," I said, "or a madman."

Nihko turned on his heel and marched away.

Prima was rigid with surpressed rage. "Perhaps it is time I had you both declawed."

I spread my hands. "In case you've forgotten, captain: *None* of us has blades with which such a thing might be done."

Which brought us around all over again to where we'd begun.

Prima's chin rose. It jutted the air. "You will have swords," she said, "as the metri has suggested. But if you press Nihko, you may well discover that a blade is no weapon at all." She stared hard at us both. "Now get off my ship."

We got off her ship. But not before I retrieved the brow ring from the deck. Only a fool refuses to use an advantage.

And I'm not a madman, either.

TWENTY-FIVE

Before Del and I had even reached the gate of the front courtyard entrance—the one where the metri had suggested Herakleio and I, wearing plaster and nothing else, should stand on display—Simonides met us. His expression was stern as stone as he put up a hand in a gesture that could be interpreted no other way save *stop*.

We stopped.

Whereupon men arrived from all corners of the courtyard, swarming into industry. A mat was laid down first, then a fine-loomed carpet was unrolled atop it. As men labored to do that, others came to Del and me with amphora, soaps, oil, and linen cloths. Another man, shaven-headed but bearing no tattoos or rings in his flesh—thus not mad, I assumed, only holy; though in my opinion a certain emphatic degree of holiness bears its own weight of madness—waited in the shade of a tree. Other men brought stools upon which Del and I were directed to sit.

We sat.

As Simonides looked on in meticulous supervision; as the priest beneath the tree murmured softly to himself; as Del and I stared at one another in baffled astonishment, we were scrubbed nearly raw from the knees down, with particular attention given to the soles of our feet. A harsh soap first, followed by scented; followed by clean rinse water; followed by oil that was, I assumed, blessed, as the oil-men first glanced to the murmuring priest for a nod of permission before pouring.

It wasn't entirely unpleasant, having rich oil worked into my flesh, except as the man's hands rose toward my knees I stiffened a little. A sidelong glance at Del showed me a bemused expression, but she did not appear entirely discontent with the direction of her oil-man's hands.

Perhaps it was time I bought my *own* bottle of oil.

Once that ritual was completed, we were gestured to rise and stand upon the carpet that was layered over the mat. Simonides escorted us with grave deliberation toward the recessed doorway. I glanced over my shoulder as we stepped out of sunlight into shade, saw the carpet- and mat-men rolling everything away; and then the priest came out from beneath the tree to begin *his* ritual.

"So," I said to Simonides, "this is why you didn't want us to walk."

Simonides said nothing, simply opened the door and stepped away, gesturing for us to enter.

"Well, look," I told him as I passed into the household, "at least we gave everyone something to do with their afternoon."

Del produced an elegant little snicker of amusement. Simonides bestowed upon me an almost mournful expression. "The metri sends to say you are to attend her in her bedroom."

That stopped me. "Her bedroom?"

"She is abed."

"That's a little redundant," I told the servant. "Why is she abed, and why am I expected to attend her *while* she's abed?"

"She has sent to say to me she wishes me to send to say to you—"

Exasperated by the circuitous manner of speech, I cut him off rudely. "Save your breath, Simonides—just point me in the right direction."

Quietly, he said, "She wishes to see her grandson."

The simplicity of the statement rocked me. Even Del marked the implications, glancing to me immediately. I nodded, offering neither commentary nor expression. Simonides led me into the depths of the household even as

Del murmured tactfully of a desire to nap, and eventually I was given entry into the metri's private quarters.

She was indeed abed, propped into a sitting position by a generous arrangement of embroidered cushions. Silvering hair had been taken from its multiple plaits and loops, freed of decorative baubles, so that it streamed down across the cushions, her shoulders, and the coverlet. It softened the severity of her features. For the first time I saw beyond the metri, beyond the self-proclaimed gods-descended woman born of and into the Eleven Families who ruled in its entirety the wine trade of Skandi, and who needed so desperately to keep every facet of her empire under control, even an individual who merely *might* be her relative. She was in this moment simply an aging woman who walked the road toward death, and knew the distance left her was shorter than for others.

"Am I so cruel," she asked, "that you feel you *must* leave?"

Not the beginning I expected. In bed with her hair loose, with her body swathed in a coverlet and linens, I had expected to hear a voice to match the impression of weakness. But her voice was the same, her tone identical to the one she used habitually: firm, clear, meticulous in its delicacy of emphasis.

She was not unlike many of the tanzeers who'd hired me to dance for them. Stern, hard, proud, possessive, but also realistic; what was undertaken was from necessity, not whim. But she was as unlike them as could be: a woman, and possibly my mother's mother. She was a stranger to me in spirit, in the large and small aspects of the heart, but potentially a woman whose bone was my bone, whose blood was my blood.

This woman had had no shaping of me, not in the smallest degree, but she could very well be *in* me. If so, I was as much of her as I was of the Salset. And without the shaping the tribe had given me, I would not stand here today to have this woman speak to me of needs and expectations.

If I left her, if I left *here,* I left myself as well.

Without accusation, I said, "You have no intention of naming me your heir."

One eyebrow twitched. "Have I not?"

"I am a tool. An adze to shape the boy you *will* name your heir."

She smiled faintly. "Or perhaps a lance point, to jab him where he is most soft."

"You admit it?"

"I admit nothing," the metri said, "beyond a promise that I will do what I have always done: whatever I perceive is required for the task."

"And Herakleio is my task."

"Herakleio is the task I have selected for you, as you have selected none for yourself."

That stung, as no doubt she intended it to. "Excuse me?"

"What are you but a man whose home is what he builds of a circle drawn in the sand? No mortar, no bricks, only air. And dreams."

"And skill."

"Oh, yes, there is skill; and I believe it not so different from the skill I employ each day for the betterment of my Name."

"Well, then we share a goal," I threw back at her. "I have a name of my own."

"Chula," she said gently.

Had I not already been standing, I'd have leaped to my feet. As it was, all I could do was contain the shame, the shock and outrage her tone and the word engendered by standing excruciatingly still. Because if I moved, if I spoke, if I so much as blinked . . .

She gave me no time to respond with anything other than quivering silence. "You are indeed skilled," the metri declared with a quietude that in no way diminished the power of personality, "and it is a skill few men have, the ability to build walls merely of the air and to abide within them, defending those walls against every enemy." One hand moved slightly on the coverlet; fingers spasmed, clenched briefly. "I asked you what you were. I have *said* what you are, and I will say this as well: you

have not been given, nor have you taken, responsibility
beyond what is required to keep yourself—and your
woman—alive."

I gifted her with a ghastly grin. "Good enough for
me!"

"But that you have taken no more does not mean you
cannot accept more. And so I give you Herakleio, that
both of you learn the requirements of responsibility. Because recognizing, acknowledging, and accepting responsibility is the hallmark of adulthood."

I wanted to smirk, but didn't; she was deadly serious,
and I owed her that much. "Is it?"

"And because the boy I have given over to you as your
task may well be your kinsman."

I studied her expression very closely. "You admit I am
a tool—and seemingly an irresponsible one at that—yet
insist I may still be a Stessa? Why? What do you gain?"

"Leverage," she answered simply.

Well, *that* was truth. "Herakleio doesn't believe any
more than you do that I'm your grandson."

"It doesn't matter what he believes. All that matters is
what I do."

"But naming a stranger, a foreigner, as heir to the
Stessa fortune is not a possibility."

She shook her head. "You still do not understand."

"Explain it to me, then."

"You may indeed not be my grandson. You *are* a
stranger, a foreigner in everything save, perhaps, blood.
But neither precludes you from inheriting."

I blinked. "You're right. I don't understand."

Her eyes were fixed on mine. "I am required only to
name an heir. The heir is heir. It is the naming that matters."

I shook my head slowly. "We know very well what I
am, you and I. A Southron barbarian who makes a living
in the circle with a sword . . . a man who builds a home
with walls of air. That makes me fit to dance for you, but
not to run your household, the vineyards, or the economics of the Stessas—Stess*oi*—which affect the economics
of Skandi."

The metri smiled. "A man who understands the mechanics of ambition is fit to do whatever he wishes to do. He finds ways to deal with such things as he does not know, and learns from those who do."

"And?"

"And," she continued pleasantly, "so I am moved to ask you if I am so cruel that you feel you *must* leave a place in my household, a position for which you are as fit as any man I know, who will learn because it is in him to learn, and who wishes to pay his debts."

I put a finger into the air. "You're forgetting: I was just down at the docks checking on the possibility of convincing Prima Rhannet to sail us away from here. Since you so kindly explained how it is no one else on the island will."

"There is nothing you may offer Prima Rhannet that will convince her of such an undertaking, when I can convince her against it." Her eyes were very calm. "Unless it is your woman."

"Del is not an issue in this!"

"Coin is minted in many shapes," she said, "not the least of which is knowledge of what another will accept. You owe me a debt; I have said you may discharge it by teaching Herakleio what it is to be a man. But you have nothing in the world Prima Rhannet will accept, *except* the companionship of your woman."

I shook my head again, shoving down the anger so I could be very plain. "Del is not coin. Del is not barter. Del is not in any way an object, nor available for trade."

The metri's smile did not reach her eyes. "Whatever it is someone else wants very badly is indeed coin, barter, and object. Availability is the only factor remaining open to negotiation, and subsequent arrangement."

"I don't accept that."

"You may reject the truth as it pleases you to do so. But it alters no part of it."

I backed away, displaying both palms in a gesture of abject refusal. "This conversation is over."

She waited until I reached the door. "And so is this test."

I froze, then swung back sharply even as I released the latch. "This was a *test?*"

"All things are tests," the metri said obliquely. "Each day as I rise, offering thanks to the gods *for* the day, I understand that the hours left to me before I retire again are tests of themselves, of my strength, of my loyalty and devotion, of my will to make certain the Stessa name survives as it was meant to survive: a piece of the gods themselves, made flesh. For they placed here upon the island a woman who was delivered of a child who in turn bore her own, and in turn another was born of that woman, until the day came that I was born to do my mother's work. It is heritage. It is legacy. It is *responsibility:* to see that one small piece of the gods, made flesh, remains whole in the world, and alive, lest that world become a lesser place for its loss." She leaned forward then, toward me, away from the cushions. Intently she asked, "Who is to say that if a single candle is blown out, the remainder of the world does not go dark as well?"

"But . . ." But. It was a debate in which I was ill-equipped to participate. And yet the argument existed of itself because it *could* exist.

No one knew.

Each time I shut my eyes on the verge of sleep, I gave myself over to trust that I'd awaken again. Because I *had* awakened each and every day.

But who was to say I would tomorrow?

Could you put coin on it?

No. Only belief *in* it. Only trust.

Only faith.

She leaned back again, abruptly ashen. One hand was pressed to her chest as she labored to breathe. Her lips and nails were blue-tinged. This was not a woman feigning illness or weakness to gain my sympathy. I had seen that look before in men with weak hearts.

"I'll call Simonides," I said sharply, and made a hasty departure.

Herakleio found me out on the terrace, moving through ritual movements designed to condition both body and mind. I had anticipated his arrival, and the accusations. I let him make them without a word spoken to stop him, because he needed to make them. And I, in his place, might well make them, too.

When he ran out of breath and I was cooling down, I finally addressed him directly. "You've said she isn't in immediate danger."

"Yes, I said that." He nearly spat the sibilants. "And no, she is not in *immediate* danger, so the physician says; she should live for another year or more. But she is clearly ill, and weakening."

"Which is why you've come to me now: you view me as a threat. And now a more *immediate* threat."

He glared. "And so you are."

"Unless she has already declared me her heir, I am no threat at all." I was loose, relaxed, sweat drying as the wind snapped against my flesh. "Has she?"

He remained hostile, if somewhat mollified. "She has not."

I took up the cloth draped over the low wall and scrubbed at my face, speaking through it. "Then you're safe. Akritara, the vineyards, the power and wealth . . . all of it is still meant to be yours."

He looked away from me then, staring hard across the land that fell away against the horizon, rushing toward the cliff face miles away. "I want it," he said tightly, "but I want her alive, more."

Prima Rhannet had said it one night in her cups: there was sunlight in him, and stone. She had not said there were tears.

I flipped the cloth over one shoulder and sat down on the wall. "Truth, Herakleio, in the name of an old woman we both of us respect: my coming here had nothing to do with hoping to replace you as heir. I knew nothing about Skandi at all, let alone that there were Stessoi, or metris, or even vineyards and wealth to inherit."

He didn't look at me, nor did he pull wind-tossed hair from his face because such a gesture would remove the shield. "Then why did you come?"

"To find out. . ." I let it go, thought it through, began

again. "To find out if there was a home in my life where the walls were built of brick and mortar instead of air."

Herakleio turned sharply into the wind to look at me. "I have heard *her* say that!"

I nodded. "She said it to me earlier today, before she became ill."

He flung out an encompassing hand. "And so you came and found that these walls were made of more than brick and mortar, but also coin and power!"

"But I didn't necessarily find my home," I said. "I found *a* home. Her home. Your home."

He shook his head vigorously. "But you want it. Now that you know it, you want it."

I drew in a deep breath, let it fill my chest, then pushed it out again in a noisy sigh of surrender. "There is a part of me that wishes to be *of* it. Yes."

"You see!"

"But being of something is not the same as being that thing," I pointed out. "There is a difference, Herakleio. You are of the Stessoi, and you *are* a Stessa. You *are* these walls; your bones are made of them. It's your home."

He was clearly perplexed.

"*I* am my home," I said. "Where I go, that is my home. My walls are built of air. There is no substance—no brick, no mortar—except the substance I give them, and that is air. A circle drawn in the sand." I hitched a shoulder. "A man born in and of a house doesn't truly comprehend what it is to *be* a house. Because there is no need."

"But," he said, "you have that woman in it."

That woman. Not *a* woman. That one. Specifically.

Herakleio understood semantics better than I'd believed.

"Because she chooses to be in it," I said finally; and that in itself was so different from what I would have said three years before, when every part of me knew a woman was in a man's house because he *put* her there.

"Does she build them of air as well, those walls?"

"The walls of my home?" I shook my head. "Del is my brick. My mortar."

His intensity went up a notch. "And if she left your house, would those walls collapse?"

This time it was my turn to stare hard across the horizon. "I don't know."

For him, for that question, the answer was enough.

TWENTY-SIX

A SPIRE OF stone tore a hole in the sky, punching upward like a fist in challenge to the gods. I poised upon the foremost knuckle of that fist, aware of the breath of those gods caressing naked flesh.

Caress. Keraka. The living embodiment of the gods-descended, sealed by spell or wish into the infant's flesh before it even knew the world, was yet safe in its mother's womb. All the colors of wine, all the shapes of the mind, staining the fragile shell before the sun so much as could warm it.

But there was none on my body. I was free of the blemish also called caress; was nothing more within or of myself than stranger, than foreigner, lacking the knowledge of gods-descended, the gifts of the Stessoi, the birthright of the Eleven.

What was I but a man born of a womb unknown to any save the woman and the man who together made a child, but who could or would not nurture that child; so that he was raised a slave in the hyorts of the Salset?

The spire beneath me shook. Bare feet grasped at stone. Wind beat into my eyes, blinded me with tears.

Skandi, they said, had been smoke made solid, then broken apart again.

If I was not to lose the spire, if I was not to let it shake me off its fist, I would have to sacrifice my own. Not to die, but to survive; not to destroy flesh, but to preserve it.

There was wind enough to do it, if I let it carry me.

There was power enough to fly, if I let myself try.

*I stretched, leaned, felt the wind against my palms.
Closed my eyes so I could see.*

Was lifted—

"Tiger?" A hand came down on bunched, sweat-
sheened shoulder. "Tiger—wake up."

*The spire fell away, crumbled to dust beneath me, took
me down with it—*

"Tiger."

*—and all the bones shattered, all the flesh split into
pulp—*

"Tiger—wake up!"

I lurched, twisted, sat up as the fingers closed tightly
into muscle taut as wire. I stared into darkness, aware of
the noise of my breathing, the protests of my heart.

The metri's heart was ailing. And I might be her
grandson.

"What is it?" Del asked.

All around me on the ground the stone of the spire
was broken.

She got up then, crawled over me, got out of bed, fumbled around in the darkness, hissed a brief oath as she
fumbled again. But I heard the metallic strike-and-
scratch, smelled the tang, saw the first flare of spark as
she used flint and steel to light the candle in its pottery
cup.

She held the cup up high so the light spilled over me.
"Gods," she whispered, "what's *wrong* with you?"

I blinked then, and squinted, then shook my head to
banish the visions. "Bad dream."

"You look scared out of your wits," Del said dubiously. "Rather like the stud when he's really spooked: all
white of eye, and stiff enough to shatter his bones."

Shattered bones.

"Don't," I said simply, then swung my legs over the
edge of the bed so my feet were flat on the floor. I
hunched there, elbows set into thighs, the heels of my
hands scouring out my eyes. "Just—a bad dream."

Del set the candle-cup down on the linens chest, then
came to sit beside me. "What was it?"

I shook my head. "I don't know." I looked up then, still squinting against the flame. "I've had rather a lot to think about, lately."

"Magic," she said grimly.

I began to object—magic was not something I gave much thought to—then refrained. Magic *was* part of it; Nihkolara was more than priest, and he had proved it. Time and time again, simply by putting his hand on me. Time and time again my body had warned me *before* he touched me, and I had refused to listen.

Some people, the priest-mage had said, were more sensitive to magic. It made them ill, he said, like certain foods or herbs.

"Magic," I muttered, and closed my hand around the necklet with its weight of sandtiger claws, and one silver ring.

Del was silent a long moment. Then, very quietly, "Do you believe he's right?"

I knew whom she meant. "No."

"In your heart."

The pounding, spasming heart. "No."

"All right—in your soul."

I laughed a little. "Just how many pieces of my anatomy do you want me to consult before you get the answer you want?"

"How about in your earlobe?"

I grinned, leaned into her with a shoulder even as she leaned back. "He has rings in his earlobes, our blue-headed first mate."

She nodded. "You always swear you don't believe in magic—"

"I said I don't *like* it. There's a difference."

"So, you mean you don't believe in *this* magic. This specific magic."

"I don't necessarily believe I have it, no."

"But—"

"But," I said, overriding her, "if what Nihko says is true, it doesn't mean I have it. It means I'm sensitive to it."

"But he has called you ioSkandic."

"I suspect Nihko has called me a lot of things."

"Besides all that. You have a history of personal experience with magic. Shall I name all the incidents?"

"Let's not," I suggested; likely it would fill six volumes to do so. "But reacting to magic doesn't mean I have any magic myself."

"Even after hosting Chosa Dei?"

"Hosting a sorcerer does not make the body of itself powerful. Only powerful by proxy." I looked at my fingernails, which had often indicated the state of my body while infested with the sorcerer who considered himself a god. They were whole, normal, not black or curling, or missing. "I can't work any kind of spells, Del. You know that."

"You sang your jivatma to life."

"So did you sing yours to life," I reminded her. "Does that make you a sorceress; or is the *tool*—in this case, the sword—the embodiment of magic?"

"No," Del said decisively. "I am not a sorceress."

"There you are, bascha. You don't like the idea any more than I do."

"But what if it *were* true? That you have magic?"

"Then I guess I'd be a sorcerer."

"You say that so lightly."

Because I had to, or admit how much the prospect frightened me. "Do you want me to say it in a hushed whisper? Shall I go out onto the terrace, thrust my right fist and sword into the air and shout 'I have the power!'? like some melodramatic fool?"

"Well," she said, "I suppose being melodramatic is better than being mad."

"Which is the problem," I pointed out. "Here in Skandi, anyone with magic is considered mad, and sent away to this lazaret place."

"Is *that* what you're afraid of?"

"What, being mad? Oh, hoolies, some people would swear I am even without benefit of Skandic blood—*if* I have any—"

"Oh, Tiger, of course you're Skandic!"

"—simply because I have the gehetties to suggest I

am the messiah who is to change the sand to grass," I finished. "Remember Mehmet? And the old hustapha? That deep-desert tribe more than willing to believe I am the one they worship?"

"And my brother," she said glumly. "Who was, according to Southron belief, the Oracle."

"Meant to announce the coming of the jhihadi." I nodded. "And so he announced me. And look at what it got him. They murdered him."

Del sighed deeply. "Likely they'd murder you, too."

"If we went back South? Oh, absolutely. If the religious zealots didn't get me, if the borjuni didn't kill me for whatever reward there must be on my head, surely the sword-dancers would track me down."

"Abbu Bensir?"

"I have dishonored the codes of Alimat, not to mention betrayed the faith and trust of our shodo," I said. "Abbu would call me out in the blink of an eye, except there'd be no circle drawn, no dance, no rituals of honor. He'd just do his best to execute me as quickly as possible."

"And if he failed?"

I shrugged. "Someone else would step forward."

Her voice was very quiet. "But if you *had* magic, no one could defeat you."

"I have magic," I declared firmly. "Sword magic. Just give me a blade, and I'll wield it."

"Then why," Del began, "are you so afraid?"

"Am I?"

"You didn't see your face just now when I lighted the candle."

"Bad dreams bring out the worst in anyone, bascha. Remember who it is I sleep with? I could tell you all the times *she's* had bad dreams. I never suggested she was afraid of anything . . . likely because she'd have knifed me in the gullet."

Del scoffed. "I'd have done no such thing." She thought it over. "Maybe planted an elbow."

"At the very least. Anyway, the point is I don't believe I have any magic, be it Skandic magic, Southron magic,

or even Northern magic—which is buried with my jivatma anyway, back beneath those heaps of rocks in the
middle of the Punja."

"You could always dig it up."

"I don't *want* to dig it up. I don't *want* any magic. I
don't *want* to be a messiah, or mad, or anything other
than what I am, which is a—" And I stopped.

"Sword-dancer," Del finished softly, with something
akin to sorrow. Because she understood what it meant, to
know myself other than what I *had* been after laboring so
long to become more than a chula. "In Skandi," she said,
"you may be a grandson, and heir to wealth, power, position. No magic is necessary, any more than a sword-
dance."

"You're telling me to stay. To let the metri name me
her heir."

"I'm pointing out potentials."

"Herakleio may have something to say about that."

"Herakleio is a boy."

"Herakleio is—" The door opened abruptly, and there
he was. "—*here,*" I finished. Then, "Knocking would be
nice."

"Knocking wastes time," he replied. "Come out onto
the terrace. Simonides has set the torches out for us."

"That must be very charming," I said, "but why am I
to go out to the terrace, and why has he set torches out
there for us?"

"The better to see by," he retorted, "while we dance."
The wooden practice blade was in his strong young hand.
Green eyes glinted hazel in candlelight. "Come out,
Sandtiger. The metri wishes you to make me a man. Per-
haps it is time I permitted you to try."

" 'Try'?" I asked dryly. "Are you suggesting you may
fail in the attempt?"

He displayed good teeth. "I may already be a man.
Shall we go and discover it?"

"It takes more than one dance, you know."

"Of course," he agreed, "as it takes more than one
man in her bed for a woman to fully understand what it is
to *be* a woman."

I felt Del stiffen beside me into utter immobility. That kind of comment had gotten me into plenty of trouble during the early days of our relationship. But then she had been the one who hired me, and had the right to disabuse me of such notions as she saw fit; now she was a guest in the metri's house and would not abuse the hospitality by insulting the woman's kin.

There are more ways than verbal of insulting another. I stood up, grabbed my practice blade from where it was propped against the wall. "Fine," I said. "Let's dance."

Imagine a sheet of ice, pearlescent in moonglow. Imagine a rim of rock made over into a wall surrounding the sheet of ice. Imagine a necklet of flames spaced evenly apart like gemstones on a chain, whipped into flaring brilliance by the breeze coming out of the night. Imagine the humped and hollowed angles of domes and arches and angles, demarcations blurred by wind-whipped torches into impression, not substance. Imagine the solidified wave of the world running outward beyond the wall as if upon a shore, then pouring off the invisible edge into the cauldron of the gods.

It was glory. It was beauty. And I walked upon it with a sword in my hand, albeit made of wood instead of beloved steel. But it didn't matter. A blade is a blade. The truth of its power lies in the hand that employs it.

Simonides, either as directed by Herakleio, or intuitively understanding the requirements of the moment, had taken care to set the torches properly. The stakes had been driven into a series of potted plants, so they were anchored against the breeze. The pots themselves had been set at equidistant points atop the curving wall, or tucked into niches formed by the architecture of the dwelling itself. Herakleio and I inhabited the terrace proper, swept clean of sand and grit and other windblown debris. White tile glowed, showing no blemish, no seams.

It was not a dance. Nor was it sparring. Herakleio didn't yet know enough to be capable of either. What he desired was contact, a way of exorcising the demon residing in him, given life by his fear that the metri might die, leaving him alone and perhaps unnamed; leaving him to deal with the only man on the island who might comprise a threat.

I gave him that contact until he was gasping, flooded with sweat even as the wind dried it; until he bent over in a vain attempt to regain a full complement of air within his lungs. Eventually he let the blade fall and stood there, bent, panting, hands grasping thighs to hold himself upright.

At last he looked at me. "Water," he rasped. "There." A flopping hand indicated a jar set atop the wall next to one of the potted torches.

Too weary to walk, was he? Or simply accustomed to giving orders?

Or, possibly, offering it to me because I was sweating as well.

Before I could decide which it might be, someone else took up the jar. I knew those hands; knew the woman who settled the jar against one hip as she stepped over the wall.

Herakleio, looking up at last, saw her and knew her, too.

She had put off the long linen tunic and wore for the first time since leaving the ship the garb I knew best of all: pale leather tunic embroidered with blue-dyed leather laces at the hemline, neckline, and short, capped sleeves. The sheer linen tunics of Skandi left little to imagine, but somehow this tunic, even made of heavier leather, gave the impression of nakedness far more than Skandic garb suggested. For one, the hem hit Del at the midline of her thighs. That left a lot of leg showing, long limbs that were, for all their femininity, sculpted of muscle refined by the circle, by the requirements of a life built upon survival in the harshest dance of all. And though the arms had been bared before by the Skandic tunics, now it was clear they matched the legs. The context had altered.

Del is not elegant, not as it might commonly be described. She is too strong for it, too determined in her movements, which are framed on athleticism and ability, not on how such movements might be perceived by a man and thus refined as a tool to draw the eyes. Del didn't *need* elegance, nor a tool; she drew the eyes because of the honesty of her body, the purity of a spirit honed by obsession: the brutal need to be better, lest being lesser kill her.

She had braided back her hair into the plait most often worn when she stepped into the circle. The shadows upon her face were made stark in relief by flame and the movement of the light, the contours and angles of strong bone beneath her flesh sharpened beauty into steel. Herakleio, who believed he had seen Del that night in the winehouse, discovered all at once he had never seen her at all.

She took the jar off her hip and handed it to me, eyes locked onto Herakleio. It was a message, though he didn't comprehend it. I smiled, raised the jar to my mouth, took several swallows of cool, sweet water. Then lowered it and looked across at Herakleio, who now stood upright with his shoulders set back, forcibly easing his breathing into something approaching calmness. Beneath Del's cool gaze, being male, there was nothing else he could do.

I drank again, then held out the jar in Herakleio's direction. He would have to come get it. "Here. And I think I'll sit this one out, if you don't mind. The old man needs a rest."

Herakleio, who had taken the steps necessary to reach the jar, looked at me hard as he took it. It was clear to anyone's eyes that I was not in need of a rest; the daily rituals on Prima Rhannet's ship and here on the terrace had restored much of my fitness. "But if you sit this one out, there is no dance."

"This isn't a dance," I explained. "This is an exercise. In futility, perhaps." I grinned, offering the sword. "Del will take my place."

She accepted the blade, looked expectantly at Herakleio. Who still hadn't drunk.

"Her?" he asked.

"Me," she confirmed quietly.

"But—"

"Drink," she said, "or don't. But *move*. Waste no more time, lest you begin to stiffen. Because then you will be easy to beat, and I prefer a challenge. Nothing is gained otherwise; time is merely lost."

Herakleio's response was to stuff the jar into my arms, to turn on his heel, to stalk out to the center of the terrace.

"Fool," Del murmured, and followed.

Me, I sat down on the wall and drank some more, enjoying the prospect of seeing the Northern bascha beat the hoolies out of a big, strong young Skandic buck who was also an idiot.

Wondering, as I settled, if I had *ever* been so obnoxious as Herakleio Stessa.

TWENTY-SEVEN

DEL, IN SHORT order, took him to the edge and pushed him over. It was not difficult for her; Herakleio was not a weak man, nor without promise, but he didn't know what she knew, including how to *use* his body. He had the potential, but he'd never realize or utilize it. He was meant to be a wealthy landowner, one of the Eleven Families, and such things did not require the learning of the sword.

She did not overpower him. She did not tease him. She did not lure him into traps. She simply used the alchemy of ability, talent, training, and a splendid economy of movement. She is peculiarly neat in her battles, is Delilah, even in her kills.

Herakleio was neither a battle nor a kill, but he undoubtedly felt as though he'd lost *and* died by the time she finished with him.

As with me, he finally pulled up, shook his head so that sweat-soaked strands of hair flew, then flopped over at the waist.

Del took one step into him, slid a rigid hand between his arms, and jabbed him in the short ribs. "Stand up," she commanded. "If you want to win back your wind, give your lungs room."

Thus accosted, no one doesn't stand up. He jerked upright, scowled at her, then walked away to circle with his hands on his hips, head tilted back, sucking air.

Del turned to me, took three strides, picked up the water jar, walked back to Herakleio. "Next time, drink when water is offered. Only a fool passes by an oasis even when his botas are full."

I smiled to hear my own words quoted. Herakleio was less amused. He snatched the jar from her, took it to his mouth, tipped his head back to drink. Then he raised the jar higher, held it in both hands, and proceeded to pour what was left over his face and head. It splashed in a silvery steam upon the clean white tiles that had hosted and honed scraping bare feet.

Del watched, apparently unmoved. She was sweat-sheened and undoubtedly thirsty as well, but she pushed for nothing. She waited.

When Herakleio handed the empty jar back, there was challenge in his eyes. "Only a fool allows the enemy to drink when she herself has not."

"I am not your enemy, nor are you mine," Del responded, clearly unwinded. "This was not a dance, nor was it war or skirmish."

"What was it, then?"

"Lesson," she said simply. "What did you learn from it?"

He flicked a glance at me, then looked back at her. "Never underestimate a woman with a sword in her hand."

"Then you have learned nothing." Del turned abruptly and strode away from him. In one step she was over the wall, and disappeared around the corner of the house.

Herakleio was baffled. Eventually he looked at me. "Isn't that what she *meant* me to learn?"

"That's a bonus," I said. "But the point was for you to learn something from the engagement. One maneuver, perhaps; even one that didn't work so you *know* it won't work." I shrugged. "Did you?"

His expression was peculiar. "No."

"Then she's right. You learned nothing." I stood up, stretched briefly, gifted him with a lopsided smile. "What woman did you *think* I meant when you asked about my scar?"

He looked at that scar immediately, and had the grace to color. "Oh."

" 'Oh,' " I echoed. "Ah, well, now you know. And it's not like you're the first to dismiss her out of hand."

He ran an arm over wet hair plastered to his scalp. "Has she ever killed a man?"

"Men," I clarified. "And I never kept count."

He nodded absently, gone away somewhere inside his head. I watched him a moment, then smiled again and turned to step over the wall.

"Wait," he said. When I turned back, his expression was calm. "Tomorrow morning?"

"Tomorrow morning is likely *today*." It was a not so subtle reminder that he'd dragged me out of bed in the middle of the night. "Get a few hours' sleep, then we'll begin again. And this time, I suspect, you'll pay attention."

He nodded, looked down at his wooden blade, nodded again.

I left him there debating his abilities, and took myself off to bed.

Life continued in that manner for the next tenday, as they reckon time on Skandi. I worked Herakleio to a standstill, pointed out his failures, guided him into small gains. Without years of study he could never match me, but he was a quick learner and not unwilling, once he decided *to* learn. His temper flared now and again and he was not beyond hurling curses at me when impatience led him into folly that I quite naturally took advantage of, but for the most part he kept his mouth shut and did what he was told.

Del, too, took part, though he shied like a wary dog the first couple of times she went at him with the sword. Me he accepted as a true challenge because I, in addition to being male, was on other levels a threat, but Del, despite his acceptance of her expertise with the blade, was yet a *woman,* and though Skandic men were not raised to believe women were lesser beings, neither were they raised to learn the sword from one.

Herakleio's natural tendency with Del was to take his punishment instead of fending it off, which occasionally led to some measure of hilarity on my part, playing spectator; a certain focused and relentless determination on Del's; and utter frustration on his. I recalled how Nihkolara had made no sound nor attempted to escape the blows rained upon him by the metri that first day. It seemed on Skandi that women in authority were permitted complete autonomy in a given situation. And while ordinarily that might be the kind of thing Del appreciated, it didn't much aid her when her express desire was for Herakleio to fight back.

The rhythm of hours, of days, of sessions settled into a comforting discipline. Herakleio and I warmed up together, performed ritual exercises designed to train the body's reflexes and control, sparred briefly; then I set about showing him techniques and maneuvers; then Del came in to test his comprehension of what I'd explained and demonstrated while I stood apart to make suggestions and comments. We trained during the day, but also at night with the torches lighted, so the eye would not be prepared only for daylight.

Occasionally I'd step back in and correct Herakleio's grip on the leather-wrapped hilt, or show him a maneuver that might offset whatever it was Del had just done to disarm him, but most of the time I simply watched and critiqued as the young Northern woman and the young Skandic man moved closer to the dance.

Then, of course, I made the mistake of shouting out for Del to correct one of *her* maneuvers.

It was growing late in the evening and the torches fluttered in the breeze. She shot me such an outraged and venomous glance that I was moved to immediate defense. "Well, hey," I said, "there's no sense in letting you make mistakes either."

Herakleio, having learned one thing, held his stance and made no assumptions as to whether this incident was unplanned, or specifically designed to catch him off guard.

"Was it a mistake?" Del asked coolly. "Or merely a maneuver different from the one you might favor?"

As she lowered her sword to look at me, Herakleio

realized it was a true disengagement. He stepped away warily, out of her reach, but did not relax completely.

"I favor whatever might help you win," I shot back. "You'd have *lost* with that maneuver. You left yourself wide open."

"To whom? You?"

"To anyone with wit enough to see the opening."

"Then come test me, Tiger."

"No."

"Come on, Tiger. Show me. *Test* me."

"No."

Herakleio asked, "Are you afraid?"

"Stay out of this," I said grimly, "or you'll end up with more bruises than you already have."

"But if she's right—if her maneuver is correct for her and merely different from one *you* might use . . ."

I glared at him. "Ten days have made you an expert, I see."

He didn't flinch; but then, he wouldn't. "Ten days have taught me that each opponent may have his—or her—own individual style, and one had better learn to adjust one's own style to it at any given moment."

Well, I couldn't argue with that. But I sure wanted to.

"Tiger," Del said with admirable self-restraint. "I'm not saying you were wrong. Only that I did it intentionally. With specific purpose."

"That's all very well and good," I returned, "but you'd have ended up dead. Unintentionally dead, perhaps, but dead. And without specific purpose."

"Then come show me."

I glared at Del, then included Herakleio in it. "I don't want to spar with you. Even with wooden swords."

"Tiger, we have sparred *many* times! Even after the dance on Staal-Ysta, where we nearly killed one another."

Herakleio, leaping head-first into stupidity again, said, "I'd like to hear about that."

I set my teeth and ignored him, speaking only to Del. "The last time we danced was in the big rockpile in the

Punja, when you wanted to lure Chosa Dei out of my sword."

"Which I did."

"Del . . ." I shook my head. "We have danced two times with intent beyond conditioning one another. Once in the North on Staal-Ysta, because the voca tricked us into it—and both of us nearly died, as you pointed out. Then again a matter of two months ago, out in the desert, when Chosa Dei nearly ate me alive from the inside out."

"Yes," Del said.

"In both circumstances, it was far too dangerous for either of us. We're lucky we didn't die on Staal-Ysta—"

"Yes."

"—and lucky you weren't swallowed by Chosa Dei when he left my sword for yours—"

"Yes."

"—and each time the threat came to life *only* when we faced one another with blades."

"Yes," she said again.

I stared at her. "Well?"

Del smiled. "It means in each case that our skills have proved equal to luck."

"I would like to see it," Herakleio said seriously.

I rounded on him then, blistering him with every foul curse I could think of on the instant. I only stopped when I became aware of applause, and noticed both Del and Herakleio had turned away from me.

I shut up. There on the other side of the wall was the metri, being seated in a chair with Simonides' aid, and beside her two people: Prima Rhannet and her blue-headed first mate. The captain was applauding.

"*Foul* tongue," she said, grinning. "One might suggest it be cut out of your head."

"Care to try?" I asked sweetly.

"Oh, no," she returned, unperturbed. "I think not. But you *will* be tried, and by the woman Herakleio is so intent upon seeing dance against you. Which means he must believe she is better." Smiling, she gestured briefly at Nihko, who bent and lifted something from the ground at his feet.

Swords.

He set them lengthwise precisely atop the wall, then took a single step away as if to repudiate any link to them. The message was clear: these were the swords the metri had hired them to find, so Del and I could enter the circle to settle my term of employment.

I looked at the metri. There was little resemblance to the ill woman I had seen in bed. Her hair was pulled off her face and gathered into a variety of plaits and loops, secured with enamel-and-gold pins. She wore a tunic and heavy beaded necklace; also a loose robe that billowed in the breeze. She sat quietly in the chair, arms folded neatly across her lap, but her expression was severe.

"Now," the metri said, "let it be settled, this argument of service."

"Here and now," I said skeptically.

"Indeed."

I looked from her to her servant. "How is she?"

He seemed to understand I asked him because she would not give me the truth, even if she answered. "Well enough," he said.

"Much improved," the metri snapped, clearly annoyed. "Now, be about it. If you win, you may be excused from service beyond our original agreement. If she wins, you will stay on an additional length of time to be decided by me."

I shook my head.

The metri looked at Nihko. "Make him."

Nihko looked at me. "I can."

Del threw down her wooden blade. "I want no part of this. I agreed to dance with Tiger, but I will not do so if he is forced. It abrogates the honor codes and oaths."

"*What* 'honor codes and oaths'?" Prima asked scathingly. "He's his own kind of ikepra. He has no such thing."

"We make our own," Del declared, stung. "He and I, between us."

Herakleio hooked a foot beneath her wooden sword and scooped it into the air, where he caught it easily. "Then do so," he suggested. "The metri has hired you.

You accepted. Is that not honor? And *dis*honor if you refuse?"

Prima's tone was sly. "You renounced your honor, Sandtiger; she has not. Do you expect her to break all of her oaths simply to be with you? Or has she none left *because* she is with you?"

The terrace was round, but we were cornered anyway. Del and I did not even bother to look at one another. They had found the holes in our individual defenses and exploited them perfectly.

I took up the blades from the wall and handed one to Del. Her eyes searched mine, asking the question.

In answer, I walked to the center point of the terrace. It wasn't a proper circle, but our minds would make it one. I leaned, set down the weapon with a faint metallic scrape, turned my back on it and paced to the wall farthest from the spectators. Torchlight filled my eyes; I half-lidded them against it.

Prima's tone was startled. "Don't you want to practice first? To test the blades?"

Del walked deliberately to the center, bent, set her sword alongside mine. Rising, she asked, "Why? If they are meant to break, they will. But I doubt that's what you want."

"Indeed not," the metri said testily. "This is to be an honorable engagement."

Herakleio grinned widely. "Then perhaps you would do better to excuse the Sandtiger. He has none."

"Enough," Del said sharply, taking position across from me.

I didn't look at Herakleio, but he knew whom I meant. "Say it."

But it wasn't Herakleio. Nihko said, "Dance."

Feet pounded, gripped, slid against tile; bodies bent; hands snatched, closed; blades came up from the ground. They met, rang, clashed, scraped apart, clashed again as we engaged. The blows were measured, but not so restrained that no damage would be done if one of us broke through. There is no sense in pulling back when one intends to win, or if one intends to learn. To do so alters the dance into travesty, with nothing learned and thus nothing gained even in victory.

We tested one another carefully. Last time we'd met it hadn't been sparring, hadn't been a contest to settle a complaint, but a dance against the magic that had infested my sword, that had wanted me as well. I had lost that dance, but in the losing I won. Del lured Chosa Dei out of my blade into hers, then purposefully broke her ji-vatma. We had not since then set foot in any kind of circle, being more concerned with surviving a journey by ship.

Now here we were, off that ship at last and on the soil of what I'd begun to believe actually was my homeland, dancing for real at the behest of a woman who had no idea what it meant to be what we were.

Or else she knew very well and used this dance to prove it.

The night was loud with sound, the clangor and screech of steel. As always, with Del and me, there was another element to the object, an aspect of the dance that elevated it above the common. We were that good together. In the circle. In bed.

—*step—thrust—spin—*
—*catch blades—catch again—*
—*slide—step—thrust—*
—*parry—again—slash—*

It was a long dance, one that leached from us all thoughts of the metri, her intentions, of Prima and her first mate, of Herakleio and his attitude. As always, everything else in the world became as water against oilcloth: shed off to pool elsewhere, while inside the circle, our dwelling, we stayed dry, and warm, and so focused as to be deaf and blind. But we were neither of us deaf *or* blind; we marked movement, responses, the slight flexing of muscle beneath taut flesh; heard the symphony of the steel, the rhythm of our breathing, the subtle sibilance of bare soles moving against stone.

—*slash—catch—scrape—*
—*the shriek of steel on steel—*

Walls of air, the metri had called it. My home was

built of walls I fashioned in the circle, because only here could I define myself, could I find my worth in the world. *Only* here had I become a man. Not in the use of my genitals, a use once copious and indiscriminatory; nor in the language of my mouth, sometimes vulgar, always ready, but inside the heart, the soul. Inside the circle I was whatever I wished to be, and no one at all could alter that.

Except me.

And I had.

One day at Aladar's palace, when I had broken all the oaths.

"No—" Del said.

I grinned.

"Tiger—"

I laughed.

With an expression of determination, Del tried the move I'd chastised her for.

"Oh, Del—" Disgust. I couldn't help it. Because now I had no choice. I broke her guard, went in, tore the hilt from her hand. "What did I *tell* you?" I roared. "Did you think I was joking? That kind of move could get you killed!"

Furious, she bent and retrieved the sword. "Again."

"Del—"

"*Again,* curse you!"

Again. As she insisted.

I stepped back, renewed the assault. Saw Del begin the maneuver again. I moved to block it, break it, destroy it—and this time something entirely different happened. This time it was *my* sword that went crashing to the tile. And I was left nursing a wrenched thumb.

"What in hoolies was that?" I asked.

"The reason I created that maneuver."

"But I defeated it the first time."

"Not the second."

"You'd have been *dead* the first time. There wouldn't have been a second."

"Maybe," Del said, "maybe not. Not everyone fights like you."

"No one fights like me," I corrected with laborious dignity, then shook out my thumb.

"Shall I kiss it?" The irony was heavy.

I bared my teeth at her. "Not in front of witnesses."

"Stop," the metri said.

I turned toward her, startled by the hostility in her tone.

"You must begin again," she declared.

"Why?" I asked.

"One of you must win. Decisively."

"I did win," I explained. "I disarmed her."

"Then she disarmed *you.*"

I shook my head. "That doesn't count."

"Why not?" Del asked.

I shot her a disbelieving glance. "Because I'd have killed you. I broke your pattern. You'd be dead."

"But I broke *your* pattern the second time."

"Finish it," the metri commanded. "One of you must win decisively."

I displayed my thumb. "I have a slight disadvantage."

"Poor baby," Prima cooed.

The metri was relentless. "Is it not true that such impasses are settled in the circle?"

"Yes, but—"

"Then settle it. Now."

I glanced at Nihko. "I suppose you'll *make me* if I don't agree." A thought. "Or will your little ring protect me from your power, and therefore this threat is nothing but a bluff?"

But Nihko made no response. He wasn't even looking at me. He looked beyond me, beyond the wall, beyond the torchlight that bathed the terrace in gilt flickering swaths of ocher and ivory and bronze. I saw the whites of his eyes, the pallor of his face; saw with disbelief as he began to tremble.

"Sahdri," he whispered, as if the word took all his breath.

The metri stood up abruptly from her chair. "You are not to be here! You and your kind are not to be here!"

I spun then, even as Del did, and we saw beyond the torches, walking softly upon the wall, a barefoot man in night-black linen.

And then I realized his feet were not touching the stone.

TWENTY-EIGHT

"YOU ARE not to be here!" the metri cried. "This ground is mine; you profane it! You soil it! You are not to be here!"

The man atop the wall—no, the man *floating above* the wall—paused, smiled, lifted a hand as if in benediction. Rings glinted on fingers, in brows, in ears, depended from his nostrils, pierced the flesh of his lower lip. In guttering torchlight, his shaven head writhed with blue tattoos.

Ah. One of *those*.

His tone was immensely conversational, lacking insult, offering no confrontation beyond the fact of his presence. "But I *am* here, because I choose to be here. And your tame ikepra can wield no power against me, even if I permitted." His dark eyes were rimmed in light borrowed from the flame. "Nihkolara Andros, you have been gone much too long. We have missed you. You must come back to us." For all the world like a doting relative.

A shudder wracked the first mate from head to toe. And then he dropped to his knees, bent at the waist, set his brow upon the ground. In clear tones, he said, "I cannot. I am ikepra."

The multitude of rings glinted in torchlight. "Forgiveness is possible."

Nihko shuddered again, hands digging into the soil. "I am ikepra."

"Forgiveness is possible," the man—Sahdri—repeated. His language was accented, but comprehensible. "You need only come with me now and begin the Rituals of Unsoiling."

"Come with you where?" I asked, since no one else seemed willing to.

The light-rimmed eyes turned their gaze on me. I wasn't sure if the illumination came from the torches, or from the eyes themselves. "IoSkandi," he answered. "Where people such as the great and gracious metrioi of the gods-descended Eleven send us all to die."

I glanced at Prima Rhannet. I expected her to speak, but she offered nothing. She stood there, locked in silence, staring at the priest-mage as her first mate knelt to him in abject obeisance.

"Well," I said finally, "it doesn't look like *you* died."

"That hour will arrive. Just as it shall arrive for Nihkolara Andros." He inclined his head toward the kneeling man. "He has returned, you see, and now is ours again. Or shall be, when he understands what lies before him, and what he is to do."

The metri too was trembling, but not from fear. "Go," she said thickly. "This man has guest-right."

The irony in his tone was delicate. "*This* man? Here?"

"This is business of the Stessoi," she said with a curtness I had never heard in her. "You are not of this family, nor do I grant you guest-right. Unless you and the others have forsworn all rites of courtesy in the Stone Forest, you know what you must do."

"Depart," he said with evident regret. "I had hoped for a cup of fine Stessa wine."

If possible, she stood a little straighter. "Save you steal grapes from the vines themselves, no wine of my vineyards shall pass your lips."

"I am desolate." But his gaze had shifted again to Nihko, who still knelt in the dirt. "You have a fine ship, Nihkolara," he said gently. "Surely you can find your way home again."

At last, Prima's voice. It scraped out of her constricted throat. "He *is* home."

Rings glinted as he lifted an illustrative finger. "His home is ioSkandi. It has been so since the day he understood what he was; was *made* to understand by such as the metrioi and the Eleven, who will not tolerate such as he, such as me. He has no place here. He came willingly to ioSkandi and embraced the service of the gods."

"He left," she said. "He *left* you."

"And so became ikepra, and abomination." His tone was matter of fact. "He was tolerated when he lived on your ship upon the seas, but he spends more time now on the earth. And so, according to the laws of the Eleven, he must be sent to live with us." He spread his hands gently. "Is this not so?"

"He has guest-right," the metri repeated tightly.

"For how long?" the priest-mage countered. "Shall you have him live among you as a Stessa? But no. Shall he go to the Palomedi metri, whom he insulted by bedding her daughter while he also bedded her? But no. Shall he go to his own folk, the Androsoi?"

From his position in the dirt, Nihko cried, "No!"

"There." The man nodded. "He knows his place."

"He's mine," Prima declared hoarsely.

Sahdri looked at her and smiled. "But he was mine first."

"Look," I said, "I'm not exactly sure what's going on here, but the metri has asked you to leave. Just when do you plan to do it?"

And he was *there,* before me, his breath warm against my face. I hadn't seen him move from the wall to the terrace. Hadn't seen any indication he would.

"Who are you?" the priest-mage asked.

I opened my mouth, shut it. This was magic, living, breathing magic in the body of a man, encompassed by no more than fragile flesh. He *stank* of power. By rights I should be spewing my dinner across the terrace, but Nihko's brow ring, still attached to my necklet, was doing its task.

Sahdri saw it. Saw me. Smiled. "Are you vermin, that I should squash you?"

The metri's voice rang out. "He is my grandson."

Every head, including mine, whipped about. I heard Herakleio's inarticulate cry of outrage, Prima Rhannet's hissing indrawn breath; saw the smoothing of Simonides' face as he donned his servant's mask.

And for some strange reason, the metri's announcement frightened me.

Nihko still knelt against the ground. Not even for such an unexpected declaration would he raise his head in Sahdri's company.

The priest-mage himself bowed in my direction. *"Kallha nahkte,"* he murmured, and the torches blew out.

I blinked into the sudden darkness, aware of the man's absence. "What did he say? What was that spell he spoke?"

Darkness was replaced with the pale, soft luminance of moon and stars, a glow from lamps inside the household. Nihko lifted his dust-powdered face from the dirt. "He said 'good night.' "

Only Del was detached enough from the emotions of the moment to find that amusing. I heard the expulsion of breath in brief, smothered laughter, glanced at her; saw how she immediately set her face into bland innocence. She met my scowl with a guileless smile.

I shook my head, drew in a deep breath, looked at the metri. "Nice timing," I said. "Do you think it worked?"

Her face wore its customary mask. "The truth often is of great effect."

Herakleio, who had been gripping the two wooden practice blades, hurled them down. They clattered against the tile. Even in muted illumination I could see how high the color stood in his face. "Truth," he snarled. "Truth, is it? *Why?*"

The metri answered steadily, "Truth is truth."

His cry was anguished. "You would put him in my place?"

She was unmoved. "No more than I would put you in his. The place is the place. The proper man shall be put in it when I am certain of his worth."

Oh, she *was* the stone, as she had told me less than a month before. Hard, sharp, brilliant, and scintillatingly shrewd.

"Let's start over," I suggested. "I take it our unexpected visitor is someone with connections to our friendly first mate?"

Nihko had risen. Having recovered much of his equanimity now that the priest-mage had departed, he glared at me. "One holds one's tongue when in ignorance, lest one lose it."

I saluted him with the sword, letting moonlight like liquid run down the blade. "Any time you like."

"Stop," the metri said. "We are done with this tonight."

"Done?" Herakleio's chopped-off bark of laughter contained no humor. "I should say we have *begun* this tonight!"

Prima Rhannet seemed to have no interest in Herakleio's concerns. Her attention was fixed on Nihko. "What can Sahdri do? Take you? Against your will?"

Grimly he said, "IoSkandics have no will. IoSkandics set no foot upon the soil of this island once one *is* of ioSkandi. We live in the Stone Forest."

"But you did set foot," she said. "This time. You've always stayed aboard ship before. But you never said *why*—"

He cut her off. "It does not matter."

"But it does, Nihko—"

"No. A brief amount of time is tolerated. More is— not." He looked at his hostess, lowered his eyes, inclined his head. "Metri, I thank you for the guest-right."

"We have unfinished business," she stated crisply. "Until it is finished, the guest-right shall apply. And then you will remove yourself from my home and my land *immediately.*"

The flinch was minute, but present. Nihko kept his head bowed and murmured an answer in Skandic that apparently suited the metri, for she simply turned away with a gesture at Simonides for his aid.

"Wait," I said, and she paused. "What happens now?"

Her mask was in place. "I have now claimed you my grandson in front of witnesses as well as a priest. He may be ioSkandic, not of the proper Order, but he serves the same gods. It has been said, and so it is."

"And—?"

Her brow creased slightly. "And you will continue to do what I have bidden you do. Teach Herakleio to be a man."

That worthy's breath hissed between clenched teeth. *"Metri—"*

She looked at him. "And you will do whatever I say you shall, without question, without hesitation, no matter what it may be. That is the term of *your* service."

All the tendons stood up beneath his flesh as he fought not to shout denials and curses at her. When he spoke, each word was squeezed out with such immense precision that I expected his head to explode. "If it is to be sword-work, then I will have the woman train me." His gaze shifted to me. "Because she is better."

Prima gulped a laugh. Nihko arched an eyebrow. I merely blinked.

It was Del who answered the intended insult. "Sometimes," she said. "Some days, some moments, some particular movements. Other times, not."

I nodded consideringly. "That about sums it up."

So, we had robbed him of that small revenge. Stiffly, Herakleio bowed to the metri, then took himself off.

"Well," Prima said when his shape was swallowed by darkness, "I would not wish to share *his* winehouse to-night."

I smiled across at her. "Or his bed?"

The captain met the gambit. "Oh, it might be worth it. Herakleio in a temper . . . indeed, it might be worth it." She fixed me with a bright, challenging eye. *"You* might even enjoy it."

"Go to bed," the metri commanded; and then, surprising us all, added: "Anyone's bed," and gestured for Simonides to escort her into the house.

"Well," I said after a moment of startlement shared equally by the others, "at least my grandmother isn't a prude."

Prima smiled sweetly. "That must mean the blood runs true."

I scoffed. "Blood? I think not. She used the tool she

had at hand: information designed to throw off that other blue-headed priestling for the moment." I looked hard at her first mate. "Who in hoolies *is* he? And what's he to you?"

Without a hint of irony Nihko said, "Secret."

I clamped my jaws tightly even as Del asked, "Need we be concerned?"

Prima shrugged. "Why should you?"

"Because we are here," Del answered steadily. "Because priests and mages often take an interest in people and topics seemingly unrelated, with dramatic effect. Because he looked at the brow ring hooked onto Tiger's necklet, and recognized it. It was then and only then that he offered a threat to Tiger. Therefore I ask, need we be concerned?"

"No," Nihko said coldly, even as his captain's expression stilled to a feral blankness for a brief, stark moment before settling once again into its normal expressive mobility. "All that concerns you now is how soon the metri will announce her heir before the priests—the *proper* priests"—he made it a derisive label—"and the assembled metrioi."

"Yes?" I invited.

"If it's you," Prima drawled, "you will inherit all the wealth and power of the Stessoi. Centuries of wealth and power." Her smile was arch. "And all the dreams you ever dreamed will come true."

"And what about *your* dream?" I countered. "Aren't you done here yet?"

"We have guest-right," Nihko snapped.

"And just what does that entail?"

Prima's smile shifted into unadulterated triumph. "It means every metri in the city must pay me respect *to my face*. It means I will gain a reputation that surpasses my father's."

"I thought you'd already accomplished that part," I retorted. "You steal men, their coin, their ships; he sells them."

Her smile vanished. But before she could answer, Del cut her off. "We're not on board your ship anymore. You can't tell us to leave the household of the woman who has now announced before witnesses she is his grandmother."

"That's right," I said brightly. "I guess I'm the one who can tell *you* to leave."

"It is not your household yet," Prima shot back.

Nihko's voice was cool. "And who says you will survive to inherit?"

With one deft move, Del tossed her sword to the first mate. Steel flashed, arced; he caught it without thought, hissed startlement, then stared at her. "Settle it," she suggested. "Man to man, here and now. In this circle."

Oh, thanks is what I wanted to say; my wrenched thumb ached dully. But I knew better. I just waited for Nihko's answer.

"I will not dishonor the metri," he said. "But, of course, I merely referred to the illness of her heart. Who is to say her grandson has not inherited its weakness?"

Double-edged blade, that. And we all of us knew it.

Prima took the sword from him, shoved its hilt toward Del. "The metri bought it for you. I suggest none of us dishonor her."

"Ah," I said sagely, "there must be some form of terrible punishment if you kill the heir of a metri."

"Sometimes," Nihko said gently, "one need not be killed to suffer the worst punishment."

Ikepra. Borjuni. We both knew the truth in his statement.

For the second time in the space of one evening, I saluted him with my sword.

Prima made a sound of disgust. "Men," she said, her sidelong glance aimed at Del. "Why is it they can fight, and then immediately be friends again? They waste a perfectly good grudge that way."

Del's eyes glinted even as her mouth twitched, and I knew none of us was going to kill one another.

Tonight.

TWENTY-NINE

FROM BESIDE me in bed, Del spoke quietly into the darkness. "You're awake."

"So are you."

"But I *was* asleep. I don't think you've slept since we came to bed."

"Long night."

"Full night," she emphasized dryly. Then, "*Is* this what you dreamed of?"

From my back, I stared hard at the ceiling I could not see. "I dreamed of no such thing in the hyorts, or even when I slept beneath the stars after a beating."

"A sandtiger," she said softly. "And freedom."

"Never beyond that. Never beyond the moment *of* freedom, when I could walk away and know myself able to make my own choices about my life."

"And now?"

"Now I'm no more free . . . no, it's not the same and I don't mean it to be, but she said something, something about responsibility, and the acceptance of it marking adulthood."

For a moment Del was silent. Then, softly, "The metri is a strong woman."

"But is she right?"

"About responsibility and adulthood?" Del sighed, shifted onto her back so that we lay side by side and flat, shoulders touching. "Taken of itself, I believe she is. Children live for their freedom, for the moment their tasks are done—if they have any—so that they may make choices about their lives. Of course, those 'lives' comprise the next few moments, little more . . . but the impulse is the same. *To* be finished, so they may be free."

When she fell silent, I prompted her. "And?"

"Adults understand that freedom must be earned, not given by someone else."

"No?"

"No. We set ourselves the tasks, we execute them, and we are free then to accept other tasks."

"What has this to do with the metri?"

"The metri decides *for others* what she believes are the tasks that must be completed. For the benefit of her house."

"In other words, she doesn't permit anyone of her household—or in her family—to seek out their own tasks. And thus no one of the—Stessoi?—is truly free."

Del tilted her head toward me. "I think the metri believes no one is strong enough to hold her place unless he be as she is."

"Ruthless. Cold. Hard."

"Is she?"

"Ruthless? Yes. Hard? Absolutely. Cold?" I fell silent. Then, "I can't say so. Because passion drives her. Her ruthlessness and hardness is framed on a passion for her household and the future of the Stessoi."

"Does Herakleio have it?"

"From the sound of it, Herakleio has enough to illuminate the island!"

"That's lust," Del countered. "Youthful passions, yes; he has never been permitted to grow beyond them. But the passion requiring coldness and ruthlessness?"

"Not yet," I answered slowly.

"You?"

We both knew the answer to that. "You're saying if I employed it now, she would hand me the household and the future of the Stessoi."

"She would expect you to *take* them."

"And Herakleio?"

Del lay very still beside me. "The first ten times you and he spar with live steel, be very careful."

"And the eleventh?"

"By the eleventh, either he will have acknowledged that you will always defeat him . . ."

"Or?"

"Or you will be dead."

In a matter of ten days, Herakleio had learned he had the body, the reflexes, the power, to be what I was. In a matter of moments, in the face of the metri's announcement that I was her grandson, he had learned he needed the mind and determination as well as the body. Because he believed now the metri favored me, and the only way he might regain that favor was not to replace me, but to *become* me.

The implications of this conviction astonished me. Not the motivation—the metri played us all like counters on a board; not the impetus—she had moved him to precisely this position on that board. But that he understood and acknowledged what it was she wanted *of* the game, and that she justified her approach because she believed it required.

And it astonished me also that he accepted it instead of railing against it as a spoiled godling might.

Herakleio may not have believed in her certainty for himself. But clearly he had done more than merely exist in the metri's household; he had learned her mind. Until now, apparently, he had never attempted to invoke and employ that knowledge. Until now, apparently, he had never felt the need.

Beyond the mechanics of technique, a sword-dancer is not required to know why an opponent moves the way he moves. Only *that he does* move, only *when he will* move, so he may anticipate and counter that move, or remove the potential for it before the idea of the move exists within the opponent's mind.

Herakleio asked for Del. He did it with premeditation, and with a deliberate shrewdness I hadn't anticipated. My opponent had won the initial pass; my first move was countered before it occurred to me I might need to make it.

He asked for Del not because he believed it would hurt me if he believed she was better—he was, surprisingly, less petty than he was clever—but because Del of anyone in the world knew best how to fight me. Knew best how to defeat me.

This move made him better than clever, and therefore dangerous.

I'd made the mistake of not judging Herakleio shrewd enough to see the option. I did not make the mistake of assuming he'd offer no contest if it came to a dance with the Stessa legacy on the line, nor did I make the assumption he could not win. Because on any day, in any circle, any man might win.

Or woman.

Abbu Bensir, on our first day in the training circle beneath the implacable eye of the shodo of Alimat, had made such assumptions about a boy with fewer than twenty years to his twenty-five; with weeks at Alimat when Abbu boasted years; with a wooden blade in a hand that had not yet wielded steel.

Abbu Bensir had lost that dance and nearly his life.

While I, in disbelief as the man lay choking from a partially crushed throat, asked what manner of magic had stood in my place, because surely there was no other way I might have defeated Abbu.

The shodo, an immensely patient and practical man, had upon the instant lost all patience and told me in no uncertain terms the only magic any man needed was that of his mind and heart; that no other existed, lest he weaken that mind and heart by setting crutches beneath them.

From that day forward the only magic in my life had been pure skill, determination, and the technique to employ both using the context I understood: I was born to and of the sword, and no other power would ever control me beyond my ability to *use* the sword.

I didn't believe Herakleio could defeat me. But neither had Abbu believed I could defeat him.

And so I won the second pass, because I accepted as truth what another might, in disbelief, name falsehood. I would not be defeated by an accident of misassumption, but by carefully constructed design, correct execution— and luck.

Technique, timing, talent. Two could be taught, refined. One could only be born. But talent without focus, without determination, without obsessive need, is wild, unchanneled, and therefore diluted. Easier to be defeated. Easier to succumb to the ravages of emotion, of excess passion, instead of controlling and using the power that could fuel technique and timing.

Del, who had more insight about people than anyone I knew, was training Herakleio. Del, who had an even greater insight into the workings of my technique, timing, and talent, was teaching Herakleio how to comprehend and counter all three.

And unlike anyone else, he had the physical tools to do it.

Unlike anyone else save Del. Who *had* done it once in a circle on Staal-Ysta, even as I had done it to her in the self-same circle.

We were a long time removed from that circle and the circumstances that put us into it. But the bones remembered. The flesh recalled. The mind retreated from the brutal honesty of that dance, because in its unyielding purity it had nearly killed us both.

And each day, as Herakleio learned from Del, he also learned from me. It was a task set before me by the woman who was, she said, my grandmother; who wanted to put into her place the man best suited to it; who believed the acceptance and execution of the task marked a boy's passage into manhood. Herakleio and I, nearly two decades apart in age, were nonetheless children in the eyes of the woman who was agelessness incarnate. And in the completion of the task, we each of us would have embraced her convictions if for differing reasons: Herakleio to prove he was worthy of her place; and *me* to prove he was worthy of her place.

It wasn't me she wanted. It wasn't me she needed. Herakleio was and always would be both. And therefore Del taught him, and therefore I taught him, so that on the day we met in the circle it would be a proper dance according to the honor codes that lived in our own souls.

I knew of men who would swear I was mad to teach my opponent. But if I didn't, if I merely watched him learn, I learned *his* abilities without offering him the same opportunity in return. That was dishonest. If I taught him with intent to sabotage his efforts, that was dishonest. Because I was already better. And the shodo had taught me to be honest in all things to do with the dance.

I knew of men who would blister Del with oaths and suggest she depart at once. But I didn't do either, because that, too, was dishonest. Del made her own decisions. Her honor was unassailable; it was one of the things I most admired and respected about her. And my honor—as *elaii-ali-ma,* as borjuni, as a Southron ikepra—was nonexistent.

In the circle, the sword-dancer with the mind that sees and creates potentials, that manufactures opportunity, is the one who wins. Anyone may kill another by stealth, by deception. But only one who invokes the honesty of the circle may call himself a sword-dancer. Because it was the circle and its inherent codes that bound our souls. No one who stepped inside could deny that, because the circle was the arbiter of our survival.

The dance Herakleio and I undertook would be honest in the extreme, because though I had the advantage of years of training and experience, he had the advantage of a peculiarly dangerous truth.

If Herakleio won, he won. If Herakleio lost, he won.

If I lost, I died.

Because I wouldn't kill Herakleio, but I believed he would kill me. And so my next move was obvious.

I stood up from the terrace wall and asked Del to halt their current exercise. It was afternoon, we were slick with sweat. Del had bound her hair back into its habitual braid, and Herakleio had tied a length of leather around his brow so wind-blown locks would not obscure his vision.

I nodded at Del, smiling, and offered a blade to Herakleio. A *steel* blade.

Once he'd have shut his hand on the hilt immediately. Now he waited. "Why?" he asked warily.

I hitched a shoulder lazily. "Only so much you can learn with wood. After a while you get complacent. Bruises sting, but they don't kill."

He nodded his head at Del. "Then *she* will show me."

I shoved the pommel of the sword into his flat belly. "Take it, boy."

It stung, as I meant it to. Color stained his face. Anger brightened his eyes as he took it as I intended: with simmering contempt. "So, you will skulk around for table scraps and wait for the metri to die no matter how long it takes."

I shrugged again. "Not like I'm a total stranger. I *am* her grandson."

"Herakleio," Del said sharply. "Be aware of what he's doing."

I shot her a glance that told her to back off. Del scowled back, telling me she refused. Herakleio, for his part, stared at me angrily, then shut his hand around the hilt. He settled the matter for us by turning to set the blade onto the tile in the center of the terrace.

"Stop it," Del hissed at me. "This is too soon."

"*He* can stop it if he wants."

"You're making it impossible!"

"All it requires is a little self-control." I saluted her with my blade. "Care to step out of the way?"

"Tiger—"

"Go," Herakleio told her. Then, belatedly, "Please?"

It was the first polite word I'd heard out of the boy. Del was no more happy for his request than she was with my suggestion, but she got out of the way.

Herakleio stood a pace from the sword he'd set upon the tile. "Well?"

I stepped to his blade, then on it. And set the tip of mine against his throat. "First mistake," I said. "You assumed this was a dance."

He lifted his chin, stretching flesh away from the steel. I let the tip drift idly up to follow. "This is how it begins," he declared. "I watched you and the woman!"

"That was a dance," I told him. "This is not. This is a lesson."

"Lesson—" he began furiously.

I hooked a foot beneath his sword, scooped it upward, caught and deflected it directly at Herakleio. He was quick enough to catch it, but in the doing of it he incurred a scratched throat from my blade. Blood trickled in a thin ribbon of crimson.

I smiled, stepped away a single pace. "Now," I said gently, and set to with my sword.

It took very little time. Very little effort. He had a firm enough grasp not to lose the sword at once, but there was no grace in his movements, no technique in answer to mine, merely desperate self-preservation. I chased him across the terrace, against the wall, *over* the wall and a good ten paces beyond before I finally took pity on him and ended it with a trap that broke his guard, caught the sword, snatched it out of his hands. I stood there before the panting young man with a hilt in each of my hands, both tips coyly resting on his shoulders. On either side of his neck.

"Lesson," I said. "Two swords are better than one. And if you can't keep yours, be certain the other man will take it."

Without waiting for his response I lifted the blades from his shoulders and turned to go; stopped briefly as I saw the woman on the terrace but a pace or two away. I heard Herakleio's hiss of humiliation; he knew she had seen the ease of his defeat.

I met the woman's eyes steadily. "Your move, metri."

She understood. She knew now that *I* knew. And it altered the strategy.

"Go," she bade me. "Herakleio and I have something to discuss."

I'll just bet they did. I raised eyebrows at Del, who turned and preceded me into the house as the metri and her kinsman discussed the repercussions of abject defeat.

THIRTY

DEL HAD the grace to wait until we were on the threshold of our room. "He is good, isn't he?"

"*Oh,* yes." I smeared a forearm against my forehead beneath a shock of too-long hair. "And getting better in a hurry. Why else do you think I did it?"

She nodded. "Scare tactics."

"A little intimidation is good for the soul. It makes you cautious before complacency can set in." I set the swords atop the linens chest, then took up the waterjar set on a small tiled table and unstoppered it.

Del waited until I was halfway through a swallow. "And sets back his training so you have more time to hone your edge."

I choked, turned away lest I lose control of the spray and soak her with it. Once I'd completed the swallow, I managed, "That obvious, am I?"

"Not to him; he doesn't know you well enough." She shook her head. "I didn't expect this of him, this attention to detail. Not yet." She paused. "If ever."

I handed her the jar. "And here we are so nicely helping him along."

She drank, handed it back. Her eyes were guileless. "You are not Abbu, Tiger, so full of complacency you forget to be cautious. And Herakleio is not you. He won't take you by surprise."

"You just never know what anyone . . ." But I let it go as the echoing sound of voices intruded. Vigorous, un-

317

happy voices just this side of anger and full of throttled consonants and hissing sibilants, trying not to shout.

"Prima Rhannet," Del said.

"And Nihko Blue-head." I turned toward the open door to listen more closely; not that it mattered, since I couldn't understand them anyway. The voices grew louder briefly, then fell away as if the captain and her first mate had moved from the hallway to another room.

"Discord," Del said, "And unsubtle."

"Subtle enough even if audible," I retorted. "Neither of us speaks Skandic."

"Others here do."

I shrugged. "Then I guess everyone but you and I knows what the quarrel is all about."

Del sat down on the edge of the bed. "But there was one word I did understand. A name."

"Sahdri." I nodded. "Wouldn't you like to be a mouse in the floorboards?"

Del said dryly, "Only if I was a mouse who spoke Skandic."

I smiled. "I know a mouse who speaks Skandic. A mouse who also speaks a language I can understand. I think maybe it's time I paid a visit to the person who is truly in charge of the household."

Del frowned. "You think the metri will tell you?"

I paused on the threshold. "Not the metri. She only gives the orders. Someone else entirely makes things *work.*"

I tracked down Simonides in a tiny suite of rooms, numbering two. A petite sitting room, a room beyond holding a bed. It was a spare, unadorned chamber of little exuberance but much meticulous tidiness, like the man himself.

If he was startled to find me on his doorstep, he made no indication. But a family servant knows how to express no emotions at all unless he is bidden to do so, and I was not the metri to bid him to do anything.

I had come full of questions, full of demands for explanations. But now that I was here, I hesitated. Even as Simonides gestured invitation and stepped aside to allow me entry, I could not cross the threshhold.

A slave's privacy is hard-won. I had claimed none of my own among the Salset, except for inside my head. This man had a place within the household, and rooms within the rooms. I robbed him of that privacy with my presence.

He read my face, as a good slave will do. One learns to survive by recognizing what even a blink portends, the slight tilting of the head or the tension in the mouth. He knew what I was thinking. And for that reason, his second welcome was warm.

This time I stepped across. This time I was more than a guest in the house, or even the metri's heir.

He set out a bowl of fruit, a small jar of wine, two shallow dishes. Poured them full, then motioned me to drink. I raised my dish in tribute to his courtesy, then sipped the vintage grown on the metri's lands. It was very good wine.

I told him then what I had come for, what had provoked my curiosity. He listened in silence, making no attempt to answer before he understood precisely what I wished to know, and why. And when I was done giving him all my reasons, he told me what he could.

It wasn't enough. But it was a beginning.

———————◆————————

It took a while to hunt her up, but eventually I found Del in the bathing pool. I couldn't remember a time when either of us had spent so many consecutive days in the water—especially considering I couldn't swim!—but I'd discovered it was a pleasant way to pass the time. Being clean was nothing to scoff at, but hanging about in warm water was far more relaxing than I'd ever contemplated.

Too bad the South didn't have enough water to build bathing pools like this.

Then again, wasn't my idea for channeling water from places it was to places it wasn't the means to afford us such luxury?

Hmm. Worth considering, that.

I added my clothing to Del's heap of same and slipped over the edge, trying not to splash too much. My skin contracted at the first touch of warm water, then relaxed. It felt good.

It felt *wonderful*.

Maybe I needed to learn how to swim.

Del, who had elbows hooked over the side and her chin resting atop flattened palms, turned her head to speak over her shoulder. "Well?"

I leaned back in the water, wishing I could float the way she could. But that required the ability to lift one's foot off the bottom without immediately sinking. "IoSkandi is an island a half-day's sail from here. The only people who live there are the priest-mages, like Sahdri."

"And Nihko."

"The 'Stone Forest' is what people call Meteiera, a place on the island full of great stone spires. The priest-mages live in and on the spires, in caves and nooks and crannies, or in dwellings built on top."

"On top?"

"On top."

"How do they get up there?"

"I don't know."

"What do they do there?"

"That I know: worship and serve the gods," I answered, "and grow crops and raise livestock, and—"

"On top of the spires?"

"The worship-and-serve part takes place on top of the spires. The growing-crops and raising-livestock part takes place down below, in the valley."

She shrugged. "Sounds peaceful enough."

I went on with my unfinished line of discussion. "—and otherwise examine, learn, refine, and implement the magic that makes them mad."

"Oh," Del said.

"It kills them eventually, according to Simonides. The madness—and magic—manifests at a particular age, and while they *can* learn to control both, it's only for a while.

Maybe ten years. Eventually the madness wins, and they die."

"Just—die?" Del was intrigued. "How?"

"They hurl themselves off the top of the spires."

Intrigue was replaced by shocked horror. *"Why?"*

"To merge with the sky."

"What for?"

"That's where the gods live. The best way to truly join the gods is to give oneself to them. Literally."

"But . . ." Her expression was perplexed.

"But," I agreed. "No surprise, is it, that everyone thinks they're mad."

"How do they explain the bodies smashed to pulp all over the ground?"

"Don't know that they bother."

"But if the bodies are smashed, they haven't merged with the gods."

I grinned. "I think it's considered merging in the strictly spiritual sense."

"Ah."

"Ah." I sank down so the water lapped at my chin. "No one really knows all the details of what goes on in Meteiera," I explained. "Simonides says it's a combination of rumor, speculation, and winehouse tales. The metrioi—I found out the 'oi' is the plural, by the way—don't talk about it at all because it's considered terribly dishonorable if anyone in the Eleven Families manifests this magic."

"But if they are gods-descended themselves, doesn't this mean a few of them might be considered more so?"

"That's one interpretation," I agreed. "Except the metrioi don't much like it. They consider madness a flaw of a rather extreme sort."

"So they send away to ioSkandi anyone who manifests this magic."

"And promptly delete from the family histories—and the histories of Skandi—any mention of these people."

"Unfair."

"Being utterly removed from existence and any memory thereof? I would say so."

"But what has any of this to do with Nihko setting foot on the earth?" She paused. "I think that's what the priest-mage said."

"It is. Simonides tells me that because the ioSkandics are themselves cast out of 'polite society,' if you will, they compensate by making up even *stronger* rules governing the behavior of anyone living in the Stone Forest."

Del nodded. "When excluded, become even more exclusive."

"Exactly. So if a man who has already been deleted from his family then leaves ioSkandi, he is considered abomination—ikepra—for turning his back on his fellow priest-mages and the gods."

"In other words, live with us and die in a few years, or leave us and die *now*."

"More or less."

"So Nihko left ioSkandi and became ikepra, but so long as he didn't set foot on the earth of Skandi itself, the ioSkandic priests didn't care."

"They cared. There just wasn't anything they could do about it."

"But there *is* something they can do about one of their own coming back here to Skandi?"

"The people of Skandi don't want to have anything to do with their mad relatives. But they won't kill them; they consider themselves a civilized society." I grinned derisively. "They have no problem with priest-mages coming back to the island briefly, so long as it's only to gather up the occasional lost chick now and again."

"So they can take that chick back to the henhouse of other mad chicks."

"And feed it to the fox."

"Dead is dead," Del said.

"Exactly. As long as the mad little chicks are *gone,* the civilized Skandics don't care what becomes of them, whether they die voluntarily merging with the gods, or are hurled off the spires after the Ritual of Unsoiling. Which of course means that even if the chicks don't want to merge with the gods quite yet, they can forcibly *be* merged. After the proper ceremonies."

"The choice therefore lies not in deciding to die, but in deciding the time and manner."

"Hurl yourself, or be hurled," I agreed. "Of course, it's not 'dying,' bascha. It's 'merging.' "

"Semantics," she said disparagingly. "Tiger—this is barbaric. It makes no sense. There is no logic in it."

"Only if you're mad."

"So this Sahdri has come here to gather up Nihko."

"And take him back to ioSkandi so they can clean him up and dump him off one of the spires."

"No wonder he doesn't want to go."

"No wonder he lives on board a ship." I blew a ripple into the surface of water. "If you don't set foot on Skandi, you're safe from Skandic repercussions and *io*Skandic retribution."

Del contemplated this. Eventually she said, "Not a comfortable way to live."

"And a less comfortable way to die."

"But so long as Nihko has guest-right, Sahdri can't take him."

"You'll recall Prima asked that very thing: could Sahdri *take* Nihko."

"Who dismissed the possibility."

I shrugged. "Nihko seems not to want to talk about any of this."

"Well," Del said, "he's been tossed out of his family, and then tossed *himself* out of this fellowship of men who think they can toss him into the sky. I don't know that I'd want to talk about it either."

"And the metri has made it clear as soon as her business with him is finished, the guest-right is revoked."

"What *is* her business with him?"

"I'm assuming it's connected to this whole discovery-and-recovery-of-the-missing-heir issue," I said. "We don't know what kind of bargain Nihko drove on his captain's behalf before presenting me as the long-lost grandson."

"Which you are."

"Which I *maybe* am—but am as likely not."

"Maybe."

"Maybe." I tilted my head back, let the surface of the water creep up to surround the edges of my face. "I don't think it really matters."

"You can't be certain of that, Tiger."

I sighed. "No. I can't read the woman."

"So she may well *mean* you to inherit."

"Maybe."

"Maybe."

"And then there's Herakleio," I said, "who stands to lose more than any of us."

"Who's 'us'?"

"You, because of me. Me because of me. Prima Rhannet. Nihkolara."

"Why do you include them?"

"Because the connection is there. It's like a wheel, bascha—the metri is the hub, and everyone else is a spoke. But the spokes fall apart if there is no hub, and then the wheel isn't a wheel anymore. Just a pile of useless wood."

"So you believe there is more to it than a simple reward for finding the long-lost heir."

"I have a theory." I smiled, staring at the arch of the dome high overhead. "And I don't believe 'simple' is a word the metri knows."

"What is your *complicated* theory?"

I had sorted the pieces out some while back. Now I presented them to Del. "That I am a threat to all of them for very different reasons."

Del, understanding, began naming them off. "The metri."

"Either I am or am not her grandson; either way, it doesn't matter. It's Herakleio she wants. If I remain, I'm a threat to him."

"Herakleio."

"Obvious. I repeat: if I remain, I'm a threat to him."

"Prima Rhannet."

"If I'm *not* the metri's long-lost heir, Prima loses out on whatever reward it is she demanded."

"And Nihkolara?"

"The same applies to him as to his captain, but there's more . . ."

She waited, then prompted me. "Well?"

"I just don't know what it is."

"If his captain lost the reward, he'd lose his share."

"That's the most obvious factor, yes. But I think there's more." I shrugged. "Like I said, I just don't know what it is."

"Maybe," Del said dryly, "it has to do with his chances of being flung off the spire. So long as you're accepted as the metri's grandson, he's got guest-right. He's safe from Sahdri and his fellow priest-mages who'd like to forcibly merge him."

"Maybe that's it," I agreed. "But I still believe there's a piece missing."

"And once it's found and all the pieces are put together?"

I stood up in the water, let it sheet off my shoulders. The name for the unflagging unease was obvious now.

Expendability.

"Once it's found, they'll kill me."

THIRTY-ONE

THOUGH CLAD again in the leather tunic, Del dripped all the way to the room we shared. She hadn't done much in the way of drying off, and her hair was sopping. "We *will discuss* this," she declared, following. "You can't announce they'll kill you, then let the subject drop."

I was considerably dryer than Del and less inclined to drip, which I had no doubt Simonides and the household staff would appreciate. "I'm not expendable *yet,*" I told her, striding along through room after room and doorway after doorway. "At least, I don't think so. But I'm just not sure there is more to say right now."

"Tiger, *stop.*"

I recognized that voice. Accordingly I stopped just across the threshold of our room, turned to her, and waited.

Rivulets of hair dribbled water down the leather. Her eyes were fierce as she came into the room behind me. "We have to come up with a plan."

"I'm listening."

She gestured. "Leave?"

"We discussed that before. No one will hire on to sail us off the island, even if we had the coin *to* hire them."

"Give up your claim?"

"I never made a claim. The metri made it for me; everyone else just *assumed* I wanted to be heir."

"Give it up anyway," she said urgently. "Reject the

metri outright. Say you aren't her grandson and you want to leave."

"Yes, well, there's a little matter of this 'term of service,' remember? The metri is likely our only way off the island, and she's not about to arrange it for us until she's accomplished whatever it is she wishes to accomplish, or I've accomplished for her whatever it is she wants me to accomplish for her."

"Herakleio?" she suggested. "Wouldn't he help? If you said you'd voluntarily give up any claim on the metri, would he help us get a ship?"

"Can he?" I shrugged. "He has no coin of his own, remember."

Del answered promptly. "He can borrow against his inheritance."

"But could he do that, and would the metri allow him to inherit if he did?"

She glared at me. "Do *you* have any ideas?"

"Play the game out."

Del was annoyed. "What game?"

"The metri's game. Give her what she wants until I see an opening."

A movement in the hallway. Del and I turned to see Prima Rhannet coming to a halt at the threshold. "I am your opening," she announced.

I looked her up and down, purposefully assessing her. "And just how is that?"

There was neither amusement nor irony in her expression. Only determination. "I need your help."

"How precisely is that *our* opening?" Del asked icily.

Prima shot her an angry, impatient glance, then looked back at me. Her expression was, oddly, guilty. "I have drugged Nihko."

That was pretty much the last thing I'd ever thought to hear exit her mouth. "You've drugged your first mate?"

She glanced over her shoulder furtively, then stepped into the room and shut the door with a decisive thud. Ruddy hair spilled like blood over her shoulders. No doubt about it; she *was* feeling guilty. Through taut lips, she said, "I gave it to him in his wine at dinner, while you took your ease in the bathing pool."

The imagery was amusing. "And is he therefore unconscious with his face in the plate?"

Prima, who was not amused, set her teeth so hard jaw muscles flexed. "He is unconscious in bed in our room," she said with precise enunciation, then let it spill out of her mouth in a jumble of words as if to say it fast diluted some of the guilt. "I want to get him back aboard ship as soon as possible, and I need your help for that."

"Why can't he just *walk* aboard ship?—that is, if you hadn't drugged his wine," I added dryly. "Isn't it his home?"

Her expression was bitter. "So long as the metri has extended guest-right, he will not leave. He honors her for her courtesy." Something glinted in her eyes that wasn't laughter. It was, I thought, a desperate pride. "You know nothing about him. You have no idea what manner of man he is—or what they will do to him."

Oh, yes, I did. "Throw him off the spire," I said quietly.

It shocked her that I knew. For a moment she stood very rigidly, staring at us both; then she set her spine against the wood of the door and slowly slid down it until she sat loose-limbed on the floor, staring blankly at the wall. I recalled the evening we'd sat so companionably upon the floor, the wall propping us up, as we shared a winejar.

"I will not lose Nihko," Prima said finally, voice stripped raw of all but her fear. "I could not bear it."

It wasn't love, not of the sort that bound many men and women. But it was a binding in its own way: friendship, companionship, loyalty, respect, admiration, dependence on one another for the large and small things, even the dependence to *not* depend, but to share in the freedom to do what they would do and be what they were. The slaver's daughter and the castrated ikepra had filled the empty spaces in one another's souls.

"A bargain," I said.

The captain looked up at me. "What do you want?"

"A way off the island."

She nodded at once. "Done."

Del scoffed. "And sacrifice what you came here for? What you brought Tiger here for?"

Pale eyes glittered with a sudden sheen of angry tears. "My father kept me fed by selling men. I would rather starve than sell Nihko."

I sat myself down on the floor and leaned against the bedframe. "Have you a suggestion as to how this might be managed?"

Her tone was steady. "You must ask the slave to get us a molah."

She meant Simonides. "And you believe he would do that."

"For you, he will. You were as he is: a slave. He has accepted his fate; you defeated yours. He will do this thing if you ask it."

I drew in a tight breath, expelled it carefully. "You seem to think you know us very well, the metri's servant and me."

Her smile was wintry. "I know slaves. And men who were."

"All right." Del sat down on the edge of the bed. "Let's say Tiger gets a molah. What then?"

Prima, seeing we were not entirely dismissing the idea, spoke rapidly and forcefully. "We put Nihko on the molah and take him down to the harbor. Once on board ship, we will sail. All of us." She spread her hands. "And you will be free of the metri, and Nihko free of Sahdri."

I considered it. "Might work," I agreed at last. "There's just one thing. One minor little detail.

Prima frowned impatiently, clearly eager to implement the plan.

I reached beneath the bed and slid out two swords, handing one up to Del. "It's a trap," I said gently.

The mouth came open slightly in astonishment, then sealed itself closed. As color drained from the taut flesh of her face, the freckles stood out in rusty relief. Something more than anger glinted in her eyes; there was also comprehension, and a bitter desperation.

"It is not," she declared, and pressed a hand flat against the floor as if to lever herself to her feet.

She did not rise after all, because Del and I were across the room with blade tips kissing her throat.

"A trap," Del said.

Prima Rhannet did not move again, not even to shake her head.

"Well?" I prompted.

"It is not," she repeated.

"Prove it."

Her eyes were cold as a Northern winter. "Go to my room. You will find Nihko there—"

"—lying in wait for me?" I grinned, shook my head. "Do better, captain."

Her words were clipped off between shut teeth. "Then we will *all* go to my room, and find Nihko there unconscious in the bed."

Del read the slight shift of my weight. We moved a step away, and I gestured Prima to her feet. A second gesture indicated she was to turn around, which she did. I pulled from her sash at the small of her back the meat-knife she carried—she wore no sword—and tossed it back onto our bed, then nodded. Del sank her left hand deep into the captain's red hair and wound a hank of it around her wrist.

"Don't want to be running off quite yet," I said lightly, and opened the door with my sword at the ready.

The corridor was empty. We proceeded down it, me in the lead and Del bringing up the rear with Prima just before her linked by hair, certainly close enough that a blade could slice through her spine or into her neck with little effort expended. It was not a comfortable position for the captain to be in, head cranked back on her neck, but she made no complaint. She merely indicated the proper door once we reached it.

I nodded at Del, who stepped against the far wall with Prima in tow. Then I stood to the side and quietly pushed the door open.

Sure enough, Nihko lay facedown on the bed, limp and unmoving.

"Just so you know," I said conversationally, "Del is prepared to cut your captain's spine in two the moment you move."

He didn't move. I approached slowly, blade poised. I could smell the wine, and a faint, sour tang of something I didn't recognize.

I thought about his magic, and how I'd reacted. Thought about the brow ring hooked to my necklet. Bent and clamped one hand around his wrist. He was alive; I felt the beat of the pulse against my hand. But he did not move.

I set the flat of the blade against the back of a thigh, bared by the short tunic. "And I'll cut *your* spine in two the moment you move."

No answer. No movement.

I carefully insinuated the edge of the blade between thumbnail and flesh. Sliced.

From the corridor, Prima Rhannet hissed her objection. But Nihkolara Andros did not so much as flinch. All he did was bleed.

I straightened, stepped away, glanced briefly at Del. "Take her back to the room. Keep her there. I'll go have a discussion with Simonides."

Prima's face lighted. "You will help?"

"I think it's likely this may be our only opportunity to get off this island." I jerked my head at Del. "I'll be back when I've made arrangements."

It was quite late when we met Simonides in the courtyard. Nihko, bowed across my back and shoulders like a side of meat, was slack and very heavy, and I thought I stood a good chance of rupturing myself before the night was through. But the molah waited for us in the deeper shadows, safe from prying moonlight, and with relief I heaved the body onto the beastie. The first mate sprawled belly-down, hands and feet dangling; I'd been hauled around the countryside in similar fashion a time or two myself and knew very well what he'd feel like when he roused: rubbed raw across the belly, hands and feet swollen, and head pounding from the throb of so much blood pooling inside the skull. And no telling what the drug would do to him.

Which didn't bother me in the slightest, in view of how often I'd surrendered the contents of my belly merely for being in his presence.

Prima complained that Del should release her. "Not yet," I answered, making sure Nihko was tied firmly onto the molah. I didn't relish the thought of picking him up from the ground if he tumbled off. "First things first."

Simonides himself stood at the molah's head, insuring the animal's cooperation and silence. Once Nihko was trussed to the beast, I stepped back and nodded. Del released Prima, who went immediately to check that he still breathed.

I looked at the servant, slim and silent in the darkness. "You're sure you won't be punished."

"The household is my responsibility," he answered. "The metri does not keep count of her molahs, or how often one goes out or comes in. Herakleio took a cart to the city earlier this evening to drink in winehouses; this will not be remarked. She will believe you simply left Akritara."

"Walking," I said dryly.

Simonides' expression did not change. "You are all of you uncivilized barbarians. I shall have to have the priests in to cleanse the household. It will be very costly."

Prima, satisfied Nihko would survive his uncomfortable journey, went to the molah's head and took its halter rope. "No more talk," she said, and tugged the animal. It stretched its neck, testing her determination, then grudgingly stepped out. She turned it to the front gate.

Del, at my nod, moved quickly to cut Prima off.

"You stay," I told her softly. "*I* will take Nihko to the ship."

She was outraged. "I will not—" But she shut up when Del's sword drifted close to her throat.

"You stay," I repeated. "You and Del will be Simonides' guests in his rooms until word is brought by one of your sailors that Nihko and I are safely on board, and I'm certain the trap isn't waiting for me down there. Then and only then will Del permit you to leave. Simonides will escort you both out of the house, and then you'll join us on the ship." I grinned at her toothily. "Call it insurance."

Prima was furious. "This is not a trap!"

"Prove it," I challenged. "Do this my way."

She stared at Nihko's slack body, then jerked her head in angry assent once and stepped out of the way. I traded glances with Del, promising renewed acquaintance later, then took the molah's halter and led it out of the gate.

Behind me, very quietly, Del ordered Prima to *move*.

Aside from a certain residue of tension, it was quiet and not unpeaceful as I led the little molah along the track from Akritara to the city. Simonides had offered me the use of a second molah, but I'd decided borrowing one was enough; the metri's servant was already risking himself. Besides, I'd found it more comfortable to stretch my legs and stride than to be jounced atop one of the little beasts, even if it was faster to ride.

Around me stretched baskets of grapevines huddled like worried chicks against the soil. Illumination was provided by the full moon and wreaths of stars. The breeze tasted of saltwater, smoke, and soil, but also of molah, wine, sweat, and the bitter tang of the drug the captain had used on her first mate. Nihko had not yet so much as snored, nor stirred atop the molah.

I wondered what Prima would have done had we refused to help. She was a small woman; and I'm not certain even Del, much taller and stronger, could have managed him this slack and heavy. Likely the captain had believed she stood a better chance of gaining our aid if the first mate was already unconscious, but it was amusing to paint a mental picture of Nihko in the morning, in very poor temper, confronting Prima Rhannet after awakening in the metri's guest bed, attempted abduction in vain. I suspected the confrontation aboard the ship would be no friendlier, but at least Prima would have the consolation of knowing she'd gotten Nihko away. Otherwise he'd still be in the metri's household and subject to Sahdri's claim once the guest-right was rescinded.

It crossed my mind also to imagine the metri's reaction when she learned we were gone. I didn't for a moment believe I was truly her grandson; she was enough of an accomplished opportunist to use the tools at hand, and I was one she could employ for multiple reasons in as many circumstances. I had no doubt anymore that I was Skandic; that seemed certain, in view of how closely Herakleio and I resembled one another, or Nihko and I, or even Nihko and Herakleio. But the Eleven Families did not have the monopoly on bastardy; they'd simply managed very cleverly to transform it into some kind of family honor instead of insult. Some Skandic man—possibly even a renegada—had sailed to the South and there impregnated a woman; I was the result. Wanted or unwanted, exposed or stolen, it simply didn't matter. It made more sense that I wasn't the metri's gods-descended grandson; especially since I knew very well I wouldn't live long enough to inherit. Herakleio was her boy.

And *he* wouldn't weep when he learned we were gone.

Ahead of me the land fell away. I saw clusters of lamplight glowing across the horizon, crowning the edge of the caldera. The molah and I plodded our way into the outskirts of Skandi-the-City, winding through narrow roads running like dusty rivulets across the top of the cliff. The winehouse district was ablaze with candles and lantern light. In one of them—or possibly in some alley awash in molah muck—was Herakleio, oblivious to the fact his legacy was safe.

I shook my head, then turned as I heard a thick-throated groan from Nihko. A brief inspection convinced me he was not likely to recover full consciousness any time soon, but neither was he as drug-sodden as before. His body didn't like where and how it was even if his mind was unaware of the offense.

I led the molah out of the streets to the track along the cliff face near the steep trailhead. Far below lay the waters of the harbor, all but one of the ships denied to Del and me by the metri herself, who wasn't, for whatever reason, finished with us yet. All it wanted was for me to lead the molah down the precarious trail to the blue-sailed renegada ship, deliver him, send someone after Prima, then wait for Del and the captain to appear. Which gave me the rest of the night and likely part of the day to somehow survive.

Nihko groaned again, stirred again atop the molah. The weight abruptly shifted; the molah, protesting, stopped short. I turned back to check on the bonds holding the first mate on the beastie, saw the half-slitted green eyes staring hazily at me in the moonlight, the shine of brow-rings.

"Go back to sleep," I suggested cheerfully, setting a shoulder under his and heaving him over an inch or three. "You don't want to see this next part."

He mumbled something completely unintelligible and appeared to do what I said. The eyes sealed themselves. Smiling, I turned back to take up the molah's headstall again—

—and there was a man in front of me.

Three men. Five.

A whole swarm of men.

Ah, hoo—

Something slammed into the small of my back and then into my ankles, driving me to my knees against the molah even as I reached for the sword hooked to my sash. Hands were on me, imprisoning me, digging into shoulders, throat, hair, wrists, dragging me away from the little animal with its load of Nihkolara; a knife threatened the back of my neck as I was forced to kneel there, head held by dint of a handful of hair snugged up tight, much as Del had imprisoned Prima Rhannet. But they didn't kill me immediately. They just *held* me.

Then they began to strip me of my clothing.

"Now, wait—" I managed, before an elbow was slammed into my mouth. The next thing that came out of it was blood.

It is somewhat disconcerting to be thrown down in the dirt as men strip the clothes off your body. It is even more unsettling when they also inspect all of your parts, as if to make certain you're truly a man. At the first touch of a hand where only my own or Del's ever went, I heaved myself up with an outraged shout expelled forcefully from my mouth, and made a real fight of it.

Something caught at my throat. My necklet. I saw the gleam of a blade in the moonlight, gritted teeth against the anticipated stab or slice even as I heaved again, roaring, attempting to break loose of the swarm. The necklet of claws pulled briefly taut, then, released, slapped down against my throat. And then abruptly everything in my body seized up as if turned to stone, and I fell facedown into the dirt.

"Throw him over," a familiar voice said in a language I understood.

I wanted to tense against the hands that would grasp, lift, heave. But nothing worked. Nothing at all—except my belly. Which relieved itself with vivid abruptness of the meal I'd eaten earlier.

Ah, hoolies, not *this* again.

"Throw him over," the voice repeated, and I heard a muttered complaint from Nihko.

From the dregs of darkness, from the misery of my belly and the helplessness of my body lying sprawled in muck left by molahs, goats, chickens—and me—and through a haze of blood, inhaling that and dust, I dimly saw the naked body on the ground grasped, lifted, heaved over the cliff. It fell slackly out of sight before I could even blink.

Thoughts fragmented as I saw the body go. The first thing through my mind: *Prima was right*—

Or else it was as much a trap for Nihko as for me.

Herakleio—?

But why would he have *Nihko* killed?

Then someone touched cool fingers to the back of my neck and I went down into darkness wondering if Nihko was conscious as he fell, and if I would wake up before I hit the bottom.

THIRTY-TWO

*T*HE SHADOW *passed across
the cliff, flitted down the sheer face with its convoluted
track folding back upon itself from harbor to clifftop. A
bird.*

*The shadow soared, circled, returned, drifted closer.
The body was a body, but broken. The skull was pulped,
the face smashed beyond recognition, limbs twisted into
positions no limb was supposed to go; nowhere was it
whole.*

The shadow fled across the body, turned back.

*It had been heaved over the edge near the track, but
not on it; and so the body was not immediately visible
from any angle. Bereft of clothing, the brown skin
blended with the soil, the rocks, the small plots of vegetation trying valiantly to cling to the cliff's face. No human
eyes beheld it, but animal nose smelled it. It was too soon
for rot to set in, but the odor of death was something
every animal recognized, and avoided. Unless it was a
carrion-eater.*

*Molahs were not. And so when a string of molahs
being led down the track rebelled, their molah-man called
out to another man to search lest a body be found, some
drink-sodden fool fallen from the cliff after stumbling out
of a winehouse; it had happened before. And so men
looked, and the body was found. It was remarked upon
for its nakedness, for the scars on its body, for the ruin of
its face and skull, but it was not recognized. It might be
one of them. It might not. But it was indisputably dead.*

The bird, deprived of its meal, soared east away from the caldera, crossed the ocean, crossed the valley, found other prey atop a stone spire piercing the sky, and there the bird drifted again, judging its meal.

And then of a sudden the bird stopped. Dropped. Hurtled out of the skies with no attempt to halt its plummet, and crashed into the body that lay sprawled atop the spire, naked of clothing, naked of consciousness; a shell of flesh and bone empty of awareness or comprehension.

The body opened, accepted the bird, closed again.

I awoke abruptly, startled out of senselessness into the awareness that I lived after all. I sat up, poised to press myself upright, saw the sky spin out from under me. I was conscious of a vast gulf of air, of a blue so brilliant as to be overwhelming, and the physical awareness of *nothingness*. The body understood the precariousness of its place even if the mind did not.

I rolled, flopped down upon my belly, realized an armspan away the surface beneath me fell away utterly into sky.

Stone bit into the flesh of my face. Naked, I was not comfortable. Genitals protested until I eased them with a shift of position, though I did little more than alter the angle of one hip. I breathed heavily, puffing dust from beneath my face. I tasted it. And blood.

Beyond one outstretched hand lay the edge of the world, such as what I knew. In that moment what I knew was what I felt beneath me, what I saw. Sky and sky. Nothing more.

I lifted my head with immense care. Rotated it so that my chin touched the stone. Saw the edge of the world stretching before me, its horizon distant.

Another rotation of the skull, to the left. Again, sky; but this time land as well: stone, and soil, and the scouring of the wind.

Even now it touched me, teased at my flesh, insinuated itself beneath the hollows of my body at ankles, knees, hips; the pockets under arms. It caught my hair, blew it into my eyes, altered vision. I saw hair and stone dust and sky.

My belly cramped. There was nothing to expel, but that wasn't the intent. From deep inside, rising from genitals, something *squeezed*.

I wondered briefly if it was fear.

As swiftly as it seized me, the cramp released me. Surely fear would last longer?

A tremor wracked me from skull to toes, grinding flesh into stone.

I shut my eyes, let my head drop. I lay there very still, save for in- and exhalations; was relieved to manage that much.

I knew where I was. I just didn't know why.

Meteiera.

Stone Forest.

IoSkandi.

Where madmen were sent to die, while they made an acquaintanceship with magic.

Not me.

Surely not me.

Wind crept beneath my body, insistent. It shifted the stone dust, drove it into the sweat-slicked creases of my flesh. I itched.

The tremor wracked me again.

I painted a portrait: me atop the spire. I lay at the edge; to my right, the world fell away. To my left, it stretched itself like an indolent cat, the bones beneath lean flesh hard and humped as stone.

It *was* stone.

This cat was neither indolent, nor stone. This cat was flesh, and afraid.

I painted a portrait. I knew where I was. Comprehended the risks, and where the dangers lay. To my right, an arm-span away. To my left, much farther.

The body gathered itself, rose onto naked buttocks, moved away from the edge of the world. It stopped when it sensed stone encompassing it: an island in the center of the sky. It sat there, arms wrapped around gathered knees, and made itself small.

Wind buffeted.

I shut my eyes against it. Hair was stripped from my face. Sweat evaporated as the wind wicked it away. Buttocks and the soles of my feet clutched at the stone.

All around me was sky, and sky, and sky.

And, according to io- and Skandic alike, gods.

It occurred to me, finally, to wonder why.

Why this?

Why not simply heave me over the edge of the caldera cliff, as they had Nihko?

Why *this?*

And then, belatedly, wondered how.

If there was a way up, there was also a way down.

I smiled then, into the face of the wind.

The spire's crown was not so small as I had initially believed. It was, in fact, approximately the surface area of two full circles, a good thirty paces across. This afforded me the latitude to move without fearing I'd fall off the edge: I'd spent half my life—or possibly longer—learning how to stay inside a circle, and *two* of them was a surfeit.

Eventually I stood up against the wind. I let it curl around me, buffet me, try to drive me down or off the edge. But I understood my place now, and how to deny the wind purchase. I used weight and awareness, and comprehension. I learned what to expect of it, to respect it, to use it. By the time I paced out the crown of stone I was no longer afraid of the wind, that it might blow me off into the sky.

By the time I had inspected every edge of the spire's crown, I knew no ropes existed.

As the sun went down, I sat atop the tower of stone and made note of the valley below, the distant glow of lanternlight, of cookfires. My spire was not the only one. I counted as many as I could see, clustered throughout the valley, suspecting there might be more beyond. No two spires were alike: some were thick, knobbed with protuberances, shelves, cave-pocked. In the dying of the day I saw light sprout atop other spires; saw the arches and angles of dwellings built there; the wooden terraces clinging to shelves and cave-mouths. As the light faded, plunging the valley into darkness, I lost definition and saw only the wavery glimmers of lanterns, the dark blocky bulwarks of stone against moon and stars.

There was no lamplight for me, no lantern, no cookfire. Only what I took for myself out of the luminance of the skies. Doubtless a priest-mage would say the moon and stars were a gift of the gods.

Before he merged with them.

I shivered. The sun took warmth with it, and I had no clothes to cut the wind. I was hungry, thirsty, and confused.

If there was a way up, there was also a way down.

Wasn't there?

Eventually I lay down atop the stone.

Eventually I slept.

In my dream Del found me. She sailed to ioSkandi, walked into the Stone Forest, came to the proper spire, found a way up and climbed over the edge to rise and stand beside me. We linked hands, stood together against the wind, and knew ourselves inviolable.

The touch of her flesh against mine granted me all the peace I knew, all the impetus for survival and triumph a man might know, were he to trust a woman the way I trusted Del. Together we stood at the edge of the crown of stone, arms outstretched, and let the wind have us. Let it tip us, take us, carry us down and down, where we walked again upon the earth as we were meant to do.

I turned to her, to embrace her, to kiss her, and felt stone against my mouth.

I sat up into wind, into light, and watched the day replace night. Dew bathed the spire, and me. Sweat joined it, welling up beneath hair to bathe my skull, my face; to sheen the fragile flesh stretched over brittle bone.

No food, no water, no way down.

Why *this?*

Why not a clean kill, a body tossed off the cliff?

I don't believe in gods.

I don't believe in magic.

I don't believe in the power of a man to float above a wall, to move without indication of it.

Yet I had witnessed the latter.

I had witnessed magic.

I had *worked* magic.

I don't believe in gods.

I believe in myself.

I put my hand upon the necklet of sandtiger claws, counted them out. None was missing. Only the silver brow ring Nihko had attached, and I had reattached when it came clear to me that no matter how much I wished to disbelieve in its efficacy against magic, it made every difference.

They had cut it from the necklet the night before.

No, the night before that.

Or the night before *that?*

How many days had I been here?

Two.

That I knew about.

Two, in which I was conscious.

Before that?

Before *that?*

I was hungry. Thirsty. Weakening.

More days than two.

How many?

Did it matter.

If I were to find a way down, it mattered.

If there were a way down.

How had I come up? How had they brought me up?

Sahdri. Sahdri, who could float above a wall, who could move across a terrace with no indication of it.

Sahdri's voice, bidding them toss the body over.

What would Prima say, to learn her first mate was dead?

What would Del say, to learn I was missing?

To learn I was dead?

More days than two.

How many?

How many left?

How long?

How many days before she accepted I was gone?

And unlikely to come back.

We had never, not once, discussed it. Because we knew, both of us, what was necessary. What I had done before, believing she would die; believing she was dead despite the breath left in her body.

I could not now recollect what emotions had led to that decision, had permitted me to leave her. Certainty that she was dead; certainty that to see that death would destroy me. But the emotions *of the moment* were long banished, and unsummonable. I recalled that I had felt them, but not how they felt beyond the memory of anguish, guilt, grief, and indescribable pain.

I had stood upon the cliff overlooking Staal-Kithra, lumpy with barrows, dolmens, and passage graves, and beyond it Staal-Ysta, the island in the glass-black lake flanked white-on-white in winter, stark peaks against bleak sky. I had bidden her good-bye; had apologized in my own fashion. Had thrust the sword's blade into turf, into soil, into the heart of the North.

I had named the sword to her, spoken that name aloud, so she would know it: *Samiel.* Now that Northern sword lay buried beneath Southron rock, drained at last of the sorcerer that had infested it. I was free of sorcerer, free of sword.

Free to die alone on ioSkandi, abandoned atop a towering spire punching a hole into the sky.

Piercing, one might hope with forgivable bitterness, the liver of the gods whom others worshiped by leaping off the spires.

That instant, with startling clarity, I knew. Understood what was expected.

I was *to merge.*

I wondered, with no little cynicism, who it was that collected all the bones found at the bottom, shattered into bits. Or were they simply left there, ignored, ground into ivory powder beneath the feet of priest-mages come to rejoice in the merging?

I tipped my head back and back, gazing up into the sky. For the first time since awakening atop the rock, I spoke.

"You're not mine!" I shouted. "You are *not my gods!*"

Because I had none. Worshiped none. Believed in none.

"Not!"

The wind whispered, *No?*

No.

No and no.

Had none, worshiped none, believed in none.

Gods, and magic.

Magic.

Had none, worked none, believed in none.

Liar, the wind whispered.

Gods, but I was thirsty.

And then I laughed. Because even a man who believes in no gods believes in the *concept* of them, believes that others believe. Or he would not rely upon a language that embraces the presence of gods.

Habit. Nothing more. One grows accustomed to others saying it, praying it, believing it. One need not believe it himself. One need not pray himself.

Would praying get me off the top of this rock?

The wind curled around me. *Hypocrite.*

Would magic get me off the top of this rock?

The wind asserted itself, but offered no answer.

Sahdri, who could float above a wall. Who could move with no indication of it. Who could require that Nihkolara Andros hurl himself off a spire to merge with the gods he had repudiated . . . but there had been no Ritual of Unsoiling, and thus Nihkolara Andros had *been* hurled. Not from the spire, not from ioSkandi where priest-mages served, worshiped, and went mad, but from the caldera clifftop.

Ikepra. Abomination.

What then was I?

I laughed again. "Fool."

The wind engulfed, embraced, tugged. I went with it; let it take me to the edge. I knelt there, supplicant to the sky. And refused.

A shadow drifted over me, across the spire. Unfurled wings. I looked up. Saw the bird. Felt something inside myself respond. My belly cramped. Genitals clenched. I bent at the waist, folding upon myself. Something within me stirred.

Grew.

Unfolded.

Felt *imminent*.

I shook upon the rock, knees ground into stone. Flesh stood up on my bones; the hair stood up on my flesh. Against my will my arms snapped out, palms flattened, fingers spread. Breath was noisy in my throat. Was expelled from my mouth, and sucked in again. Loudly. And as loudly expelled.

Sweat ran from me. I felt it roll down flesh; saw it splash against the stone. Every inch of that flesh itched. I knelt there, shuddering, aware of the rattling of my bones, the quailing of my spirit.

So easy to let go.

So easy to lean forward.

So easy to tip myself off the rim of the world.

So easy to fall.

So easy to *end*.

"Del!" I shouted. Louder, again, *"Dellllllllll!"*

She was my walls. My house.

Did Herakleio want her so badly?
So easy.
To let go.
To fall.
To end.

———◦┼————

Night found me there. Kneeling. Denying the gods. Repudiating magic.

Putting my faith in Del.
Find me.
Find me.
Find me.
Bascha. Please.
Find me?

———◦┼————

I lay atop the spire, spine pressed into stone. I was heavy. All of me, heavy. And yet it seemed impossible that I should be so, because there was no food, no water. Only wind. Only sun. Only endless skies, and endless days, and nights that fed me on stars.

In the South, I would have died days before. Here, with moisture in the air, with morning dew, with the breath of seawater against my flesh, death was tardy. But it came. The carrion bird above me, inside me, assured me of that.

Del hadn't come.
Couldn't.
Did not know where, or how.
Or even *if* I lived.

Had anyone else died atop the spire? Did the carrion bird feast upon the body, scattering the bones? Did the wind blow them off?

Could the wind lift a body?
Carry it?
Could the bird lift a body?
Carry it?
Could I rise and try the skies?

Flesh itched. Bones burned.

Emptiness abounded, save for the imminence.

I was glass, and I would break.

Lift me, carry me, drop me, and I would shatter.

Better *I* lift me. Better *I* carry me.

Better I shatter myself.

Hollowness.

Spirit honed to an edge no one could see, but it would cut; oh, yes, it would cut through the flesh before anyone knew.

And kill.

Cut. Slice. Pierce.

Like a sword.

I was a sword.

I *was* the sword.

The sword.

Conceived in the skies, of the metal made into steel; given birth above the earth.

Falling.

Falling.

Found later, and smelted. Folded. Hammered. Heated. Cooled in the waters, and blessed. And honed.

Wielded.

Jhihadi. Messiah. Slave. Sword-dancer.

Wielded.

Broken?

And heated again. Folded again.

Hammered.

Honed.

Wielded.

My eyes snapped open. I stared up into the skies, aware of but not blinded by the sun. A shadow passed across it, across me. Wings unfurled.

The noise I made sounded not unlike the cry of a carrion-eater.

I rose from the stone and stood upon it for the first time in days. Gazed upon the doubled circle and the world beyond it, the endless skies filled with wind, and gods.

And a bird.

Conceived in the skies, found later, and smelted. So

that the essence of *me* was retained, worked, heated and hammered and honed.

There was nothing left of me but steel.

Sword-dancer.

Dancer.

Sword.

Imminence was a *presence*.

Wings unfurled.

Shadow passed, darkening my eyes.

Heal me.

Anneal me.

Wings within unfurled.

Anneal me.

I stood on the edge of the spire and unfurled arms, palms, fingers. Felt the wind upon my flesh. Felt it enwrap, enfold, engulf.

Anneal me.

Heels lifted from the stone. Toes gripped. Clung. Balanced.

Anneal me.

Skull tipped back. Sun warmed my face; wind kissed it. Seduced, I let the lids drop closed; saw the red brilliance behind them, filling my head with light.

Comprehension.

Acknowledgement.

I poised there, a man at the edge of a stone circle, the only sword available the one I made of myself.

Shadow winged over me.

"Anneeeeeeeaallllll meeeeeeeeeeeeeee!"

No gods.

Only me.

Only me.

The shadow within unfurled.

The wind came again. I felt it in my eyes, my nostrils, my mouth; felt it enter throat and lungs and belly. Felt it bind my bones, so brittle, so hollow, so light.

And imminence *arrived*.

And power.

Comprehension.

Acknowledgment.

I whelped it there upon the rock; gave birth to the child I had carried for more than three decades, now labored in pain to bear upon the spire in the skies. The child I might have been had I been born in Skandi. The child thrown away in the sands of the Southron desert. The child I was never permitted to be; the child I never permitted myself to be. To conceive. To bear.

I whelped it there upon the rock and screamed out the pain and rage: that the choice was taken from me. Decades after the vessel had been shaped of a man and a woman, the child was born at last. The vessel was annealed. The flesh was strong enough at last to contain the child.

Oh, it wanted freedom!

I spun then and ran.

Ran.

To the edge of the circle.

The edge of the spire.

The edge of the world.

And beyond.

No gods.

Only me.

Leaping into the day.

The shadow passed across the spire, flitted down the sheer sides. A bird.

The shadow soared, circled, returned, drifted closer. The body was a body, unbroken. The skull was whole, the face recognizable, the limbs untwisted.

The shadow fled across the body, turned back.

It had leaped near the edge, and so the body was not immediately visible from any angle. Bereft of clothing, the brown skin blended with the soil, the rocks, the small plots of vegetation trying valiantly to cling to the spire's footing. No human eyes beheld it, but animal nose smelled it. The odor of impending death was something every animal recognized, and avoided. Unless it was a carrion-eater.

Molahs were not. And so when the molah pulling the cart rebelled, its molah-man looked, and the body was found. It was recognized for its nakedness, for the scars on its body, for the shape of its face and skull. It might be one of them. It might not. But it was indisputably alive.

THIRTY-THREE

SOUND. THE WIND, rustling vegetation. Lifting sand and dirt. The scratch of grit, rolling. The tickle of air in the hairs on arms, and legs, and head. I could hear it. *Hear* the hairs rising.

Could feel it.

Feel.

In a single spasmodic inhalation my lungs filled, expanded my chest; I was afraid to let it go again, lest it never be repeated.

My head was filled with light.

Breath whooshed out again. Came back, like a dog, when I called it.

I breathed.

Sound. The clink of stone on stone, the dig of hoof into soil, the whuffing snort of an animal.

And a person, walking.

Eyelids cracked. Daylight filled my eyes; I lay on my back. I saw the animal: molah. Saw the shape: male. Black against the sun.

The molah was stopped. The man tied its lead-rope to a scrubby tree, then came to me. Knelt down beside me. Inspected me, though he put no hands upon me.

"For forty years," he said, "you have been dead. Only now are you born. Only now are you whole."

Forty?

Had I so many years?

No one had known. No one had told me. All of it a guess.

Forty.

"Only now are you whole," he repeated.

I realized then he was speaking Skandic.

And that I understood it.

His smile was ironic. "I know," he said. "But now you comprehend what a newborn baby encounters. So much of a new world. So much to overwhelm it."

I opened my eyes fully. Saw the shaven, tattooed head; green eyes in sun-bronzed skin; the glint of rings in his brows.

"Dead," I said.

"You were," he agreed.

"You."

"Ah." The ironic smile deepened. "No."

"Saw it."

"You saw *a body*. It was dark, you were in some distress—and the magic was in your body, once they took this from your necklet." A finger indicated the healed cut where the ring had once resided; had been sliced out. "A body," he said. "Nothing more. A dead man, and convenient: your height, your weight, your coloring; we are all of us similar."

"You?"

"Me they pulled from the molah; I was in no position to argue."

No. He had been drugged to insensibility by his captain.

"Why?" I asked. "Why present a body?"

"Because of your woman," he answered.

Del?

"If she believed you lived, she would search for you. They wish her gone."

"Who?"

And how many?

"Sahdri, lest she come looking. The metri, lest she become what Herakleio desires. Prima, because—because she hopes in grief Del might turn to her."

"Who did this?"

"Any one of them."

"You."

"No."

Certainty. "Del will come."

"But she believes you are dead. Your body was found."

"Not mine."

"They believe it is yours."

"They?"

"The metri. Herakleio. Prima."

Disbelief was manifest. *"Prima?"*

He did not smile. "She believes you are dead. She is meant to believe it, as are the others."

"But she knows you're alive."

"No."

"No?"

"I disappeared."

"How convenient."

"They assume I am dead. They know you are."

"Not Del."

"And Del."

"No."

"They are priests," he said gently, "*and* mages. Do you believe a body would be found that did not resemble yours even in certain details?" For the first time he touched me. It was brief, impersonal, without intent beyond indication. "Here." The travesty of an abdomen reshaped by Del's jivatma. "And here." The claw marks graven deeply into my cheek. "Not much skull left, nor face, but enough for the scars."

"I don't believe it. Neither will anyone else." Certainly not Del. "Even a smashed body bears specific blemishes."

"They are mages," he said with infinite precision. "This is not beyond them. They simply lifted the scars from you and set them into another man's flesh."

It robbed me of breath. "Lifted—?"

"No scars," he said, "beyond those they left you. A dead man bears them. And so *you* are dead."

I wanted desperately to move, to lift a hand to my cheek, but the body betrayed me.

"Dead," he repeated. "To everyone who knew you."

"*You* know me."

Nihko smiled sadly. "But I am a priest, and I am a mage, and I am a madman."

"Ikepra."

"Not any more."

"*How?*"

"Payment," he said, "for this."

"For—?"

"This."

"This?"

"The first steps," he said, "following birth. You have ten years. Possibly twelve. You are a candle now, burning brighter and hotter than any other. You will consume yourself with the heat of your spirit, with the power in your bones. You have no time to crawl, but must be made to walk."

I lay sprawled against the ground, unable to move. "Am I—whole?"

"Better than whole," he answered. "Now you are *complete.*"

I knew what I was. "Sword-dancer."

Nihko said, "Not any more."

"I danced atop the spire."

"You had no sword."

"I *am* the sword."

"No."

"You can't take that from me."

"I will not. They will."

"No one can."

"You are a child," he said kindly. "The magic is wild. These are men who have learned its nature and how to control it. Trust me in this: you will do as they say, become what they decree."

"You didn't."

"And they would kill me for it."

"You're alive."

"Payment," he said. "For this."

I laughed then; was shocked that I could. "I'm dead. *Really* dead. This is not real. You're dead, and I'm dead, and this is not real."

"Well," he said philosophically, "I said much the same myself."

"And did you leap off a spire?"

Nihko's face was serene. "We all of us leap," he said. "It is how we know."

"Know what?"

"That the magic has manifested."

"To me," I said, "leaping off a spire suggests *madness* has manifested!"

"Yes," he agreed. "Any man may do so, and die of it. But those of us who survive are something more than simply mad."

"Magic," I said in disgust.

"Mages," he clarified. "Men who are made of it, and who learn how to wield it."

I stirred for the first time. The body—did not cooperate.

"Be still," Nihko said. "The body has used itself up."

"Used up—?"

"It was a circle," Nihko said, "for you. But in truth it is what each man makes of it. He learns himself up there, learns what and who he is. He must recognize it, acknowledge it, comprehend it, and employ it. Rely upon it. Use it up."

"Then if it's used up—"

"Gone," he said. "Extinguished."

"Then I *am* dead."

"The man you were. The slave. The messiah. The sword-dancer."

"No."

"You surrendered it in the circle. You *left* the circle. You flung yourself out of it."

"Elaii-ali-ma," I whispered.

"You are not what you were. You are what you will be. You are not *who* you were. You are who you shall be."

"Sword-dancer."

"Mage."

I laughed; it tore my throat. "Would you have me be a priest? Me?"

"You gave yourself to the gods."

"They aren't my gods."

"You gave yourself to gods, be they mine or yours."

"Semantics," I muttered.

"You survived," Nihko said. "You are what you are."

"Mad?"

"Indisputably."

"I don't feel mad."

"You don't feel anything. Yet. Come morning, you will."

"And what will I be in the morning?"

Nihko said, "Mage. And aware of it."

I shut my eyes. I did not echo him. I named myself inside where no one else could see.

"Mage," he repeated.

Sword-dancer, I said.

In, or out of the circle.

In the morning I wasn't a mage. I was merely a man sick unto death. Fever burned my bones, wasted my flesh, turned my eyes to soup in their sockets. Lips cracked and bled. A layer of skin sloughed off. My belly, bowels, and bladder expelled what was left; after uncounted days atop the spire without nourishment, little enough *was* left. I was weak and wracked, joints ablaze. What moisture remained spilled out of my eyes. My tongue swelled and filled my mouth, then cracked and bled like the lips. I drank blood, until Nihko gave me water.

He bandaged my eyes, because I could not close them.

He splinted fingers and toes, because I could not open them.

He restrained the skull that risked itself in frenzy against the ground.

He did what was necessary to bring me across the threshold, and when that much was accomplished he did even more.

He made me rise.

I stood upright again for the first time in days. Felt the earth beneath bare feet, felt the wind in my hair. Saw— everything.

Nihko heard the ragged gasp that was expelled from my mouth. "Clarity," he said.

It was too bright. Everything, too bright. Too rich. Too *brilliant*. I thought it might well blind me. My skin burned from the sun. Ached over the bones. Everything hurt. Everything was *too much*. I quivered like a child, trying to sort out things I could not comprehend. Things I had comprehended for most of my life, such as taste, touch, odor, sound, light.

All of it: too much.

"What do you hear?" he asked.

It thrummed inside my head. The whisper was a shout. I recoiled. "Too much," I said, then hissed. Then winced.

"All the senses," he said, "Everything is *more*."

More was too much. I stood for the first time in days and was blinded by the world, deafened by the world, filled with the scent of the world, tasted all of its courses, felt it impinge so much upon me that the flesh ached from it.

Everything was *more*.

I sought escape inside. But *more* existed there. I beat against the cage that was my own skull, attempted to withdraw, escape. And knew defeat.

"You cannot," Nihko told me. "It *is* you, now."

I barely spoke. "What is?"

"Everything."

I stood there and trembled, while the man's hand steadied me.

And then I knelt. Sought solace in the soil. Its scent was overwhelming. "I can't," I mouthed.

"You can."

"I *can't*."

"You will.

I bent, pressed my hands into the earth. Put my brow upon it, so that the sun beat on my spine. It made its way through flesh into muscle, into viscera. Into my very soul. It illuminated me, betrayed my frailties.

"You can," Nihko told me.

The world was too large. And everything in it too bright, too loud, too *much*.

To the earth, I said. "I want . . ."

Nihko waited.

"I want," I said with difficulty, "to go back."

"You are dead."

"I'm *alive*." I rolled back onto my haunches then, rose to my feet. Confronted him. "I'm too alive to be dead. I feel it in me. *Taste* it in me. I can hear my blood!"

"Yes."

I clamped palms across my eyes. "I want to go back. To be what I was."

"You are what you were."

My hands fell away so I could see his face. "You said I wasn't!"

"You were unborn," he explained. "For forty years, the vessel was shaped as it was shaped. The magic was dormant. But it began to rouse two or three years ago. The seeds of it were in you. As you approached the threshold, the seeds began to sprout. Atop that spire, you celebrated your birth forty years before. And the magic manifested."

I remembered unfolding. Unfurling. Within me, and without. The imminence that burst into being as I whelped it on the rock.

"You knew," I said abruptly. "That day on the ship, when you first took us aboard. You *knew*."

"As you will know it in another. Others will come. And you will serve them as I have served you: lift them up, nourish them, help them across the threshold."

"I want to go back."

"There is no 'back.' "

"I'm not you, Nihko!"

It echoed against the spire. I recoiled and slapped hands over my ears.

Nihko smiled. "Quietly," he said. "Control is necessary."

"Like yours?" I threw at him; but very quietly.

"My control is negligible," he said with irony. "It is why I deserted my brothers."

"And now you're back?"

"Am I not here?"

"Helping me," I said bitterly, "across the threshold."

He extended his arm. "Take my hand," he suggested, "and cross."

"Haven't I already?"

"A step or two."

I laughed at him, though there was no humor in it. "The first step I took off the spire was a killer."

"Yes," he agreed. "For many men, it is."

"Then if they have no magic, why are they up there?"

"They have magic," he answered, "and it manifests. But some vessels are not strong enough. They do not survive the annealing."

"Gods," I said, remembering. Recalling how I begged.

Anneal me.

Nihko smiled. "Precisely."

"No," I blurted. "No, not that . . ." But to speak of what happened wasn't possible. It was too new. Too—large. "How did I get up there?"

"Sahdri."

"He took me up there?"

"Took you. Left you."

"How?"

Nihko's brow rings glinted. "He is a mage, is he not?"

"I want to know how. How *exactly?*"

His tone was devoid of compassion. "And how *exactly* did you come down from the spire?"

"How did I—?"

"Come down," he repeated. "Should you not have broken to pieces here upon the ground?"

I inspected a hand. "Didn't I?"

"How did you come down?"

"I leaped." I grimaced. "Like a madman."

"Should you not be dead?"

"Aren't I?"

"Be in no haste," he said grimly. "You have ten years left to you."

"You told me twelve."

"*Possibly* twelve."

I looked into his eyes. "How many have you?"

"Two," he said. "Possibly."

"How do you know?"

"I know."

"How can you tell?"

"I can."

"This is ridiculous," I snapped. "You feed me this nonsense of scars being lifted and put onto another man; of Sahdri using magic to set me atop this rock; of me *being born,* as if once wasn't enough; of me surviving this leap that only a madman would make—"

"A madman did."

"—and then you expect me to believe this nonsense?"

"This nonsense will convince you."

"I don't think so."

"Look at yourself," he commanded. "Look at your flesh."

I scowled. "So?"

"He *lifted the scars from you.*"

I looked at myself. Peered down at my abdomen, where the Northern blade had sculpted flesh and muscle into an architecture I hadn't been born with.

The flesh was whole. Unblemished.

I clapped a hand to my face. The cheek was whole. Unblemished.

I looked then at my hands, seeking the cuts, the divots, the over-large knuckle where a finger had been broken, the nails themselves left ridged from hard usage. All of me was whole. All of me was new.

I stared hard at Nihko. "*You* have scars."

"You begin anew," he answered. "What damage you do to yourself from this day forward will be manifested in your flesh—it can even kill you—but you were reborn on the spire. A child comes into the world without blemish."

I knew better. "Not all children!"

He conceded that. "But not all children are ioSkandic."

"And the ones who are?"

"Are mages. Are mad."

I laughed harshly. "You tell me I have power, now;

that I'm a mage, now. And also that I'm mad? What advantage is that?"

"None."

"Then?"

"We are transient," he said. "We burn too brightly. We burn ourselves out."

I stabbed a finger at him. "This is not helping."

He grinned toothily at me. "I live to serve."

"Clothes," I said, focusing on nakedness; on what I could understand.

"In the cart."

"Good. Get them."

"Ah. I am to serve."

"You said that's what you were here for."

"For the moment." But he went to the cart, found a bundle of linen and tossed it at me.

I caught and shook it out. "What is this?"

"Robes," he answered, untying the molah's lead-rope. "But you need not concern yourself with how they suit you."

Slipping into the linen, I eyed him irritably. "Why not?"

"Because you will not be wearing them for very long."

The hem of the robe ended just above my ankles. "Why not?"

"Because," he said, "Sahdri will have you stripped."

I froze. "Why?"

"Rituals," he said briefly, leading the molah over. Cartwheels grated on stone.

"*What* rituals?" I asked suspiciously. "No more leaping off of spires!"

"That is done." He gestured. "Get in."

"Little chance of that," I retorted. "There's only one thing that will convince me I should."

"Yes?"

"That this cart is going to a ship that can take me back to Skandi."

"No," he answered.

"Then I guess I'm going nowhere. Not to Sahdri. Not *with* you."

Nihko sighed. "Do you believe I cannot make you?"

"If I'm a mage," I said promptly, "you can't make me do anything."

"But I can," he said, and touched me.

I tumbled into darkness.

And into the cart.

THIRTY-FOUR

SENSE RETURNED with a rush. Ropes cut into me, rubbed wounds into newly sensitive flesh; I felt everything as if it were hot as wire. The pounding of my heart filled my skull, reverberated in my chest. I heard the hiss of blood running back and forth in its vessels, as if my skin were too thin.

I flailed, felt ropes give; realized it was net. I was cradled, captured. Bundled up within the ropes fashioned into nets. And I was suspended.

From a spire.

I flailed again, spasming. Felt the net, harsh as wire. Felt the sway of the rope used to haul me up.

I depended from the spire. Depended *on* the spire.

Movement. I was being hauled up, winched up; I heard the creak of wood, the rubbing of the rope. Was this how Sahdri had taken me up the other spire?

There had been no rope. And nothing to which rope might be attached. There had only been stone. And spire. And me.

This was different.

I was meat in a net, hauled up. If my flesh wasn't eaten, my spirit would be.

Sahdri. Who had known the moment he saw me. Saw the brow ring hooked in my necklet.

I snatched at necklet. Found it. Caught it. Closed my hand upon it. Ten curving claws, strung upon a thong. I had cut them from the paws. Pierced them. Strung them. Wore them as a badge: see what I have become? I am the boy that killed the sandtiger; that saved the children; that saved the tribe; that freed himself.

Twenty-four years I had worn the necklet.

I knew that, now. I was forty years old. Nihko had told me. The magic had manifested. Sixteen when I killed the sandtiger; sixteen when I conjured it. And thirty-seven when I met Del.

Not thirty-six. Not thirty-eight.

I had a name. An age. One I gave myself. The other was given to me.

Sandtiger.

Sandtiger.

They would not take it from me.

"There is no magic," I said aloud, "and I am no mage."

Wood creaked. Rope rubbed as it was wound.

"There are no gods," I said, "and I am no priest."

Sandtiger.

Sword-dancer.

No less.

No more.

This spire was taller than the one I had roused upon, danced atop, leaped from. This spire was wider, thicker, shaped of twists and columns and shelves and pockets and caves cut into the stone by wind, by rain. Trapped in my net I stared at the stone. Saw *through* the stone. Saw deep into its heart where the minerals lay, wound within and around the bones.

I blinked. The stone was stone again.

Wood creaked. Rope rubbed.

Higher by the moment.

I swung in the net. Spun in the net. Saw the sky encompass stone, stone overtake sky. I shut my eyes: saw it. Opened them: the same.

I lifted a hand. Studied it. Saw no blemishes. Saw only flesh that had existed for forty years. Not young. Not old. Somewhere in the middle, were I to survive to be as old again as I was now.

I turned the hand. The palm was lined, callused. It was a hand, not a construct. Rebirth had renewed the flesh, but not leached away the time.

The flesh of a sudden went white. Stark white, like snow. I blinked. In shock, I watched flesh thin to transparency. Saw the vessels pulsing beneath, the blood running in them; the sinew, the meat, the bone.

"Gods," I blurted, and clamped my eyes closed.

When I opened them, the hand was a hand again. Whole. Normal. The bones were decently clad in human flesh once more.

My own.

I touched my face. Felt the cheek that had borne the scars for so long. Rubbed fingers across it. Stubble had sprouted; I was not so much a child newly born that I couldn't grow a beard. I needed to shave. I needed a haircut. I needed to eat, to drink, to empty bladder and bowels—though nothing was in them—so I knew I lived again as a man is meant to live.

And I needed Del. To know I lived again as a man is meant to live.

Gods, bascha. I want you.

No scars met seeking fingers. I dug them in, scraped fingers across the stubble. No marks of the sandtiger.

I sealed my eyes with lids. Clamped a hand around the necklet. Let the claws bite into palm.

Bleed, I said. Bleed.

There was no blood.

Nihko had said I could manifest such wounds as a man might, were he given to injury.

Bleed, I said, and shut my hand the tighter.

When two mage-priests hooked me into the winch-house, undid the net, pulled me free of rope, I at last unclamped my hand and displayed the palm to Sahdri, who waited.

"Bleeding," I said.

His eyes were dark. They were not rimmed with light.

It had been a trick that night. "Then you must have wanted it so."

"I'm a *man*," I said. "I bleed. I can die."

"Is that what you wish?"

Blood ran down my hand. It dripped to the floor of the winch-house. I followed the droplets, saw them strike the stone. Saw them swallowed by the stone. Saw them go down and down through stone until they reached its heart, where they were consumed. Changed to mineral.

Transfixed, I knelt upon the stone and tried to reach through it, to recapture the blood. It was mine.

"You are very young," Sahdri said gently, "and very new. But give me time—give *yourself* time—and you will understand what it is to be one of us."

I looked up at him. "I saw through it," I said. "This hand."

He smiled. "It takes some people so." He gestured briefly, indicating two shaven-headed, tattooed men with him. "This is Erastu." The man on the left. "And this is Natha." The man on the right. "They are acolytes here, as you shall become shortly. They shall assist you."

I stood. I ignored Erastu and Natha. I looked into Sahdri's face. "I can see through *you*."

And I could. I saw the rings in his flesh melt, saw the flesh of his face peel away, saw the bones of the skull beneath tattooed flesh glisten in a bed of raw meat. Beneath the meat, the bone, I saw the brain. And the light of his madness, pulsing as if it lived.

The shudder took me. Shook me. I fell. Pressed a bleeding palm against the stone; felt blood and substance drawn away, pulled deep.

"Lift him," Sahdri said to his acolytes. "He is far gone, farther than I expected. But he is not to merge yet. There is too much for him to learn; he is as yet soiled with too many things of the earth, and the gods would repudiate him."

Merge. Not me.

Only madmen did such things.

"No," I managed.

"No." Sahdri's voice was gentle as the hands of Era-

stu and Natha were placed upon me. "Not yet. I promise
you that."

I looked into his face. It *was* a face again. "I'm not
mad."

"Of course you are," he said. "We all of us are mad.
How else could we survive? How else would we be
worthy?"

"Worthy?"

"To merge." He gestured to the acolytes. "Bring him
to the hermitage. We shall leave him food and water and
let the sickness settle."

"Sick," I murmured. I could not walk on my own. The
body refused. Natha and Erastu held me up. Natha and
Erastu carried me.

Sahdri said, comfortingly, "It takes us all this way."

They took me deep into stone, beyond a door. Gave
me food. Water. And left me there.

I drank. Ate. Slept.

Dreamed of Del.

And freedom.

*The boy crept out of the hyort. It was near dawn; he was
expected to tend the goats. But he did not go to the goats.
He risked a beating for it—but no, it was no risk; he
would be beaten for it. Because if he failed—but no, he
would not fail. He had only dreamed of triumph.*

*He took with him the spear shaped painstakingly out
of the remains of a hyort pole. It was too short, the spear,
but better than bare hands; and they permitted him nothing else save the crook to tend the goats. A crook for
goats was not meant for sandtigers; even he knew that
much.*

Even he who had conjured the beast.

*In the hyort, Sula slept on. Mother. Sister. Lover. Wife.
She had made a man of him before the others could, and
had kept him so that others would not use him. He was a
likely boy, she told him, and others would use him. Given
the opportunity. He was fortunate they had not already*

begun. But she was a respectable widow, and the husband, alive, had also been respected. The old shukar muttered over his magic and made comments to the others that she was foolish for taking to bed a chula when she might have a man; but Sula, laughing, had said that meant the old shukar wanted her for himself. And would not have her. The chula pleased her.

Son. Brother. Lover. Husband. He had been all of those things to her.

And now he would be a man. Now he would be free.

He had only to kill the beast.

I woke up with a start. Dimness pervaded; the only illumination was the sunlight through the slotted holes cut out of stone into sky. I flung myself to my feet and stumbled to the stone, hung my hands into the slots, peered out upon the world.

Sky met my eyes.

None of it a dream.

All of it: real.

I turned then, slumped against the stone. In the wall opposite was a low wooden door, painted blue.

Blue as Nihko's head. Blue as Sahdri's head. Blue as the sails of Prima Rhannet's ship.

Prima. The metri. Herakleio.

Del.

All of whom thought me dead. Had seen the body bearing my scars: the handiwork of Del's jivatma; the visible reminders that the beast conjured of dreams had been real enough to mark me. To nearly kill me.

Sula had saved me. When the sandtiger's poison took hold, she made certain the chula would live.

As the chula made certain the beast would die.

Its death had bought my freedom.

What beast need I kill to buy my freedom now?

I shut my hand upon the claws strung around my throat, and squeezed. Until the tips pierced. Until the blood ran.

When Sahdri came for me, flanked by his acolytes, I showed him my palm.

"Ah," he said, and gestured the two to take me. Natha and Erastu.

I shook myself free of their hands. "No."

His tattooed brow creased. "What language is that?"

I bared teeth at him, as I had seen the sandtiger do. "The language of '*No.*' "

The brow creased more deeply. Rings glinted in slotted sunlight. "What language is that?"

"Don't you speak it?" I asked. "Don't you understand? I can understand you."

"Tongues," he said, sounding startled, even as Natha and Erastu murmured to one another. "Well, it will undoubtedly be helpful. You can read the books for us."

I stared. "Books?" This time in words he knew: Skandic. That I had not known the day before.

He gestured. "We speak many languages. But not all. There are books we cannot translate." His eyes were hungry. "What language did you speak a moment ago?"

"I don't know," I answered, because I didn't. I merely spoke. What came out, came out. I understood it all. "What do you want with books?"

"We trade for them," he said. "We are priests, not fools. Mages, not simpletons. We were born on Skandi and raised in the ways of trade. We value books, and we trade for them." Dark eyes glowed. "You can read them to us, those we cannot decipher."

I laughed at him. "I can't decipher anything. I never learned to read."

He, as were his acolytes, was astonished. "Never?"

"Maps," I conceded. Any man in the South who wishes to survive learns to read a map.

"But you have the gift of tongues," Sahdri said. "It has manifested. Undoubtedly you can read." He paused. "Now."

A new thought. It stunned me.

Rings glinted as the flesh of his face altered into a

smile of immense compassion. "Did you believe it would
be terrible, our magic? That all of it should be painful?"

With difficulty I said, "I saw the bones of your skull
break open. I saw what lay beneath."

"Control," Sahdri soothed. "A matter of control. The
gift is beautiful. The power is—transcendent."

"I don't want it." The truth.

Ring-weighted brows arched delicately. "Surely once
in your life you wished for magic. For a power that would
give you the aid you required. Everyone does."

Testily—because he was so cursed right—I asked,
"And does everyone get what they wish for?"

"Only some of us." He gestured. Natha and Erastu
laid hands upon me. "There is much for you to learn. We
had best begin now."

I struggled, but could not move the hands. "Just what
is it I'm supposed to be learning?"

"Who you were. Who you are." He stepped aside so
the young men might escort me out of the chamber he'd
called the hermitage. "Did the ikepra not tell you?"

"He told me he's not ikepra anymore."

"Ah. But he is ikepra. He will always be ikepra. He
turned his back on the gods."

"Maybe," I said tightly, "he didn't want to merge."

"Then he will only die. Alone. Quite mad." He shook
his head; rings glinted. "All men must die, but only we
are permitted to merge. It is the only way we know ourselves worthy, and welcomed among the gods."

"That was his payment," I said. "Freedom. Wasn't it?
For bringing me to you."

Sahdri offered no answer.

"He's free now, isn't he? No longer subject to your
beliefs, your rules."

The priest-mage's tone was severe. "He does not believe in the necessity."

"Neither do I!"

"Most of us do not," he agreed, "when first we come
here. But disbelief passes—"

"It didn't for Nihko."

"—and most of us learn to serve properly, until we merge."

Abruptly I recoiled, even restrained by strong hands. My lips drew back into a rictus. "You stink of it," I said. "It fills me up."

Sahdri studied me intently. "What do you smell?"

"Magic." The word was hurled from my mouth. "It's—alive."

"Yes," he agreed. "It lives. It grows. It dies."

"Dies?"

He reconsidered. "Wanes. Waxes anew. But we none of us may predict it. The magic is wild. It manifests differently in every man. We are made over into mages, but until the moment arrives we cannot say what we are, or what we may do."

"At all?"

His expression was kind. He glanced at the acolytes. "Natha, do you know what each moment holds?"

"I know nothing beyond the moment," the man answered.

"Erastu, do you know what faces you the next day?"

"Never," Erastu said. "Each day is born anew, and unknown."

I shook my head. "No one knows what each moment or day holds."

"This is the same."

"But magic gives you power!"

"Magic *is* power," he corrected gently. "But it is wholly unpredictable."

"Nihko can change flesh. Nihko can halt a heart."

"As can I," Sahdri said. "It takes some of us that way. It may take you that way."

"You don't know?"

"I know what I may do today, this moment," he answered. "But not what I may be able to do tomorrow."

" 'It grows,' " I quoted.

"As the infant grows," the priest-mage said gently. "On the day the child is born, no one knows what may come of it. Not its mother, who bore it. Not its father, who sired it. Certainly not the child. It simply lives every hour, every day, every year, and *becomes.*"

"You're saying I'm one thing now, this moment, here before you—but may be something else tomorrow?"

"Or even before moonrise."

"And I'll never know?"

"Not from one moment to the next."

"That's madness!" I cried. "How can a man be one thing one moment, and something else the next? How can he survive? How can he live his life?"

"Here," Sahdri said, "where such things belong to the gods. Where what he is this moment, this instant, here and now, need not reflect on his next, or shape it. Where a day is not a day, a night is not a night, and a man lives his life to merge with the gods."

"I don't want to merge with anyone!"

"But you will," he told me. "You have leaped from the spire once, with no one there to suggest it, to force it, to shape your mind into the desire. Do you really think there will fail to come another day when you wish to leap again?"

"*Nihko* has no desire to leap."

"He will leap," the priest-mage said. "One day it will come upon him, and he will leap. As it will come to Natha and Erastu."

They inclined tattooed heads in silent assent. Rings in their flesh glinted.

"Then why does it matter?" I asked. "Why does it matter *where* a man lives?"

The dark eyes were steady. "A man such as we may love his child one moment, and kill it the next. It is better such a man lives here, where he may serve the gods as he learns to control his power. Where he may harm no one."

It was inconceivable. "I don't believe that. What about Nihko? Why did you let him go if you believe he will harm someone?"

"He keeps himself aboard ship. He sets no foot upon the earth of Skandi. He may harm himself, or his captain, or his crewmates—but mostly he harms the people he robs." His tone made it an insult: "He is a *renegada.*"

"You're saying anyone with this magic is capable of doing anything, even something he finds abhorrent?"

Unexpectedly, tears welled in Sahdri's eyes. "Why do you think we come here?" he asked. "Why do you think we desert our families—our wives, our mothers, our children? Why do you think we never go back?"

I scowled at him. "Except to gather up a lost chick."

"That lost chick," Sahdri said plainly, "may murder the flock. May bring down such calamity as you cannot imagine." His expression was peculiar. "Because if you *do* imagine it, it will come to be."

"You're saying you come here willingly, but only after you've been driven out by the people on Skandi."

"We do not at first understand what is happening. When the magic manifests. It is others who recognize it. A wife. Perhaps a child." He gestured. "It is unpredictable, as I have said. We know only that symptoms begin occurring with greater frequency as we approach our fortieth year."

"What symptoms?"

He shrugged beneath dark robes. "Any behavior that is not customary. Visions. Acute awareness. A talent that increases for no apparent reason. Or one may imagine such things as no one has imagined before."

Such as turning the sand to grass.

Such as conjuring a living sandtiger out of dreams.

Such as knowing magic was present and so overwhelming as to make the belly rebel.

Sensitivity, Nihko had called it. When the body manifested a reaction to something it registered as too loud, too bright, too rich.

Too powerful.

My voice rasped. "And once here, you make a decision never to go back. To stay forever. Willingly."

"Would you kiss a woman," he asked, "if you knew she would die of it?"

"But—"

"If you *knew she would die of it?*"

I stared at Sahdri, weighing his convictions. He was serious. Deadly serious.

I would not kiss a woman if I knew she would die of it. Not if I knew. How could I? How could any man?

"Know this," Sahdri said clearly. "We are sane enough to comprehend we are mad. And mad enough to welcome that comprehension—"

"Why?"

"Because it keeps us apart from those we may otherwise harm."

Desperation boiled over. "I'm not a priest! I don't believe in gods! I'm not of your faith!"

Sahdri said, "Faith is all that preserves us," and gestured to the acolytes.

Too much, all at once. Too bright, too loud, too painful. I ached from awareness. Trembled from comprehension.

Not to know what one might do one moment to the next.

Not to know what one was *capable* of doing.

Not to know if one could kill for wishing it, in that moment of madness.

Understood fear: Imagination made real.

It ran in my bones, the power. I felt it there. Felt it invading, infesting, infecting.

How much would I remember?

How much would I forget?

How many years did I have before I leaped from the spire?

"You will find peace," Sahdri said. "I promise you that. Only serve the gods as they deserve, and the day will come when you will be at rest."

Erastu and Natha put hands upon me. This time I let them.

THIRTY-FIVE

THE WINCH-HOUSE WAS built into a cave in the side of the spire, whose mouth opened to the skies. The hermitage was also a cave, but lacking a mouth: it was a stone bubble pierced on one side with slotted holes to let the light in, and closed away by a door. From these places Sahdri took me up to the top of the spire, into and through a proper dwelling built of brick and mortar and tile. So closely did the dwelling resemble the spire itself that it seemed to grow out of it, a series of angled, high-beamed rooms that perched atop the surface like a clutch of chicks, interconnected as the metri's household was.

Men filled it. Men with shaven, tattooed heads, faces aglint with rings. All seemed to be my age, or older, but none appeared to be *old*. They attended prayers, or had the ordering of the household. Some worked below in the valley, going down each day by rope net, or crude ladders, to work in the gardens, the fields, to conduct the trade that came in from foreign lands.

The crown of this spire was much wider than the one I had leaped from. There was room for the dwelling. Room for a terrace. Room for a man to walk upon the stone without fearing he might fall off.

Room for a man, standing atop it, to realize how very small he is. How utterly insignificant.

I walked to the edge and stood there with the wind in my face, stripping hair from my eyes and tangling the robes around my body. I gazed across the lush, undulant valley with its multitude of spires springing up from the ground like mushrooms. The valley itself was rumpled, cloaked in greenery; we were far from the sere heat of the South, the icy snows of the North. Here there was wind, and moisture, the tang of earth and seasalt, the brilliance of endless skies. A forest of stone, like half-made statuary stripped of intended images.

"Beauty," Sahdri said from behind. "But outside."

Distracted, I managed. "What else is there?"

"*In*side," he said. "The beauty of the spirit, when it works to serve the gods."

I looked at the clustered spires, the inverted oubliettes. "Are there people in all of them?"

"In and on many of them, yes. This is the *iaka,* the First House, the dwelling of those who must learn what they are, what they are to be. How to control the magic. How to serve the gods."

"And if one doesn't?"

"One does."

"Nihko," I said, denying it.

"Ikepra."

I sighed. "Fine. Let's say I'm ikepra, too—"

He came up beside me and shut his hand upon my wrist. "Say nothing of the sort!"

"But I might be," I said mildly, trying with annoyance to detach my arm, and failing. "I may make that choice."

"Do you think you are the only one who has pleaded with the gods?" As if aware of my discomfort, he released my arm. "Those who go home die of it."

"Die of what?"

"Of going home."

I turned to look into his face. "But Nihko is free. Alive."

Sahdri's expression was still. "The ikepra will die. He has two years, perhaps three. But he will not stay on Skandi, and so he does not risk harm to his people."

Because it mattered, I said, "Skandi isn't *my* home. I would go there only so long as it took to collect Del, and leave. What risk is there in that?"

"She believes you are dead."

I grinned. "Faced with the flesh, she might be convinced otherwise."

From stillness, Sahdri turned upon me a face of unfettered desperation. "You would risk their lives? All the folk of Skandi?"

It burst from me, was torn upon the wind. "How do you *know* I would? How can you *swear* I am a danger to them?"

His expression was anguished. Unevenly he said, "There has been tragedy of it before."

I blinked. "From ioSkandics who went back?"

Sahdri nodded, too overcome to speak.

"What happened?"

He drew in a harsh breath. "I have told you: the magic is random, the madness unpredictable. When you marry the two . . ." He gestured futility, helplessness. "And I have told you why we remain here."

I stared out across the vista with the wind in my hair, mentally making a map of the spires thrusting from valley floor to the sky. Marking their shapes, their placements. An alien land, alien people. Alien gods.

Desolation was abrupt. "I want to go *home.*"

With great compassion Sahdri said, "We all of us wish to go home. The welfare of our people lies in not doing it."

Even as I shook my head I felt myself trembling. "This is not where I belong."

"You can belong nowhere else. Not now."

I swung on him. "I'm not one of you! I wasn't born here, wasn't raised here . . . I know nothing of Skandi beyond what I have learned since I came. There is nothing of Skandi *in* me—"

"Your blood," he said. "Your bone. You were bred of this place, even if you were not born here. Skandi is in you; how not? How can you believe otherwise? *You leaped from the spire, and survived.*"

"And I don't even remember why, let alone how!" I shouted it. Heard the echoes amid the spires.

Gently he said, "You will."

I turned away again, to stare fixedly at the Stone Forest. "There is only one life that matters, and I would never harm her."

"You may believe so. But you are wrong. Others have been wrong before."

"I would never hurt Del—" And then I stopped short. I *had* hurt Del. Had nearly killed Del.

"Trust me," Sahdri said, seeing my expression. "I entreat you to remain here, and I pray you will be brought to wisdom—"

I shook my head.

"Afterward," he said earnestly, "after you understand what you truly are—"

I interrupted. "Sword-dancer. There is nothing else in the world I am or wish to be."

He closed his eyes. I marveled again at the trappings of his order: ornate blue patterns tattooed into shaven skull, ring after ring piercing lips and ears, brows and nose. He glittered in the sunlight, features aglow with a haze of silver. He was not an old man, but neither was he young. Lines of character and strength of will shaped his features.

When he opened his eyes again, the darkness was rimmed with fire.

I fell back a step. Stared at him, transfixed by the expression of his face, the transcendent power in his eyes.

"Who are you?" he asked.

I swallowed. "Sword-dancer."

"Who are you?"

"Sandtiger."

"Io," he said. "Io. Who are you?"

"Sandtiger. Sword-dancer."

"Io."

"No," I said. "Not mad. Not *io*."

"Kneel."

"I'm not kneel—" And I did. Without volition. One moment I was standing, but the next I knelt. I could not connect the moments, could find no bridge between them.

Sahdri stood over me and put his hands upon me. Settled them into my hair, captured the skull with his grip.

Tipped the skull up so I had no choice but to look into his face. "Who are you?"

I opened my mouth to answer: *the Sandtiger.* But the world was ripped away.

—————————◆—————————

The bird drifted. Below it stretched the endless sands, the Southron desert known as Punja, alive and sentient. It moved by whim of wind, swallowing settlements, caravans, tribes. It left in its wake bones scoured free of flesh, and tumbled. Buried later, unburied later yet. Scattered scraps of bone, eaten of flesh; stripped by sand, by wind; clean of any taint of life.

No meal here; others had feasted before it. The bird flew on, winged shadow fleeing across the sands. And then it came to an oasis, a cluster of trees around a well framed in stone. Men were there, gathering. A circle was drawn in the sand. Blades were placed in the center, while two men stood at the inner rim, facing one another.

A man said "Dance," and so they did. Ran, took up swords, began the ritual so pure in its intent, so splendid in execution, that even the death was beautiful.

One man died. The other did not. He was a tall man, a big man, with dark hair bleached to bronze from the sun, skin baked to copper. His strength and quickness were legendary; he had come to be reckoned by many the best. There was another, but he was older. And they had never met to settle it since one bout within a training circle, beneath the eyes of the shodo. This man wondered which of them might win, were they to meet again.

With meticulous care, he cleaned his blade. Accepted the accolades of those who watched. As one they turned their backs on him and walked to their horses, to depart. He expected no more. He had killed one of their own.

One man threw down a leather pouch: it spilled a handful of coin into the sand. The victor did not immediately take it up but tended his sword instead, wiping it clean of blood. Or the leavings of the dance.

Not always to the death, the sword-dance. Infrequently

so; ritual was often enough, and the yielding. But this dance had been declared a death-dance.

He survived. He cleaned his blade, put it back in its scabbard, slid arms into harness straps. He wore only a leather dhoti, leather harness. From the ground he took the coin, took the burnous, took the reins of his horse.

He had won. Again.

The bird circled. Winged on. Watched the man, watched the dances, watched him win. So many dances. Nothing else lived in the man but the willingness to risk himself within the confines of the circle. He was the dance.

The bird circled. Winged on. North, to mountains, to water, to winter. To a circle in the lake: the island named Staal-Ysta; to the circle on the island, drawn by Northern hands. The man in the circle, dancing. The woman who danced with him.

Pain there, and grief. Desperate regret. The wish to leave the circle . . . the capacity to stay, because it was required. Because honor demanded it.

The man and the woman danced, hating the dance, loving one another. Each of them wounded. Each of them bleeding. Each of them reeling to fall upon the ground. Each of them believing there was no better way to die than in the circle, honoring its rituals. Honoring one another.

The circle. The sword. The dance. And the man within the circle, dancing with a sword.

Dancing against the beast. Dancing for the beast.

The sandtiger he had conjured to also conjure freedom.

The bird circled. Swung back. South to the desert, southeast to the ocean, east to the island. To the Stone Forest, and the spires of the gods.

It knew. It understood. It acknowledged.

I roused to the rattle of claws, the tautness of leather thong against my throat. I meant to set my hand to the necklet, to preserve it and my throat, but I knelt upon the stone with legs and hands made part of it, encased, and I could do nothing.

A hoarse sound escaped me. Sahdri said, "Be still." And so I was.

He took the necklet from my throat. Leather rotted to dust in his hands, was carried away by wind. All that remained were claws.

One by one he tossed them into the air. Into the skies, and down.

With each he said, *"The beast is dead."*

They fell, one by one.

Were gone.

He knelt before me. Set hands into my hair, imprisoned the skull. *"The beast is dead."*

Unlocked from stone, I stood as he raised me. I was hollow, empty. A husk.

"Come inside," Sahdri said. "There are rituals to be done, and the gods await."

The bird perched upon the chair. It watched as the hair was shorn, then shaved. The flesh of the skull was paler than the body, for the Southron sun had only tantalized it, never reached it. When that flesh was smooth and clean, men gathered with dye, with needles. The patterns were elaborate, and lovely. Blood and fluid welled, was blotted away. The canvas on which they painted made no sound of complaint, of comment, of question. The pupils had grown small; the eyes saw elsewhere. The house of bone and flesh was quiescent as the spirit turned away from the world and in upon itself, to consider what it was now that the beast was dead.

When the patterns were complete, rings were set into his flesh. The lobe of each ear was pierced three times and silver rings hooked through. Three rings also were put through each eyebrow. Then the man was taken out upon the spire, was shown the wind, the world. He was made to kneel again; was blessed there by the others. Was made to lie facedown upon the stone. The arms were pulled away from his sides and placed outstretched upon the stone, palms down.

He lay in silence, rapt. Seeking the beast perhaps; but the beast was dead.

Shadow winged across the man's back. His head was blue, and bloody.

The bird circled. It watched as the fingers of the hands were spread with deft precision. Saw how the thumbs and first three fingers were sealed into stone; how the small finger on each hand was left as flesh, and free.

Two knives were brought. Two men, Natha and Erastu, priests and mages, knelt beside the man who lay upon the stone.

At Sahdri's brief nod, they cut off the smallest finger of each hand.

At Sahdri's brief nod, they lifted the severed fingers and gave them into his keeping.

He turned to the rim of the world, to the wind, invoked the blessing of the gods, and threw the fingers away.

One by one they fell.

Were gone.

The man upon the stone made no sound until Sahdri knelt beside him, put a hand upon his neck, and let it be known what had been done to him.

The man upon the stone, rousing into awareness, into comprehension, began to cry out curses upon them all.

"Be at peace," Sahdri said kindly. "The beast is dead, and you are now a living celebration of the gods."

The man upon the stone—shaven, tattooed, flesh pierced and amputated—continued to cry out curses. To scream them at Sahdri, at the brothers, at the gods.

The bird winged higher, to catch and ride the wind.

———◆———————

I roused into fever, into pain. And when the fever was gone, I lived with pain. The stumps were sealed, so there was no blood, but pain remained. As much was of knowledge as of physical offense.

For days I lay upon the floor of the hermitage. I was given food and water; wanted neither. But eventually I drank, though I spurned the food. And when I drank, cup held in shaking hands now lacking a finger each, I tasted blood and bitter gall.

Sahdri said they had killed the beast. The sandtiger. The animal that freed me, that gave me identity and purpose, a name. The animal I *was* in the stories of the South: the Sandtiger, shodo-trained seventh-level sword-dancer from legendary Alimat; the man who lost no dances; who had, as a boy, defeated Abbu Bensir.

I was all of those things, and none of them. I understood what was done, and why: rob a man of his past, of the ability to live in it, to continue it through present into future, and he has no choice. He becomes something else. Other.

But understanding came fitfully. There were other times it deserted me. Times when *I* deserted me, left the abused body and went into the stone, plunged my spirit into the blood and bone of it, seeking escape. It was not difficult to do. I detached from the body, and left it.

And while the spirit was housed in stone one day, men came and took up the body.

It walked with them. The flesh of the skull had healed, no longer wept blood and fluid. The scabs of the brow piercings had fallen away, so the rings shone clean and bright; the earlobes were no longer swollen. The hands still trembled, still curled themselves, still pressed themselves high against the chest, crossed as if in ward because the stumps were yet tender, but the flesh there healed as well. The body went with them out onto the spire and saw how they restrained one brother. How he fought to be free; how he cried to be released.

When all of them gathered there upon the spire beneath the vault of heaven, the brother was released. Sobbing his joy, Erastu thrust both arms up into the skies in tribute to the gods, and ran.

And leaped.

And fell.

The priest-mages of the iaka, the First House, of the

Stone Forest of Meteiera on ioSkandi, sang blessings unto the gods, begging their acceptance of the newly merged spirit.

The body knelt. Was still. And the others left it there as they left the spire, went back into the dwelling still singing blessings. To gather together and worship. To conduct rites and rituals.

The body, alone atop the world, remained. And when I let the spirit flow back out of the stone and into the flesh, *I* knelt there alone atop the world.

For the first time I looked at my hands. They were— unbalanced. Out of true, lacking symmetry. Four fingers were three, and no counterbalance to the thumbs.

I had no sword. No broom handle. Not even a stick, here atop the spire. But I had two wrists.

I stretched out my left arm. Placed my right palm against it, from underneath. Both hands trembled; the spirit quailed from anticipated pain. But I closed the thumb and three fingers of my right hand around my wrist.

Imagining a hilt.

Imagining grip, and balance.

Imagining a sword.

Imagining a dance.

"You will forget," Sahdri said.

Startled, I stiffened. Gripped the wrist, and hissed against the pain.

"You will forget."

"I can't."

"The beast is dead."

"No."

"The memory survives, for now. But that, too, will die."

"No."

"You have a very strong will," Sahdri said. "Stronger than I expected. To be stripped of the beast . . . to be stripped of the means to *be* the beast within the circle—"

I snapped my head around to look at him. "You're saying *I* am the beast?"

"The sandtiger," he said, "And so you were, since the

day you conjured and killed it. But it is dead, that beast. And the man who killed it, who became it, will forget what he was. He will be what he *is*."

"And what *am* I?"

"Mage," Sahdri answered.

"What?" I arched eyebrows; felt the alien weight of rings depending from flesh. "Not priest?"

"Not yet. But that will come."

"When I'm willing to 'merge' as Erastu did?"

"Oh, long before. You will understand why it is necessary, and you will accept it. Willingly."

"I will, will I? Willingly?"

"Within a year."

"So certain of me, are you?"

"Certain of the magic. The madness." Sahdri's robes whipped in the wind. "Surely you understand the need for discipline."

"Discipline!"

"The beast," Sahdri said, "learned of rules, and codes, and rituals and rites. Was circumscribed by such things, even as it was circumscribed by the circle. As it was taught by its shodo."

I stared at him as I knelt upon the stone.

"It understood that without the rules, the codes, lacking rituals and rites, it had no discipline. And without discipline, it was merely a beast. A boy." He paused. "A chula."

I flinched.

"Discipline," Sahdri said, "is necessary. Tasks, to fill the hands. Prayers, to fill the mind. Rituals and rites. All of the things we do here, how we fill our days, our nights, our minds." His eyes gazed beyond me. "To keep the madness at bay."

I sat back on my heels. "*That's* why—"

"With discipline," he said before I could finish my comment, "we may last a decade. Possibly even fifteen years, as I have. But without it . . ." He looked once more beyond me, stared into wind and sky. "Without it, we have only power without control, without purpose, and the madness that will loose it."

"Wild magic," I murmured, thinking of seeing through flesh, through bone; of seeing the heart of the stone from the inside.

"If you let it," Sahdri said, "it will consume you. Burn you up. And in the doing, you may well harm others. Magic and madness, married, is calamity, given form. It is catastrophe. But here upon the spires, with rituals and rites, *with discipline,* we keep it contained. Lest there be tragedy of it."

"Erastu killed himself."

"Erastu merged with his gods."

"But died doing it."

"A man without faith may choose to believe so."

"You're saying it would have happened anyway. Someday."

"Better it should happen here."

"But if he would have gone mad no matter where he was—"

"Here, he filled his hands with tasks. His mind with prayers, rites, rituals. He was a *disciplined* man—and thus he harmed no one."

"But himself."

"He went to his gods."

"And killed no one doing it."

Sahdri inclined his head.

In disbelief, incomprehension, I clung to one thing. "You let Nihko go. For me. In payment for me. You let *him* go."

Sahdri smiled. "Did we?"

THIRTY-SIX

Discipline.
I learned the prayers.
Said the prayers.
Discipline.
I learned the rites.
Performed the rites.
Discipline.
I learned the rituals.
Performed the rituals.
Discipline.
I believed in no prayers, no rites, no rituals.
I acknowledged and invoked one god.
Whose name was *Discipline.*

When stubble bristled, they shaved it. Face and head. There were no claw marks now to make it difficult, lest the scarred flesh be cut. And when Sahdri saw I had learned the prayers, and said them; learned the rites, and performed them; learned the rituals, performed them, he had more holes pierced, more silver shaped, more rings set into my flesh. Two more for each brow. Two more for each ear.

Discipline.
I said nothing.
Did nothing.
Beyond what was expected.

And I forgot nothing.
Beyond what was expected.

Magic, Sahdri said, was bred in my bones, knitted into flesh. Was as much a part of me as the heart that beat in my chest. No man, he said, considered the heart's task until it failed; the heart simply was. And magic was the same.

I believed in none of it. I acknowledged none of it. To do so gave power to those who wished to use it. I believed in myself. And I fell asleep each night invoking no gods, only myself. The essence of who I was, and what. Sworddancer. Sandtiger. No more. No less.

Each night.
Discipline.
No more.
No less.

I stood atop the spire. Wind blew in my face, but it moved no hair; there was no hair to move. I waited. Feeling it. Knowing it. Hearing it in the stone.

She came. She climbed over the edge of the spire, rose, and stepped into the circle. Set both swords into the center.

Pale hair glowed in the sun. Blue eyes were ruthless.

"Dance," she commanded, in a voice of winter water.

I moved then.

Ran then.

Took up the sword.

Danced—

—and nearly died, when her blade sheared into ribs.

My eyes snapped open. I lay in my hermitage, arms and hands as always—now—tucked up against my chest. With effort I let go the tension, let the body settle. Felt the stone beneath my cheek.

The memory of steel. Of a man in the circle. Of the woman, the sword, the song.

I lay very still upon the stone, not even breathing. Tentatively I slid one hand beneath the fabric of the robe and felt the flesh of my abdomen, recalling the pain, the icy fire, the horrific weakness engendered by the wound. Touched scar tissue.

Breath rasped as I expelled it in a rush. Scar tissue, where none had been after Sahdri lifted it from me. Knurled, resculpted flesh, a rim around the crater left by the jivatma. My abdomen burned with remembered pain.

Sweat ran from me. Relief was tangible.

Magic. Power. Conjuring reality from dreams. Using it without volition even as Sahdri had warned.

But for this? Was this so bad, to find a piece of myself once taken away and make it whole again, even though this wholeness was a travesty of the flesh?

Yes. For this. For myself.

I shut my eyes. *Thank you, bascha.*

From the winch-house I took a length of wood, carried it to my hermitage. From the wall I took a piece of stone. Made it over into the shape of an adze. Then dropped it as I fell, as I curled upon the stone, and trembled terribly in the aftermath of a terrible magic.

Discipline.

When I could, I sat up and took the stone adze, took the wood, and began to work it. To shape a point of the narrowest end.

Discipline.

When the spear was made, I lay down upon the stone and gripped it, willing myself to sleep. Willing myself to dream.

—sandtiger—

At dawn the boy crept out of the hyort. He was to tend the goats, but he did not go there. He carried a spear *made out of a broken hyort pole, painstakingly worked with a stone, and went instead to the tumbled pile of rocks near the oasis that had shaped itself, in falling, into a modest cave.*

A lair.

He knelt there before the mouth and prayed to the gods, that they might aid him. That they might give him strength, and power, and the will to do what was necessary.

Kill the beast.

Save the tribe.

Win his freedom.

He received no answer from the gods; but gods and their power, their magic, were often random, wholly unpredictable. No man might know what or when they might speak. But he put his faith in them, put his faith in the magic of his imagination, and crept into the lair.

The sandtiger had fed only the afternoon before. It was sated, sleeping. The boy moved very carefully into the cave that was also lair, and found the beast there in the shadows, its belly full of girl-child.

He placed the tip of his spear into the throat, and thrust.

And thrust.

Bore the fury, the outrage. Withstood even the claws, envenomed and precise. One knee. One cheek. But he did not let go of the spear.

When the beast was dead, he vomited. The poison was in him. Retching, he backed his way out of the lair that reeked now of the death of the beast, its effluvia, of his own vomit.

He stood up, trembling, and made his way very carefully back to the cluster of hyorts. To the old shukar, maker of magic. And claimed he had killed the beast.

No one believed him.

But when he fell ill of the poison, Sula took him in. Sula made them go. And when they came back with the dead beast and the clawed, tooth-shattered spear, she bade them cure the pelt even as she cured the chula. When he was healed, when he could speak again de-

*spite the pain in his cheek, he asked for the sandtiger. It
was brought to him. With great care, with Sula's knife,
he cut each claw out of the paws, pierced them, and
strung them on a thong.*

*It was argued that he was chula, and thus claimed no
rights for killing the beast. But Sula insisted; how many
men, how many women, how many children now would
survive because of the chula?*

*Wearing nothing but the necklet, he stood before the
tribe and was told to go.*

*Sula gave him clothing. Sula gave him food. Sula gave
him water.*

Sula gave him leave to go, to become a man.

I fell back in the dimness, gasping, cheek ablaze with
pain. Blood dripped; I set the back of my hand against it,
felt the sting of raw and weeping flesh. Then fingers, to
seek. Examine.

I counted the fresh furrows. Four. Welcomed the pain,
the tangible proof that I was I again. With or without
magic.

I looked then at the sandtiger in its lair, where I had
tracked it. Where I had killed it, so I might win my
freedom.

Sahdri, in a rictus of astonishment, lay dead of a spear
through the throat.

Sahdri, who had served his gods with absolute dedication, so absolute as to amputate fingers, pierce my flesh,
tattoo my scalp.

To see nothing wrong in robbing a man of his past, his
freedom, so his future would be built on the architecture
of magic, and madness.

The shudder wracked me. I bent, cradled hands
against me. Felt the heat running down my face to drip
upon the stone. To trickle into my mouth.

I straightened slowly. Licked my lip and tasted blood.
Tangible blood.

I welcomed the pain. And I gave myself leave to go,
to become a man. Again.

Sword-dancer.
Sandtiger.
Again.
Still.

In the winch-house I weighted the net and sent it plunging downward. When it reached the bottom, I tied the winch-drum into place and took hold of the rope that spilled over the lip of stone.

I had leaped from a spire. I could surely climb down a rope.

At the bottom I released the rope. Walked four paces. Saw the world reverse before me: everything light was dark, everything dark became light. Black was white, white was black. With nothing in between.

I knelt down, shut my eyes, prayed for the fit to pass.

When I could stand again, walk again, I sought and found seven of ten claws. Gathered them up. Tied them into the hem of my robe. And walked through the Stone Forest to the edge of the island.

At the ocean I looked for boats, for ships, and found none. That they came to ioSkandi, I knew; Sahdri had said there was trade of a sort. But none was present now.

Wind beat on the waves. Weary, I knelt upon the shore, let sea spray cool my burning face. Gripped the claws through linen, counting seven of ten.

I sat down then in the sand. Waves lapped, soaked me. I didn't care. I took the claws from the hem, pulled thread from the fabric, and began to string a necklet.

When I was done, when the necklet was knotted around my throat, I sat in sand, soaked by wave and wind, and gripped the curving claws. Pain flared anew in the stumps of the missing fingers. It set me to sweating.

Abdomen. Cheek. Claws. Bit by bit, I would fit the pieces of me back together again.

Magic or no.
Madness or no.
Discipline.

Sahdri and the others made of it a religion, a new and
alien zealotry I could not embrace. So I embraced what I
already knew, renewed in myself *that* zealotry: the rituals
and rites of Alimat. Lost myself in the patterns of the
dance, the techniques of the sword. Stepped into the circle
of the mind, and won.

Discipline.

I took seawrack, driftwood, a tattered piece of linen,
and after four days of desperation, futility, and multitudinous curses, vows, and promises made to nonexistent
gods, I finally conjured a ship.

Discipline.

A half-day and blinding headache later it sailed me into
the caldera, where I saw no blue-sailed ships. No red-
headed women captains. No fair-haired Northern baschas.

They believed I was dead. All of them.

Except the one who had set the trap.

I left behind seawrack, driftwood, and tattered linen.
The basin-men, the molah-men, spying the shaven, tattooed head, the rings in ears and brow, fell away from me
without offering their services even at exorbitant prices.
Instead they shouted, called out curses, made ward-signs
against magic, madness, and the ikepra.

Discipline.

I climbed the treacherous track to the top of the cliff,
where basin-men, molah-men, women, wives, children,
and merchants made ward-signs against the ikepra.

The ikepra, who by now was exhausted enough to
want nothing better than to tumble into bedding and sleep
for two tendays, ignored it all and walked.

In truth, the ikepra did more wobbling than walking, but
the end result was the same: I reached Akritara. By sundown.

Simonides came out of the house to tell the ikepra to
leave. Then blanched white as he truly *saw* the ikepra.
"Alive!"

I wasted no time. "Where's Del?"

He swallowed, closed his eyes, stared at me again. Said, in Skandic, "Praise all the gods of the sky!"

"Where's Del?"

He set a trembling hand to the wall, as if he might fall without the support. "Gone. Both of them. They sailed."

I had expected it. Had prepared for it. But the despair was profound.

The ikepra showed none of it. Only cold control. "When?"

Simonides took his hand from the wall and gathered himself. "A threeday ago."

"At whose behest?"

His face was strained. "Mine."

He meant the metri's. "I was dead, so why extend the guest-right to unnecessary people?"

"There was no place . . ." He attempted to regain self-control, began again. "There was no place here for the renegada woman."

"Del?"

"She said—she said this was not her home. Nor yours." His expression was anguished. "She would not stay in the place that had killed you."

"Well," I said, "that's settled for the moment. Time I saw the metri."

"Wait!" His hand extended to stop me, fell away limply. "She is unwell. The shock . . ."

I offered neither diplomacy nor compassion. "Too bad."

His eyes sought my face, examined the ring-pierced brows, the tattooed patterns on my skull. Had the grace to comprehend some small measure of the shock *I* had been subjected to.

"Of course," he murmured, turning to escort me into her presence.

The metri stood in the center of an arch-roofed room, surrounded by pools of rich fabric—tunics—draped over the bed, the chair, the chest, puddled on the floor; a scattering of jewelry glinting of gold and glass in the lamplight; a handful of old flowers, dulled by years into brittle, pale, dusty semblances of what once had been bright and lively, and fresh.

As I came into the room she looked up from the flowers. Saw me. And the blooms were crumbled into dust and ash by the spasming of her fingers closing into trembling fists.

Even her lips were white. *"Alive."*

"Despite every effort to insure otherwise," I said, "and somewhat more and certainly less than I was"—I held out my hands, palms up—"but incontestably *alive*."

She was transfixed by my hands, by the evidence of mutilation. The stumps had healed, but were pink-and-purple against the tanned flesh. I have big hands, wide palms, long fingers; anyone, looking at my hands, would see at once something was missing.

Her pupils swelled to black as she stared into my face.

"A man born to the sword," I said, "is somewhat hampered by an—*injury*—such as this." I watched the flinching in her eyes. "Is this what you intended?"

She exhaled it. "I?"

In some distant, detached way, I appreciated the delicacy of her tone, the reaction honed to just the right degree of shock and denial. "Your boy," I said, "was feeling threatened. Your boy was truly afraid you might name me in his place. Your boy was on the verge of stepping outside your control. So you removed a piece from the board. A piece that had served a very important, if temporary, function, and was now viewed as unnecessary. Possibly even dangerous to the overall intent of the game." I paused. "Could you not have told him the truth from the beginning?"

The metri said, "He would not have played his part properly."

"Ah." I nodded. "And when will you teach him the rules?"

"There are none. Only an object: to win."

"Whose body was it that came in so handy?"

The tilt of her head shifted minutely. "*I* believed it was yours."

I laughed sharply, a brief blurt of sound. And in pure, unaccented, formal Skandic, the kind spoken only among the Eleven Families, I told her she was a liar.

The Stessa metri began to tremble.

"What did you think would happen?" I asked. "Did you think I would *merge,* thus removing all possibility I might return to complicate your life? Did you think I would forget everything I knew of my life before I was put atop the spire? Did you think I would be *unchanged,* and therefore not even due a momentary memory of my presence in your world?" I shook my head slowly. "I am as I always was. A sword-dancer. The Sandtiger. But with a little extra thrown into the pot. A pinch more seasoning than I had before."

Simonides, behind me, said very quietly, "Mage."

The metri met my eyes. "Mad."

"If I am either, or if I am both," I said, smiling, "perhaps you should be afraid."

The metri gazed down at her hands, still doubled into fists. Slowly she opened them, saw the crushed remains of ancient flowers. After a moment she turned her hands palm down and began to shed those remains. Dust, and bits of stem and petal. Drifting to the floor.

Tears shone in her eyes as she looked at me. "This was my daughter's room."

Tunics, jewelry, the keepsakes of a woman's life. Surrounding the woman who had borne her.

Who had banished her.

"My daughter," she said, "has been dead for forty-two years."

And I was forty.

"Go," the metri commanded.

The ikepra went.

———◖━━━━━━━━━

I stepped out of the house into the courtyard, bathed in moon- and starlight, and the sword arced out of the darkness.

I caught the hilt one-handed. Hissed as pain kindled into a bonfire in that hand.

"Alive?" Herakleio stepped from shadows into moonlight. "Well then, perhaps we should remedy that." And brought his own blade up.

I thought of laughing at him. I thought of saying no. I thought of pleading fatigue. Pain. Inability to even grip the sword properly.

But all of that was what Herakleio wished to hear.

He came at me then, as I had gone at him the evening Sahdri arrived in our midst, floating atop the wall. This was no circle, no dance, no sparring, but engagement with intent. No rules, no codes, no vows, no honor.

I had meant to intimidate, because I knew the difference. Herakleio meant to take all of his anger and frustration out on me. To punish me. Put me in my place. Render me defeated.

Kill me? No. Unless he got lucky.

Of course, I had two fingers fewer than before, and all wagers were off.

I heard Simonides' blurt of shocked denial from the doorway. But Herakleio was on me, and I had no time for servants, metris, or magic. All I had was myself.

A sword.

And the dance of the mind, contained within its circle. *Discipline.*

When I was done, Herakleio lay sprawled upon the courtyard tiles. He bled from a dozen cuts. His blade had been flung well out of reach against a wall, hidden by shadow; he had only himself now, winded, wounded, humiliated, and that was not enough.

Not for me. Not for himself. Possibly not for the metri.

But she had no one else.

I tossed my sword aside, so he would not see me shaking. "We're done," I said. "I bequeath to you all of the things you believed I had taken from you, or would. I want none of them. None of you, none of her, none of this place. I am due nothing as a son or a grandson; I am neither. I am a seventh-level sword-dancer, trained by the shodo of Alimat and sworn to the rites and rituals of the circle. That is all. And that is more than ever I dreamed of."

Because all I had ever dreamed of was freedom.

And, one night, a sandtiger.

I turned from him then, and walked. Out of the courtyard. Away from the household. Down the track toward the city, the cliff, the caldera.

Simonides found me. I had collapsed at the side of the track, overtaken by pain so intense it bathed my body in sweat and set tears in my eyes; by reaction so profound I could not even manage to sit. I lay curled on my side, arms tucked in against my chest in vain attempt to ward my hands from further offense. I rocked against the soil, smelling saltwater, grapes, and blood from a bitten lip.

The hand touched my shoulder. "I have water," he said in a rusty voice.

Eventually I sat up. Let him give me water, since I dared not even hold the jar, or the cup. A rivulet ran down my chin and dripped onto the dusty linen of my robe.

"I have food," he said, "and clothing. And coin."

"Sword?" I rasped.

"No."

Ah, well. I had come without one. Why expect to leave *with* one?

"They sailed a threeday ago," he said. "The metri owns swift ships. I will pay your passage and inform the captain he is to take you wherever you wish to go. But there is only one renegada ship boasting blue sails. He will know it."

"Is this at the metri's behest?"

"It is at my behest."

In the moonlight, the slave's face was both worried and compassionate. "You're risking yourself again, Simonides."

"This is no risk."

"Or is it you think it's owed me, slave to slave?"

"Slaves," he said, and stopped. Then began again,

with difficulty. "Slaves do what they must to survive. To make a life, and to find the freedom within. But there need not be dishonor in it, if there are ways to find a measure of dignity and integrity."

Dishonor lay in what one thought of himself. Not in what others believed.

I nodded. "Will this captain take orders from you?"

Solemnly he said, "I am the eyes and ears of the metri."

I drank again, nodded thanks for the aid. Stood up with effort, but got there. "So, what kind of clothing did you bring?"

The smile was slight. "What you arrived in."

In mock horror I cried, "Not the *red* clothes!"

"Well," he said, "red does suit you."

Del had said that once. Maybe she would approve of the garb when I caught up to her.

Or maybe she wouldn't notice at all.

Or maybe she'd notice, but I wouldn't be wearing them long enough to matter.

I grinned into moonlight.

I'm coming, bascha.

THIRTY-SEVEN

WEARING Nihko's dreadfully red tunic and baggy trousers—and a necklet of seven sandtiger claws newly strung on leather—I hiked through waves, wet sand, dry sand, and vegetation. My head itched abominably, but I had hair again. About half the length of an eyelash.

And here I'd been complaining about needing to cut it only a matter of weeks before.

The metri's ship lay anchored behind me. The lookout had spotted a blue-sailed ship two hours before and the captain laid in a course to follow it. Prima Rhannet's vessel now was anchored on the other side of the island, near the only fresh water available; as I did not want to risk the metri's ship being taken by renegadas—not because it was hers, but because we needed it—I requested the captain to stay clear. And anyway, this was for me to do.

Although I had an idea what *Del* was trying to do.

I grinned. Shook my head. "Never work, bascha. You and the stud have worked too hard at cultivating a mutual dislike."

Of course when I finally broke through the vegetation and found them near the spring, the stud was standing with his head shoved against Del's shoulder, rubbing hard, resembling for all the world a very large, brown dog. Del was attempting to stop him from rubbing, apparently in a vain effort to hug that big jug-head.

Silly bascha.

Prima Rhannet and her first mate stood very near Del.

All of them had their backs to me, except the stud. Who stopped rubbing against Del's shoulder when he noticed me, stuck his head high in the air, and snorted his alarm. Loudly, and with typically emphatic dampness.

Too bad he hadn't done that the first time Prima and her blue-headed companion mate showed up. The warning might have been useful.

"So," I called, "I guess they didn't see fit to merge you after all."

Nihko spun, even as Prima and Del. The stud snorted again, this time in disgust, and wandered off, as he was wont to do; everyone else just stood there. Gaping.

I didn't look at Del. My first hard glance as she turned had surmised she was fine, if white and wobbly with shock. But there was time for a proper reunion later. Now that I knew she was safe, and she knew I was alive—at least, I *think* she knew it was me—other business came first.

I looked at Prima and Nihko. "Surprise."

The captain's hand was plastered to her left breast where, if she had a heart, it lay beneath flesh and bone. Pounding hard enough, I hoped, fit to burst her chest.

In Skandic, Nihko told her, "There is nothing he can do to us."

In Skandic, I retorted, "Care to wager on that?"

He had the grace to color. His eyes flickered a moment, then stilled again into implacability.

"What I would like to do," I told him, "is forget all about this magic and beat you to a pulp. But maybe later." I held up my hands. "For now it'll have to wait."

I heard Del's blurt of shocked anguish. Wanted to say something, to console her, but my attention was on Nihkolara Andros.

"Did you think," I began, "that I couldn't follow the same road you did? That I would not repudiate the magic, the madness, and leave Sahdri and the others atop their rocks? *Oh*—" I paused with deliberate drama. "—and by the way, Sahdri's dead. He had a sore throat. Little matter of a spear stuck into it."

Nihko blanched to a sickly grayish pallor.

"Was he the one?" I asked with acid solicitude. "The one who found you at the foot of the spire, after you had leaped? The one who lifted you up, nourished you, led you across the threshold?" Pointedly I added, "The one who named you ikepra?"

"And you." His grin was a ghastly echo of what I had seen before. "Ikepra."

"But I've been that," I told him. "In the South, we call it borjuni. In the circle, we call it *elaii-ali-ma,* for an oath-bound man cast out of the circle forever." I shook my head, affecting pity. "Did you *really* believe a man such as that would shrink from adding one more bad name to his collection?"

"But you," he said with a brittle honesty so edged it cut, "are yet a man."

I opened my mouth to answer yes, I was, because I had seen fit not to sleep with the daughter of the Palomedi metri while I also slept with the Palomidi metri—and then I understood.

Sahdri and his brothers had cut only fingers from me.

"Stop." It was Prima Rhannet, very white of face. "Stop."

I looked at her, saw the fear in her. For Nihko.

"He did not do it," she said. "It was not Nihko's plan."

"Nor yours," I told her.

It startled her that I believed her. "The metri," she declared firmly. "The metrioi of the Eleven are capable of anything."

"No, not the metri. Not even Herakleio, though I don't doubt he wished for it."

Del spoke for the first time. Her tone was ice and steel. *"Who is left?"*

For a moment I looked over her head into the sky beyond, unable to meet her eyes. Then I did, swallowing painfully. "Simonides."

They none of them believed that answer.

" 'Slaves,' " I said, quoting him, " 'do what they must to survive. To make a life, and to find the freedom within.

But there need not be dishonor in it, if there are ways to find a measure of dignity and integrity.' "

Dishonor lay in what one thought of himself. Not in what others believed.

I sighed. "He did it for her. Because he saw no other way to be true to his household. I think after sixty-odd years beneath her roof, he really perceived no choice."

"How can you say that?" Del cried. "We believed you were dead! And he let us!"

"But I'm not." I smiled crookedly. "I'm a bit more *colorful* than I was"—I brushed a hand over my tattooed, stubble-fuzzed skull—"but I'm also not dead. And he was genuinely glad of that. I think he felt there was a chance I'd survive."

Del's eyes were full of tears. "Your *fingers* . . ."

It hurt to see her anguish. Softly I said, "Let it go, bascha."

She did. Because I asked it.

I looked at Prima and her first mate. "Go. We have our own ship. We won't be needing yours."

Her chin shot up. "And are you giving the orders now?"

"Ask Nihko if I can." I let him see my eyes. "Ask."

Prima, being Prima, remained unconvinced. "Perhaps we should simply *steal* your ship, like we did before."

"You broke it, you didn't steal it." I grinned. "And certainly you may try."

Nihko put one big hand on the small woman's neck and aimed her toward the blue-sailed ship. "Go."

She was outraged. "Nihko—"

"Go."

When she had gone, he inclined his head briefly. "Young," he said, "and strong. You would have killed Sahdri anyway, eventually. The iaka would have been yours."

"I never wanted the First House," I said. "I never wanted Meteiera, Akritara, the vineyards, the ships, the slaves. All I ever wanted was to know who my people were."

"And so you know."

I shook my head. "I'm not of Stessa blood. Skandic, undoubtedly—and *io*Skandic, so it seems—but not the metri's grandson. Her daughter was dead two years before I was born."

"The metri," he said calmly, "lies."

I smiled. "So do we all, ikepra. When it suits us."

The shift of his body was minute. He was prepared. "Shall it be now?"

I arched ring-weighted brows. "You really want to merge that badly?"

"I do not wish to merge at all."

"Then don't. You have two, possibly three years left. Go and live them." I paused. "Although it might be suggested for the sake of innocents that you find other employment."

Nihko displayed his teeth. "I am what I am, what I have made of myself. It is what I wish to be."

"Ah." I bared mine back at him in a ferocious grin. "Then that makes two of us."

He inclined his head again in brief salute, one ikepra to another, and turned to go.

"Wait."

He paused, looked back.

"How do you do it?" I asked. "How do you control it? Suppress it?"

He flicked a glance at Del briefly, then met my eyes. "With discipline," he said, "and the aid of the gods."

I laughed harshly. "And does it work?"

Nihko said, "Sometimes."

When he was gone, Del came to me. Took each hand into hers, kissed the palms with infinite care.

"There is not," I said, "that I know of, any medicinal value in that."

"Gods." She wound her arms around my neck, pressed herself against me. "Gods, Tiger—you're shaking."

"So are you, bascha."

She turned her face into my neck and began to cry.

I was a little damp myself as I carefully locked both arms around her, sealing myself against her.

After a moment, I said, "I hate these clothes."

She laughed, pressed herself harder against me. "Red suits you."

"I kind of thought you might prefer me without them. You know. *Out* of them."

Her breath was warm against my throat. "You are being terribly unsubtle."

"Subtlety has never been one of my great gifts, ba-scha. As you have said yourself."

Del slid to her knees. Untied the drawstring of the baggy trousers. Tugged them away. They fell into a heap at my feet.

"So," she said, "is this to be just for you?"

"I wanted you to see I still had all of my working parts." I paused, turning my palms into the light. "Well. Most of them."

And then I bent down, knelt, and took her into my arms.

EPILOGUE

LATER, as we lay in warm sand beside the rock-rimmed pool, Del amused herself by tracing the tattoos on my head. At first it tickled. Then I decided it felt rather good.

Idly she asked, "Will you keep your head shaved?"

I grunted drowsily, sprawled belly-down in blissful abandon with eyes closed. "Not likely."

"It isn't *un*attractive."

She had said something similar about Nihko, months before. Sternly I said, "It also isn't me."

Her fingers stroked. "It is now. Unless you think you can take them off, these tattoos."

I thought of Sahdri, lifting the scars from my body. "No," I said, suppressing a shiver. "I think I'll just let the hair grow back."

"Are you sure you want me to cut those rings out of your eyebrows?"

"I am."

"It will hurt."

I grunted again.

"Maybe you could leave the ones in your ears."

I opened my eyes, frowned thoughtfully, rolled over onto my back. "Are you saying you *like* me like this?"

Del, looking down on me, smiled winsomely. "I like you any way I can get you."

I thought about it. "All right," I said finally. "We'll leave one ring each in my ears—"

"Two."

I scowled. "Two. Just for you." I fixed her with a firm stare. "And that's *all.*"

She nodded, tracing patterns on my head again. "Such a pretty blue," she said. "Except for here." Her hand stopped just behind my left ear.

"Why? What's different about there?"

"You have a little smeary bubble here"—she tapped it—"like spilled wine."

I sat bolt upright.

Del blinked at me. "It's only a birthmark, Tiger. And once your hair grows back out, it will be hidden. I never saw it before."

I swore. Lay back down. Thought about it.

"Tiger—?"

Then I began to laugh.

"Tiger, what is it?"

I hooked an elbow over my eyes to blot out the sun. "Nihko said it."

"Nihko said what?"

"That the metri lies."

"Yes," Del agreed emphatically. "She said you were dead."

I was thinking of other things. Of caresses called keraka, formed of any size or shape. Found anywhere on the body. A Stessa-born body. "Well, I'm not dead."

Not yet.

Her hand moved down my abdomen. Closed. "I can tell."

I tried not to flinch. "Be careful with that."

"I rather think—not."

I thought about the implications of *that* a moment. "All right." I sat up, hooked an arm around her, pulled her down on top of me.

A fterward, Del asked, "What do you want to do?"

"Go home."

A delicate pause. "Where is home?"

"Where it's always been. The South."

"But—you said if you ever went back there—"

I interrupted. "I know what I said. I don't care. It's home. And it doesn't matter if there's a price on my head, or if borjuni and sword-dancers come hunting me—"

Her turn to interrupt. "Abbu Bensir?"

I hitched a shoulder. "Him, too. Let 'em all come."

After a moment she asked, "Why?"

We lay on our sides. I scooped an arm beneath Del and dragged her closer, fitting my body to hers, ankles entwined. I set my lips against cornsilk hair. "Because," I said, "it's time I built my home of something more than walls of air. I want brick, stone, wood, tile. I want *substance*."

"What kind of substance?"

"Alimat."

Del stiffened. "I thought you said Alimat was destroyed years ago in a monstrous sandstorm."

"So it was, most of it. But the bones are there. I'll rebuild it."

"Will they let you?"

"Who?"

"Abbu. The others."

"That will be settled in the circle. And once I'm done settling things, the students will come."

Astonishment was profound. *"Students?"*

"I taught Herakleio, didn't I?"

"Yes, but—you?"

"Why not?"

"You've always been so . . . independent."

"Well, maybe it's time I accepted responsibility." I pondered that a moment. "*Some* responsibility."

Del snickered politely. "And how long do you think this will last?"

"Ten years," I said evenly. "Maybe twelve. Fifteen if I'm lucky."

She poked me with an elbow. "Be serious, Tiger. You?"

I wanted to smile, but didn't. "Trust me, bascha, I have never been more serious in my life."

She closed a hand over one of mine, carefully avoiding the sensitive stump. Her voice was rusty. "Can you?"

"Oh, yes. It will take time—I have to learn new grips, new balance, new techniques and maneuvers; strengthen my wrists and remaining fingers—but yes. I can." I smiled. "It's called discipline."

"And until then?"

I knew she was thinking of Abbu. "Until then," I whispered into her ear, "you'll just have to protect me."

The stud, grazing contentedly on a patch of nearby grass, snorted.

I glanced across at him. "She can, you know. She's better than I am."

This time it was Del's turn to snort, albeit with more delicacy.

"Well," I conceded, "sometimes. Some days, some moments, some particular movements. Other times, not."

Del laughed softly. "That about sums it up."

"And speaking of particular movements . . ."

In mock disbelief, she asked, "What—*again?*"

I grinned. Then the grin fell away. I pulled her very tightly against me, held her there. Set my face into her hair. Told her I loved her.

In uplander, downlander, Northern, Southron, Desert, and every tongue in between. All the tongues of the world.

It took a long time.

But Del did not complain.

Geography

The model for "Skandi" is a Greek island called Santorini (from "Saint Irene.") Originally named Thera, Santorini was a large round island until approximately 1500 BC, when catastrophe struck in the form of a massive volcanic eruption. (It is believed Thera and its destruction may be the historical foundation for the stories of Atlantis.) Though the residents of Thera had enough warning to flee, thereby not becoming memorialized in lava and ash the way the victims of Vesuvius were, most of the island exploded. Chunks of what had been arable land collapsed and sank to the bottom of the ocean, leaving only the rim of the island above the waterline. Akrotiri, one of the settlements buried by the eruption, was discovered in 1967 by Greek archeologist Spyros Marinatos. Excavations continue to this day, peeling back the layers of an advanced civilization that may have been a direct offshoot of Minoan culture. The "living islands" described briefly in the novel are still-steaming portions of the volcanic cone visible in the center of the water-filled crater.

Geographically speaking, Santorini and its primary city, Fira (perched atop and built into the cliff), is as I have described it, even to the switchback donkey rides up and down the face of the caldera (which is especially interesting when one is lugging along a case of Boutari wine) and the grapevine "wreaths" grown against the ground. However, it should be noted that I have freely adapted elements to suit my story, and if anyone visits Santorini subsequent to reading this novel it should be noted that the most significant threat to them lies not in wading through molah muck, winehouses, dark alleys, or being tossed off the cliff to merge with the gods, but in surviving winding streets full of jewelry shops catering to tourists.

The model for Meteiera, the "Stone Forest," is an extended cluster of startlingly dramatic rock formations in Thessaly. Collectively called Meteora ("in the air"), the massive spires form a complex of monasteries, retreats, and cells built atop the crowns, and the home of traditional Orthodox monasticism founded in the eleventh century. (It is also the birthplace and home of Asclepius, classical antiquity's first and finest physician.) The crowns of the spires were originally accessed by rope and wooden ladders, scaffolding, and nets attached to winches; today the monasteries, with drivable roads to several of them, continue to function as retreats for contemplation and worship.

After The Fact, or:
"A Final Note From The Author"

Any series tends to spawn its own mythos, including misconceptions, assumptions, and inaccuracies, not to mention Frequently Asked Questions. For instance, when *Sword-Dancer,* the first volume in this series, was initially published in 1986, I was a relative unknown in the f/sf field and for a while a rumor circulated that I was actually a male writing under a female pseudonym. Now that I've returned to the world of Tiger and Del after a significant hiatus, I'm going to answer some of the most frequent of the Frequently Asked Questions.

No, I am not a man.

No, I do not want to be a man.

No, Tiger is not based on anyone I know, be he friend, foe, or ex-husband. [*If anything, there are pieces of me in Tiger: I'm fortysomething, have bad knees, bear a few scars from such things as ski poles, 50-gallon oil drums, swimming pool aerators, and dog teeth, and my joints regularly produce all manner of sounds not unlike percussion instruments.*]

Yes, I know horses. [*I used to rodeo, albeit on the amateur level.*]

No, the stud is not based on a horse I once owned. [*If I'd had a stud like the stud, I'd have gelded the sucker.*]

No, the stud will never have a name. [*He is what he is: a stud. Which horse people understand.*]

No, I am not personally trained in the use of Sharp Pointy Objects. [*Although I do own a replica of the* **Highlander** *katana and have been known to flail it about rather unconvincingly in the privacy of my home, affording all manner of consternation to dogs and cats.*]

And for the Qs to become FA'd following the publication of this book:

No, my publisher did not request me to return to a known universe because it would be commercially profitable. Tiger and Del are great fun to write about, and having given myself a breather with a few other novels, I was fresh and more than ready to play in their world again. In fact, I insisted. [*Just ask my editor.*]

No, I am not gay. [*I simply believe in an individual's right to a personal choice in lifestyle, and in the respect due those choices.*]

Yes, I have a personal agenda in writing these books. [*I'm revolutionary enough to want to* entertain *readers—and to believe that "commercial genre novels" can also educate with regard to specific issues, be it gender equality, freedom of choice, or dozens of other topics.*]

Yes, there will be another novel featuring Tiger and Del. [*Sword-Sworn, which will probably appear somewhere around the millennium.*]

About The Author

Since 1984, with the debut of *Shapechangers,* Jennifer Roberson has published twenty novels. In addition to fantasy, she has written two mainstream historicals: *Lady of the Forest,* an award-winning reinterpretation of how the Robin Hood legend came to be, emphasizing Marian's role (with its upcoming sequel, *Lady of Sherwood,* featuring the classic ballad-adventures); and *Lady of the Glen,* the documented story of seventeenth-century Scotland's Massacre of Glencoe, similar in theme to the film "Braveheart." She has also contributed short stories to collections, anthologies, and magazines, has herself edited two original anthologies, and collaborated with Melanie Rawn and Kate Elliott on the 1997 World Fantasy Award-nominated novel *The Golden Key,* a historical fantasy. Her works have appeared in translation in Germany, Japan, France, Russia, Poland, Italy, China, and Sweden.

Jennifer has a Bachelor of Science degree in mass communications journalism from Northern Arizona University, with an extended major in British history. In 1982 she spent her final semester in England at the University of London, which enabled her to do on-site research. In 1996 she visited Greece and Turkey on a research trip for *Sword-Born* and future novels.

Though born in Kansas City, Missouri, Jennifer Roberson grew up in Arizona, where she used to compete in amateur rodeos. Her primary hobby now is the breeding, training, and exhibition of Cardigan Welsh Corgis (the Corgi with the tail) and Labrador Retrievers in the conformation, obedience, and agility rings of AKC dog shows

and trials. She is the Cardigan Welsh Corgi breed colum-
nist for the AKC *Gazette* magazine, and lives near Phoe-
nix with (currently) seven dogs and three cats.

The author may be reached via her website at **sff.net/
people/jennifer.roberson/**

THE GOLDEN KEY
by
Melanie Rawn
Jennifer Roberson
Kate Elliott

In the duchy of Tira Virte fine art is prized above all things. But not even the Grand Duke knows just how powerful the art of the Grijalva family is. For thanks to a genetic fluke certain males of their bloodline are born with a frightening talent—the ability to manipulate time, space, and reality within their paintings, using them to cast magical spells which alter events, people, places, and things in the real world. Their secret magic formula, known as the Golden Key, permits those Gifted sons to vastly improve the fortunes of their family. Still, the Grijalvas are fairly circumspect in their dealings until two young talents come into their powers: Sario, a boy who will learn to use his Gift to make himself virtually immortal; and Saavedra, a female cousin who, unbeknownst to her family, may be the first woman ever to have the Gift. Sario's personal ambitions and thwarted love for his cousin will lead to a generations-spanning plot to seize total control of the duchy and those who rule it.

• Featuring cover art by Michael Whelan

☐ Hardcover Edition   UE2691-$24.95
☐ Paperback Edition   UE2746-$6.99

Jennifer Roberson

THE NOVELS OF TIGER AND DEL